CIRCLE OF LIGHT 4

Squaring the Circle

Don't get left behind!

STARSCAPE

Let the journey begin . . .

CIRCLE OF LIGHT 4

Squaring the Circle

NIEL HANCOCK

A TOM DOHERTY ASSOCIATES BOOK
NEW YORK

SQUARING THE CIRCLE

A Starscape Book
Published by Tom Doherty Associates, LLC
175 Fifth Avenue
New York, NY 10010

www.starscapebooks.com

ISBN 0-765-34618-4
EAN 978-0765-34618-6

First Starscape edition: August 2004

Printed in the United States of America

0 9 8 7 6 5 4 3 2 1

For all my fellow travelers
everywhere on this journey.

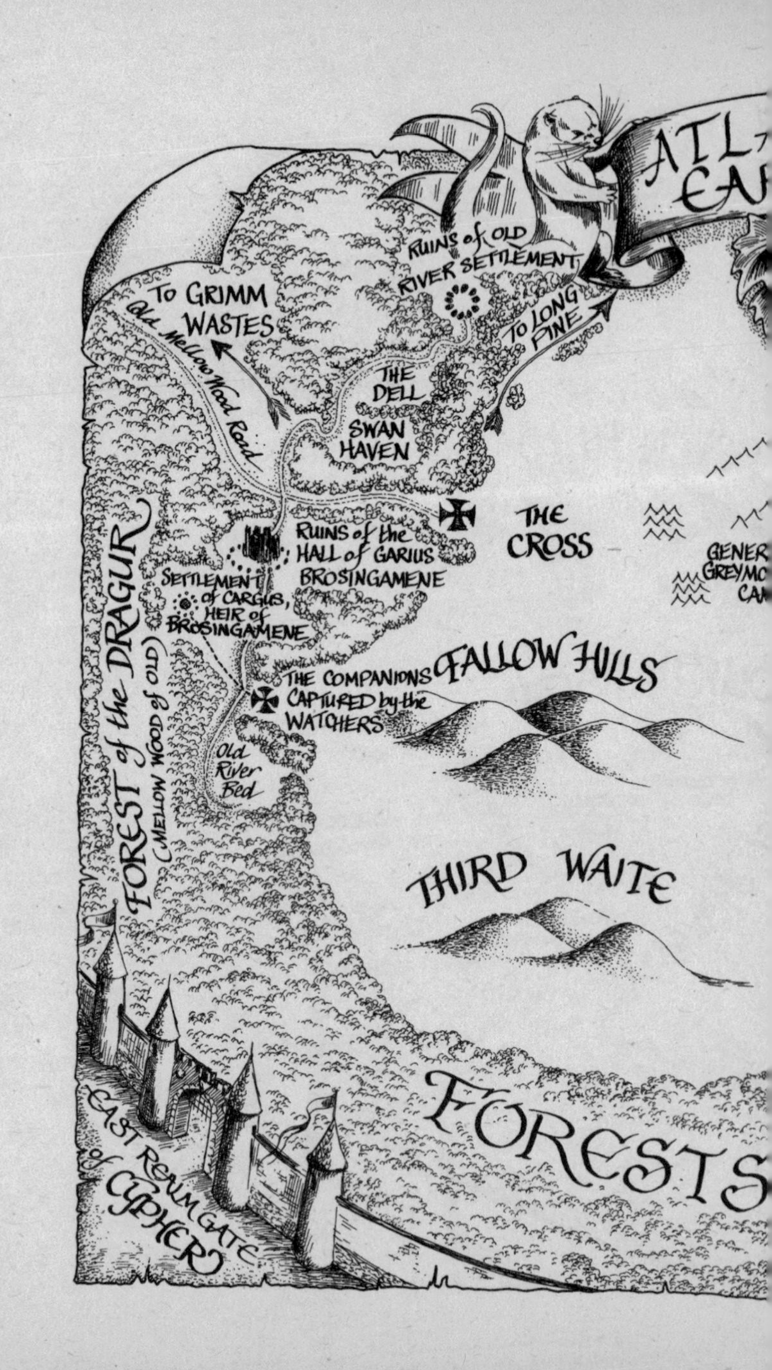

RUINS of OLD RIVER SETTLEMENT
TO GRIMM WASTES
Old Mellow Wood Road
TO LONG PINE
THE DELL
SWAN HAVEN
THE CROSS
RUINS of the HALL of GARIUS BROSINGAMENE
SETTLEMENT of CARGUS, HEIR of BROSINGAMENE
FOREST of the DRAGUR
(MELLOW WOOD of OLD)
FALLOW HILLS
THE COMPANIONS CAPTURED by the WATCHERS
Old River Bed
THIRD WAITE
FORESTS
EAST REALM GATE of CYPHER

FALLOW HILLS
BATTLE of SEVEN HILLS
HILL
CROWN of HAVAMAL RUINS
MELODIAS STARSON'S FORCES
GORGOLAC ARMIES
ASHGNAZI WORLUGHS
OLD WATER WAY to RUINS of CODA POOL
HAVAMAL
CYPHER
NORTH REALM GATE of CYPHER
Alisa Mitchell 2003

Echoes of the Past

Lights and Voices

Through a great roaring of storming lights and exploding sound, Flewingam heard a voice beside him calling out his name.

"Flew! Flew, old fellow, can you hear me?"

It was faintly familiar, yet blurry at the edges, and Flewingam sensed that he was angry, and he did not want to be awakened at this particular moment, for he was just remembering, for the time in a long while, how good a long nap in a soft bed was.

"Flew! Wake up, we've crossed the River."

At those words, his eyes blinked open, and he stared straight into the worried frown of his friend Otter.

"Calix Stay?" repeated Flewingam aloud, trying to take in the full meaning of the thought.

He felt odd indeed, and could not quite put his finger on it, until he saw the broad smile cross Otter's features.

"We're here, Flew. The Meadows of the Sun. Or at one end of them, at any rate. I've never been in these particular parts, but it doesn't take much to tell we're across the River again. It's just like I was always trying to tell you."

Flewingam sat up and looked about, fighting the confusion and fear that he felt. "But what happened?" His voice carried a trace of doubt.

"I'm not sure, except that there was a lot of water and noise. I'm not one to complain about too much water, but I think there was a flood. I keep thinking we were in an underground river, or something about rocks that walked."

"The Roots," said Flewingam. "And Bear was washed away first. And Thumb, and the rest?" he said excitedly, remembering at once the events that had happened. He could not say how long ago it had occurred, or exactly where, but he distinctly remembered the flashing bright lights that exploded through his memory, and the noise of the flooded cavern, and the greater noise and brighter flashes that followed. He seemed to remember Otter's descriptions of this River, so long ago now, yet it all seemed so familiar.

Otter had raised himself up, and was studying their surroundings, his small muzzle worked into a frown. "I don't remember these parts much. Or I do, but then again something's changed. I think the light isn't so bright."

He squinted away into the direction that the golden sheen of mellow warmth seemed to come from, and he gasped aloud and pointed. "It's almost setting," he breathed. "It wasn't that low before."

"Do you think the trouble has spread even here, friend?" asked Flewingam.

Otter turned a frightened glance on his companion. "And where is Bear, and Thumb, and Lilly, and their friends?" His eyes darkened, and a wave of sadness tore at his heart. "And will we never see our Dwarf again? He was the one that needed to be here, to deliver the Chest. But we're here instead, and lost, and alone, to boot."

Flewingam got up from the soft ground where he'd found himself sitting. "I don't know what's been happening here, but I don't like the feel of it."

"Let's look for the others," suggested Otter, trying to cheer himself. "Perhaps they've landed somewhere nearby."

Flewingam sighed wearily. "I can't see any point, my friend, but then it's better than just sitting here. And we might come across our supper while we're at it. If we're to be here with nothing to show for it, I hope we can at least find a bite or two, and a warm place to lie down."

Otter plodded along a few paces ahead of his friend. "It seems like we were taken on a wild-goose chase, Flew," he went on after a moment. "And goodness knows I'm fond enough of those, except this time we've been up one side of the world, down another, without so much as a handkerchief or a decent meal, and now this again. And I've lost Bear and Dwarf, on top of it all." Otter had stopped and stood staring at his friend. A great tear shone in his eye, and his chin whiskers quivered.

"Well, I did get to see Cypher, and meet the Golden Lady, and Cybelle. And I got to have a companion like our Dwarf for a time. And I have known some of the Masters, and seen more than my share of good water." He choked back a sob. "And I've been a long mile or two with you, Flew, and we've seen some foul times, we have, between us. And we had good comrades in Cranny and Ned."

Flewingam had stopped, and was staring at the little gray fellow.

"Not to mention the fact we were with Dwarf, who was

carrying the Chest back to safety here," continued Otter, his voice tight. "Only now here *we* are, and nothing really matters now, because it's all changed here, and I don't even want to stay here anymore."

Flewingam went to his friend and gave the little animal a gentle pat. His own eyes were glistening, and his voice shook as he spoke. "That's the way it looks, on the face of it, old fellow. But we must go on and try to find the others. I don't think there's a choice now."

Otter bit back a sniffle, and wrinkled his brow. "Well, let's just walk on awhile, and see if we can find out what's happening. I think if we just try to do that, we won't have far to go to our next plan."

Flewingam had started to agree, when the sound of voices reached the friends. They froze to the spot, and tried to listen to what the voices were saying. A loud humming seemed to grow from the very air, followed by a faint, faraway rattle of drums. And then, quite distinctly, came a rather feathery voice, right at Otter's elbow.

"What have we here, and what errand are you on that you're traveling about in those silly forms? Speak quickly, before we deal with you as we should have the moment we detected you cross our borders." There was something irksome in the tone of the invisible voice, but it was frightening all the same, coming as it did out of thin air.

Otter's hackles quavered, and his lips crept back to expose his fangs, and he stepped back a pace so that he could go into his fighting stance.

"Ooooch, ouch! You silly thing, you've crushed my stump. Watch out, please, so as not to mash me."

Otter whirled, but there was nothing to be seen.

"And why won't you look at me when I'm speaking to you? I don't think you're nice at all, you know." The unseen voice was constrained and teasing, and more irritating than ever.

Otter, being the shorter of the two, had glanced at the ground, for the voice was coming from somewhere low down, and he could have almost sworn it was near the small plant that Flewingam had just roughly brushed with his foot.

On his stomach, with his muzzle almost touching the small green thing, Otter spoke. "Is this you?"

"Of course, silly. Who did you think I was?"

"Well, I'm not sure," replied Otter. "But I guess we've seen stranger things."

"What, may I ask, is so strange in the figure of an elf?" The voice was highly indignant.

"An elf?" echoed Flew and Otter together.

"Naturally, you thickheaded beasts. Or are you? I can see right enough one of you is human, at any rate. Not that that means anything. What do you want here, and who are you? Or did I ask that? We have orders that none shall cross the River without plain and proper reason to be here. Speak up, speak up."

"And we might ask the same of you," shot Otter, trying to address the small green plant that the voice seemed to be coming from.

"I'm quite sure you have two good eyes. An elf, as you see, at your service, an elf in charge of these borders, along with my men. That is my errand."

As the voice ceased, a dozen or more of the same feathery voices piped up all around the two friends. "Hear, hear, and what's your errand?" demanded one.

"More's the pity we don't have permission to shoot 'em," said another.

A chorus of confused voices went on.

"Let's have it. What's your tricks?"

"A likely lot, and full of their shoddy doings."

The first voice rose a tone above the others. "Later, later, men."

It waited until the others had died down somewhat, then went on. "Well, out with it. Let's have it."

"If you're really elves, you don't look like any I've ever met," snapped Otter.

"And where would the likes of you ever have the honor of meeting an elf? Such drab creatures. I hardly think you would have a need to meet anyone at all who didn't go about in a poor human's form, or down on all fours."

"Hear, hear," piped up the other voices, coming from the grass, and other plants near the friends.

Flewingam had raised himself to his fullest height, and was on the verge of smashing down one of his booted feet to flatten the small plant below him.

"Wait, Flew," chittered Otter, and he turned and addressed the invisible voice.

"Now, friend elf, if elf indeed you are, which I wonder from your tongue, to answer your questions. We met elves at the court of the Golden Lady of Cypher, and those fellows were ever so polite and generous, and sang such music as I doubt you've ever heard. And we have traveled with Broco, gypsy dwarf, on his quest for the Circle, and spoken with and fought beside Mithramuse Cairngarme, better known as Greymouse, and have been befriended by Greyfax Grimwald and Froghorn Fairingay. And we would have you for friends, if you will, or enemies, if you won't, but think twice about your answer to the companions of the Circle."

There was an unbroken silence for a space of time, then Flewingam and Otter detected a heavy fog like mist that began to rise from the ground, swirling and gray, turning silver in the golden sunlight as it slanted through the stillness of the meadow. A faint tinkling of a bell was heard, and then the humming sound again, like a wind through an old forest, and there before the bewildered friends stood a dozen green-clad elves, long bows in hand, and short mithra worked swords hanging from their belts. They were smaller than the elves Otter had met in Cypher, yet they had the same fair features, and the same clear blue-gray eyes.

One of the elves stepped forward and made a low, sweeping bow, doffing his hat as he did so.

"You are asked to pardon our rudeness," said the elf, his voice taking on a sudden oily smoothness. "There can be no excuses, except that we had hardly dared hope ever to meet the Otter from the stories of Cypher. Those were never supposed to have been anything more than someone's fancy at making a good tune. More times than not, we often scoffed at the elf kindred who traveled through our woods here, on their way to havens, and even when our own kindred, who had been in or about Cypher, told us these stories, we hardly believed them. But since you say you are indeed that very Otter, we have instructions to take you to our camp, for there is someone there most anxious to see you."

Otter gasped, and Flewingam's eyes grew wider.

"But in the meantime," the elf went on evenly, "I beg your forgiveness for Belwicke, poor host that he is, and the poor woodland folk at your noble service."

Otter returned the elf's stiff bow. "We're very pleased to make your acquaintance, Belwicke, and honored to have such friends. But who ever do we know that is still here, on this side of Calix Stay?"

"We call him by many names, some you've heard, and some you've not. And it's no one you've known here before. You will probably recognize him best by the name . . ." The elf paused for a long moment. "Froghorn Fairingay."

Before the stunned companions could reply, the elfin company had set off at a great pace, and the two friends were hard pressed to keep the small figures in sight.

The Iron Crown at Cypher

A low, gray sun shone bleakly over the tower of the swan, and the sound of a lonely wind echoed over the moldering ruins of the once golden Cypher. In the study Lorini had once used, a much different figure now paced to and fro over the lifeless, mute rugs, glaring at the ashen, dead tapestries. Below, in the singing fountains, small, broken dirty chunks of ice floated in the brackish water.

Dorini halted before the cold fireplace and looked up at the engraved stone above the hearth. It was a crown, with five stars.

Dorini touched her own crown, an iron affair, with five dark circles at each sharp, jagged edge.

"Indeed, indeed, we shall see who has the upper hand now. I head my forces from the very seat of Cypher, just as I promised my weak sister I should do. This victory is not sweet enough. Nothing can stop my plans now. I shall have these worlds and all who go upon them forever, as it was intended."

Dorini laughed, a low, malignant sound that came from

the dark light of her secret heart, like a beast growling warning. As she turned her attention to a battle map laid before her, a Urinine captain, coldly handsome, and clad all in black, entered the room brusquely and saluted.

"There is a visitor for Your Majesty," he reported, clicking his heels smartly.

Dorini raised an icy stare to the man's face. "Who wishes to see me?"

"He says you will see him, Your Majesty. It is one of the wood elves. He has news that he says might be of interest to you."

An ominous smile crept across Dorini's lips. "Bring him to me, then."

She folded the map and placed it in the top drawer of the writing desk. As she turned, the slight figure who had entered bowed low and strode to stand beside her.

"Your Highness, Tyron the Green, at your service," said Tyron, bowing low once more.

"Speak, elf. I know your name. What news have you that would be of interest to me? And why have you risked your wretched life coming here?"

"I find we may have a common bond, Your Grandness," said Tyron. "I ask you to hear me out before you risk harming me. What I have to say could prove to be mutually beneficial to both our causes."

Dorini laughed icily. "What cause have I that includes a miserable elf?" she sneered, yet still encouraging Tyron to continue. She was intrigued by the elf's bearing, although she did not show it.

"You seek certain information as to the whereabouts of a certain object. And I seek to rid myself of certain persons.

Perhaps in the trade, we might be immeasurably of service to each other."

"And why should I not have you flayed alive to gain your information? Or why shall I not gather it in other ways?" Dorini's eyes became a frozen gray color as she spoke, and seemed to open onto fathomless darkness as she turned her cold gaze on Tyron.

The elf's hand went into his cloak and returned with a small object that barely covered the palm of his hand. He held it out to her, very slowly. The bottomless darkness of her eyes crept dangerously near him, then retreated.

"It is but a momentary advantage. You cannot keep me away forever with your small trinket."

Tyron replaced the small, elfin-worked mithra mirror, upon which he had printed the single word of the Secret he carried. "But long enough to keep your power from touching me until I have said my say."

"Speak on, then. I have urgent matters," said Dorini, smiling inwardly that the fool of an elf thought he could protect himself from her so easily.

"I shall, if you wish it. For you see, there is one here across Calix Stay who may have the very thing which might put all your plans to waste."

"The miserable box," she spat fiercely. "It's crossed, then?"

"It has. And Greymouse and Melodias, along with others. They are preparing even now to drive you from these realms and throw you back across Cypher's borders, where they say you belong."

"I belong wherever my power leads me," replied Dorini coldly.

"But these aren't your natural realms, and you know it, as well as I. I have done my share of lore work, you see. I know what is written. You have overstepped the boundaries you were given in the beginning, and now seek to keep these lower worlds of Windameir for yourself, along with all those dwelling there. And that's your own affair. My affair is the holding safely of the Gilden Wood, and Gilden Far. Those areas have been mine and my sire's since the beginning, handed down hand to hand by all my forefathers, and all theirs before them. It has always been elf haven, and always shall be, if I have my way. But it's changing dangerously in these late times, and all manner of things are seeking refuge in these woods. We have long found that dealings with other kinds have always been at dear cost to us, and all associations have always left us the less for it. What I propose is a trade."

"An exchange?" snapped Dorini, somewhat taken aback. "What have you that I would seek?"

"A certain object, or rather a dealing with a certain object, in return for your word and help in making Gilden Wood and Gilden Far beyond all beings other than those of elfish kin. You desire to hold these lower three worlds. My desire is to have a safe elfin haven that is sealed for all time from those snooping, prying fools of the Circle. And from you, Your Grandness."

"What you ask is impossible," snapped Dorini angrily.

She had been badly shocked to find that this ignorant elf had known the fact that one of the defenses against her terrible gaze was one of the Secrets written across a simple mirror. And that was the horror she faced in all the lower creations, for if once it was known that the way to protect oneself from her power could be something so insignificant and simple as a mirror with a word of hope turned on her, then all would be lost, and the gates would be opened for all to escape as they might.

"I think not," went on Tyron. "If you gain your ends upon these lower worlds, you will have the final say of what is or isn't. And if the Circle is banished beyond your borders, as it well could be, and if you were in possession of a certain object, or had dealt wisely with that object, you would have the power to vouchsafe the haven I ask for."

A plan began to formulate in the deeper recesses of Dorini's mind, and the thought of its simplicity brought a slow smile to the frozen beauty of her proud face.

"Then we shall agree, in principle, and work out our differences."

"We must do more than agree, I fear, Your Grandness," went on Tyron boldly. "We must strike a bargain that will hold each of us to our word."

"As you wish, elf. What do you propose?"

"Simply this. You will set apart Gilden Wood and Gilden Far to be governed by me, and me alone. And your oath that you shall never try to retake it, or trick your way back in."

"And how shall we seal this bargain, my good Tyron?"

"We shall seal it in this manner. I propose to take with me into the haven you will give me the same object you so despise and fear. All you need is for that object to disappear, without a chance of it cropping up to plague you again in your schemes. And having it safe with me will ensure that his lordship, Doraki, will never begin to have certain ideas about replacing Your Grandness. If you meet my demands, and give me the thing I ask, your worries with the Arkenchest will be over, for I will hold it and the Secrets across my borders, where none shall dare come, or who, if once there, can never leave. It is a perfect solution to your problem, and mine. My folk have no desire to do anything beyond manage our own affairs and be left in peace."

Dorini's frigid glance took in the confident elf. "Why should I trust you?" she asked at length. "And what would keep you from becoming more ambitious than Doraki, once you hold the Chest?"

Tyron laughed. "Because, dear lady, I am an elf. You well know the makeup of my folk. We are close-mouthed, and stingy when it comes to dealing with others. We are also more concerned with our own affairs than most. All we ask is our haven. An elf's ambition is never more than to have his haven."

"Indeed. I am aware of the shortness of vision in some. Go on."

"If you keep the Chest here, Your Grandness, you well know the risks. Sooner or later there would be the attempt by your Doraki to oust you, and to take your powers. The Chest is capable of generating hope in even the blackest of hearts, and if the hope in that heart is to overcome one's mistress and rob her of her powers, even that hope can be generated. And I think, from all my lore learning, that the more dreadful hope that the Chest would generate would be to return it to its rightful place, and surrender."

"That would never be!" snorted Dorini, although she turned over in her mind what the elf was saying. Deep within herself, she knew he spoke the truth. Doraki was not to be trusted beyond the realm of the threats and promises she made him. And she knew he hated her with every beat of his dark heart. Keeping him that way made him more useful to her.

The thought of holding the Arkenchest sent thrills of delight through her, although she feared it and the unlimited power it could in truth generate. The elf spoke the truth, she knew. It could generate the power to desire to surrender it back to the cursed Circle, and to give up all her schemes and desires of these lower worlds, but knowing that only made the wish sweeter.

She gloried in the power it would give her over the wretched brutes of the Circle, and over Greyfax Grimwald most of all. She also knew that it was created by the High Lord himself, and that if she were in possession of it, she would eventually be tempted to give in to its power. And that, in essence, was no more than total surrender, and the greatest challenge of all to her. If she could resist the cursed, miserable Chest, she would truly be on equal footing with the High Lord of Windameir himself.

Tyron had begun to fidget and become uneasy.

For the moment, and without further ado, she agreed to Tyron's plan, and the two sat long in the now cold sunlight that fell through the darkened windows of Lorini's old study in Cypher, drawing up the scheme that would give Tyron the Green unchallenged hold of Gilden Wood and Gilden Far, and provide him with his precious haven.

And it would give her, Dorini, the chance once and for always to know the true power of her most dread enemy, the

Arkenchest, the symbol of the Five Secrets of the High Lord of Windameir, and the guide to the Pathway that would lead all the beings now in her realms back to their true Home, far from the prison worlds she so jealously guarded and held for her own.

Across the River

Bear sat in dazed wonder, watching the hot tea simmer in the mug in his hand, and the broth slowly boiling on the fire. His head was reeling with confusion, and he stared wide-eyed at the bustling camp about him.

Three tall elves sat across from him near the fire, talking among themselves and occasionally stirring the big pot of broth. Next to them sat two men, dressed in the uniforms of Melodias Starson's armies.

The wild river and the terror of the time in the tunnels had passed into an uneasy memory, and he was not certain that he had not been here forever. The warm sun felt good, and the odd, familiar feeling he had felt comfortable.

It was all spinning crazily in his head when a figure approached and sat down at his side.

"Well, my friend, it has been something of a few miles between us since last we met."

Bear looked at the gray-cloaked figure leaning over the fire now and pouring himself a mug of the fragrant herb tea.

"There is much news we have to exchange, Bruinlen. Come, let's go to my tent."

Without questioning the command, Bear rose and followed the gray-clad figure through the center of camp and into the deeper, cool shadows of a large tent. At a desk covered with charts and strewn papers, the cloaked figure drew up a camp stool and motioned for Bear to do the same.

"You hardly recognize me, my good fellow. Have I changed so much since last you saw me?"

A slight change of tone pulled Bear's ears up straight, and he knew whose voice it was, and recognized its owner.

"Froghorn Fairingay!" he blurted out, trying to stand. "I mean Faragon."

"Froghorn, still," chuckled the young wizard, motioning for Bear to sit. "And things have come a long piece since we had opportunity to see one another. Many things have passed since then. But come, tell me of your news, and what you know of passing interest."

"I don't know," mumbled Bear, still amazed and flustered. "I was with Otter and Flewingam, and some other friends of mine, Thumb, and his band, when we ended up in some underground tunnel, and there were Roots, and a river called the Under Tide, and then I got swept away, and there was an awful darkness and voices and music, and light, and the next thing I knew I was being chased again. I don't know whether I'm back in the Dragur Wood, or where, but I do know I'm full of a thousand things, and tired and hungry. I've lost Otter, and Dwarf is gone, and the Chest, and now I don't know what to make of all this. But I'm glad enough to see you. I was beginning to think all you fellows had taken leave of us, and gone on without giving us another thought." Bear ended with a hurt note in his voice.

"Not just yet, old fellow," laughed Froghorn, refusing to let Bear feel sorry for himself. "I know you have had a time of it, but it all seems to be coming to rights now. I talked with my men who found you on our outer perimeters. They said you had crossed Calix Stay there, and were being pursued by the Darkness as you landed in our little wood. You see, and this I have gathered from talking to Greyfax and Melodias, you have landed not far from where you dwelled before you made your crossing of Calix Stay that day, and ran upon Greyfax and me."

"You mean this is the Meadows of the Sun?" asked Bear, gazing about incredulously. "But it's all different somehow. I mean the light. The sun isn't so high, and why is there anyone here who would be chasing me, if it *is* the Meadows of the Sun? It wasn't that way before. No one could cross if they weren't the right sort."

"Well," began Froghorn, stroking his chin, "you see, things have changed considerably. We have been pursued even into these regions by the Darkness. Dorini resides in Cypher now, and directs her war against us from there. Of course, she could not bring her beast armies across Calix Stay, for the River would not allow that, but she has other allies here that have been here all along, awaiting her crossing. As long as Lorini resided in Cypher, she could not move in force in these realms, but since the lady is gone, and Cybelle is taken, Dorini has struck here hard and quickly. These armies you see here are half General Greymouse's men who have crossed the River, and half the elfin host of

Urien Typhon. Melodias has his own forces farther up, toward Gilden Tarn. And Greymouse is there with him."

"But I don't understand," moaned Bear. "Cybelle taken? I mean, how could that be? And what's happened here that Dorini can bring her hordes and get over too?"

"First things first, Bear. It is difficult to understand in some ways, but quite simple, actually. Dorini took Cybelle from the very halls of Cypher while all the rest of us were away on our errands. And Dorini has used that chance to force Lorini from Cypher, and to move in force across Calix Stay. And these men you see in my camp here have died, as you might say, to the other world across Calix Stay. That isn't the proper term, but it shall have to suffice. We've merely changed planes. Nothing changes except the outward form. Nothing changes, on the true level. And Urien and his men have long since mastered the art of form changing at will, just as all men will, sooner or later. It is all a part of the natural order of the One we all follow, whether we are aware of it or not. It is simple, if you remember the Circle. You start, and follow the line outward, then reach the bottom of the arc, and then you are following on back to where you began."

Bear frowned, knotting up his brow and starting to ask something else, when Froghorn went on.

"It's as simple as the trick I showed you and Otter on the form changing, long ago, in your old valley. And as for the Dark Queen, she got here by the same method. Except she has all the same powers as all the Masters, for she, too, is the daughter of the Lord of Windameir. She was given the lower three worlds to govern, along with Lorini, in the name of the High Lord, and therefore has all the same powers as any of us. And more in these lower worlds in some cases, because they were given to her and Lorini, and it is Law that each plane is ruled by its own natural forces, so she therefore holds something of an edge, as far as regulation of these planes goes. But the Five Secrets are the key, and since she has gone to war to gain the control of these lower worlds, and wrest them from Lorini and the High Lord, she must have control of the Five. She knows that a dwarf holds the Chest, and that she once held that very dwarf in her grasp. That has made her throw herself into the fray totally. If she cannot capture the Arkenchest, then she has lost her bid for supremacy, for as long as the Secrets exist, then she cannot hold these worlds in darkness."

Bear shook his head slowly. "You mean I've really been drowned across Calix Stay, but I'm here now, and my trick of changing shapes is a simple thing just like all the wizards use? And here I am, just exactly in the same fix I was in before I got washed into the River?"

"The Under Tide is one of the entries into Calix Stay, although there are many, and they go under many names. And not all of them are rivers. You may be washed into Calix Stay by a sword stroke, or a bullet, or a bomb, or from a fall, or heart seizure, or brain tumors, or mere old age. All things lead to the River."

Bear thought silently for a moment. "I think I'm beginning to understand a little. But it's still so confusing."

"You'll understand more as you progress, my friend. For now, we have had enough of these ponderous subjects. I must pass on more cheerful news." Froghorn smiled, and leaned back on his stool.

"Soon we shall be with our friends, and shall go up toward

the Beginning, where Lorini awaits us. And we must gather our forces here, which we are doing now. Your friends shall be with us soon, and we'll move on as the moment strikes."

"You mean Otter? And Dwarf? And Flew, and Cranny, and Thumb, and all his band will be here?"

"All as you say, but Thumb and the other bears. They have had to return to beyond Calix Stay for another turning. They have not finished their time there. They have more lessons to see, and more roles to play."

Bear's face fell, and he felt the sadness wash through him. "He seemed a good sort. I hate to lose him now. Isn't there anything you or the others could do?"

Froghorn smiled gently. "He is progressing at his own rate, as are all things. And they are no longer bears. They have returned in the human form, this trip. They, too, are beginning to learn the forms and changes that go along with the One."

"You mean they won't go back to being bears?"

"No, they have fulfilled that role. They now have other parts to complete their education beyond Calix Stay. They shall come up in their own time, to return to their True Home."

"All the same, I shall miss them," mumbled Bear.

"As well you should. If you didn't feel that, you would not have come such a long way, and we wouldn't be having our little chat here now."

As the young wizard fell silent, an orderly entered, carrying a large tray covered with bowls and loaves, and a pot of fragrant herb tea. He placed it on top of the desk, saluted, and went out.

"Come, let's fill our hunger, and then we shall be at our tasks."

Bear, hungrier than he wanted to admit, and still pondering all Froghorn had said, fell on the broth and loaf, and remained as silent as possible. He did not dare ask what tasks they had yet to perform, but from all past experience, Bear knew it was most likely to be something that would carry him yet further into all this strange business the young wizard had been describing. And the oddest part of it all, Bear thought, spreading honey on another thick slice of bread, was that Froghorn's talk of all the strange things had begun to make sense, and that he was not surprised too much at anything that had been said.

"I guess all this comes about as a result of getting mixed up in this business to begin with," muttered Bear, half aloud. "If I'd had any sense, I'd still be back in my old cave, tending bees, as likely as not." He snorted. "And the next thing I know, I'm probably going to be as odd as all the rest."

He shook his head, and tried to remember what it was he had always been told about mixing with others than your own, but the words were not there. And he had begun to feel that he was, in spite of himself, at last truly with his own.

Old Friends

"You're the last one I expected to see here," said Lorini, addressing her old friend in a teasing, lilting voice.

"I find that disheartening, madam," replied Greyfax, bowing low, and taking her hand.

"Cephus Starkeeper and Erophin have been kind. They've showed and answered me my questions, and caught me up on matters that had puzzled me sorely." She paused, then went on. "But this meeting puzzles me greatly, too."

"It shouldn't, my lady. It is all as written. We are here awaiting the carrying out of our roles."

"And those being?" asked Lorini.

"You know as well as I. We shall have guests before too much longer. I have word that even now they have flown through Calix Stay, and have begun their journey this side of the River."

Lorini faced the hearth and stood a moment looking into the empty firedogs. "And what news have you of the return of Cybelle?" She did not dare turn to Greyfax, for she was not quite in control of her features.

"My dear Lorini," said Greyfax quietly, "we know of the return of our dear Cybelle. It is written. You need not concern yourself with it more. And it only makes it the more difficult when you think of it. There is nothing more to be done for the moment. Her return is written in the Book. And we have much to do, now that you've finally arrived. There is the matter of Cypher to be handled, and preparations for the arrival of your dark sister. She has become active here at last on these planes, for after the fall of Cypher, there was nothing to guard against her wielding her power in these upper spheres of Atlanton Earth."

"Have you seen Cypher since your return here?"

"I have, my lady. It is as if it never were, at least not to my mind. But yet it is still Cypher. I was disguised, and scouted out the lay of the enemy there before they were aware of an intruder. Doraki holds his court there at times, and Dorini has been seen, and heard, and it is common knowledge that she is moving her headquarters there. The only thing missing is a troop of Worlughs or Gorgolacs feasting on some slain foeman. But the River will not allow those kind across. They come now in the forms of men, although they are still the same beasts inside."

Lorini gazed on into the invisible fire, looking hard at the hearth. "And do we now set up our new Cypher here?" she asked at last, in a voice so low Greyfax wasn't sure he had heard.

"Not you or I, dear lady. No. You and I are to be here purely as advisers for now. I think we shall have some help soon from that hotheaded young whelp of a Fairingay. It is rumored he is somewhere about."

"Then what are your plans? Do we merely sit here, helpless?"

"Not quite helpless, my lady. As you know, our power here is quite strong, much more so than in the lower physical realms of the World Before Time, across Calix Stay. And your sister's powers are lessened here. She has not the power here she holds in the lower planes. So we have a definite edge, as far as that goes. But we cannot control her use of treachery or deceit." Greyfax grew somber, and paused before going on. "Our danger in these parts lies in the fact that Dorini may take on any guise she wishes, and although she commands no great army here, she does command the powers of cunning disguise, and has many an ally in unexpected places. And the beings here aren't so concerned with anything more pressing than new forms of magic, or music. They suffer no physical pain, so they do not fear much. In the worlds below Calix Stay, though, they are easily swayed with a mere display of simple tricks, and fear is Dorini's greatest whip there. But here, those are nothing, for almost everyone in these realms possesses those powers to a small degree. Of course, it avails them nothing, for they all must return to the planes across Calix Stay for further lessons, but they can prove dangerous to us in their miseducation. They might find Dorini's games to their fancy upon these worlds, as a bauble to entertain themselves. She is yet capable of doing great harm, although not so much in the way of physical damage or unleashing great hordes against us."

Greyfax sat at a simple desk, carved of wood and painted a cheery green with a yellow chair. He withdrew from the hinged top a large chart, and spread it out before him. "Here, you see, is our disposition now." He indicated a place on the chart with his forefinger. "And here are the borders, guarded by Calix Stay. There is Cypher, and beyond this forest, where the foothills begin, is the camp of Tyron the Green. He still holds one of the Five, and that chap is one reason we are here."

Greyfax looked up, and smiled. "Only one of the many reasons, for the courses of many paths converge here, or begin to converge. Seeds long past begin to bear their fruit now, and we shall be in for a busy time of it soon."

"I'm glad," said Lorini simply. "I've forgotten myself in my grief over Cybelle, and begun to feel as if I have no real control over what's going to happen. I haven't felt this way since I first crossed Calix Stay, whenever we first began the journeys away from Home, exploring."

"It is to be expected, Lorini," replied Greyfax, in a softer voice. "Otherwise, how would we ever learn, or remember? And I have felt the same yearning, to control these events, so that I can at last return Home. I told Cephus of these thoughts when I was with him last. And Erophin, too. They laughed, and agreed. I think we are all weary of this, and our hearts begin to call us to our rest."

"That does sound wonderful," Lorini sighed. "But I know we must finish this as we must. We are responsible for those left to our guidance, and we must safeguard the Secrets, and hold them ready for all those in that lower darkness, just as those before us held them safe for us."

Greyfax turned slowly, and gazed at Lorini for a long moment before answering. "I had quite forgotten those times, you know, until you said that just now. It's almost as if

I'd allowed myself to forget thinking of them at all." He pushed back his chair and stood up. "I had wondered what it was that was sitting oddly with me, and you've hit upon the truth of it."

"How is that?" asked Lorini, looking at her friend with worried concern.

"I had merely forgotten where it all began, and what I had to go through there upon those lower planes. What we *all* had to go through there. And that I have the task of helping all those others upon the Path that will lead them out of that darkness Home."

"I hardly believe that of you, Greyfax. Of all those of the Circle, you are certainly the last one to forget your duties. I have known you long and well, and it cannot be said you have ever been guilty of neglect or carelessness in carrying out your errands."

"No, what you say is true. It is not neglect, exactly, but something very near it. Those were the hardest years, and the goal always seemed so far away. But now, with things as they are, and after my last visit with Cephus, I find I have the feelings. Just as you spoke of, when you mentioned Cybelle. I was beginning to believe that I had no sort of control over what was happening, or going to happen."

Lorini's eyes clouded, and her lips trembled. "I know it's all as it should be, and to the Purpose, but I yet have this ache in my heart about my daughter. Until I see her safe with my own eyes, I know it shall be there. I am sure it shall come to pass, and that all things that are to be shall be. It is just that I have this difficult lesson to learn that he has given me for my own growth. And that alone tells me it is yet but a short time before we are to leave these lower spheres."

"As you say, my lady, we get our lessons before we progress. I am learning mine twice over with you, first with the abduction of Cybelle, then with my feelings toward you."

"Oh, don't, dear Grimwald. Let us leave that here, on this level. You know I have loved you all this time, even as I loved Trianion. But those were old wounds, and debts from before our entry into the Circle. Yet it has taken us long to pay off those hasty moments of pleasure we sought before."

"But it is well enough, I agree. We have learned, I hope, to love each other in a better way. Just as we are loved by our Lord do we love one another. And it is that love I feel for you now."

Greyfax stood beside Lorini, and took her hand in his. He started to say something further, but she shook her head, and gazed at him in silence, her eyes clear gray-blue and full of the wonder of all Windameir.

She leaned closer, and kissed him tenderly on the cheek. "Dear, dear Grimwald, the things we have seen, you and I. It is beyond hope of ever expressing. And now, we shall, after all, be here at this together. We were kept long apart, while I yet carried on in Cypher and you were forever at your errands upon Atlanton. But now, it seems, and by His grace, we shall see this part unfold together."

"And unfold it shall. I think I hear news arriving now," said Greyfax, releasing Lorini's hand and stepping to the arched window that overlooked a small, simple courtyard.

"What is it, Galen?" called out Greyfax. "Have we a report from the River?"

"More than that. A group of Tyron's elves have showed up here claiming your favor and saying that they seek to parley with you."

"Then show the good fellows up. We'll have a chat over our lunch."

"They won't come in. They're at the edge of the wood, and say that if you wish to treat with them, they'll wait there an hour, no more."

Greyfax withdrew from the window, and a frown crossed his face.

"I wonder what this is all about? Has Tyron decided to relinquish that which he holds? That would be most unusual."

"I think Tyron has other plans," said Lorini, standing beside the desk and looking down at the chart unfolded upon it. "And I wonder that Urien Typhon has not angered Tyron before this, for I sent him to Tyron upon the errand of staying Tyron's hand, to keep him from striking across Calix Stay, and thereby putting one of the Five in grave danger. It would have been easy prey for my sister. And Tyron has always had much ambition. I wonder?" Lorini fell silent, looking at the chart.

"Perhaps he has yet fallen prey to her here," suggested Greyfax. "It seems he is sure of my accepting his offer to parley. Otherwise he would have come here himself."

"Then you must go to his meeting. Only be careful, Greyfax. If it is some scheme of my dark sister, it could be dangerous."

"Then we shall get to the bottom of this at once," he said,

and as he rolled up the chart to put it away, his eye fell upon the place marked as Tyron's camp. It was colored a brilliant green, and stood near where the Under Tide flowed into Calix Stay, from across the boundary's border.

"I wonder," he half muttered to himself, "if this has anything to do with a certain crossing?"

"A crossing?" echoed Lorini.

"Of some friends of ours I have been expecting."

He hastily rolled up the map and strode from the room.

In the chamber below, Galen Isenault waited before the stairwell, and at seeing Greyfax, he hurried forward. "I think it's a trap, Grimwald. They sent word to all the other settlements saying there would be a council day tomorrow, and that all who desire a peaceful life will be there to listen to a plan proposed by Tyron the Green, governor of Gilden Tarn."

"Governor of Gilden Tarn?" snapped Greyfax, running his hand over his beard thoughtfully. "This is indeed interesting."

"That's what he is calling himself now," replied Galen.

The two looked at each other a moment more in silence, then Greyfax walked to the door and selected a stout walking stick. "Indeed. Perhaps I shall have more use for this cane than to keep my knees from aching."

"He is growing more intolerable by the hour."

Greyfax touched Galen's shoulder. "I know, my friend. But perhaps things have been going his way a bit overlong now. There are definite patterns of change now. I smell it in the wind." Greyfax smiled, and giving Galen another gentle pat, repeated, "Yes, my friend, I can already smell it in the wind."

Before departing, Greyfax outlined his instructions for

Galen, and firmly sure the elf understood, he set out upon his own immediate errand.

He stepped off briskly, whistling an old and favorite walking tune he'd always fancied.

And the snoring breeze that stirred the wizard's cloak as he passed beyond the courtyard blew gently against Broco, cooling his burning dreams as he awakened in the calm green shadows of the Meadows of the Sun.

His eyes went wide in wonder, and it took him a moment to comprehend that he was beyond all the despair and terror of the Delvings of his sires, and the light reached gently to his aching heart, and eased even those darkest dreams which lingered there. It was, as the thought had just occurred to him, simply another beginning of the old journey he had set out upon on that long-ago morning in his old home beneath the mountain.

Tyron the Green

"Welcome, Tyron. We hadn't expected the honor of so esteemed an ally," said Froghorn Fairingay, addressing the elf who stood before him, bowing.

"My good Master Fairingay," said the slight figure politely, "I've come offering my services, and those of my company. It seems we are in discomfiting times indeed, with the enemy pressed so close upon us even here, beyond the boundaries."

Froghorn nodded. "It is as you say, Tyron. But it is all but a piece of the puzzle. It will fit rightly, one day, and then all will be as it should be with us."

A flickering moment of unease swept across the elf's face, but if the young wizard saw it, he did not show any outward sign.

"I have it on good word that there is an enemy battle camp not far from Gilden Far, sir," said Tyron, his voice becoming more relaxed. "I have thought perhaps it might be wise if I moved my band into the Gilden Wood, so as to block any forays upon that flank. We are scattered now, up and down the boundaries, on patrol, and are stretched far too thin to be of any use should we be attacked in force."

"I thought you were but scouting there, Tyron. We had no plan for you to be a main portion of any battle line unaided. My forces are drawn up nearby, so that your men would have the safety of friends if close set by an attack in force."

"It is as you say, sir, for now. But I have a feeling the face of this battle plan is changing, even as we speak. We have seen the gathering of forces now for more than a few days, and although there are many war camps, no move has been made as yet. That is not a natural state of affairs. One does not gather men and arms and then take pleasure walks, admiring the beauty of the countryside."

Froghorn did not speak for a moment, and seemed to be pondering what the elf was saying. "What you say is true, Tyron," he said at length. "We are in a strange time now. I can't imagine what the Darkness is waiting for, but they seem to be waiting for some sign, or word. And we will have need of having Gilden Wood blocked to movements of those we don't want lurking about where they should not be. I think that is an excellent plan. Call your men in from their patrols, and take charge of the Wood. That should seal out any undesirable travelers from crossing our lines without our knowing of it."

Tyron smiled widely, and raised his hand in salute. "We shall see to it the Wood is impassable," he said. "But I shall leave my patrols out a bit longer while we make the transition. It will take some rearranging to regroup all my company into the fastness of the Wood."

Bear, upon waking from a short, troubled nap in the adjacent tent, had listened to the whole conversation unnoticed. He slipped off the cot, padded outside, and went in next door, lifting the tent flap and entering softly.

"Well, so there you are," greeted Froghorn. "I began to wonder if you would ever catch up on your sleep."

"Hullo, sir," muttered Bear, raising a paw to the wizard.

"Good tidings to you, Bruinlen," said Tyron. "And how is our good dwarf companion today?"

"Well, thanks," grumbled Bear, his hackles trying to rise, although he could not put his finger on what was troubling him.

"We have been laying our plans, and have discovered a weakness in the Gilden Wood," explained Froghorn, walking to a camp table and pointing out a place on one of the many unrolled charts that lay there.

Bear's ears picked up. "Gilden Wood? Why, that's where I had one of my old shelters, before we crossed Calix Stay."

He crossed and stood beside the gray-clad form of Froghorn, looking over the wizard's shoulder at the confused colors and drawings on the map.

"I don't think that's a very good likeness of the Wood," said Bear at last. "There isn't any stream there, or at least not to my knowledge. Or unless it has all changed since I was there last."

Froghorn bent forward and studied what Bear had pointed out.

"And here there's a thicket so dense you couldn't get anything through, unless maybe it was smaller than a chipmunk. It's like a fence in the wood. I knew a hedgehog that had crossed that once, and he said it went on, all the way through the center of Gilden."

Froghorn nodded, and made a small note on the margin with a pen he had taken from a holder on the table.

"And over here, where these lines are, that's what's left of some ruins or other, left over from some other time, I guess. It's mostly just old caves now. That's where I had my home there. It wasn't bear digs, but it was snug. And full of all sorts of handy tunnels, already dug, and with two or three very sensible spare doors."

After another moment, Froghorn straightened.

"This isn't the most accurate chart I have put my eye to," he said, turning to Tyron. "I thought you had corrected all this before you gave me the map?"

"I did, sir," explained Tyron hurriedly. "I didn't think it could possibly matter about that stream bed or those ancient caves. They are of no matter in this instance, and only the main lines and routes of travel are here, which is all we are concerned with. I had no idea you wanted a tree-by-tree description of the Gilden Wood. When you said a rough sketch of the terrain there, I naturally assumed you wanted it for a battle map."

"And that's precisely what I wanted," replied Froghorn, in a chilly, even tone. "I see here before me something I had not taken into account. Caves, where men or arms could be hidden, a route that could be taken that would be concealed from scouting parties who would not know to look for a stream beyond this natural barrier. And there is no telling how much else has been overlooked in this hasty draft."

Froghorn turned to Tyron.

"I realize you had no idea of all that I wanted, Tyron. But this will not do at all. I need a more detailed map if I am to lay my plans and take all the factors of a battle into consideration. This oversight could cost us a victory, if the chaps on the other side are more familiar with the Gilden Wood than we are. My men have been removed from their familiar surroundings, and aren't at all on terms with these climes. I'm not even sure myself about the lay of the terrain, and until I have a chance to talk with Melodias and Greymouse, I'm not at all certain that we are anywhere near where we are supposed to be."

Froghorn then addressed himself to Bear.

"I would like you, Bruinlen, since you are somewhat familiar with these parts, to go with Tyron, and fill in this rough sketch of the Gilden Wood, and Gilden Tarn, and any place in between you might think of that could at all be important to our battle plans. We have no reports of any imminent action, so I'm sure you'll have time to complete at least a fuller description of those places I have asked for before we have any need of the information."

Bear moaned to himself, but said nothing. He nodded, trying to work up some enthusiasm for the task Froghorn had just given him.

Tyron the Green stood before the camp table, glaring at his boots, but he, too, remained silent for a moment before he spoke. "I am sure you have other more urgent matters for the stout Bear, sir. I can re-sketch the map for you myself, now that I have clearly in mind what you require. There is no need to send along our friend here, before he has fully rested from his ordeal of the crossing."

Bear tended to agree with Tyron, although there was something about the elf that he did not quite like.

Froghorn dashed his hopes before he could decide what it was he did not trust in Tyron.

"I'm afraid you will have your hands full, good Tyron. And Bear can return by way of Greymouse, and deliver him my messages, and return to me when he is done. It will free you to your work, and speed up your grouping of your elves in Gilden Wood."

"Then as you wish," snapped Tyron. "I shall set out in an hour to begin my task. I would ask my companion to be ready to accompany me then." The elf bowed curtly, and stumped out of the tent.

Bear watched, slightly aghast that anyone would be so rude to one of the Masters of the Circle.

"Now, good Bruinlen, as for you," smiled the wizard, "I've got a very important errand for you to run, without our fair elf knowing of it."

Bear felt the uneasy, familiar twist of fear in his stomach as Froghorn outlined his plan.

A High Elfin King

As Bear moved along behind the stealthy Tyron, his great hackles crept up and down on his back, and he could not rid himself of the feeling that he was in the presence of some danger. He sniffed the air repeatedly, and cast his huge head about as he paced along, but there was no outward warning signal, or any of the usual signs that would define an enemy or unseen hazard.

There were a number of other elves in Tyron's band, and Bear could see most of this party, although he knew the largest part of the company was out of sight in the darker eaves of the woods, and without knowing how, or why, Bear felt that the number of the elves was growing as they went along.

He ran over in his head the instructions Froghorn had given him, and tried to recall what it was that had seemed to amuse the young wizard so.

"You will go with our ambitious elf, and do just as he says. Whenever he tells you his new map is complete, or that your mission with him is finished, make your way to General

Greymouse. He is camped not far beyond the Eastering Dell. You will remember that. It isn't far from Cheerweir."

Bear remembered all that portion of the Meadows of the Sun well, and told Froghorn he would be able to find it.

"Tyron has his own plans, and we have others which are going to bode no good to our fanciful friend. Feet that come in small boots can often make the most noise of all when it comes to dancing on a drum. And that is what it all seems to be leading to."

Froghorn had paused, and thrown back his head in a long, rippling chuckle.

"The pure simplicity of it," he went on. "And I would never have suspected any of it, or guessed at anywhere near the truth of what he had intended to be the resolving of it all."

Bear had studied the problem from every angle he could see, turning it over and over in his mind, but it still seemed rather vague to him, and it certainly didn't seem anywhere near as funny as Froghorn had thought it, especially as he lumbered along behind Tyron, who kept casting nasty glances over his shoulder in Bear's direction.

"Well, it's beyond me," muttered Bear, trying to make the best of the situation, and shaking his head now and then as he recognized old, faintly familiar marks.

Gilden Wood was more sparsely settled than Bear remembered, and seemingly large swaths of the woods had been burned, or blasted out. Great black tree trunks rose like shattered hulks as they neared a particularly dense section of the Wood, and Bear saw long rows of burnt trees stretching their dead limbs skyward, marching on away into a distance he could not see an end of. He remembered that it had been in these realms that men had had settlements, and other kinds. They now looked wasted and dead.

And as if by some sort of wizard's spell, immediately beyond the closest stand of charred trees there began a green and thickly growing wood that looked to Bear almost too thick and overgrown to walk into. It was this green wall that Tyron made directly for, and it was at this moment that Bear noticed how large the elfin host had grown.

All about him marched the small woodland elves, who looked not at all like the ones he had met in Cypher, and it appeared to Bear that the very earth was parting to reveal more and more of Tyron's clan. Upon looking more closely, Bear saw that some of the elves were coming from concealed stairways that led up from the earth, and that the clever trapdoors were hidden amid clumps of hurryback bushes and tinwhistle brambles. He watched in amazement as scores of these elves hurried from their hiding places and made their way toward Tyron, whose face had taken on the smug look of one who is in complete control of his surroundings. Bear looked back at the earth whence the elves had arisen, and to his surprise, all was once more merely impassable thickets of undergrowth.

A noisy din had begun in the vanguard of Tyron's elves, and this uproar drew Bear's attention once more to where the elfin leader stood. Bear's thoughts raced, and he began to have a distinctly uneasy feeling in the pit of his stomach. Whatever Froghorn had found amusing in the entire situation escaped Bear, and he sincerely wished that he were with the young master at the moment, sitting before the breakfast fire and reaching for another loaf, and full of the good comb honey, rather than gawking awkwardly at an elfin host beyond count, led by the now strutting Tyron, who was riding about at the moment on the shoulders of a dozen or so of his followers.

A great cry was going up from clumps of elves here and there, and at last the entire throng, which stretched away in both directions until Bear could only make out the tiniest forms in the distance, took up the chant.

"Tyron of Gilden,
Tyron of Gilden,
Holder of the Secret,
King of the Wood,
Ruin of the Circle,
And Light of the Dark,
Tyron of Gilden,
Our High Elfin King.
Tyron, Tyron, Tyron,"

sang the lifted voices, and the earth trembled as feet pounded in time on the ground, and Bear's ears began to hum and throb with the high-pitched cry of the elves.

He was too stunned for the moment to realize what was occurring, but like a slowly rising bubble in the clear depths of a stream, a vague, faint finger of fear touched his heart. He looked about him, seeking an avenue of escape should the need arise, but in every direction line upon line of Tyron's clan stood drawn up as if in formal formation to a high prince's coronation. Uneasily, Bear began easing toward the long shadows of a stand of ancient trees that mysteriously stood unharmed amid the ruin and rubble of the fire-gutted wood. His hackles tickled his neck, and he felt an overwhelming desire to bolt, but he fought to control that urgent compulsion, and slowly made his way toward the only visible area that wasn't overfilled with Tyron's hordes.

After a huge commotion at the front of the demonstration, the voice of Tyron was heard, raised into a high, staccato scream, so that he could be heard by all. "You needn't worry, my slinky friend," shouted Tyron. "You are not to be harmed. We are releasing you so that you may take word back to that imbecile Faringay, and the other connivers of the wretched Circle, that Tyron the Green is sealing off forever this wood of Gilden, and that no traveler of any kind shall pass these boundaries, either in or out. My kingdom begins at this moment, and I have taken measures to ensure that none of the meddling thieves of the Circle shall ever again be able to try to take back from me what is rightfully mine." Tyron gasped for air, then went on with his harangue. "I am taking with me what my father willed me, and this one of the Secrets will I set my throne upon. None shall have its power but me, and I shall use it for the good of all my kind and kindred, and it shall remain with me forever."

A great ragged cheer went up as Tyron paused, and another outburst of chanting drowned out everything for a short time.

At last, Tyron's voice rose again. "Greyfax has had his last chance to treat with me, and my emissaries are with him even now. And beyond acceptance of my terms, there is nothing to be hoped for. And even the dreaded Queen of

Darkness hears my plans, and agrees that Tyron the Green has just and worthy cause to rule these realms of Gilden, and that he has all power to make his own elfin law forever in this wood."

More cheering broke out here, and Bear felt himself shoved and pushed, and only by the greatest forbearance did he manage to overcome the great urge to rear and claw his way to freedom. The rude hands seemed to be casting him away from the center of the throng, and Tyron's voice was fading and being drowned out by the roaring of the chanting crowd.

"Give him a poke, there, and set him out," jeered one of the small elves of Tyron's band.

"His likes don't deserve to go free," chimed in another. "Animals are all alike. If you don't keep them controlled, they go wild, and then you're back where you always were, having to hunt them down one by one and slay them."

"Tyron says he's to be set loose, so that's the way of it," snapped another, who slapped the hand of the one who was holding Bear roughly by a handful of fur.

"Then fling him out, and good riddance," snorted the other elf.

"He won't ever be able to come into our woods after this. Not by what Tyron says. Even the Dark Lady has agreed with him on taking the Wood for our own, and from all I hear, she has promised Tyron the rest of the Five to hold here in Gilden. Seems as if she hasn't no taste for being too close to the Arkenchest, and she's going to let King Tyron be steward of all the Secrets."

"Hear, hear," voiced another of Tyron's band, and interest

went from their prisoner to the conversation, and soon Bear found himself beyond the boundaries of the sprawling throng of elves, and loping hard, away in the direction he remembered his destination to be, where, with any luck at all, he was to find General Greymouse, and there to tell his friends of the terrible news he had heard in the uproar of Tyron the Green's mutiny, and his denial of the Circle.

And Dorini had been named aloud, and all the clan of Tyron seemed to know of the Arkenchest, and the hopes that it held, and that it was somehow to be captured by Dorini and turned over to Tyron, the traitorous elf of old, whose father had gone on before him, refusing to turn back the Secret he held to the safekeeping of the Council of Elders, and who had passed on to his son the seed of distrust and doubt that now threatened all the hopes and plans of the Circle.

Bear raced on, his drumming heart full of dark thoughts, of his wasted journey and the disappearance of Dwarf and Otter, and the grim certainty that the end was indeed near if the Meadows of the Sun were invaded by the enemies of the Light and if Gilden Wood, where his old home had been, was no longer safe for travel.

He was past the sentry before he heard the surprised warning snapped at his hard-running form, and before he could explain anything at all to the startled man, he was suddenly face to face with General Greymouse, who seemed to keep smiling more and more broadly as he related his terrible news, until at last Bear thought that worst of all the things he'd seen and heard, worst by far was the sudden inability of anyone to understand the grave news he was relating.

As he finished pouring out his devastating tale, his heart jumped to his throat when his old and trusted friend General Greymouse threw back his head, slapped a hand to his knee, and was convulsed with long gales of laughter.

In the Woods of Gilden Far

"We has done it now," moaned Ned, feeling his thin body carefully, searching for something broken.

Cranfallow, sitting dazedly beside him, stared blankly at his friend. "Where is we?" he finally blurted.

"Blast it if I knows," mumbled Ned, trying slowly to get to his feet.

Cranfallow looked about at his surroundings and whistled. "It don't seems like no place I has ever touched a boot to. Look at them trees. And feel how fresh the wind is."

Ned Thinvoice's eyes widened, and he smashed a fist to his palm. "It were our dwarf witch. I knows he has done us some new trick or other. And he wasn't nowheres near wherever this is. We was in a worm's cupboard, or a snake's hole of some sorts." He paused, frowning. "At least, it seems like we was?"

Cranfallow pursed his lips, thinking hard. "You is right, Ned. But what has we blundered into now? And where is our Dwarf?"

Ned Thinvoice sat back down heavily and put his head in his hands. "I doesn't know, Cranny, and I isn't so sure I is in no such of a hurry to finds him. We is always in the soup when he's about, and I loves the little fellow and all, but I isn't up to no such goings-on as these is, and waking up halfway to I doesn't know where." He groaned softly into his sleeves. "Maybe I is ready to take up a nice quiet clerk job somewheres, and leaves all this to-do to someone who can stands up to this sort of rousting around."

"I guess you is right, Ned, but I doesn't think we is going to gets to try out that sorts of life, least-ways not yet. Here comes our Dwarf yonder, and it looks like he has got hisself some more help."

Cranfallow pointed away to the border of a dark green line of tall trees that opened out into the meadow where Ned and Cranfallow found themselves sitting. A band of ten or twelve tall, fair elves followed along behind Broco, and a taller, fairer elf, who seemed to be in command, strode along beside Dwarf, talking in a determined voice, and making quick gestures in the air with his hands. Dwarf seemed to be listening very closely.

Upon spying his two companions, Broco brightened, and hurried to their side.

"Good Cranny, and Ned," he huffed, giving them loud thwacks upon their backs and almost toppling over the startled Thinvoice. "We've gotten ourselves through and across Calix Stay, after all. When the Foundation broke, I guess the old underground river there, the Under Tide, swept us back into from whence it sprang, which was the root of the Endin, or so says my friend Galen."

"I knows we is in it now, sir, but doesn't we has no way to gets back? I mean across this whatever river you says we has crossed?"

"I'm afraid you're here, and shall have to be happy with it. At least, unless we are supposed to go back over." Broco turned to the elf beside him. "Galen Isenault," and he held a hand toward Ned and Cranny. "Ned Thinvoice, and Corporal Cranfallow, my two close companions for quite a long while now."

A small smile crept over the elf's face. "And you have been through the halls of Brosingamene, I hear? And met Alane? And nosed out the escape route through the ancient waters of the Foundation Stone? It is an adventure worth the retelling, and I look forward to hearing all of it. But now, we must find our camp, and leave these borders. Things are hard upon us, even on this side of Calix Stay. It has not gone well since Dorini has taken hostage the fair Cybelle. And Cypher lies in the hands of the foul Doraki, and even these shores are no longer safe havens for anyone, whether dwarf or elf, or animal or man."

Dwarf halted in mid-stride. "Cybelle taken?" His voice choked off in the beginning of tears, and the cold splinter of icy fear that he had carried away from the Dark Queen's dungeons took his breath and sent a searing, frozen pain across his chest.

"Aye, from the very halls of Cypher. It was an unexpected move on Dorini's part. And all the others of the Circle had been at errands elsewhere. Froghorn was across here, staying the move of Tyron the Green, who had proposed to strike his own blow and gain Cypher for himself. He has not forgotten the grudge his father carried at the Council, and would stop at nothing to take what he feels is rightfully his. Even now, he is proclaimed governor of Gilden Tarn, according to the news I had as I left to come to fetch you."

Dwarf had slumped heavily down as the elf was speaking, and looked up now, great tears welling in his eyes. "Then this has all been for naught," he moaned, "and getting the Chest safely across Calix Stay come to nothing. With Cybelle taken, what can they do against Dorini?"

"For one thing, the Darkness only knows who holds the Chest, but not where the Chest is. That is the only thing that would assure their success. As grim as it seems, even Cybelle could not buy for Dorini what she is asking."

"But what of Froghorn now? And Greyfax, and the lady Lorini? Are they safe?"

"Froghorn is about somewhere here, still at his chores," said Galen, smiling broadly, "and Greyfax was off to treat with Tyron's advisers, the last I heard, and that was as I came to guide you back to him. Lorini is there, in the new mountain fastness where we are heading now."

Dwarf's hopes rose. "You mean we are going to her?"

"Just as quickly as our feet will carry us," assured the elf, reaching down and touching Dwarf gently on the shoulder. "But come, you all must be famished and exhausted. Come along. We'll find a fire to dry you, and food to fill you, and then you can catch us up on all that's been going on across Calix Stay."

"And is we agoing to gets a nap, to boot?" asked Ned shyly. "I thinks I could sleeps a month or two, the way I feels now."

"And fine sleeping hammocks for those that want them,"

reassured Galen, turning and leading away in a direction that carried them from the still roaring nearness of Calix Stay, off on a new bearing that seemed to point directly toward the white-capped mountains far ahead and asleep in a misty blue patch of horizon that dimmed in the golden shadows of the lowering sun.

As Broco walked along beside Ned and Cranfallow, he began to point out landmarks he was familiar with, or had read of. "It has all changed, of course, but these woods lead on until Gilden Tarn, and beyond, to Gilden Far. Bear had his old camp not so very far from here, in the days when our friendship was new. And I met Otter first at Cheerweir. That's away and downstream from Gilden Tarn a bit."

Ned Thinvoice yawned. "Them is all wonderful tales you is spinning, sir, and I is always one to knows a scrap or two of news about where I is, but I thinks I is plumb wore out on my hoofs, and needs a snooze. Isn't we anywhere near where Master Galen was talking about when he said we was agoing to gets a nap?"

"I is with Ned," groaned Cranfallow, stumbling awkwardly along, his eyes hollow and dark with fatigue.

Dwarf started a huff, but saw the exhaustion in his friends' faces, and remembered that he hadn't slept in what seemed like days. "It's only a bit farther on, and we shall have our fill and rest. And Galen has said there is word up and down the Wood to keep an eye out for crossers. He even has word that Bear crossed before us, and is already on his way to Lorini. So wherever Bear is, Otter is sure to be close behind. We all must have somehow gotten into the Delvings of my sires, and when the Foundation broke, we all got swept here."

"We has been swept, we has. I isn't going to be no good for hoofing, though, if we doesn't gets some solid food in us afore long."

Galen strode back to the friends, and pointed an arm in the direction of a clearing ahead. "There is our camp, and there we'll find refreshment for you."

"Anything, as long as it are grub," complained Ned.

"Or looks like a cot," put in Cranny.

"My friends and I have come far in these past hours," said Dwarf, addressing Galen in a voice tinged with fatigue. "It seems we've come across not only miles, but worlds as well, and I'm aching for a chance to rest and ponder on what's to be done now."

"We're almost there. It's not far now. And then we shall go on after you've regained your strength."

"That might takes a bit," yawned Ned. "And after all I has been dragged through, I may has to nap a week."

"Oh, Ned, you is always on the damp side of anything. You was plenty glad for a peek at sunshine not too long back. And we wasn't expecting no sorts of welcome like this."

Ned, walking now beside Dwarf, turned. "And how is it we *is* here? I mean I sorts of recalls a lot of dark, and noise, and then some sorts of river busting aloose, but how is we here? I mean, it don't all tot up, the way I sees it."

Dwarf looked at his friend briefly. "Well, Ned, you see," he began, then shook his head. "I mean it's hard to explain, yet it's all so simple. We are what you might call changed. Crossing Calix Stay as we did, we have entered another world. It is only a part of the one we were in, but on a higher level."

"Like we is out of one country and in another?"

"Exactly, old fellow. We've changed countries, that's all. And I don't think we'll be going back, now."

"You mean we isn't going to see our homes no more? Or where we was bread and buttered?" asked Ned.

"They ain't none of them folks left, no ways, Ned," replied Cranny.

"We shall be going on, Ned. You'll understand a little more, perhaps, after we've been here awhile."

"I think what he is after saying is that we is dead, Ned," went on Cranfallow, looking hard at Broco. "Or leastways, something like that."

Dwarf stopped before he answered. "Yes, and no. For you can plainly see we're not what you would call dead."

"Not unless ghosties and such is flesh and bone," agreed Ned, looking perplexed.

"But then, when we left the kingdom of Underearth of my kindred, we did change forms. You might say we died there, to that old life. Or one form of us died."

"But I doesn't feel dead," argued Ned, pinching himself.

"Of course not, you silly lug. You are you, just as always. We don't change anything but the outward form."

"You mean I is still Ned Thinvoice?" he asked, incredulously.

"And shall always be, whether you go by the name of Ned Thinvoice or Butterbean."

"This are all too much for my head," moaned Cranny. "And all I knows is if I is a ghostie, I is a hungry and tired one."

"That makes two of us, Cranny," said Broco, and they followed on again after Galen, who started forward once more after they had finished their talk.

They passed through the first soft green apron of the woods, fragrant with resin scent and green leaves, and on into the deepening cool shadows of the trees, going slower now, as the way became more difficult. A circle of open clearings came into sight, and Dwarf saw what looked to be sentries posted in the upper boughs of two tall trees.

A few steps farther on, and a low whisper reached his ears, and the dull metallic sound of a rifle safety bolt being flicked on.

"Greetings, Galen. We didn't expect you back so soon."

The figure that went with the voice materialized out of almost thin air, and extended a hand to Broco.

"And you're the one we've been waiting for, Broco, Dwarflord."

"My service is yours," said Dwarf politely, although more than a little confused. "And these are my companions Ned and Cranny."

The sentry clasped hands with Ned. "A brisk task, sir, traveling with the likes of this stiff-necked fellow."

Before Ned could reply, the sentry had grasped Cranfallow by the hand in his turn. "And you, good Cranny, aren't you taxed to exhaustion with the forever huffing of your traveling companion?"

Dwarf's face fell into an ugly scowl, and he drew himself up into a threatening position. Before he could speak, the sentry threw back the hood to his cloak, and for the first time Broco realized the voice had been vaguely familiar, but his exhaustion and hunger had kept him from noticing it.

"Is that you, Froghorn?" he blurted out, suddenly overwhelmed with fatigue and relief. The past hours had been long, and the crossing of Calix Stay had further weakened him. He fell on the young wizard and buried his face in Froghorn's cloak.

And Cranny and Ned, standing struck silent in their place, turned as another figure loomed out of the shadows of the trees and raced toward them. Before they could cry out, Bear, in his man form, had grasped the two of them by the shoulders in a terrific hug, and fallen on the helplessly sobbing Dwarf.

"Well, if this don't fry the cakes," breathed Cranny. "If this are what it's like being deaded and all, I wonder what in my great-grandgeezer's straw hat it are like to be alive and kicking?"

He fell silent, scratching his head, and with further snorts and snuffles from Broco and back-thumping from Bear, the reunited friends followed Galen Isenault on into the busy elfin camp, deep in the woods of Gilden Far.

A Dark Wind Across The Sun

Despair and Terror

An amazing change seemed to have come over Froghorn Fairingay as he stood before the two friends, his arms outstretched to them.

"Welcome, old friends. It is well met that I have found you here so soon after your crossing."

Flewingam looked hard at Otter, who was openly staring at the worn figure of the young master. His hair was rather longer than they remembered, and his face seemed to carry an almost bitter look. "Fatigue and worry, no doubt," Otter hastily explained to himself, although he could not explain away the joyless laugh or the cold hand that had shaken his paw in greeting.

Froghorn was saying something to Flewingam about his travels, and how he had come to be this side of Calix Stay, but Otter did not hear the words. He watched Froghorn move about as he spoke, and gestured to make a point, and slapped the top of his boot with a riding crop. This, to all appearances, was much the same Froghorn as Otter had seen him last, yet something had altered the young wizard terribly.

Flewingam felt the change had taken place entirely in Froghorn's face, for it was there that the fire had died, as if Froghorn were weary beyond words. An ashen pallor replaced the old, high color of the young wizard's cheeks, and his eyes seemed to be sunken and lifeless.

"And so, good Otter, we find our paths crossed again, and pleasantly so," Froghorn concluded, and turned to Belwicke. "Let us have some refreshments, good elf, and see to it we're not disturbed for a bit. I have much news to impart to my friends, and they to me."

"We'll see to it, Your Excellency," mumbled Belwicke, bowing stiffly.

Otter and Flewingam followed Froghorn into a rather large shelter, fashioned from logs and vines, and grown over with moss.

Otter stopped suddenly and put his muzzle close to one of the walls. "Why, this was here from before," he chittered. "I think one of the chaps from down below Gilden Tarn must have built this. What was that fellow's name, anyhow?" Otter puckered his whiskers and scowled as he tried to recall the misplaced name.

"It was a woodchuck," said Froghorn over his shoulder as he settled down to a crude wooden table that was a size or two too small for him. A roughly constructed human-sized chair had been built of new wood and stood out sharply in contrast to the older, smoky interior of the shelter.

"Why, that's right," agreed Otter, standing still and whistling out his cheeks. "And a right cheery sort of fellow, too, if I remember right. Always full of some story or other, and forever forgetting what he was saying." Otter sat as he finished speaking, then continued. "Is he still about? I'd like to speak to someone who has been here all this time we've been away."

"I wouldn't know," replied Froghorn, who had stopped speaking as Belwicke and two other of the woodland elves had come into the low shelter with pots of herb tea and fresh loaves of bread and combs of honey. Another of the elves brought in a covered pan, which was placed before Froghorn.

"Well, my good comrades, what of yourselves? I have given you a rundown of my whereabouts since last we met; now let me hear your tale. How is it you're here, and wherever have you lost the rest of your company?"

"Well," began Otter, slightly confused, for Froghorn had told them nothing, "I'm not very sure at all of how we got here, but before that, it was all simple enough. Or not simple, but on the other hand, not easy to explain, either."

"What he means," burst in Flewingam, "is that it's hard to say what's happened since we saw you last. We've been lost more often than not, and split up from our Dwarf and friends most of the time. We were trying to reach Fair Crossing so we could reach you, or Greyfax, or Melodias, and give the Chest back, but with one thing and another, we lost Broco and ended up in some snake's den, and there were the Roots, then there was all this noise and light, and here we are."

Froghorn's face had changed as Flewingam spoke. "Then Dwarf has the Chest still?" he asked, a faint light glimmering in the depths of his exhausted eyes.

"He had it the last I know," said Otter, between mouthfuls of the elfin bread and honey and long sips of the sweet tea. "Only now none of it makes any difference at all, for were here, and we don't know where Broco is, or Bear, or Ned, or Cranny, or Thumb, or any of the rest."

"But anyway we've found each other," said Flewingam to Froghorn, his spirits trying to rise. "And that makes some of it all right, at least."

"Yes, my friend, I think our finding each other was a stroke of fortune indeed." Froghorn turned, and called out to the elf who was waiting outside the shelter door. "Belwicke, I think perhaps you should have your men warned to expect the arrival of a dwarf and some others, if they're not already among us. They shall be brought to me immediately."

Froghorn beamed a shallow smile at Otter. "We want to see our good Dwarf as soon as he arrives. After all, his burden has indeed been one that has been hard to bear."

Otter hardly had time to agree, for he was busy with the honey and bread. It wasn't the best he'd remembered from his old home, although it was good sweetcomb, and it seemed it had been forever since he had eaten.

Flewingam had poured out his third cup of the hot tea, and sat back, his hunger appeased for the moment. "Do you think he'll find his way here?" he asked Froghorn, who had at last uncovered his own dish, and now began to eat.

"I'm sure we shall find him, if he is to be found at all," said the young wizard. "And if what you say is so, then we should probably be expecting him anytime now."

Otter's nose had begun to twitch an odd twitch, and for some reason his hackles curled on his back. A slightly giddy sensation crept into his full stomach. "I'm awfully tired all of a sudden," said Otter, looking strangely at his friend. "Is there anyplace we can rest up a bit? We've been up and going so long I can hardly remember what a good rest is like." He yawned, and patted his tummy. "And finding you again has been a shock, and now a good meal has worn me out."

"Of course, my friends. Belwicke will show you where you can lie down a bit. We'll wake you if we have news of the arrival of our other companions."

Froghorn rose and gave them a cool hand and paw shake as they left the shelter, and instructed Belwicke, who had been waiting at the door, to see to sleeping arrangements for the friends.

They hadn't far to go to reach a rather large underground room which Otter rightly suspected was the woodchucks' root and herb cellar. Along the walls were dried roots and aging herbs, and in the far corner of the dim hole were neatly stacked cots.

"Old Whistlepig must have had a lot of company to have a supply of beds like this," said Flewingam, pulling down a large hammock and stringing it onto the hooks that were buried in the walls.

Flewingam's queasiness had subsided somewhat, and turning to make certain that the elf who had shown them into the cellar had left the lamp and gone, he lowered his voice to a low whisper and put his mouth next to Otter's ear. "Did you see what I saw in the dish Froghorn was eating? Or am I having visions from crossing this river of yours?"

Otter chittered, and said aloud, "My, oh my, this cot does look good indeed. I may sleep all week." Under his breath, and leaning near Flewingam, he nodded and said, "It couldn't have been a mistake. And it wasn't a vision, unless were both seeing the same ones, and unless they stink."

"But what can have happened to Froghorn that he would

do such a thing? Or even allow it to be tolerated in his presence?" asked Flewingam, confusion and anger creeping into his urgent whisper.

"Shhhhh!" cautioned Otter. "I don't know about you, but I'm not even sure it *is* Froghorn."

Flewingam's eyes widened and shone in surprise in the golden glow of the lamp.

"He was too different, somehow. I can't put my paw on it. The eyes, and the touch. It was cold, and all funny. My hackles could barely stay down."

"Why didn't you say something? Or give me a signal?"

"Because I didn't want to give ourselves away. If this *isn't* Froghorn, and I'll lay my last chin whisker it isn't, then who *is* it, and why is he here?"

"And that Belwicke character, and his cronies. I know they're elves and all, but they seem odd, if you know what I mean."

"These must be woodland elves," mused Otter. "I have heard of the elfin clans being divided into two camps, the woodland and the waterfolk. And these elves haven't laughed. All the elves I ever met at Cypher were always full of cheer, and that beautiful music. I think they must have been of the waterfolk sort."

"These elves look almost like men. Or something akin to there. Smaller, but they don't seem like real elves at all."

Otter lay back heavily on the small cot he had prepared for himself. "And I'll wager you there is one of those fine fellows on guard at the door, to boot."

Flewingam crept silently to the lamp and extinguished it, and moved along the wall to the short dirt steps that led outside. Otter, his eyes still full of the glowing lamp, could barely make out Flewingam's form.

After a long moment, Flewingam's voice spoke right at Otter's ear. "There are two of them. And I don't think they're there to keep anyone from disturbing our sleep."

Otter whistled low in his throat, and chittered a rapid whisper. "I don't understand this at all, Flew. I don't know who this Froghorn really is, or what these elves are up to, but I do know we've landed ourselves into a stewpot of trouble." He shuddered violently. "Poor old fellow who lived here never had a chance. And I guess he ended up on his own table, just like that poor thing today." Otter's voice trailed away. "I wondered why we hadn't run across more animals in the woods. Of course they wouldn't make themselves known if they were being hunted."

"I think I knew before that," whispered Flewingam. "Our Froghorn would have been happier to see us."

"I wonder," said Otter aloud, then lowering his voice, "Will any of them be glad to see us, if we ever run into any of them again? It seems like we're always bad news to anybody concerned with us. Poor old Thumb found that out the hard way. And I guess Dwarf, and Bear, and Ned and Cranny, too. Wherever they are, if they're still alive."

Flewingam gave his little friend a gentle pat, and felt the small gray animal's body tensed and quivering. "Here, here, old fellow, this won't ever do. We're in a pickle, and no doubt about it, but we'll find some way out. I don't think this is all going to end here."

"I don't either, but then I can't truly say where I think it will. But Flew, it's all over for us, can't you see? What are you and I going to do alone? We don't have the Chest, and anyhow, if we did, this fake Froghorn, or whoever he is, would take it away from us. And I don't imagine he's got anything more in mind for us except that I'll sooner or later end up on his dinner table, and you'll probably be kept for labor."

"Whoever can he be?" mulled Flewingam. "I haven't ever heard of any of the Circle turning bad, or anything like that. Has that ever happened, or anything like it?"

"No, not to my knowledge, or according to any of the stories I've ever heard or read."

Otter fell silent a moment, then grabbed Flewingam's hand. "What you just said, Flew. About one of the Circle turning bad? Well, while we were in Cypher, one day Dwarf was reading a story to me out of one of the books there. You know Dwarf and his lore books. Well, it was just what you said, only it was so long ago people don't remember, and it's the only thing that could explain any of it."

"What ever are you babbling about, Otter? What story? What books?"

"The books in Lorini's library, and the story of how it had all begun. When Lorini came down from Windameir to rule the lower three worlds, she had a twin, Dorini, the Dark Queen, and they were to have shared the kingdoms equally, but Dorini was jealous, and didn't want to let any of her people leave her kingdoms to go back to Windameir, and so she set out to take over. That's what started all the Dragon Wars Dwarf was always talking about, and all the other business. That's where the Worlughs and Gorgolacs came from, too. The people she kept couldn't get back to Windameir, so they began to get all funny."

"There's nothing funny in a Gorgolac or Worlugh to my way of thinking," snapped Flew.

Otter ignored his friend and hurried on, breathless. "Well, she had a friend, who was once a part of the Circle, just like she was, and he joined up with her, and the two of them have been trying ever since to overcome the Light."

Flewingam was silent, and Otter went on half aloud.

"Could it be the one we saw fighting with Greyfax that night on Havamal?"

"I think it must be. None of the other things have anything like that kind of power. Or at least none of the Gorgolacs or Worlughs Dwarf ever told me about had any of those powers."

"Doraki!" whispered Otter, between clenched teeth.

An icy wave of fear froze the friends into silence, and a greenish tongue of yellow flames seemed to crackle alive in the cold darkness of their prison, for they now knew they were indeed captives, and held by the dark Doraki, who had somehow taken on the identity of one of the Masters of the Circle. A darkness such as the two friends had never known before settled over their hearts, and any hopes they had held onto were devoured in the frozen wastes of their despair and terror.

A Woodchuck's Cellar

Flewingam was awakened by a persistent whistle in his ear. He sat up, blinking his eyes in the darkness, trying to pull his reeling thoughts together. For a moment he thought he was in the eerie tunnels beyond Calix Stay, but Otter, chittering excitedly into his ear, soon brought him full awake.

"I've found the back way out of poor old Whistlepig's cellar. I knew I'd find it if I kept at it. Always a very sensible thing to have, and woodchucks are always very sensible sorts, for the most part." Otter lowered his whispering chirp a shade. "Except the poor bloke here ended sadly enough. I'm sure he never suspected the elvish clans would be a part of any deception. And I certainly wouldn't have believed it of them either, before now."

"I've never had any dealings with them, except that once when Froghorn's elves took me to the field hospital after Seven Hills. These sort certainly don't seem like they would have been of any army Froghorn would have led."

"They're not. I think I overheard Lorini telling Greyfax

once that there had been some trouble among the Elders of the Circle and the elf lord who was part of the Council. Erehorn, or Eiorn, or something like that. And he had a son, Tyron. All this was a long time ago, I guess, when the Circle was fighting the dragons. But that elf handed down to his son the grudge he bore the Circle, and I guess he planted the seed of distrust. Tyron doesn't like anyone too much, except the elves of his own clan."

"Sounds like a cheerful sort," mumbled Flewingam.

"And I think we're dealing with some of his men here. Belwicke doesn't seem the sort you would find in Cypher."

A sound of stealthy feet approached, and the two friends fell silent, straining to hear.

"I think they're changing the guard," breathed Flewingam. "This might be our best chance to use your back door. I don't fancy staying about, waiting for whoever it is that is disguised as Froghorn. It reeks of the Darkness, and my blood is cold inside me."

"Come on, then. It's going to be a bit close for you, Flew. But there's nothing for it but to squeeze. I do wish you'd have learned how to change into a bit more sensible form."

Otter led Flewingam to the very rear of the cellar, beyond where the cots were stored and shelves of jam and marmalade were kept. Farther back, the sloping roof lowered toward the floor, and Flewingam had to go forward on his hands and knees. It got misty, and a damp smell of freshly dug earth filled their senses.

"I'm getting tired of crawling around in shafts," groaned Flew, having to lean forward yet more and get onto his stomach.

"This is only a short tunnel. It comes up clear of the

camp. Good old clever Whistlepig dug right up in the clump of a berry patch. We can get our fill of dewberries, as well as escape."

Flewingam grunted, having to strain now to drag himself painfully along on his stomach. Already his elbows and knees were sore, and they had hardly begun their journey. Breathing heavily, Flewingam panted in a choked voice. "I don't think I can go on, Otter. You go on without me. I can barely move my nose now. It's too small for me. I'll stay behind and try to do what I can to cause a diversion."

Otter came back to where his friend seemed hopelessly stuck in the close shaft. His paws flashed in the dark, here and there, and he busily pushed and patted and piled the soft, damp earth, until at last he had the hole widened enough so that Flewingam, using all his control not to cry out in the smothering darkness of the shaft, shot forward a few feet, where the walls broadened out somewhat, and the friends were able to make better progress.

"I must say, I'm not bad as a mole," sneezed Otter, the damp earth tickling his whiskers and threatening to make him sneeze again.

"Shhhhh!" cautioned Flewingham.

It seemed he had heard footsteps directly over them. Otter put his paw to his muzzle and stifled the new explosion of sneezes he felt coming. And having to be quiet only seemed to make it worse. The footsteps, or what appeared to have been footsteps, stopped also.

A thin chill began to crawl down Flewingam's spine. "Otter, do you think they knew you would find this escape hole? Do you think they meant for us to use it, and try to get away?"

Still holding his paw to his nose, Otter tried to swallow the sneezes. When he felt it safe to speak, he whispered softly. "I don't know. But it's for sure we can't go back. There's nothing there to do but wait until they serve us up on a chafing dish, or worse, just like they did the poor fellow who dug this hole. And even if they do know we're escaping and have some reason to allow us to, it can't be worse than it already is. And at least we have a chance outside to throw them off our trail. I'm more familiar with these parts than they might be, and I might just know some hiding place they're not aware of."

"What about the impostor?"

"I don't doubt he thinks we'll flee straight to Dwarf to warn him. That would save him the task of having to hunt Dwarf up and down these borders of Calix Stay. That's a lot of territory. But if he thinks we know where Dwarf is, perhaps we may help Dwarf escape, if he is across, as our false Froghorn seems to think. We'll set off as if we know where we're off to, and see if we can't take these fellows off on a wild otter frolic they won't soon forget."

Flewingam was silent a moment before he answered. "That may well be the case, Otter. This all seems too easy. And he may indeed be sure we know where Broco is. So why disencourage him? I know whoever he is, he wishes Dwarf no good. It is the Arkenchest he is after, for my money."

"There couldn't be any other reason," answered Otter, turning it over in his head. "But things have certainly changed since last I set foot here. I just hope things haven't changed so much that I can't find my way."

"Whichever way you choose can't make a difference,

friend. We'll just set off whatever way we can, and act as if we know where we're bound."

Otter screwed his face into a small scowl. "I do wonder where the silly asses have gotten off to," he said gently, and a sudden loneliness washed over him, and a slight feeling of hope he had had earlier at finding the cellar door vanished, leaving him drained and exhausted. "Bear, and Dwarf, and Thumb's band, all gone," he said, very near crying. "And Ned and Cranny, too. All lost, and here we are stuck in a rat shaft, with nothing to do, and no plan to go on except to run like rabbits until we're caught, without food or water, or anyplace to turn."

Flewingam let Otter go on until he fell silent.

"I know how you feel, my friend. It does look pretty grim, although I think we'd feel better about it all if we were to talk it over in the fresh air, and away from here."

Without replying, Otter began moving forward. The soft, almost inaudible shuffling began over his head again, and Flewingam was sure they were being followed aboveground. He did not let on to Otter, and refused to let himself think of anything more than the next shove of his hand forward, turn on his side, kick with his leg that slowly and painfully inched him along the rough floor of the stifling closeness of the shaft.

A new sound reached him from somewhere ahead, and his eyes automatically blinked shut as a bright shaft of golden light exploded into the tunnel. Otter, a small way ahead, had opened the back door to the woodchuck's cellar.

Whatever he had expected to occur had not, and he carefully poked his head up into the fresh air of the late afternoon. Looking around him, he could make out that the forest surrounding the escape hole was dense and silent, and if any eyes watched, they were well hidden.

Then Otter remembered Belwicke and his unusual talent of going about under the guise of a small bush.

"Well, there's nothing for it now," he muttered under his breath, and struggled through the tight opening, turning as he did so to help the floundering Flewingam stand in the cramped opening.

Flewingam was squinting painfully about at his surroundings, and said in a half whisper, "Looks like it's all clear."

Otter did not remind him of Belwicke's amazing capacity to disguise himself as part of the forest. There was a feeling he could not put his paw on, but he knew that they were watched, and hoping it would disconcert the unseen watchers, he turned quickly and began to make as if signaling some distant companion. What effect that act had on the invisible onlookers Otter did not know, but it startled the shaken Flewingam visibly.

"You gave me a fright. I thought you had really seen Dwarf, or Bear, or the others."

"Never mind," hissed Otter through clenched teeth. "Just pretend you're making some sort of hand signals to someone off in this direction. Then we'll wait a moment as if we're reading some answer, then we'll go."

"Are you sure this is a smart thing to be getting into?" asked Flewingam, waving an arm up and down in short, jerky motions. "I mean won't they suspect?"

"So much the better," snapped Otter, who had just crossed his paws over his head and brought them sharply down before him.

"Well, we're in it now. We may as well go on like we know

what we're doing," said Flewingam softly, his voice taking on a resigned quality. "Whatever else happens, Otter, when all is said and done, I can't say that my life has been overly dull since that night you first found me and began telling me all your farfetched tales. And if I live to be a gray-beard, I don't think I'll ever be fully convinced that I'm not dreaming all this yet."

Otter's quick motion with his paw pointed toward the camp where they had been a few moments before. A small movement there had caught his eye. He was certain he had momentarily seen the features of the imposter, so cruel in that being reminded of the young wizard only made Otter aware that if this new pretender could so easily go about as a member of the Circle, then it was evident the Circle, and its members, were not to be found anywhere in the near vicinity.

"Let's go," he said, turning to Flewingam. "I want to be away from here."

Flewingam gave his friend a reassuring pat on the back as they moved rapidly away, talking as if with a purpose, but neither of the friends felt in the least comforted, and Otter could not shake off the feeling of hidden eyes watching him. He clenched his teeth and increased his speed, pretending to himself he was hurrying to keep an appointment with Greyfax Grimwald. That thought, although vague and only fancied, somehow cheered him.

Bearer of the Arkenchest

As Otter and Flewingam made their way through the outlying edges of Gilden Wood, Dwarf was in deep conversation with Froghorn Fairingay.

"And then again, I beg you," went on Broco, "I must hear it again. It's all a mess in my head, and I'm confused on all the points except that I think I'm here, talking to you, but I can't be sure of even that. I had those feelings at times, but I would always wake up and find I had only been dreaming."

"You weren't exactly dreaming, my friend," laughed Froghorn. "We do have ways, at times, of reaching those who may have their thoughts pointed in our direction."

"You mean I actually was seeing you? Or talking to you?"

"Most assuredly, good fellow. I think Greyfax spoke to you of Fair Crossing, and told you you were to cross the River, did he not?"

"Well, yes. But we didn't exactly come the way I imagine he had in mind that we should come."

Dwarf paused long enough to fill his mouth with another journey cake, covered with honey and sweet jam.

"No?" Froghorn asked, glancing up from the fire and meeting Dwarf's eyes in a long, even gaze.

"You mean he knew we were to recross Calix Stay the way we did? Trapped in my sire's Delvings?"

"We won't press him on the matter, and the most important thing is that you've safely reached us. Things are as they should be. But now we have a hard journey ahead of us, and much more to do before we tarry long at our rest."

Dwarf had risen, and reached gingerly into his cloak. "Before we go on, you must take the Chest. It's too much for me to bear any longer. I had never intended to lug it this far, except for how things seemed to fall out after Melodias and Greyfax disappeared after Havamal, and after we got lost in the Dragur Wood, and ran into Garius and that strange kingdom of his."

Froghorn's eyes softened, and he looked long at the tiny figure of the Chest as it rested in Dwarf's outstretched hand. "It is not for me to bear it again, old friend. I have had my time at that duty. This is meant for you alone, until a time as we shall both know is the proper moment for you no longer to carry it. I cannot help you, except to be with you on this part of our errand."

Dwarf pressed the Chest into Froghorn's hand, but the young Master smiled sadly and shook his head. "I cannot, Broco. You are the Arkenchest Bearer, until your time is come. I cannot hold it for you. There are yet things to do that only you may do. And your part to play is not ended yet."

"But I'm tired, blast you. I've carried this long, and it's wearied me beyond words. I can't stand this any longer." Dwarf tried to prise open Froghorn's hand and press the Chest into it. "You've got to take it, don't you see? I almost lost it. Did lose it once, and I can't stand the thought of it. It's too much for me to carry any longer."

Broco's eyes had widened, and he frantically groped at Froghorn's fingers, trying to fasten them around the tiny Chest. "I can't hold it anymore. I was told to bring it across Calix Stay and turn it over, and here I am, and you must take it. It belongs with the Circle, not with the likes of me."

Without realizing it, Broco had begun sobbing, and he tried pathetically to force Froghorn's hand to hold the Chest. After a moment he gave up and sat down heavily, letting the small object fall to lie at his feet. His shoulders trembled violently, and a long sob escaped him.

"I'm sorry, Froghorn. I don't know what's wrong, except I'm tired, and I've lost Bear and Otter, and this Chest has given me more grief than I ever dreamed existed. I remember just before we were swept away in the old Delvings, I thought I had failed the Circle and lost the Chest forever. It was too much to bear, that thought. Please, please take it, if you love me. I can't stand the load anymore."

Broco had fallen at Froghorn's knees as he choked and sobbed the words.

Froghorn knelt beside his hysterical friend and placed an arm on his shoulder. He had picked up the Arkenchest and placed it back into Dwarf's knotted fists. "I know, old fellow. I, too, have borne that weight, and know the terrible price it demands. But you must carry on a bit longer. The fate of Cybelle depends on it, and our very errand upon the edges of the old Cypher. Lorini, and Greyfax, and all the others know that it is you who must do this thing, and it must be you who yet carries the Chest a while longer. It is so written."

Broco had stemmed his tears, and looked down at the

small object he held clutched to his chest. "What has a dwarf to do with anything such as this?" he asked, choking back a fresh bout of sobbing.

Froghorn grasped him by the shoulders and looked deeply into his eyes. A slight change came over the clear features of the young wizard, and a cloud seemed to pass overhead, for it grew darker upon the borders of the wood where they sat. A chilling wind seemed to spring up from the deeper heart of the forest, and Dwarf's vision dimmed.

In a faint, shadowy, mist-covered dream, Broco saw Cybelle, lying cold and lifeless on a frozen breath of ice. And after that came a troubling, familiar face, an elf, but none of the elves such as he had seen in Cypher. This face was pinched and troubled, and it seemed to Dwarf the elf was carrying a secret deep within the haunted windows of his eyes. And then there came Lorini, but not the Lorini he remembered, and she was dressed in a simple gray cloak, and appeared under a dark, star-strewn sky.

Following these visions, a fleeting array of dizzy sights flew across his sight, and Greyfax stood up, offering his hand, followed by Lorini. There were visions of Melodias Starson and George Greymouse, followed by raging battle fires that howled and bellowed, and these firest burned even in the Gilden Wood, and a dark presence seemed to creep out over the ruined tower of the swan in Cypher, and Broco cried aloud in black terror as an icy hand groped out toward him, clutching for the warm beating of his heart. As the suffocating darkness began to drown him in its awesome depths, a beam of light, high up and distant, began to shine, and it grew and shone until the terrible darkness was gone, and before him stretched the vast and sun-filled sky of a land so bright and shining it hurt his eyes to look upon it.

"There, old fellow, is why you must yet bear this burden." Froghorn's voice reached him from far away, and his eyes were unable to focus for a moment.

"But why was all that?" he muttered, stammering.

"You will find all your answers in time, my friend. For now, think only that it is necessary for you to carry the Chest in order that we may save Cybelle."

"If that is so, then I shall carry it," gulped Dwarf. "And more, if need be."

A strange, new feeling had begun at the bottom of Dwarf's heart, and grew stronger with each breath.

"You needn't carry more, Dwarf. You have done this well, and all the Elders of the Circle couldn't have done it better."

"But what of Otter and Flew? Are we to go on without them? I don't feel that I can carry that without feeling sad about it. It doesn't seem right, after all we have been through."

Froghorn clapped Dwarf briskly on the back, and glanced away into the woods. "I think perhaps if we wait here until Ned and Cranny awaken, we may have a pleasant surprise in store for us."

Froghorn smiled mysteriously, and hinted at odd events, but would not speak plainly. And Dwarf, for all his questions, could not draw the wizard out.

Greyfax and Thailwicke

"The Light," said Greyfax Grimwald as he approached the silent figures of the elves who sat sprawled about the remnants of a fire and a meal.

Greyfax reached the group and stood a moment longer before a sharp-featured elf arose and raised a curt hand of acknowledgment.

"In the name of the Governor and High King of Gilden, I am bid to bring you this message. Tyron the Green offers safe conduct to all those who are not of his clan from the new kingdom of Gilden, to a location of their choice. And beyond this date, no further commerce with any outside the boundaries of Gilden will be carried on, and the boundaries shall be closed to all but those of elvish blood and who are of the clan of Tyron."

The small features of the elf seemed to harden as he repeated his message, and as he paused for breath, an ugly scowl spread over his face.

"Further, the organization of Elders which call themselves

the Circle will be forever banned from entry into Gilden, and all those who ally themselves with this organization will suffer the same fate as their leaders. Anyone seeking entry, either by force or trickery, will be executed on sight."

As if to stress this last announcement, the other elves drew nearer in a tight knot, and a few laid their hands to their short swords or bows or firearms.

Greyfax remained silent until the elf finished, his level gaze on the eyes of the nervous spokesman. "Is this all I have come to hear, good Thailwicke? I don't suppose you will remember, but I once visited in your grandsire's house, not long after Eiorn returned his clan to these parts, after the last troubles of the Dragon."

Thailwicke, for it was indeed the elf Greyfax named, went red to his ears, and began a bluster to save face in front of his comrades. "Aye, it is Thailwicke you address in so loose a term, and it is a long season since the shame of those dealings with the Circle, who robbed us of all that was rightfully ours and who tried to steal away by conniving and force what was by right Eiorn's, and now belongs to Tyron, High King of Gilden. And there's no need denying the truth of any of what I say, or of trying any soft speech to cajole us to listen to your bald-faced lies. Urien Typhon has tried long enough, and elf though he is, he is a traitor kind to our royal blood, for he has thrown over his own, and now casts his lot with our enemies."

"Ah, good Thailwicke, you surprise me in your new role. Rudeness doesn't sit well on you at all. We must deal with each other as common partners in this crime of ours, as you describe it, and see what is to be treated with, and see if we can't make some sense of this affair you've been describing."

Greyfax moved forward in a tired motion, and sat heavily beside the fire the elves had made to brew their tea. His hand went forward to pick up the small, bright green teapot, and he brought out an object from beneath his cloak and made as if to pour out a cup of tea for himself.

Thailwicke, confused and flustered at the unmoved Greyfax, stepped nearer the sitting wizard and sneered as menacingly as he was able. "Our tea is at your disposal, sir, and it is the last of our good Gilden herb brew you'll have. May you enjoy it well."

"Thank you kindly, Thailwicke, I shall," replied Greyfax good-humoredly, and as he spoke, a tiny fleck of sparkling blue-white light leapt from the tip of his finger into the fire, and without warning, a fiery, blazing hot wind came whistling out of the flames, whipping dust into the faces of the elves and setting their cloaks flapping madly in the angry breeze.

Thailwicke had to lean forward into this small cyclone to keep his balance, and he shouted angrily at Greyfax, who sat placidly in a perfect calm, sipping slowly at his cup of tea.

"Tyron warned us about your behavior," shouted the elf, barely able to make himself heard.

At the moment he stopped to draw another breath, his hat was blown off his head, and the force of the wind blew him backward into one of the other elves standing behind him. He grappled wildly with his companion, regained his feet, and turned once more to shout at Greyfax.

"It won't do you any good, all this wizard's work. Tyron has warned us all about you, and we know you won't harm us. We're not afraid. And you won't gain a thing by insulting us with your fancy spell weaving."

Greyfax chuckled softly to himself, and as quickly as it had come, the blazing inferno of wind settled upon itself, and Thailwicke toppled forward onto his face in a rather awkward manner. He had been leaning so far forward into the stiff breeze that when the wind stopped, he was far overbalanced.

Greyfax helped the disconcerted elf up and handed him back his rather badly crushed hat. "Here, here, let me help you," insisted Greyfax, and in placing the hat back on the elf's head, it somehow got smashed down over his ears, and Thailwicke was thrashing around blindly, cursing Greyfax loudly.

"You'll pay for this, you hired puppet of a magician. Tyron was being very lenient in his terms, and extremely fair on everything he proposes to set to his law. We shall see, now, after I tell him of this outrage. Tyron is a holder of a Secret, too, and just as powerful as any of you. We all know the code. Any holder of any of the Five Secrets is a full and equal ruler, just as your precious Circle decreed so long ago, when Tyron's father was given one of the Secrets to hold in trust."

"You are doing well with your history lesson so far, good Thailwicke, but go on. Does Tyron now tell you he alone knows the key to holding that Secret? And that by keeping it safe, the Circle will never be able to move upon any holder of any of the Five, so long as it is in the hands of the one it was entrusted to?"

"Of course, we all know that," snapped Thailwicke.

"Has he explained how it is he is going to wrest Gilden Wood from its boundaries and close off his kingdom? Or why? Has he explained to you that in order to do so, he is having to deal with Dorini and her dark underlord?"

"Tyron has to explain nothing, you dratted hexmonger. We all know that Tyron is the rightful ruler of Gilden, and we have all seen and heard of the outrageous treatment the elfin clans got at the hands of your greedy, self-centered Circle."

"I am glad you are well read, Thailwicke. Now come, tell me, what was the reason Tyron sent you to me? And why would he not come himself? Is he afraid that we would take by force what he holds? Or is this some ruse of his to keep me here, rather than someplace else he would not wish me to be?"

"Tyron fears nothing at your hands, or at the hands of any of your bungling magicians. And he sent me because he is at this moment seeing to the business of closing the boundaries along Calix Stay. And to give you fair warning that Gilden Wood is no longer open to travel, and that all caught trying to meddle across our borders will be dealt with on the spot, by summary execution. And any act of trespass will be looked upon as an act of war, and dealt with as such."

Greyfax stood, and his figure towered over Thailwicke, who, in spite of his brave speech, fell back a few paces from the wizard.

"I shall long lament this unfortunate day, Thailwicke; if what you say is true, and if Tyron has indeed taken leave of his senses in the manner you describe. I know that the only way he would ever be able to carry out any of those threats is if he has been dealing with Dorini, and if his ambition has caused him to treat with the Darkness, then we shall indeed have reason to grieve before all is over and done. But you tell him this. Greyfax Grimwald is willing to reason with him, and more than happy for the union of his clan and the other allies of the Circle. We are not cutting Tyron adrift. When he comes to his senses, you tell him he is always welcome in the camp of the Circle."

Greyfax paused for a moment, and touched the shoulder of the elf that stood uncomfortably before him.

"And you tell him to be extremely prudent with spreading that loose information about concerning the trust he holds. And that if he has been to treat with Dorini, then she will know the truth of it, and he is indeed in dire jeopardy. She will stop at nothing to gain control of the Secrets and the Arkenchest. And she also well knows that if she gains control of even one, she can call the others to it. And tell the good Tyron he may have a bit more than he bargained for if he is going to try to cut off his boundaries, for there are going to be many crossers from now on. It would take quite some doing on his part to close off the River."

"They can do it together," shot Thailwicke, then immediately went silent.

"Then he has been dabbling with fire," sighed Greyfax. "I had hoped the Secret wouldn't weigh so heavily upon his ambitions, but I can see that it would be too sweet a dream to overcome. Especially in the light his father painted the picture. And yet, I still see the wisdom in having Eiorn carry the Secret. I begin to see it all plainly now. Still, I don't like the idea of Tyron trying to play about in affairs that are beyond his depth."

Greyfax had placed his hands behind his back and was pacing to and fro, almost unaware of the elves that surrounded him. They looked at one another, then at Thailwicke, and back to Greyfax.

"It is odd planning, but then I can see it," he was saying aloud, although obviously to no one in particular. "But how does this tie in with Dwarf's arrival? Or the return of Cybelle?" Greyfax whirled in a sudden motion that startled the speechless elves. "Of course," he said, his face breaking out into a broad smile of relief. "It must be. I think I begin to see the pattern to it now."

His gaze cleared, and the blue-gray eyes focused once more on Thailwicke.

"You tell Tyron I've heard you out, and I am accepting his decision for now. We shall respect as we shall the boundary of Gilden Wood for the moment, and spread the news of his punishment of trespassers. In return, I will ask simply that you tell Tyron that the Bearer of the Arkenchest shall be among us soon, and that as holder of a sacred Secret, he cannot refuse a call from the Chest Bearer, if the Chest Bearer so desires his presence. Should he refuse, the Secret he holds becomes free from his trust, and shall return to its rightful place with the others."

Thailwicke glowered at the wizard, and without further word, was gone. Grayfax watched the retreating figures until they disappeared, and then studied the dying fire closely. A face, smiling and serene, was reflected from the pure blue-white heat, and Greyfax smiled in return.

"It is done, then, my friend?" asked the figure in the flames.

"Yes, Erophin, it is done. He will hear our story, and if he believes it, then we will be seeing things move at a quicker pace. There is nothing quite so explosive as putting gunpowder on a hot flame. And the idea that he could lose the precious Secret, which is his throne maker, is going to set him in action quickly. And I am sure our Dark Queen is going to hear all about this business, and set her hand to the plan, too. She cannot resist the bait."

The figure of Erophin faded and blurred for a moment, then cleared and came more brightly into view. "Then the first small stone has been cast into the pond. Now we shall watch our ripples, and wait. Still, this is a perilous undertaking."

Greyfax Grimwald looked deeply into his friend's thoughts, and then smiled. "I was almost on the brink of frivolity with those overfed elves. Something I haven't allowed myself in I don't remember how long. And it was fun when Thailwicke lost his hat, and fell down flat on his nose when that little breeze I conjured up quit. Quite a delightful exchange, I think. And yes, it is dangerous, my dear old comrade, but not if we play out our hand as it has been dealt us. The only true danger to this course lies in the risk of exactly what Tyron has fallen for, and that is the wielding of the power of the Secrets for a selfish gain. That could happen, you know."

Another flickering shadow crossed the fire, and as the figure of Erophin cleared once more, the blue-white flames leapt into a dazzling brilliance that seemed to reach up and touch Greyfax on the brow.

"Yes, it is a dangerous road, then. But one worth the traveling. I think I can begin to see the reasons for it now."

"Whatever comes, it seems the stage is set, and our lot cast," said the fading figure of Erophin, as the fire began to dim.

"Our lots have been cast since long before we remembered, old friend. And Tyron the Green is embarking upon a much larger adventure than he ever dared dream of. And playing a much bigger part."

"And still, an unenviable role, for all its importance."

"Still, old fellow, I think we have all played it, in our

own times," Greyfax said, smiling sadly. And the light in his eyes dimmed for a moment, as if an old echo from some long-past suffering had faintly lingered, and then was gone.

After another moment, the fire flickered and fell silent, and Greyfax, taking one last look into the smoldering embers, smiled inwardly, and felt glad within, and felt the onrushing joy of the knowledge that at last an unseen tide had turned, and that beyond all shadow of a doubt, they were all, friend and foe alike, bound irretrievably in a direction that would lead at long, long last to the soft and gentle answers they had all been seeking for so long that Greyfax faltered at the measuring of it. It was, he concluded, a very long time on the one hand, but no time at all on the other.

"And time enough," he chuckled to himself. "For I've even gotten into the habit of answering myself with riddles."

He carefully put out the fire, and strode quickly away in the direction of the camp where Lorini stood anxiously gazing out into the eaves of the wood, awaiting his return from his meeting with the messengers of Tyron.

A False Wizard

Flewingam crept silently into his perch in one of the taller trees, signaling Otter as he did so with a movement of his hand. From his high vantage point, he scanned the surrounding wood, or what he could make out of the wood through the lush green foliage, and beyond the edge of the forest, where a grassy meadowland ran down smoothly to the banks of a river that was covered with a silver mist that boiled angrily and rose away into the bronze-blue sky. Although Flewingam could not hear it well from so great a distance, he knew the noise that this river made would be deafening.

Just as his eyes left the troubled vision of the great River, he caught sight of a slight movement. When he began the search to find it again, he saw nothing, and he was on the point of deciding he had been letting his mind play tricks. And then, as he gave up the search and started to look away, it came again, this time unmistakable. He squinted hard, and put a hand to his forehead to shield his eyes, and he scoured the clearing in the woods, not more than a good stone's throw away.

The third time the movement came, Flewingam recognized it as one of the band that had been in the service of the false wizard. The elf seemed to be trying to keep out of sight, although Flewingam knew they had the power to be truly invisible to an untrained eye if they actually wished to escape detection. Flewingam then noticed this elf was limping, and appeared to be hurt.

And right at the moment that Flewingam began to climb down from his scouting perch, he saw the men who emerged from beneath the dark green shadows of the trees. They darted out from their cover quickly, and were gone from sight in barely a fraction of a moment, and Flewingam was almost unsure he had seen them at all, until he heard a faint call, a single note, as that of a forest bird, that repeated itself after a moment, then settled into silence.

Otter waited anxiously for Flewingam to descend. "Where are we? Did you see anything?" he chittered, still in his animal form.

"Shhhhh!" warned Flewingam, as he jumped down the last few feet to the ground. "We have our company still. I saw one of them, which was strange. He was wobbling about, pretending to try to be hiding, and a band of men came out of nowhere and carried him away."

"What sort of men?" asked Otter, remembering all too well Garius Brosingamene and his strange army of grim-faced men.

"I couldn't tell. They were out of sight too quickly. But they were in that direction," said Flewingam, pointing away toward where he had seen the elf and had a momentary glimpse of the men. "And there was a river, all silver, with a great cloud of mist above it, like it was above a falls or rapids."

"Calix Stay," confirmed Otter, nodding his head. "It's like that."

"Frightening enough to look at," agreed Flewingam. "I don't think I would fancy having to try to recross it."

"It was bad enough," chirped Otter, and his eyes turned the same silver mist-gray as the River. "But that was going in the other direction. I don't remember much of it coming back this way."

He knitted his muzzle whiskers and looked up at his friend. "But who could the men have been? And on whose side? I don't know who to turn to or trust now. If those others can take on even the look of a Master of the Circle, how will we know who we're dealing with? Or how will we know before it's too late?"

"And I still want to know why we were allowed to escape so conveniently. It makes no sense, unless they thought we knew where Dwarf was and would make our way back to him."

"I'm sure that is the only reason we left alive, Flew. And I'm afraid that the minute they suspect we're not making for some specific place, they may have more than a second thought about us."

"We could try the River," murmured Flewingam. "I don't like the thought of it, but it might be the easiest. We have no food, no weapons, we're lost, and I'd much prefer having a hand, even though a small one, in my own undoing."

Otter shook his head. "It only works if you know the words to hold it. Or if it is time. I don't think we could get close to it, anyhow. And our friends would suspect long before we could begin to reach it."

Flewingam leaned against the tree, his head lowered to his chest. "Then what's left for us, my friend? Do you have any other ideas?"

Otter's eyes closed, and he began listening very hard. There was something he had been hearing since they had entered the deeper silence of the forest. It wasn't the occasional call of birds, or animals, and he noticed that those were fewer than in the old days across the River that he remembered so vividly. And with a false Master who made supper of woodchuck, and other things, he understood why there weren't many of them about, and if they were there at all, why they were so silent.

Again it came, just below his grasp, lilting and fine, like bubbling water in a high, clear mountain stream. Flewingam started to put a question to him, but he held up a paw for silence. Now it came stronger, washing over his senses in a smooth, flowing motion. His small body began to sway in time to what he heard, and his eyes blinked open. At once the sound was gone, and he was still standing beneath the tree Flewingam had climbed, and his friend still stood before him, very still, with a worried frown pinching his face tight.

"I thought I heard something," explained Otter, his voice full of his disappointment.

"What was it, Otter?"

"I can't be sure. Something I've almost forgotten. Maybe it'll come to me."

"I hope that's true. Our time is running out for staying here. If our friends are watching, I'm sure they will begin wondering at our long halt."

"Then let's go on, Flew. Perhaps it's just as well if we make for where you saw the men and the elf. We have nothing to lose or gain by it. And if we've any luck at all left to us, if they are from the Darkness, they may end our worries on the spot."

Flewingam looked hard at his small friend, who had clutched his hands tightly into tiny fists. A grim, cold hardness had replaced the soft look in his eyes.

"With any luck," repeated Flewingam, and he held out a hand. "I didn't ever dream we'd end this way, but if it is to be so, we shall face it together."

Otter shook Flewingam's hand firmly, and standing a little taller, he started away in the direction Flewingam had indicated. He had gone no more than a few paces when the sound reached him again, lifting his heart, and flowing through him in gentle waves, dispelling the fear and helplessness he felt. This time it was stronger, and unmistakable. He was on the point of a wild otter reel when the full impact of this new discovery flooded over him. He had to grit his teeth and hold his paws shut tight to keep from sobbing aloud.

"What is it?" whispered Flewingam, now standing beside him.

"Oh, Flew, it's here, close by. And we can't go, don't you see? They're waiting for us to do exactly that."

"Do what?"

"Lead them to Dwarf."

Flewingam's face brightened, then fell. "You mean he's near here? How can you know that?"

"I've felt the Arkenchest. Or at least I'm sure that's what it is. I guess being here again, across the River, you can feel things, and see things so much clearer."

"And if we go to it, then there will be Dwarf, and exactly what our invisible trackers are waiting for." Flewingam fell silent, thinking hard.

When he spoke again, it was in a lower whisper. "If you can feel it, do you think they can? I mean, I don't seem to feel anything different, although now that you mention it, I think I can see what you mean. But would *they* be able to feel it?"

Otter studied his friend. "I don't know, Flew. It's all so familiar to me because Dwarf sang a part of the music that the Chest makes before we left here before. Or hummed it. But I remember it now, since I'm back. It was part of what the Arkenchest is all about. Still, I don't know whether or not those others can feel it. I guess if it was right under their noses, they might."

"They probably won't be able to know it's anywhere nearby, then?"

"No, I don't think so. And I'm just assuming that Dwarf has it still." Otter turned to Flewingam, his muzzle worked into a small, hopeful smile. "And if that's so, it means he's gotten here, after all, and that he's not lost."

The two friends stared at each other, hardly able to hold themselves in, or keep from crying aloud.

"Then we know what we must do," said Otter at last. "If he is to have a chance to escape, we must lure them after us." He turned to Flewingam as his voice trailed away.

"Is there no other way, Otter?" Flewingam asked, hoping to find some reason for not believing what he knew was true.

"I wish there was, Flew. But we can't risk it, not with those things that call themselves elves watching us. I didn't think when we got away that we would be faced with this problem.

I thought Dwarf lost, perhaps beyond Calix Stay. It's a bitter stroke. It was easier thinking our Dwarf was gone."

"Well, come on then," said Flewingam. "We won't help him by sitting here any longer. What direction?"

"Away from here," replied Otter, struggling to keep the tears out of his voice.

The two friends stole away as briskly as they were able, and after a time Otter began talking as he ran along at Flewingam's feet.

"Perhaps we can lose these things that are trailing us, and double back and find Broco," he said, never breaking stride.

"Then let's see to it," answered Flewingam, although he felt doubtful of being able to shake off the invisible watchers that seemed to loom all around them. The crawling skin at the nape of his neck told him they were still there.

"At least we can try," chittered Otter, his heart breaking with every step he took away from the music of the Chest, which had grown fainter, although still audible.

Without further word or warning, he abruptly repeated the spell Froghorn Fairingay had given him that distant day in Bear's cave in their old valley, and stood beside Flewingam in his man form.

"Now, Flew," he cried. "We're for it!"

And the two friends crashed headlong into the denser undergrowth at the side of the faint track they had been following. The startled noise of a voice called out in a strained whisper, and it was answered by hissed mumbling rumors of speech, and the two companions knew that they had but a moment of surprise to try to make good their escape.

Running hard, almost out of breath, Flewingam did not see the hidden figures in the trees and bushes about them, and Otter crashed along behind in his clumsy man form, on the heels of his friend. As they passed a small, open glade in the green silence of the Gilden Wood, the figures in the trees formed a line behind the fleeing friends, as if a gate were shutting, and neither Otter nor Flewingam heard the abrupt halt of their pursuers.

A few moments later, Flewingam had bowled into a dense, canopied forest niche, with a soft pine- and wood-scented floor, the tall arms of the trees making a roof of golden green leaves above them. Otter bumped painfully into Flewingam, who had drawn up abruptly, and his heart fell. Bitter tears welled to his eyes, and he gritted his teeth painfully.

"You!" he finally managed to choke out. "You won't live to defile Froghorn's likeness again."

With a gasping cry, he leapt forward, brandishing the crude weapon, his voice suddenly strong and clear.

"The Light!" he cried, his arms above his head, ready to strike.

Flewingam, seeing they were lost, leapt into the fray behind his friend, his small dagger drawn. He did not see Otter fall, nor feel the strong arms that grasped him, for the dark walls of the shaded place burst into a sudden, flashing golden fire, and then there was nothing but warm darkness and echoing voices that dimmed gradually and went out, like candles guttering in a breeze.

Revelations of George Greymouse

Bear sat staring numbly at the laughing wizard, and his anxious looks only made Greymouse gasp for breath and slap his knee twice more before he could gain sufficient control of his voice to speak.

"You must forgive me, good Bruinlen. This comes, I'm sure, as somewhat of a shock to you. It has not been often in the past that you have found an Elder of the Circle with so much to find amusing in the news you have just given me. But it is news indeed to make a tired old man lonesome for Home, and it seems that every piece of the play that falls into line only speeds the day when we'll be able to draw a free breath at last, and be rid of all this business. It is wearisome work, and sometimes I can hardly remember where or why it all began. Of course, we can't forget that, but it has dragged on now for ever so long, and I imagine everyone but Dorini is growing a bit out of sorts with it. She, of course, might find all this war and confusion to her fancy, but I really even wonder about that at times."

Greymouse drew Bear up from his seat by the camp table

and led him outside, where a cloth had been spread, tea prepared, and fresh journey cakes laid out, with honey and fresh apples to go with them.

"I guess I just don't grasp any of what you're saying, sir," mumbled Bear apologetically. "I mean all you're saying is true, I'm sure, but it seems awfully confusing. You mean you think maybe even the Dark Queen might give up now? And surrender to the Circle? Why, that would be great. And then Dwarf wouldn't have to hide the Chest anymore, and we could all forget about all this, and just go on simply doing whatever it was we were doing before all this came up." Bear's face took on the beginning of a hopeful smile, then ended in a troubled scowl, and he knitted his great brows together. "I mean, I suppose one would want to take up a simple life. Keep a few bees, or jot down some notes in one's journal, or maybe even do a bit of gardening, if one had a fancy."

Bear fell silent, studying the far-distant peaks that lay low down on the horizon, their gold and silver tops winking softly in the late afternoon sun. A thin ring of high white clouds circled the taller mountain range, and Bear could see the grayish-blue fringe of the foothills that led on upward toward the Beginning, and beyond.

Greymouse did not speak for a moment, but watched as Bear's eyes seemed to be seeing some other moment or season.

"It is a very great thing to settle down into a routine," said Greymouse after a moment longer. "I found it particularly pleasant when I was between my travels, or long before this last business of the Circle brought me out and left me here, as you see me now, all this time after. "I had written most of the Chronicles of the Lower Order of the High Guild, and was well into depicting certain exploits of a twice-removed cousin whose experiences in the Dragon Wars were most remarkable. It filled the time for me, and I could ask no more. I was living then in a very quiet place, much like this used to be, doodling and doing a bit of landscaping in a back garden, or watching the watercraft in the afternoons. It was a most delightful existence, and I had grown rather fond of it."

Greymouse leaned forward and refilled his teacup with the spicy berry tea, and cut himself another slice of the warm journey cake.

"And then word came that I was to drop all that life and report myself to the service of the Circle, by the command of the High Lord of Windameir himself. No refusing that. And then I found out that I had been waiting for quite some time for that call. Oh, I wasn't exactly what you would call restless with my life, but there was something I couldn't put my finger on that was waiting to be done. I couldn't exactly say what that feeling was, but I knew it when the time came, and I realized I had been waiting all along for that call."

"I know exactly what you mean, sir," agreed Bear shyly. "That was just the way I'd have to say I felt, all that time ago when I was here before, and Dwarf found me, and then all of a sudden, without so much as a tote keg of honey, I was off with him on a journey, without so much as asking where or how far. But I knew I had to go. And I guess I still feel that way now. I wouldn't know what to do if the Dark Queen *did* stop. I don't really think I'd want to stay on here anymore. It's still beautiful and all, but I've seen it, and been here before. And I don't think I could remember the spells to get back across Calix Stay into the World Before Time. And I don't think I want to go back there, anyway. I feel like all that life is gone, and this one, too, if I really look at it. So I'm not sure what I feel. I guess I should be happy. I mean, I would be happy if Dorini were to stop, and let Cybelle go, and then all the wars would be over with, and everyone could settle down to a peaceful life. Then there wouldn't be all the upsets and misery there has been, at least."

Bear fell silent.

"It's true, Bear, what you say. Then everyone could go back to a life just like we were describing. Except it's not enough anymore. It leaves something to be desired. Somehow it leaves one feeling a bit flat."

"Well, more or less. I'm not sure I wouldn't be a little bit happier if I didn't have to worry about Worlughs or Gorgolacs trying to put a hole in my hide, or men forever after one thing or another, for all that. And things like Seven Hills, when we were in that battle. Those sorts of things I don't think I'd miss at all."

Greymouse laughed softly, and nodded. "No, I don't imagine anyone would like to have those sorts of things as everyday affairs."

"But I still feel like it's all been good. It feels like it, anyhow. I mean, Dwarf's journey, and all the things that have happened to us. And it doesn't really feel like it's over yet."

"No, old fellow, it's not quite over yet, not even if Dorini and Doraki were to give themselves up and go back to the natural order of Windameir this very instant. Great things don't get put into motion in a moment, and they aren't stopped so easily, once they gain momentum. Look at the snowball on top of the hill. Small and so easily moved. But push it over the side, and soon it gains force and size, and before long it is impossible to stop, and dangerous to try.

And our little affair is like that now. Things have been put into motion that will play themselves out in their own time. We rest now on the crest of the tide. We've been swept out of the mainstream into a quiet eddy. It is still the same River, but we find ourselves resting in a protected cove for the moment."

Bear had finished the last of the journey cakes, and was working on the honey.

"Then Tyron the Green has done something that is going to be helpful?

I don't see how, with all those elves, and all those threats."

"Helpful, yes. A problem? Yes to that, too. Yet it is still but the setting of the stage. It is necessary. And until I heard your news, I wasn't sure of exactly what way the event would turn. I had a vague notion of it, but I did not know for sure if the way I had imagined would be the way it would eventually work out."

"How is having a half-mad elf with a large army loose in Gilden Wood going to allow anything to work out?" asked Bear sourly. "They weren't the friendliest sorts I would want to meet, and I don't doubt but that they would take great pleasure in ventilating anyone's hide who was messing about in their precious forest."

"No doubt they would," agreed Greymouse. "And we shall have a nasty time of it before the whole thing is said and done. And I don't think it's going to end with Tyron simply taking Gilden Wood. I don't think he will be satisfied with so small a prize when he finds that he has the support and aid of the Dark Queen. I am fairly convinced that the news you have brought me means that good Tyron has seen fit to make a trip or two to Cypher to closet with the new mistress there. And I am sure she is aware of what our esteemable elf holds in trust, and that she has some design of her own to use that to her own advantage."

"It doesn't sound to me like you really think we have much reason to start planning our peaceful pursuits. Bee-keeping, it seems, is going to have to wait."

"For the moment, I'm afraid it is. Tyron is probably going to keep our hands full, and we've got another journey to prepare for."

Bear moaned.

"We must meet up with our good Froghorn, and get you back to your companions," continued Greymouse.

"It seems I'm fated to wear out my pads on this business," groaned Bear. "First with one thing, then another, I'm not even sure whether I'm sleepy or starved anymore, or if I've had anything for my stomach or a pillow for my head since the last time we were in Cypher."

Bear's eyes met Greymouse's.

"And now there isn't any rest to be had even there, since Cybelle and Lorini are gone."

"You'll be seeing Lorini soon enough, old fellow. She's waiting for us, and Greyfax is there, too. It'll be a jolly good bang-up time, once we all meet up. Melodias is marching to join us now, and we're off with the hour, or sooner."

Bear's hopes of getting another meal and a nap fell, but he felt oddly at ease, even though his stomach was signaling that it was growing uneasy once more. His eyes turned restlessly toward the distant mountains, and he could make out the faint, flickering shadows on the earth as the clouds drifted slowly in front of the sun and made moving patterns of deep shadow over the dark green fingers of the gentle slopes of the foothills. Even if it meant going on in the same manner, he suddenly realized within himself, it was what he truly wanted, in his secret heart, and felt was right. There would be no stopping here to root about the old shelters, or lying about under one of the fine nap trees that grew so abundantly in these woods of Gilden Far. His thoughts turned to Cheerweir and Otter, and all that had passed since their meeting long ago, and a warm feeling settled over him. It had, for all of it, certainly been something of an adventure. And it had led them up one side and down the other, but it still felt the right thing in his heart, for something there, deep down, told him that the journey which had taken them so far was now taking them without fail toward Home.

Bear was thinking pleasantly on this last discovery when General Greymouse bounded across the short distance between his tent and the table where they had had lunch, and with an urgent signal of his hand to follow him, had gone bolting on, head down, gray cloak flying out behind. A flurry of other movement caught Bear's eye, and he saw the rest of Greymouse's army scattering into the nearby trees or sprinting away over the small meadow off in the direction of where Greymouse had said Melodias Starson's camp was.

"What is it?" called Bear after the rapidly moving wizard. He had to run hard in order to catch up to Greymouse, and breathlessly he asked the question again.

"I just learned that Tyron has already made his move," shot Greymouse. "He's sent elves to find us here. And he has claimed that his kingdom now has the guidance and blessing of Froghorn Fairingay and the lady Cybelle, of the Circle."

Before Bear could question the wizard further, they had

plunged into the depths of the woods, and the noise of their hurrying feet and the dense growth made speech impossible. Every time Bear would begin to ask a question, Greymouse would shush him and take a new course, until finally Bear's head was dazed by all the doubling back and sidetracking, and the woods grew darker and thicker, until at last they were creeping slowly along, inching ever deeper into the silent forest. As the time wore on, Bear realized with an already pounding heart that Greymouse had been leading him farther and farther into the forbidden boundaries of Gilden Wood.

Breaking Point

Otter plunged through a long, narrow tunnel that spun and turned in brilliant white and blue lights and then dimmed into a throbbing blue sound that called his name over and over.

"Otter, Otter," the voice called, and he answered aloud, "Whater, whater."

The voice began to irritate him, for it went on, droning monotonously.

Without realizing when exactly he woke up, he found himself staring into the worried eyes of his friend Flewingam. After a moment of confusion, he struggled to get to his feet, and found he was in his own familiar form.

"We must fly here, Flew. He's here, too. We've got to escape somehow." Otter feebly sat up and put a paw to his head. "Didn't we attack him just then? And didn't something happen to us? Or someone else come up?"

Flewingam helped his little friend to his feet. "Yes, we did get rather heated up there for a moment, and we did fall on some people," said Flew, holding Otter steady as he walked slowly along, trying to clear his head.

"Are we free?" asked Otter suddenly, jerking to a halt. "I mean, are we free of *him?*" He did not name whom he meant.

"Well, as best as I can make out, we are free, and as for the him you're speaking of, no, we are not. Nor are we rid of a wizard, or a rather pesky dwarf, or two fine fellows going under the unlikely names of Cranfallow and Thinvoice."

Otter's eyes widened, and he looked hard at his friend. "Don't tease me, Flew. I'm in no mood to be reminded of my lost comrades."

"Lost, indeed," blustered an injured voice. "I guess you could says we was lost, but then again, I isn't so sure we was ever in no shape that could be called found."

"I is plumb sure you is right on that account," chimed in another voice.

"Leave it to infernably lazy water dogs to be caught napping in time of a crisis," huffed another, coming almost at Otter's ear.

He wheeled, and staggered forward weakly, blundering directly into Dwarf's arms.

"No!" cried Otter, his voice shaky, and on the verge of sobbing. "This is too much. I mean if we must lose our lives trying to battle this thing, that's as it should be, and I'm ready to use my last breath in service of the Circle. But I won't have any more of this. I know you're not my friend, or you," he said savagely, pointing at Cranfallow. "I know you're nothing more than a trick, too, and I won't have it," he shouted, and he bent forward in a flash, then rose, stumbling toward the figure of Dwarf, a large rock clutched in his paws.

Before Cranfallow or Flewingam or Ned could move to cut off the small animal, a gray-cloaked figure stepped into the space between Otter and Dwarf. A crazed look came over Otter, and a great thin war cry escaped him, and he bared his tiny fangs in a frightening way, and with a deafening explosion of chirps and whistles, he darted forward, the wicked-looking stone raised above his head to strike.

"Stop him!" shouted Cranny, making a vain attempt to snatch the rock from his small friend's paws.

"Lord save us," gasped Ned, who had darted sideways to avoid being smashed by Otter, "the poor little blighter has come aloose from his wits. Here, grabs him, Cranny, afore he hurts hisself, or us with him. That there rock is as big as a horse. I swear, I never thoughts the little bloke could have toted up nothing like the size of that."

Cranfallow had intercepted Otter, and was struggling with him for control of the heavy gray stone Otter brandished aloft. Otter's eyes rolled back in his head, and with another shriek and flurry of whistles, he tore free from Cranfallow and lurched forward toward Broco.

"Easy, lad," warned Cranfallow, although Otter heard nothing, and renewed his war call.

The stone in his paws became airborne, and flew with great velocity directly at Dwarf's head, hissing through the air with an ugly crackling sound. Broco, transfixed by his friend's behavior, stood frozen, watching as the deadly-looking stone flew at him. A soft snap of air and a louder splintering noise, followed by the sharp clap of an explosion, sent showers of the crushed stone pelting over the friends, who had to cover their faces from the sharp hail of the shards of rock.

Froghorn, who at the last moment had flung up his hand and touched the missile, sending it exploding into pieces, uttered a short command in a stern voice. He spoke to Otter in a high form of Otter's ancient tongue, the timeless language of all living things, and at once the small animal quieted down, and looking about himself, came abruptly to tears and fell on Dwarf with a long, high, forlorn whistle that had all the friends thumping the little animal's back in an effort to reassure and console him.

Long blubbery chitters and whiskerfuls of tears made any speech impossible for Otter, but he continued to hug hand and paw alike, and let himself be picked up by Flewingam and carried to the shady coolness beneath a large tree, where everyone tried his best to soothe the hysterical creature. Dwarf, the tears pouring down his face in a continuous stream, patted Otter's paw, while Froghorn knelt beside him and poured the contents of a flask he had removed from a fold in his cloak into a tiny mithra worked goblet and held it to Otter's muzzle. There were snorts and sneezing wheezes, and a great deal of the drink was caught in Otter's whiskers, and reflected the bottle-green shady light of the sun, but some of the cool liquid reached his tongue, and a smooth, blue silence began to grow inside him, and Otter's trembling stopped, and his eyes cleared, and his crying slowed, then ceased altogether.

At last, in a trembling, unsure voice, he spoke. "I'm sorry, friends, I've had a start, and I couldn't face knowing it was him again. I mean the one who looked like you, Froghorn, and who had eaten poor old Whistlepig, and was following us so we'd lead him to Dwarf. And they're looking for you, Dwarf. They know you've got it. And I thought we had stumbled right back into his hands, and that all of you were just tricks. I didn't know what to believe, until Froghorn spoke to me in the old tongue. I guess that's what gave the other one away. When he talked to Flew and me, he didn't say anything at all in any of the other tongues, only the common one. And I know wizards always use whatever tongue they like, but they almost always are polite enough to speak in the tongue of whoever they're talking to. And he didn't. And he didn't say anything at all about any of it, or ask us any questions except about Dwarf, and when those horrible elves brought in that covered dish, I knew something was wrong. And then he didn't even say anything."

Otter drew a long, shuddering breath.

"Brrrrr," he trembled. "It gives me the bumps just to think about it."

Froghorn rose, and replaced the flask into his cloak. "We know who your friend was, Otter. And we know he is operating now out of Cypher, at the orders of the lady Lorini's sister. They can bring none of their beast armies here, but they don't need to. On these planes, they are able to take on whatever appearance suits them. Their war, for the most part, on these levels is one of trickery and deceit. They have no great hordes here, and neither does the Circle, for that matter, so the war in these realms is mostly played out in the minds of the combatants."

"You means we is up toe to toe with someone what's able to just ups and poofs hisself into someones else?" asked Ned Thinvoice, taking off his hat and scratching his head.

"It ain't no different than none of what you is used to, Neddy," chided Cranfallow. "You has been atraveling with them sorts of weird birds ever since you runned across these here friends of ours."

Ned shook his head. "Well, blow out my candles, but I guess I has," he whistled.

"I guess we is just getting used to all this here sorts of goings-on," said Cranny, " 'cause I isn't upset nohow about none of it. Why, you could march up here right this minute and tell me my old geezer what's been croaked now for ten years was acoming for supper, and I wouldn't think nothing of it, but just puts out another plate. I think we is agetting the hang of all this, Ned, I does. As like as not, one of these days we is agoing to be able to wrinkle up our brows real good and bust out in a spell that would scare the warts off a toadfrog."

Ned Thinvoice looked blankly at his friend, but remained silent.

"That's quite a mouthful, Cranny, and I'd wager you it shall all come to pass," agreed Froghorn, smiling. "But what you say is true, Ned, these enemies of ours have certain advantages in these realms, and are able to throw us off the track with their disguises. We may not know where they are, or who they are posing as, but the one thing they cannot stand up against here is the power of the Chest, and as long as we hold that, and keep our Dwarf with us, we shall be able to make that test of all we chance across in our journey to reach Greyfax and Lorini, and I'm sure we're going to have opportunity enough to try it." Froghorn paused, then went on in a lighter voice. "And speaking of coming across someone, I feel sure we're going to find our path running to Melodias, and Greymouse, too. And we all have a friend who is with Greymouse at this moment, who is going to be very glad of knowing of some certain travelers' arrival."

"Who is that?" asked Flew, curious to know who or what else they might expect in the seemingly ever changing flow of events that surrounded them.

"A rather stout fellow who answers to the name of Bear," smiled Froghorn, "and a fellow who, I'm sure, is somewhat perplexed at the moment because the news he has to tell has been received in a rather unseemly fashion." Froghorn gave a little laugh. "There have been events that have taken place that have been long awaited by certain parties, and the announcement of a certain elf we know who has proclaimed himself king in Gilden Wood is one that has brought good cheer to more than one soul in these parts." He laughed again, and raised a hand to fend off Dwarf's question.

"You mean Bear is here, too? But how?" exploded Otter.

"We will have our explanations soon enough, but for now, we need to make our start toward Greymouse. He is anxiously awaiting our news, and our good Dwarf. And I think he may be hurrying to meet us in a place we have long sought."

Froghorn, to everyone's dismay, would say no more, and with almost rude abruptness, he led the companions off in the direction of the lowering sun, which burned with a shadowy, shimmering light over the burnished gold tops of the distant trees in the newly closed fastness of Gilden Wood.

A Pact Is Sealed

In the fading silence that hung grimly on in the gray pall that had fallen over Cypher, a faint and uneasy laughter rang, shrill and hollow, and without trace of joy or humor.

"Well said, well said, Your Eminence," shot Tyron nervously. "It is as well put as I have ever heard it."

Doraki's burning, blank eyes fell on Tyron, and the elf felt himself grow faint with fear. The most terrible thing about the Dark Queen's underlord was his eyes, which were perfectly empty, just as his queen's were full of the dreadful menace of the Darkness she commanded.

"You speak most lightly, Tyron. I have made no decisions about what should be done with you. I have a fair mind to send you to the boundaries beyond light. Yet I still find you amusing, you and your silly little scheme." Dorini spoke from the shadows of a tall wing chair, which was carved in the likeness of a huge dragon's head. "Yet," she went on, "your sniveling scheme to gain a throne for yourself interests me at the moment. I have held greater kings than you dare ever hope to be in the palm of my hand, and destroyed far mightier plans than the paltry things you dream." Dorini snorted. "And it is just that that makes it hold its weight with me. It is novel, this shriveling knot of a being daring to cross my path, and actually thinking he might by some far reach of the imagination have something to bargain with me for."

A shuddering storm of icy, dark laughter broke from the unsounded depths of Dorini and echoed over again through the once bright dining hall in the heart of Cypher. Tyron's knees trembled, but fortunately he was sitting, and he raised himself a small bit before speaking.

"I realize Your Darkness is all-powerful, and far beyond the likes of anyone so humble as myself, yet it is as I have said, Your Darkness, it is because of that very fact that I am in the best position to serve the ends you seek. You could, as we both know, take from me a certain property by force. But as we both know, that certain property, if taken by force, does not hold the Law any longer, and cannot call those others that are a part of it. And only the holder of that property can do that, which would rid you of the thing you need to be rid of most. And it would give me what I most desire, and that is a realm beyond all interference, where all my clan shall forever more grow and flourish unhampered."

"Sit nearer here," crooned Dorini, a sudden, disconcerting smoothness in her voice.

Tyron looked up sharply, and saw that she had moved to a smaller table, and was indicating a chair that stood close by her. He hesitated for a moment, but at length went and sat, clutching tightly the small mirror in his cloak.

"What say you to all this, my love? Does this suit your fancy?"

Dorini had turned to Doraki, and addressed herself to his shadowy form as he stood near the fireless hearth.

A cold, chilling wind seemed to fill the room each time he spoke.

"I am on the verge of gaining the prize. I have found out from the gnome's traveling companions that he is across the River. And I have located the camp where they now stay. But that beast Foulingray protects them, and the others are all across, too. I don't like this business here. I belong with our other armies, where I may be of most use."

"You don't take well to going about in the guise of our Foulingray, my pet? Doesn't it suit your fancy to imitate those horrible things that want to send us back to the nothingness we were before, when we had nothing, and controlled nothing?"

"These games of yours shall end in mischance, Your Darkness. I loathe being here, this side of this accursed River, and amid these crawling, sniveling things that call themselves beings. There is nothing to be gained here. Our power is lessened here, and I am longing for the treat of going out with Fireslayer and Cakgor and riding among the cringing hordes we control in your lower dominion. I long for the bite of the whip to sting deeply in the shrieking herds of craven things we have below."

"You have begun to get a bit ambitious, my love. For that, you shall stay here yet awhile. I am going to deny you your playthings still longer. Your errand here is not complete. And you promise me empty promises, my pet. You have told me time and again that you will deliver me the accursed box of those murdering thieves who follow my weak sister, but always there is some lame excuse or other that you give me, instead of bringing me the one thing I must have. That we *both* must have, for if this pesky tunnel rat of a dwarf gets by us now, then the wretched box is beyond our grasp. We can go no further in our cause of freeing these lower dominions from the grip of those monsters of the Circle. We are at the end of our realms here. So we must succeed this time. And I think this ambitious elf is going to help us achieve our goal."

Dorini turned on Tyron, and the terrible beauty of her struck him, and she reached out a smooth, pale hand and touched him, and her eyes became deep, dark pools that went on forever. Tyron, too frozen and helpless to resist her, could not hold out his small defense in time, and felt himself dragged into the nothingness of her eyes and pulled farther and farther away, into the depths of a sleep that was dreamless and deep.

Tyron's unfeeling body rocked to and fro in the chair beside Dorini.

"Are you going to take the cursed thing's life?" asked Doraki, his cruel lips curled back in a savage smile.

"No, my tender one. And I am not yet ready to take from him what he holds, for what he says is true. I could gain the one, but without the Chest, the others would still be a threat to our plans. I shall need them all safely within our grasp."

"If you say that the wretch of a dwarf might get through, and beyond our boundaries, then what harm? The box would be gone, and we would be free of any of those beasts trying to drag us back to that miserable hole of a prison they call home."

"You outdo yourself this evening, my pet. Yes, what harm, and why not let that wretched thing through, and be rid of the both of them, box and all, for good?"

Dorini threw back her head and snorted a low growl of laughter.

"But do you think *they* would let that be the end of it? Do you think *they* would leave it at that? No, my slow one, if we allow this one to escape, he will only cause more to come in his place, and then more, and more. As long as they have their miserable slaves here, like Greyfilth, and Foulingray, and all the rest of those beasts, we shall not find a moment's peace. Our only chance at achieving the dream we have for these kingdoms is to destroy or capture the miserable box once and for all, and to drive out these puppets who call themselves servants of the High King of Windameir. All lies, and weak-willed idiots, bowing and scraping to some doddering old fools who are forever muttering in their whiskers about peace, and joy, and being at one with the Lord. Bah!" spat Dorini. "We have created our own world here, and seen it come alive with action, and feeling, and felt the supreme power of being all-knowing and controlling our destinies as the High King meant us to."

Dorini had risen as she spoke, and now paced up and down restlessly.

"He has given us our chance," she said, jabbing a finger in the direction of Tyron. "What we have been unable to get by our campaigns below we shall achieve by our brains above. We are going to become bystanders here, as prim and well-mannered as mice, for the moment. And our good elf here is going to set the trap for our most glorious triumph. And then we shall have not only that sniveling brat of my sister's, but we will have the last ingredient in total victory in our hands, and these lower worlds will never be taken from us again, and we will be free of ever having to return to any dungeon cell the miserable fools of the Circle call home."

"Then this thing is to be used?" asked Doraki, who paced beside Dorini and gazed with his horrible, empty eyes at the still form of Tyron.

"Yes. And now you will assume your former guise. And I shall take on one as well."

The cruel features of Doraki softened, and a wreath of pale green light hovered about him for a moment, until after another second or two, he stood forth as Froghorn Fairingay. The eyes were somewhat dull and lifeless, and there was none of the young wizard's good humor or thoughtfulness, but Dorini looked at the hated, familiar face and drew her lips back in an ugly smile.

"You do that very well, my love. You look enough like that foul thing that I could almost carry out the vengeance I have plotted for them upon you."

"I don't like this, Your Darkness," snarled Doraki. "Why can't we smash these hateful things, and bring the rest of our armies here, like below? There isn't enough fighting here for me."

"You'll have plenty soon enough, my pet. Patience. And in a little while, you'll be able to have your playthings without worry of losing them, and even have a new toy, all for your own." As Dorini finished speaking, she turned to face her underlord. "And you would like this, wouldn't you?"

Cybelle, or a very near likeness of her, stood smiling at Doraki.

Only the hardness of the eyes gave away the startling change that Dorini had worked upon herself, and Tyron the

Green, who was released from her spell at that moment, noticed not at all that the beautiful young woman who stood beside him was not what she seemed, and found it strange that Froghorn Fairingay, supposedly one of the Elders of the Circle of Light, would be found in the old halls of Cypher, with the same intentions in mind as those plans of his own.

And it did not seem strange, or out of place, that Dorini and Doraki were nowhere to be seen.

They fell into conversation then, and Tyron found that the ambitious young wizard was plotting on his own for the very reasons that moved him, and that Cybelle, daughter of Lorini, the sister of the Dark Queen, was in on the treachery that would overturn the Circle and cast the lower worlds of Windameir into the eternal darkness of Dorini.

Storm Gatherings

A Parting Glance

In the gray light of the dark gloom that hung like heavy smoke over the ruins of Cypher, Lorini turned to Greyfax, her eyes brimming with unwept tears. He cushioned her head on his shoulder, and patted her gently.

"It is as I told you, sister. But it is still Cypher in our hearts. Nothing can change that. And it is still Cypher, even in its ruin. And it is still Cypher on this side of the River. That is as it is written. See, even the chill of the Dark Queen can't quell the light of the place."

"I am glad you brought me, dear Greyfax. It is what I needed to rid me of the last lingering hope that I would someday return to Cypher. I see it is only as Erophin and Cephus tried to tell me all along. When you know of nothing but what you have, you do not seek anything more, even though you may find something finer. I had filled my heart with Cypher for so many turnings that I had quite forgotten the rest. It is a hard lesson, but one that I have so dearly needed for so long. And the loss of Cybelle has brought home to me that she is not mine. I have acted very unwisely about her, and I find that even I, who should know better than to become attached to anything or anyone for selfish reasons, have become selfishly attached to my daughter. But that is over now that I have seen Erophin. I now it is all playing itself out. I lost my faith for a while, it seems, and tried to put myself on even footing with Windameir himself."

"A common mistake, my lady," Greyfax chuckled softly. "But come, we must remove ourselves before our hostess returns. I have no doubt that her absence, and the absence of her underling, shall spell some mischief or other before too much longer. It has been relatively quiet here, all things considering, and taking into account that both Dorini and Doraki have crossed the River and are here. But I don't like the lay of it. Too quiet, for my liking. It's not a proper state of affairs, if you know what I mean."

"If you feel it odd that more is not happening because of their presence, I agree. I do find it extremely distressing that the entire scope of her operations has drawn quieter, and even the reports we have had from beyond Calix Stay indicate things have settled down, even there. The Worlughs and Gorgolacs have been retreating all along every front, and no beast has been seen on any battleground since we have made the crossing this time."

Greyfax remained silent for a time before answering Lorini. His eyes studied the gray ruins of Cypher, but his thoughts were far from there.

"An enemy you can't find is always more distressing than the one who is asleep in your pocket," he mused aloud.

"Yet we know she is across Calix Stay," continued Lorini. "We know she has been seen in Cypher, and that Doraki is here with her also."

"Here, and still we don't know where they are, or what new trick they are up to."

The two were silent and motionless for a moment longer, and as they gazed on the ruined halls and gardens of Cypher, a subtle change seemed to come over the place, and for the barest of moments, the gray light brightened into the full glory of a spring day, bright and golden, and the grim silence that hung like a dark curtain over the gardens and fountains burst into high, trilling laughter and music, reed pipe and soft voice, accompanied by the hushed voice of a lute, turned and spun on the face of the day, and the memories of Cypher of old came alive to the stately, moving tunes that painted the wind a brilliant silver-white and rustled the dead leaves in the gardens to dance and turned the murky, stagnant fountains into rippling waterfalls of rainbow lights that glistened and turned in the air, leaving a fine halo of spray lingering after all the music and light were gone.

Lorini, eyes shining, and fighting hard to hold herself in check, turned to Greyfax. "You didn't have to remind me of things better left as they are," she managed, unable to meet his steady, even gaze.

"It was not I, my lady," said Greyfax. "Cypher is alive of itself. It does not need the paltry designs of a bumbling fool such as I to waken the magic there."

Lorini lifted her tear-stained face to Greyfax.

"Even after all it has suffered?"

"Cypher has not suffered, my lady. I fear that you and I and all the rest who have ever seen Cypher of old have suffered. Cypher is as it was and shall always be. Only those who come and go are altered."

"I like to think of it that way," said Lorini softly. "And that even my sister's presence will make no difference. And that perhaps even the magic of Cypher might somehow reach her."

"I think perhaps that may have already occurred. And her presence there shall probably make Cypher that much more dear, in many ways. Only after we have seen the coin from both sides do we truly know all that is concerned with a matter."

"I think I know what you mean. But let's go, shall we? I feel we must be getting on with the parts we have been given."

"And that is right enough. I have word that our good Froghorn is going to rather upset Tyron's plans for Gilden Wood, by stopping up one of those odd crossings that were left over from after the Dragon Wars. It's a good thing Tyron is such a close-mouth, for if that crossing had ever been made known more widely, I'm sure we would have more of a problem to deal with here than we do. As it is, Tyron is too smart for his own good, in many ways. By keeping that secret, not even Tyron's closest adviser knows of it. Dorini would delight in it, for it is capable of bringing or sending anyone at will, as long as the medium is in control of its workings. I remember we had quite a time of it cleaning up the Meadows of the Sun before, when the last of the dragon hordes crossed and had to be hunted down this side of Calix Stay. We thought all these crossings had been closed, and that only Calix Stay remained, and the other boundaries, but of the single one that was left, leave it to a rather ambitious elf to find. And oddly enough, the one elf who holds the Secret that comes from the Chest."

"Tyron will be very angry at the loss of that. Eiorn must have given him that along with the Secret. It is a very powerful thing to have up one's sleeve."

"Too powerful, just as the Secret is. I think perhaps it has driven Tyron to overreach himself, not only with the holding back of the information of the whereabouts of the crossing, and the use of that crossing for furthering his own designs, and other schemes, but it has caused him most likely to think that he will be able to rid himself of Dorini and Doraki. The crossing is capable of that, naturally, although they would not long be kept at bay by it. He has, I fear, a somewhat enlarged idea of what the crossing, in conjunction with the Secret, can do."

Greyfax paused as he spoke, and the two, who had been walking slowly away from the pale shadow of Cypher, turned for one last look at the faintly glimmering ruins.

"And that was the danger of carrying the Chest too long. It was the danger that the Circle feared the most," he went on, as they began walking again. "And that was the reason none of us ever carried the Chest too long, or even one of the Secrets. It was fine when the Arkenchest was complete and the Five were there in full, but after the separation of the Secrets, it became a temptation to wield the power in unwise ways. Eiorn held for too long the Secret put in his trust, which was to have been but a short-term move to ensure its safety. How little time it took to corrupt even the good Eiorn into knowing what was best for the Secret, and too assume responsibility for it, even to the point of passing it on to his son, who, being subject to his father's opinions and oddness, took up right where his father left off."

"You know, I honestly think Urien Typhon almost had

Tyron talked into surrendering up his trust. Froghorn said that Urien holds terrific sway with those elves who yet remain in these lower realms. They seem to look up to him as an elder, or guide."

"That may be. Yet the woodland folk have never fully trusted the waterfolk, which is Urien's clan. There have been many disputes among the elvish clans on that issue, ever since the first of them began to appear in these lower creations. Tyron, I think, is also jealous of Urien. And Urien is on his last turning in these worlds, and does have great power to attract goodness of heart. And that might also create just the opposite in one who is envious of such a being. But you can see the whole question as it has been fought for all these ages. You look at Urien, and then see Tyron. For some reason the woodland folk have always felt inferior."

"But they are both the same. And I remember when our feast halls were full of the likes of them." She shook her head, frowning. "Has it all been so long ago?"

"Not so long that I've forgotten it," replied Greyfax. "But if you remember, Urien's kin were indispensable in the later years of the Dragon Wars. And as like as not, you'd find his clan on any errand that had the smell of danger to it. They served faithfully, and well, and were all given the freedom to act as they chose about going on beyond these lower borders. The woodland elves never really took too well to mingling with others, although Eiorn served honorably as Elder, and contributed many invaluable suggestions, and played his own part well, as did all his kin. Yet somehow, someway, the woodland elves broke away from the flow of things, and began retreating into their havens and having nothing to do with the other elvish folk, or the Circle, for that matter. And the final stroke was Eiorn's deciding that he was going to keep the Secret he had been entrusted with. It was too much for him, it seems, and he saw it as a way to outdo the waterfolk, who were not given the errand of guarding a Secret, for they wisely refused it. And it seems that Tyron's father planted that idea in his head."

Greyfax smiled gently.

"And naturally, the waterfolk, for the most part, have chosen to go on beyond these lower realms and leave these troubled times behind. Now it is mostly the woodland elves, led by Tyron, who remain, seeking to find the perfect haven, when the only real haven is Home. Yet I see that it is all working out as it should."

Having come some way from the ruins of Cypher, the two had increased their pace slightly. Without warning, Greyfax suddenly halted and gave out a long, soft, whirring note of a whistle that sounded almost like the cry of a dove. Immediately ahead of them, in a small clearing of the remnants of the old Forest of Cypher, there stepped the great silver-gray horse An'yim and his brother, Pe'lon. The two horses bowed their noble heads twice to Greyfax and Lorini, and An'yim buried his nose in his old friend's arm, neighing in long, chuckling noises that made the wizard laugh.

"Good friend, I have long missed you. Our last parting was sudden, and I hadn't planned in being so long away."

An'yim nickered and put his muzzle at the wizard's back, giving Greyfax a playful shove.

"But come, we must find our feet now, and make our start for the Beginning. There is much to be done there, and many scenes to set."

Lorini mounted An'yim, who stood unmoving while Greyfax handed her up to his high saddle.

"Do you think my sister will show herself soon?" she asked, holding tightly to the sturdy saddle horn, although An'yim stood so still he might well have been stone.

"I greatly expect that she shall," answered Greyfax. "We have the sudden appearance of our two friends here to speak for the fact that something is afoot. They have not been in our plans for quite some span of time now, and I think perhaps we have had the good fortune of Someone sending them back to us, to enable us to do what must be done here with as little slowness as possible. And being able to travel with the ease and speed of these steeds is a boon in any chore, no matter what the task at hand."

Lorini was quite taken with the great silver-gray animals, and she leaned forward and gave An'yim a tender stroke on his long, powerful neck.

"I have often talked to this noble being, when he was visiting Cypher with his master," she said, "but I never dared dream that I would one day be upon his back."

"And it is well we have these speedy allies;" said Greyfax, turning away for a moment, his head poised in listening. "The quiet is as bothersome as a cannon blast. I'd prefer some noise to this. I don't like the set of it. Your dark sister is at her work, I don't doubt. But I think instead of taking both our friends here, it would be wise to send Pe'lon to search out Froghorn. If anyone can find our impetuous young pup, it's this fellow. I daresay he's known Froghorn as long or longer than most of us, and he might likely know of the hotheaded young scamp's whereabouts."

"Are we to seek out Fairingay, then?" asked Lorini, looking down into the worried glance of Greyfax.

"Not now. It would spoil a plan that has been set into action, I fear. And I have heard nothing as to its misfire, so we shall leave well enough alone. And I think we must be at our journey. Perhaps we shouldn't have left at all, except that I wanted you to have that look at Cypher. I can't say that I didn't want one more look myself."

Lorini laughed quietly. "You sly devil," she teased. "You never mentioned that."

"Well, it's true enough. I spent many a gay hour within those walls, and I can't say that those memories don't give me much pleasure when all else is grim and of a less fortunate nature."

Lorini squeezed Greyfax's hand and smiled softly. "Then thank you for bringing me. It has been something that I needed for a boost. I do feel much better now."

"I think we'd best send our good Pe'lon on his way. He seems anxious to be off."

The tall animal paced nervously at An'yim's side, his neigh a low chuckle of urgency.

"Go on, then, old fellow. Find your Froghorn. We shall await you all, and see you when best we may."

Pe'lon bowed once, then unable to contain himself longer, he blurred into a moving wind and was suddenly gone from sight.

"He seemed very much in a hurry," laughed Lorini. "I think he has already discovered the whereabouts of his young Froghorn."

Greyfax, mounting An'yim behind Lorini, nodded. "Even Pe'lon has his part to play."

"What is that supposed to say, my sphinx? Are you saying you know more this moment than you're telling me?"

Before Greyfax could reply, they had crossed the long, deep green meadow that lay in the middle of the thickly wooded stand of trees, and the great horse wheeled high up in the silver-blue reaches of the sky and rose away upward on a ray of late afternoon sunlight. And in another reach of the wood not very far distant, Pe'lon began his errand, even as Lorini and Greyfax touched down lightly in the heart of their latest camp, high up the back of the blue-colored mountains. They did not hear the distraught cries of the comrades of the Light as they searched the surrounding woods of Gilden in vain for an ominously missing companion.

Settling Down for a Wait

Broco, along with Cranfallow and Ned, had been left as a lookout while the others went with Froghorn to destroy the crossing of Tyron. They waited uneasily as the minutes dragged on into seemingly endless hours and still their companions had not returned. Dwarf's instructions had been to keep an eye out for any sign of Tyron's forces, in which case he was to signal with a small, finely carved ivory ring, which Froghorn had said would alert him if rubbed in a certain manner and worn on the third finger of the left hand. And he was also to keep watch should any others of the Circle pass on in their journey to reach the Mountains of Beginning, and beyond.

Dwarf, who had not liked being singled out for this unpleasant, frightening task, wailed and complained bitterly. "Why can't I have someone stay to help keep watch, if it's so important? As they say, four eyes are sharper than two."

"You are perfectly capable of keeping a close eye out, old fellow. And I need Otter and Flewingam to help me in a task that needs very much to be taken care of before we leave these parts. Otherwise, I fear we'll be going on with this nonsense until we all have gray beards past our bucklers. But stout Cranny and Ned will keep you company."

"Why can't I go, and Otter stay? Or Flewingam?" persisted the truculent Broco, who was more sure than ever that Froghorn was marking him out especially for some sort of punishment.

After all, he thought, the young wizard had refused to take the Arkenchest, and had given him feeble excuses to justify it, and now he was leaving him in the middle of an enemy-infested wood, totally at the mercy of any who wished him harm.

"You could go, old fellow, but I'd rather have the Chest safe here, should anything go awry at the crossing. Sometimes these things are very tricky, and I've seen and heard of these very things that have somehow reversed the spells of those who are evoking them, and catapulted everything back into another space, forward or back. It can be most dangerous sometimes if one isn't careful of all the counterspells that may have been put into use. And we don't know what Tyron may have done to protect this prize of his."

Froghorn's voice took on a harder note.

"And that, my lump of a gnome, is why you are remaining here to keep watch for us. First, because I am expecting company, perhaps, and I want them to know where I'm bound, and what my errand is. And secondly, because I want the Chest out of harm's way, at least until I can determine to what extent the danger is with the gate of Tyron's that we are going to close."

"We isn't no sorts of anything like company, but we does has our good sides," assured Ned Thinvoice rather testily.

He was irritated and saddened by the change that had seemingly come over Dwarf since their arrival in these new surroundings, for Broco often treated both him and Cranfallow as if they were no more than passing strangers now. At times he seemed to forget their experiences together and the common dangers they had shared.

"I know you and Cranny are staying," shot back Dwarf, just as sharply. "I want to know why *I'm* staying. It's not fair, having to always take the worst jobs to be done."

Flewingam and Otter looked at their friend closely, trying to see if he were teasing Ned, but Broco was perfectly earnest.

Froghorn addressed Broco in a slightly softer tone. "I know it's hard for you to stay behind while your friends face all the danger, but there is good reason that I ask you to do this. I can only say that as a personal boon to me, it would please me greatly."

Dwarf huffed importantly, and cleared his throat. "In that case, I shall do this, as a personal favor to you, Froghorn. I admit I don't like the idea of my friends having to face possible danger without me, but I am sure they understand that I cannot, with honor, refuse your request."

"They do, I am sure, understand," said Froghorn.

He looked the companions squarely in the eyes, and asked, "You understand this, don't you?"

Without comprehending what Froghorn was attempting to do, or what strange mood had come over Broco, the friends nodded.

"Good. Cranny and Ned, I shall expect you to stick close to our Chest Bearer, just as faithfully as you always have in the past."

Cranfallow merely nodded without looking up from his boots, but Ned Thinvoice spoke up loudly.

"A fine lot of thanks we gets for that," he pouted. "A fat-headed lump of a dwarf gets sets in his ways, and I knows that, and I isn't after asking no one for no special favors for Neddy Thinvoice. What I *is* after asking is that once we gets out of this kettle of brew we has stumbled into, or *if* we ever gets out, that I isn't ever reminded no more of dwarfs, or of any of their goings-on."

Cranfallow looked up quickly from the ground at his feet upon hearing the bitterness in his friend's voice. "He don't mean that," put in Cranny, addressing himself to Broco, who had huffed himself into a purple-faced rage. "He's just after blowing off a bit of that steam we has all been abuilding up since we has ended up in these queer parts where we is."

"You don't have to speak for this illiterate, lazy lout of a worthless jackanapes," shot Dwarf in a dangerous, even tone. "I have felt he is after a certain something I'm carrying, and has been plotting to attain that end for some time now. I can even recall once or twice when he almost succeeded, when I was gravely injured and could not defend myself."

Broco turned to Cranfallow.

"I owe to you the fact that he did not carry out his plan, although I'm not entirely convinced that you yourself aren't in on the scheme, since you seem to be such bosom companions."

Froghorn interrupted the ranting Dwarf. "Enough, you lummox. This is a matter to be settled in a time and place much more suited to it than this. You will stand watch here, as I've asked, and if you don't find the thought of standing it together particularly pleasing, then you stand your watch on this side of the trail, and Cranfallow and Thinvoice can cover the other side."

"That's all as fair," muttered Thinvoice angrily.

"And it suits me very well," blustered Dwarf.

Froghorn gave his final instructions, and set out in the direction of the thickening wood, where the trees grew even denser and the air seemed to be filled with the sticky green smell of endless trees, growing on forever in all directions.

Otter, his heart still pounding from the scene earlier, finally caught up with the quick-striding wizard.

"What's gotten wrong with everyone, Froghorn? I mean Ned and Dwarf have been the best of comrades, always. And now they're on the point of boxing each other's ears."

Froghorn replied without changing stride or taking his eyes off the invisible markers he used to guide himself through the closely grown green canopy of trees.

"A thing that someone cherishes, say, a prize of some sort or other that one likes above everything else, will sooner or later work one's mind about until one thinks that everyone is most certainly, and beyond a doubt, after that prized possession. And that may or may not be the case in truth, but one's mind assures one that every single being is after that treasure. That is what is happening to our dwarf, Otter. The Chest is beginning to make its weight felt."

Froghorn glanced down at the troubled Otter, whose muzzle had worked itself into a broad frown as the young wizard had been speaking.

"Say it this way, then," he went on. "The Chest is the hope of all the lower worlds of Windameir. We depend upon the Secrets to enable us to break free of Dorini's hold and go

Home. But the Chest now is only partially whole, and the Secrets are divided. Too much knowledge is sometimes a dangerous thing, my little friend. Just as is too little."

Otter wrinkled his whiskers and wiggled his ears to make sure he was hearing right.

"But what's all that got to do with Dwarf? And why has Ned gotten so testy?"

"There are things here at work, old fellow, that aren't easily explained. Let me just say that certain forces are at work here in these woods, and that Tyron's dealings with Dorini are already paying off. We're feeling the long reach of the Dark Queen. Negative power is her energy, and that energy generates strong ripples in the very air around us. Ned and Dwarf were fighting because they were feeling the negative thoughts that are put into motion by the Dark Queen's energy. She feeds off strife. And you must remember, our good spanner has been captured and held in the very depths of Dorini's prisons."

Otter's eyes opened wide.

"You mean she can do all this even when she's not around?"

"Oh, it is one of her very best, most effective weapons, on some planes. She creates a fear and plants it in the heart, and soon that unsuspecting person is firmly sure that his neighbor is out to rob him, and before long the neighbors have built fences, and dug moats, and if that doesn't do, they'll invent some weapon or other for knocking each other's brains out. That is one of her most widely spread weapons, that fear."

"I still don't see why Dwarf would be so sharp with Ned," Otter persisted.

"It is all a little scene that has to be played out, Otter. It is nothing to be overly concerned about."

Flewingam, who had been silent as the two talked, spoke up. "I've noticed something different in Dwarf. He seems to be a bit huffier than I remember. Almost defensive."

"Yes, that's so," agreed Froghorn, nodding.

"And I've noticed that he keeps his hand inside his cloak almost all the time lately. I thought at first he had hurt his hand or arm, but when I asked him about it, he just muttered something about he wasn't going to show it to me, and that I might as well forget trying to trick him into it."

"Show you what? His arm?" asked Otter.

"That's what I thought," went on Flewingam. "Except that then I saw him with both arms out of his cloak for a moment, and neither of them seemed injured in any way."

"Then what was it he wouldn't show you?"

"The Chest," said Froghorn. "He is feeling the weight of bearing the Chest, as I said."

"The Chest?" repeated Otter. "What on earth has the Chest got to do with it?"

"Our good Dwarf is beginning to feel a certain pull," replied Froghorn. "It happens to us all. And it is a thing that must happen, for our own growth, so we can overcome it."

"And while we're at overcoming things, what sort of a gate is this we're going to find?" asked Otter, who did not want to lose a chance of getting replies from an unusually verbal Froghorn.

"It's a gate of sorts, or otherwise known as a crossing, and this one has been overlooked for a long time now. It's been here since before the Dragon Wars, but no one has known its exact whereabouts or had a chance to do anything about it until now."

"Would it really be dangerous for Dwarf to be here? Or were you just making him stay behind for some other reason?" asked Otter.

Froghorn shot a sideways glance at the little animal.

"What do you think?" he asked in an amused voice.

Otter blushed gray.

"I don't know."

"Don't you?"

"Well, he told me you were trying to punish him, and that you were doing things to try to make him give up the Chest and let you take it back."

"He said that, did he? That's very interesting."

"And he said that if we weren't all careful, we'd be caught like fish in an eel net and hung up to dry, and that we needed to be moving on out of these woods."

Flewingham, walking beside Otter, spoke again. "And he seemed to think that the place we should be making for is not the Beginning, but back in the direction of wherever it was he used to dwell, beneath the mountain, he said. It's the only safe place, so he says, where the Darkness would never think to look for the Chest."

Froghorn's face was a mask, and neither Otter nor Flewingam could tell what the young wizard was thinking. He strode on in silence, and try as they might, they could get him to say nothing further about the Chest, or the gate of Tyron's that he was so concerned about closing. And at last, as they made their way deeper into the darkening wood, they had to give up their questioning and watch where they were going, for the footing grew somewhat tricky from a ground dew that left the short, tufted grass below the trees smooth and slippery. And the two friends no longer dared raise their voices, for this new, quieter part of the wood seemed to grow more and more foreboding, and the light that before had been much as the light in any densely overgrown wood now seemed to be altered, and looked more and more like the light that filters down through a pool of deep, undisturbed water.

They had gone on a bit farther when Froghorn made a signal with his hand, and all three of the friends dropped to the ground and waited in a breathless silence for something to pass. Otter and Flewingam had seen nothing, but they felt the presence of something, and the rasping, raw way it beat against the heart and the tingling sensation it made on the back of the neck made them feel that whatever it was it was not of a benign nature.

After another moment they went on, but soon Froghorn stopped them again, this time in the stifling green stillness of the deepest heart of Gilden Wood, and the three friends looked out into an odd clearing, right where there should have been none, filled with carven stone pillars higher than most of the trees, and odd stones that seemed to take on the appearance of some sort of bridge, although they obviously went nowhere, and crossed nothing that could be seen. And then the high, thin music began, and Froghorn gave them a hasty, warning scowl that silenced all the questions they were ready to ask.

They took up their positions behind the young wizard and settled down to wait.

Relics of the Dragon

Through a dense green window of branches, Otter and Flewingam looked out into the small clearing that was deep in the very heart of Gilden Wood. Otter, when he had lived in the Meadows of the Sun long ago, had heard rumors of this glade, but he had never cared to venture so far from his beloved river or weir, and so had never known if the story was fact or merely someone's fancy. He had never had reason to doubt that the ancient crossing did exist, somewhere, and since he had no interest in it then, he let it go at that. Now, crouched by Froghorn's side, he saw for himself that the secret place was real, and was there before him.

A ring of huge stones circled the fringe of the glade, right where the trees began, and each of the great stones had the likeness of a man, or elf, or animal, or dwarf, or dragon on it, and many of the stones had carvings of things that Otter could not make out. A faint, thin reed pipe swam softly over the heavy air, making the mind drowsy and the thoughts all turn to lazy summer afternoons on the river, with fat honey-bees dancing their slow tune to the yellow, red, and blue flowers at the water's side. Otter's body began a slow swaying, and he was rudely jostled by Froghorn, who scowled and signaled him to be silent.

Flewingam, his pale face close beside Otter, looked on the strange sight with wide, frightened eyes, and tiny drops of sweat crept down his nose and dropped onto his mustache.

The air was laden with the smells of the deep forest, and hard to breathe, so full it was of pine resin scent, and old growth, and decay, and yesterday's rain.

Otter's nostrils flared, and he had to work hard at not becoming closed in by the atmosphere of the place.

Froghorn seemed not to notice his friends' raspy breathing, and stared intently into the clearing and at the woods that circled it. The young wizard tensed once, and his eyes seemed to take on a rippling gray-blue fire and his mouth set into a grim mask, but it passed after a moment, and whatever he had seen, or thought he had seen, passed, and his features fell once more into an eager, watchful anticipation.

Twice Otter jumped as Froghorn stiffened, then relaxed. Fairingay had explained nothing, which by now Otter knew was only to be expected. The Elders of the Circle seemed to him to be a closemouthed bunch on most occasions, and he had learned after a time that they would tell him everything he needed to know when he needed to know it, and not a moment before. As irritating as that had often been, Otter resigned himself to it and tried to keep alert to any movement in the glade or the wood.

He turned to give Flewingam a pat to reassure him, and as he did so, his eyes caught the barest glimpse of a movement behind them, somewhere in the wall of green that rose upward and away until almost all the sunlight was filtered into a deep, blue-green halo, almost as if it were a shadow of light. In the gloom Otter couldn't be sure of what he thought he had seen, but as he concentrated on looking, it seemed as if every bush moved. He blinked, and tried looking out of the corner of his eye. The movement came again. This time it seemed as if what had moved was a grayish-blue cloud of fog, dense and low on the ground. As Otter watched, another small cloud seemed to inch its way closer to the three friends. Otter tried to get Froghorn's attention, but the young wizard thrust a hand to his mouth to indicate silence, and went on with his study of the woods across the clearing.

Flewingam tapped Otter urgently on the back, and pointed with his hand at the advancing sea of grayish mass, whose ugly, coiling body was moving in the still air like limbs of trees being blown about in a woodland storm. Otter nodded, and again tried to attract Froghorn's attention. As he raised a hand to try to touch his shoulder, he heard a dim roaring, as if a thousand drums began to roll, and the already fading light in the clearing began to flicker and flash, first dim, and then bright, and a reddish haze began to grow over the clearing, almost like the dull, leaden red glow of battle fires. Without warning, the harsh red cloud was gone, replaced by a pale golden halo that seemed to be not only a color, but a sound. It sounded golden, and felt golden as well, and Otter would have sworn it even tasted golden. And the drums had been replaced by a single stringed instrument that sounded like a violin, accompanied by a flute that played on unceasingly.

Flewingam had grabbed hold of Otter, and Otter, not knowing what else to do, grabbed hold of Froghorn's cloak. The young Master's face seemed transformed, and his eyes danced with a golden, glowing fire. He seemed to be speaking, although no words escaped his lips, and after a time, he sat as if he were listening.

Otter did not recall how long he had been looking into the calm gray-blue eyes of General Greymouse, who now stood beside him. Half a moment later, Otter saw the hulking form of his big friend Bear, and the remembered splinter of pain and sorrow that had lodged in Otter's heart in the tunnels of the Roots melted and passed away into forgetfulness and joy, and he raced toward Bear in a clumsy-footed gallop that almost toppled Bear over on top of Greymouse.

And Bear, busy at trying not to trip over Otter, knocked the wizard's hat askew as he fought for balance, all the while trying not to step on his little friend's paw or tail as he darted in circles about him.

Another roar and change of light brought Otter up short, and the friends stared at the sight that now filled the glade before them. The woods had disappeared, and all that was visible was the silver-gray mist that seemed to be consumed with a white fire that licked and curled wildly at the edges. Confused visions tumbled and turned in the mist, and it seemed that everything, everywhere, was going on there in the swirling gray, burning cloud. Great armies clashed, and the roar and din of battle shook the earth until their senses spun, and the friends found themselves thrown to the ground by a fierce blast of wind and noise. Then great cities came and went, and cool, even-flowing scenes of wood and river, and forest animal.

These visions were followed by many more, of elf and dwarf, and man, and times changing, yet unchanged, Otter saw a fleeting glimpse of what looked to be the other side of

Calix Stay, where they had landed long ago when they had crossed the Great River with Dwarf. And then, immediately after, it was gone, but the tide of images flowed on unending.

The air seemed to grow heavier, and the golden light and sound and touch seemed to falter. Otter looked wildly from Froghorn to Greymouse.

The two wizards were looking anxiously at each other, and Froghorn looked up in the direction of the sky, made a sign, and then peered back into the confusion of the swirling gray mist. Greymouse moved closer to Froghorn, and the two of them stood together, arm in arm, and the golden sound and light seemed to strengthen, but only for a moment.

Slowly, so slowly at first that he was not aware of feeling it, Otter sensed the trembling of the ground, and heard the sharp, discordant noise of drum and horn, and high, shrieking whistles. He cast a frightened glance at Bear to see if his friend had heard, and saw Bear's eyes opened wide in horror and revulsion.

"Quickly!" called Greymouse. "Join hands with us, and repeat after us the names we shall give you."

Hardly knowing that they did so, the three comrades linked hands with Froghorn and Greymouse and began repeating the names the two Elders of the Circle were saying. Over and over they said the names, and still the air about them was filled with harsh and ugly clamorings of iron bell and anvil, and great, coughing horns whose notes were like barbs to the ear. And the light had dimmed and turned a rusty, dirty orange, as if it were the reflection of a burial pyre.

Completely unnoticed, Melodias Starson had appeared

beside Flewingam and now joined in the small ring the friends had formed and began repeating after them the names they were speaking. Otter, Bear, and Flewingam were too frightened already to be upset with anything to do concerning the appearance of another wizard, although Flewingam did flinch and jerk away for a moment when Melodias put out his hand, but the friends were too involved with the horrible din to notice anything much at all, and all they knew was that more than anything in their wildest dreams, they wanted the shrieking darkness to stop and to leave them alone, in peace.

Great winged forms whirled and spun madly about their heads, and Bear's ears lay flat back against his huge head as the flying things dipped and darted about him. His hackles were straight out, and if he had not been holding so tightly to Greymouse and Otter, he would have been greatly tempted to swat away whatever the ugly things were. He could not make them out clearly, but he felt they were trying to gouge out his eyes, and he was forced to dodge and twist as the shadowy figures soared and plunged all about him. He felt Otter pulling and tugging at his paw, and knew the little animal was trying to get away from the unseen attackers too.

Greymouse, on the other side of him, did not struggle to loosen his hold, although Bear watched as the wizard turned into a fiery blue shaft of light and began to throb loudly, even over the uproar of the dark noise.

A deafening crack of thunder split the afternoon wide open, and the rattle of rifle fire and cannons flooded the glade, and then as it faded, the soft reed pipe returned, along with the golden light. The mist began to clear, and went from gray-red, to blue, to the rich golden sound that seemed to be growing in strength every moment.

Otter's grip relaxed in Bear's paw, and for the first time Froghorn seemed to look relieved, and gave Greymouse and Melodias a quick, somewhat hurried smile.

"I think we've done it," he sighed at last, and his voice was edged with fatigue.

The young wizard's speaking made Bear jump, which in turn frightened Flewingam into giving a sharp little moan.

"I think we have," agreed Melodias. "This is going to put our newly crowned king of the elfin clans into something of a tizzy, I'm afraid. Now there is no gate for those who would come to reinforce Tyron, nor any threat he can hold over those who might rebel against him."

Melodias wiped a hand across his forehead before continuing.

"This place has long been known to the Circle as one of the places that Eiorn used, and one of the crossings that he kept secret and handed down to Tyron. But it will be of no further use to Tyron now, for it's been sealed off on this plane, and that's an end of it here."

"What on earth was all that?" squeaked Otter, having to work at making his voice sound even.

"Well, our friend Tyron, it seems, being in possession of one of the Secrets from the Arkenchest, which his father Eiorn handed down to him, had learned his lessons well, and made use of some of the power that the knowledge of the Secrets gives. Only Tyron has been using that power to build what he calls a haven for himself here, and to help him seal off the Meadows of the Sun."

Melodias paused, and looked to Froghorn, who took up the story and went on.

"You see, this all has to do with the power of the Secrets, which are the Law. A holder of these Secrets, whether it's one or all, is able to do many unusual things. One feels a great sense of control over things, and because one is able to disappear at will, or change forms, or materialize objects, or control the wind, one begins to run the risk of feeling as an equal to the High Lord himself."

"Except, of course," broke in Greymouse, "that once you get to the point that you're able to do anything that the High Lord can do, you don't really want anything to do with any of it, except to stay near him."

"The trouble lies," said Melodias, "in one having only part of a Secret, or miseducation on the use of a Secret. That's where the disharmony usually begins, when one is about to discover the Secrets, or after one first gets on to them. Then, it seems, at that point, it is very easy to become overwhelmed with the power the Secrets bear, and to fall prey to the common danger, which is the misuse of them in the interest of one's own selfish desires."

"Was that what you were hinting at, Froghorn? That our Dwarf might be falling under the spell of the Chest?" chittered Otter loudly.

Froghorn smiled at the little animal, and studied him a moment before answering.

"We each one fall prey to the misuse of the Secrets," he at last replied. "Whether we wish to or not, it, too, is a part of our education."

"That may be so with some I know," put in Bear, "but our

Dwarf is too stubborn to get into that sort of trouble. If it were something to do with old lore, or delvings, then I suppose he might be in for a time of it." He snorted, and laughed. "And it seems like he's a little too stubborn about seeing to it a bear's paws are worn down to a nub trying to keep up with him."

As the companions had been talking, the air had cleared and become lighter and easier to breathe.

Flewingam had been on the point of asking a question of Froghorn when a high, shrill voice broke the air with a strident cry of alarm. It seemed to come from only a short distance away, in the thick woods that surrounded the now silent glade.

"Quickly!" snapped Melodias. "That sounds like our companions who are waiting by the trail. While you find them, we shall make good our plan of not getting caught in Tyron's net. We shall set our course for Greyfax and Lorini, and meet again when we shall."

"We shall split up for the moment," said Greymouse hurriedly. "That will confuse our good elf, and give him more than one hare to chase. I shall move my camp on and meet up with you again soon, Melodias. And now I see no reason why Froghorn shouldn't go on with Dwarf and his comrades, and see them escorted safely to their destination."

As Greymouse finished speaking, a flickering silver-gray shadow appeared beyond the clearing, causing a moment's fright, but Froghorn quickly stepped forward and whistled a joyful, rippling note. In another instant, the great steed Pe'lon stood beside his friend, chortling and neighing softly, and bowing politely to the others.

"It seems we have been sent a welcome ally," said

Froghorn, "and one we can well use now. We'll send him on ahead to pick up Dwarf and the others. I think our cries are from there. And good Pe'lon is worthy of driving off whatever it is that is a peril there."

Another mournful, worried call echoed behind them, cutting short any further talk.

Pe'lon disappeared in a blur of gray speed, and Melodias Starson vanished as quickly and completely as he had come. Froghorn set off at the head of his group, with Bear next, Otter, and then Flewingam. Greymouse followed along after for a moment or two, but he was gone when Flewingam next turned to glance behind him.

From the hidden glade they had just left came the angry, crackling voice of a signal horn that filled the afternoon air with hot, savage notes that clearly said the companions were not welcome callers in the Gilden Wood, and that someone had discovered them, and was in pursuit of the trespassers of the forbidden kingdom of Tyron the Green, the elfin monarch who had fallen prey to his selfish dream of power that would be made possible by the wielding of the Secret from the Arkenchest that Dwarf carried.

And Dwarf, at that moment, was upon his own road, toward the only safety he knew, which was his old delving below the mountain, higher and away in the direction of the late afternoon sun that spun golden shadows across its lofty, cloud-crowned peak.

Tyron and Doraki

"They'll pay dearly for this bit of treachery. I'll see them all staked on the highest tree in Gilden Wood for this piece of their infernal meddling," shouted Tyron, pacing madly about in the long, dark hall that he was using for a dwelling until the newer, more opulent Kings Hall could be finished. For much of it, he had detailed many of his subjects to transport parts of the old Cypher into Gilden Wood, and reconstruct the towers and halls there. What was left of the tower of the dove was being made into his reception hall and private study, and the ruins of the turtle were his sleeping quarters and dining hall.

But at the moment, all work had been halted while the elves were out in search of marauding members of the Circle, who had stolen into the sacred fastness of Gilden Wood and destroyed one of the crossings, ancient doors between the lower worlds of Windameir which were no longer so numerous in these parts of the Meadows of the Sun, and whose absence was sorely felt by Tyron. In times of great need, he had always been able to use the crossing for calling up other elves for his armies, or to banish those subjects whose allegiance was doubtful.

Tyron had mastered well the use of the Secret his father had handed down to him. His "legacy," as his father had referred to it, was but a simple truth, and for years Tyron did not understand its depth, or that it was indeed one of the Five that comprised the Five of the Arkenchest. All he knew was the bitterness his father felt toward certain Elders of the Circle and their decision to return the Secrets to the Chest at a time when Eiorn felt it was folly to do so. He was also angered that none of the Circle agreed with him in his insistence that both Lorini and Dorini be returned to the Fields of Light in Windameir, thus eliminating the danger once and for all to the lower three worlds in the Meadows of Creation.

Tyron believed, as his father before him, that the High Lord of Windameir had made a serious blunder in leaving the two sisters to their own devices, and he had seen his beliefs proved true time and again, until now, after the complete loss of Maldan and Origin, over which Dorini had gained complete reign, the third lower world was in grave peril also. There would be no salvaging what was left, to Tyron's way of thinking, and he sought to retreat beyond the ruined borders of Atlanton Earth and create his own more perfect kingdom, where justice and order ruled supreme. And to that end, Tyron felt more than up to the job of administering to the needs of his subjects, and to ensuring the smooth workings of a government that would be the most beneficial to the greatest numbers.

Again Tyron's anger flared, as he remembered the loss of the crossing, for that was one of the most effective bulwarks he had against revolt, since the threat of knowing one could be sent back across the boundaries was a most effective way of reducing any line of thought that might mark one out as an undesirable. Tyron stamped a foot, and drove a fist into a palm.

"They will pay for this," he said aloud, for the fourth time.

He was reaching for a revenge sweet enough to inflict upon the blundering fools of the Circle when a page announced the arrival of the Dark Queen's second-in-command. Tyron's blood ran cold, for he could barely tolerate being in the presence of this icy man, whose dead eyes struck dumb terror into the hearts of most, although Tyron did not fear him greatly, for he held the Secret before him like a shield, and he knew enough of the histories of the Arkenchest and the Five Secrets to know they were powerful defenses against the Darkness.

He was recalling the futile attempt his father had made to convince the Circle to return the two sisters to the Fields of Light, and the Circle's refusal, when Doraki suddenly appeared in the room.

If Tyron was startled, he did his best not to show it.

"What is it, sir, that you seek of me?" snapped Tyron irritably.

A cruel light flickered across Doraki's dull eyes, and for a moment an ugly smile lingered at the corner of his lips.

"My lord has a tongue today, doesn't he?" crooned Doraki, in a low, pleasant voice. "Perhaps you will use it to explain why you did not tell us of this crossing you held, and how you let the blundering wretches of the Circle destroy it. It is impossible to keep an army here, and we can't bring the regular troops from our other units across these borders without the help of a crossing. We could have done so, with the use of the thing you have just bungled away. Her Darkness has been greatly upset by your lack of trust. To make up for your blunder, you will send an escort to do some traveling with our queen. I think she is to do some visiting at certain of the settlements in the areas below your wood, and on toward the mountains. There are some certain ones there who will join us if we but let them know we are moving even in these realms. And it will be certain that others will follow our lead if they see you in our vanguard, and see your loyal subjects following us."

Doraki, whose back had been to Tyron as he spoke, turned and smiled coldly on the elf.

"What need has she of any of my subjects? I wish no dealings with those beyond this realm. And my people have had no commerce with those who have settled here in these last times since the big crossings after the Dragon Wars. Tell her she will have to find some other way of swaying these beings," said Tyron, keeping his voice as even as he could make it. "And she need have no hopes of most of those who have settled beyond Gilden Far, or of those farther up toward the Beginning Mountains. I have word that none of those who are settled there are interested in anything to do with war or fighting."

Doraki threw back his head and gave a sharp bark of laughter.

"She has ways to interest them. And she wants you to be the one to spread the word that she is on the march beyond Calix Stay." Doraki's tone was brittle and menacing. "What we have in mind is something far more useful than to parade a few haughty elves in weaponry. No indeed, what we have in mind is just revenge for the treacherous closing of our crossing."

Tyron fought down anger and fear at the insulting tone of Doraki. He had need of those two for the moment, for they were going to help him gain a haven for his people. He knew the risks involved in dealing with Dorini and her underlord, and knew, too, that she was dangerous and cunning, and had so far successfully captured control of two of the lower creations of Windameir, and was fighting for total dominance, and that she was an enemy to be feared and respected.

His father had instructed him in all the workings of the Circle, and as part of that, there had been a long course on the two sisters, Lorini and Dorini, and the struggle that had evolved from the presence of these sisters, both beautiful, and both extremely dangerous. If he thought he would stand a chance at attaining his end, Tyron thought to himself, he would go to Lorini as well, if he knew of her whereabouts or how to reach her. He did, however, think Lorini was the weaker of the two, and felt that if he were to have a choice of either of them, he had dealt with the more powerful one, the one who had the greatest ambition.

He knew Dorini wanted possession of the Arkenchest more than anything else at the moment, for the third world, Atlanton Earth, held on stubbornly against her all-out attack. She knew the only way utterly to crush the fools was to destroy completely, or capture, the Arkenchest and the Five Secrets. And she also knew that her only hope along these lines was to deal with the holder of one of the Secrets. He had what she wanted, and she also knew that the one Secret would be of little use to her if she forced it from him, for to be of full power, the Secret had to be wielded by the bearer it was entrusted to by legal representatives of the Circle.

And his father had received his Secret from the hands of

none other than Melodias Starson, who was also the one who had angered Eiorn, by asking for the Secret back once the Circle felt the danger was over. Yet Eiorn never felt the danger had ended, and so kept the Secret to himself, and withdrew across Calix Stay after the time of the trouble of the Dragon Wars, and raised Tyron, and shared the Secret with him. When the time came, he fully entrusted the safe-keeping of the Secret to his son, and instructed him in the care and use of it, among all other things.

Doraki was a formidable foe, thought Tyron, and his insides crawled at the revulsion he felt at the presence of the one who was the keeper of Fireslayer and Suneater, the last spawn of the great dragons. Tyron knew he was as cold and ruthless as a viper, yet he also knew that he held the one thing Dorini wanted most of all, and that was his safe-conduct ticket and his most important weapon in dealing with the deadly underling of the Dark Queen.

"We shall have useful errands for your soldiers, I assure you," snarled Doraki, "And there are ways of dealing with an enemy without having to have superior forces. With some degree of forethought and clever planning, one could immobilize a much larger army with the good design and conception of a well-laid plan and plotted moves. The game becomes very subtle here, in your realms. I am more accustomed to a rather more vigorous and realistic environment than what I find here."

The frigid smile fell once more on Tyron.

"I can't tell you how pleasant it is to savor the physical aspects that are experienced below. They are most exquisite."

"Whatever, it is neither here nor there, those points. I am still unconvinced that I should comply with her request.

What she asked is a thing my loyal subjects aren't going to like, since I have promised them that not a single one of them will ever have to leave Gilden Wood again, or deal with anyone else but our own elvish clan."

"I'm afraid I'm not making myself quite clear," explained Doraki, picking up a small mithra worked globe from the desk Tyron had been using an hour before to lay out some charts of the borders of Gilden Wood and Gilden Far. "Her Darkness will expect your full cooperation, to make up for the mess you've already made. And she wishes you to present your own explanations to her immediately."

Before Tyron could protest or disagree, Doraki went on.

"Otherwise she will see fit to destroy your little scheme for an undisturbed kingdom here."

Tyron reddened, and held his silence for a moment. "And what else does she require?" he asked at last.

"Only that. It is a small price to pay for all you are getting. And she is letting you off very lightly. Why, it will require nothing of you but a small amount of your subjects' time. We'll leave it to you to convince them they must go, and why you have broken your word to them. That will please Her Darkness very much. It is always well to please her. She is a dreadful enemy to those who oppose her just and all-encompassing will."

"How do I know this is all that she will ask?" questioned Tyron suspiciously. "I can't go on doing this, and making my folk go beyond Gilden Wood, not after I've promised them that as their king I will put an end to it."

"This is all she requires. Her Darkness is merely trying to help you in expediting your ambitions. And we must move quickly to punish the traitorous behavior of the infernal Circle. We must not let them think for a single moment that we won't repay their beastly acts with equal force."

Tyron moved from his place at a low window that overlooked his courtyard. After a further silence, he spoke without looking at Doraki.

"All right. I'll concede this once. I shall send her her escort and help her gather these men she wants."

"Her Darkness will be heartened to hear of your desires to carry out her wishes," sneered Doraki, thrusting his cape over his shoulder and extending a gloved hand out from under its folds. He placed an object on the table that stood before the rough wooden hearth and strode from the room without speaking further.

"Good riddance," breathed Tyron, his heart heavy with the knowledge that he was going to have to break his word so soon after he had faithfully promised his subjects that there would be no more dealings with anyone but themselves.

Tyron moved to the table and studied the object that lay there. It took him a few moments to make out the small, gnarled black object, and when he did he uttered a cry of abject horror and grief. There on his breakfast plate, amid the leftover crumbs, was the sacred ring of the sign of the Oak, which his father had always worn, and had taken with him in his crossing to Upper Havens, where only those who had mastered the Unknown went, and once there, never had to make any crossings again. It was the Havens, just as he planned to make his own haven in Gilden Wood.

His father had worn the sacred ring, and no one had ever been allowed to touch it, and on the day he departed, just before being lowered into the secret gate of the earth where Tyron and his closest friends had sheltered him, he pointed to the ring and smiled, saying that the power of the Oak was carrying him across to his last reward. Somehow, someway, Doraki and Dorini had found the vault where Tyron had buried his father. And if they had found the vault and stolen the sacred symbol, then something was greatly amiss, for that was not the truth that Tyron's father had given him, and something was very wrong if his father's Havens was no harder to reach than the effort it took to shovel away the dirt that lay on the surface of the gateway.

With a leaden sinking of his heart, he realized that the haven he was seeking to make of Gilden Wood was as vulnerable as the hidden door his father had gone through.

And he still had to face Dorini, as she had commanded, and make his excuses for the loss of the crossing, which he had held secret from her.

Thinking of that, and holding the encrusted ring of his father, a tremor of doubt swept over Tyron, and for the first time, he was very frightened of the Queen of Darkness who could so easily brush away the layers of defense and clutch at the very beating of one's heart.

At the same time, a faint glimmer of light crept into that black void that had devoured him, and he brightened somewhat, for he felt sure he would be able to find an ally in Froghorn Fairingay, and the lady Cybelle. They were powerful too, and equals with Dorini and the dark Doraki. That thought eased the sharp dagger of fear that had buried itself in Tyron's soul as he thought of having to face the fury of the Dark Queen.

A Disappearance

Watching the unending late afternoon sunset, Ned Thinvoice retreated further into his thoughts and moved somewhat apart from Dwarf and Cranfallow, who sat beneath the wide green shade of a large tree. He was thinking of something that had been said to him long ago, when he was first in the company of the huffy, stiff-necked dwarf who sat not far from him, and who had led him on a trail of danger and misery from the moment he had first laid eyes on him that far-distant day when Dwarf had come upon the gates of the fortified town, at the beginning of his journey to find his two lost comrades, Otter and Bear.

"You'd best leave them sorts to themselfs," warned his friend, who had later been slain by the beast warriors who had attacked the town. "They is never no good for none of them what follows after 'em, and as like as not, they'll for sure run you to an early tomb."

Everything was coming true, just as he had heard it said, as long as he remained with those "with them powers," as he called it.

Looking at his predicament at the moment, Ned realized that he had somehow been "deaded," and that he was in some place that was beyond his imagination to grasp. It did not seem odd to him, however, that the sun in this place did not rise or set, or that there was no darkness, like that he had known before. And as strange as it seemed to him at the time, he did not need to sleep nearly as much as he was used to. It was, it seemed to him, nothing at all to lie down to what would have been a long nap had he been across what Broco called Calix Stay, or the River, and sleep for six, or eight, or ten hours straight. Here, however, where he found himself at the moment, he would hardly have shut his eyes and he would be awake again, refreshed and ready to go on with his business.

It was odd, he thought, but not nearly so odd as the way the dwarf had been acting since their arrival, and even Cranny, who was the most loyal of friends and the last to raise a complaint, was heard mumbling under his breath about the haughty way Broco had been treating not only themselves, but others he came in contact with.

Galen, captain of an elfin host, and who had come from Greyfax himself, made light of an insult Dwarf had dealt him as they sat eating around the fire, gathering news of interest and catching up on the goings-on of the wizards, and hearing reports on the whereabouts and activities of the enemy. Froghorn had looked sharply at Dwarf, although he said nothing, and Dwarf, minding his plate more than his manners, had been unaware of the eyes upon him, and seemingly unaware that his remark had embarrassed the elf and those others gathered around the fire. It had not been a barbed comment with an intent to injure, but rather something that one might have said without thinking. Still, it was injurious, and Broco had not withdrawn the remark, or seemed to have been aware of it having been taken amiss by Galen or any of the others seated in the circle of friends.

Then the insults had become more and more frequent, directed at everyone, and yet no one, and Ned had taken it at first as simply fatigue, and that Broco needed rest, after carrying the heavy load of the Arkenchest for so long. Cranfallow felt the same, and the two comrades overlooked the constant nagging comments of Dwarf and the almost perceptible swelling of his self-importance. More than once, Broco had shouted Galen down while the elf had been attempting to outline a plan or explain a detail of an operation.

Even Froghorn, in going over a fine point on a map, had been interrupted rudely by Broco and informed that the information he was giving out was in fact wrong, and entirely out of date. On that occasion, Froghorn had ignored Broco and gone on with his briefing.

And now, as they waited for the rest of their company to return, Ned looked at the last few moments of the parting, and the stinging remarks of Dwarf.

"He don't even know we is real bone and blood, he don't," said Ned half aloud. "And I doesn't guess he cares none, one way or other."

Somewhere down in his secret heart, though, Ned knew that this part of Dwarf was not the real Broco, and that he was upset and disturbed because he did not like this side of his small dwarf witch.

Cranfallow got to his feet and stretched, and wandered over to stand by Ned.

"I doesn't sees no signs of nothing, does you, Ned?" he asked, turning his head and gazing all about him.

"I hasn't seen so much as a gnat's whisker move none since they has slipped away. And I doesn't like that, neither."

"I is with you there, Neddy. I hates it worst of all when I doesn't knows what it is I is alooking for, and I doesn't knows where it is I is supposed to be alooking for it."

"If we keep our tongues still, we can use our eyes just that much better," said Dwarf caustically.

He had risen and come to stand beside the two friends. Without looking at them, he went on.

"I realize it is a lot to ask of you, but I would greatly appreciate it if you two could stop running your jaws long enough for one of you to go up one of these fine lookout posts and see if you can make anything out."

"What he is after asking," sneered Ned in a singsong voice, "is that he wants to know if you or me is agoing to shinny up one of these here trees and take a gander around at the countryside."

"I knows I isn't no good at that sorts of carrying on," said Cranny, reaching down to hold a knee. "I has hurt myself something fierce awful, and I isn't able to go barking my shins on no tree."

"I isn't neither, Cranny. I has a plumb terrible fear of them high places. I'd as like fall out on my head as not," went on Ned.

"Oh, blast you both," snorted Dwarf indignantly "I knew it was useless even asking you. There's no respect of your betters anymore. If I wasn't exceptionally kindhearted, I'd take half an hour with my cudgel to teach you some proper manners."

"Well, Mr. Snooty Nose, I might just tells you the exact same thing," snapped Ned.

"Leave him alone," warned Cranny. "We isn't out here to hold no shouting contests. And I has a suspicion that Froghorn left us here to watch out for something that might just has something to do with something that don't has old Cranny or old Ned's best interests at heart."

"That's what I'm trying to tell you," shot Dwarf angrily. "And that's why I think it would be a good idea if one of you would climb one of these trees here, and see if you can spot anything, or see if you can locate the others."

Cranfallow looked at Ned for a moment, then turned to Broco. "Better yet, just so's we don't get in no dither about who is agoing to shinny a tree, I thinks we has better both go."

Ned started to protest, then saw that Cranfallow's idea was irritating to Dwarf. "Right you is, Cranny, my lad. You takes that one there, and I'll crawl up this here one."

"And if you see anything, you report to me immediately," huffed Dwarf, fingering something on the inside of his cloak. "If it's danger, I have to warn Froghorn."

"Well, don't you worry none, we'll holler it up, all right, if it's something that might be nasty," said Ned, and the two friends moved away from Broco and began ascending the wide-trunked trees.

Amid pants and grunts, Ned and Cranfallow made good progress, and soon they were high up and able to look out over a portion of their surroundings. On two sides, for as far as they could see, the thick, dark green wood ran on, from one horizon to the next. On either side of this band of trees, they could detect small glades and clearings, and away toward the dim outline of the mountains in the distance, they could barely make out what looked to be open, rolling country, with a bright, thin silver ribbon of a river running through it, and low, round shrubs that dotted the lighter green of a grassy lawn.

Ned could hardly see Cranfallow, who faintly resembled some large, awkward bird, sprawling in the upper branches of the tree. After another moment, Cranfallow turned and waved to signal he had found a solid seat, and Ned signaled back his acknowledgment. The two friends settled down to watch, and Ned, although he did not like to admit it, was feeling glad that he had made Broco angry.

Below, Dwarf fumed and raged at the mutiny that had taken place, and he plotted terrible, swift justice for the two disrespectful ingrates who had dared let themselves think that they were his friends. He could see that all along they had been merely attempting to gain his good grace and favor, to use him as they could, and get the benefits of his protection.

"I don't know why I haven't seen through them long before this," huffed Dwarf, aloud. "They've tagged along after me now all this time, taking every advantage they could, and returning me nothing in the way of even so much as a thank-you or much obliged."

Dwarf snorted disdainfully, and smiled ruefully to think that even Froghorn, after refusing to take back the Chest, was plotting to use him as well, and schemed to have him risk all the dangers and go through all the agony and pain of bearing the Arkenchest, and then, because he was an Elder of the Circle, he would ask for it back when the proper moment arrived, and all the glory would be his, and he, Dwarf, would be left in the lurch as merely some pesky gnome who was forever getting underfoot, or at best, a highly amusing dwarf from across the boundaries, who could spin yarns and make good dwarf cakes.

A slow sneer spread across Broco's face.

"But I could spoil the plans of the lot of them," he said aloud, his hand gone once more inside his cloak, and clutching the tiny form of the Arkenchest. "It wouldn't be so difficult for me to reach Greyfax and Lorini from here. All I need is my two good feet. I'm more familiar with these parts than most of the rest of this bunch, and most likely they were going to use me as a guide to boot. But if anyone is to save Cybelle or get the Chest safely to Greyfax, it's me."

After another moment's pause, he went on aloud.

"And why should I surrender the Chest at all? Tyron the Green has gotten away with holding a Secret all this time, and I was given a Secret to hold by my own father, who had it from Greyfax himself. It is just as much my right to hold what is rightfully mine as it is for Tyron."

A slow, dim shape of an idea was beginning to take form in his mind, and he smiled broadly as he turned it over and over, this way and that, and looked at all the pleasant aspects of it.

"There would be my own Cypher," he said aloud, going on. "And perhaps Cybelle might be persuaded to see me in a different light, if it were known that I am Arkenchest Bearer, and holder of one of the Five."

Broco chuckled to himself and rubbed his hands together.

"And there would be rewards for those who have been loyal to me and served me well," he said, stroking his chin thoughtfully. "Bear and Otter have been with me from the first, and I think I shall find a spot for them as ministers, or perhaps advisers."

His face clouded over in anger.

"But there'll certainly be no place for those who have disobeyed me or refused me."

Dwarf glanced significantly up into the green shade of the trees above him, trying to spot Ned and Cranfallow. They were nowhere to be seen, although he had watched closely as they had ascended into the leafy heights, and knew which trees they were in. He studied the trees carefully, and at last, after quite some time, thought he could make out the outlines of their forms against the other patterns in the limbs, but if he hadn't known where to look, there would have been no way ever to detect the presence of anyone in the tall, cool green boughs of the gently snoring trees.

Dwarf was beginning to go on in his thoughts to where he would fashion his kingdom, and what name he should call it, when a faint, almost inaudible whistle drifted softly from Cranfallow's perch. It was answered from Ned's, and then all was silence.

Broco had started a huff and was upon the verge of calling out to get them to answer up and stop all the nonsense, when the thought struck him that if it had been anything friendly they had spotted, they would have called rather than have used such a deceptive signal. Unable to see what new danger approached, and blocked off from view of the two friends in the trees, who were trying to signal him, Dwarf gathered the folds of his cloak about him, and clutching the Chest tightly to his wildly pounding heart, he took a bearing on where he remembered the distant peaks of the Beginning Mountains to be, and making his last decision on what to do, he chose to leave Cranny and Ned and all the rest, and reach the hidden fastness that was his old home beneath the mountain. He felt the others would be able to reach safety without him, and he, not they, was running the most terrible risk of all, for the Darkness was after the very thing he carried with him wrapped in his cloak.

In his hurry to reach the safety of the inner woods, where he planned to travel for a time, Dwarf could not see beyond the clearing he had just left, nor catch more than a glimpse of the fleeting gray shadow of the great horse that approached at a joyful gallop. That vision frightened Broco badly, and he hurried on and was beyond earshot when Ned Thinvoice called out loudly that the others were on their way back.

Neither Cranfallow nor Ned Thinvoice suspected that anything below was amiss, or that Dwarf, misinterpreting Ned's whistle to get the attention of his friend, would think that some danger was nearing them, and take action to remove himself from the area of peril. And neither of the two friends could know what had happened to Broco when they came down from their lofty posts to greet Pe'lon, and found their stuffy friend had disappeared.

Their cries of dismay and distress brought Froghorn and the rest of the company on the run, to find Ned and Cranfallow searching futilely about in the small clearing for Broco, who had, it seemed, simply vanished without a trace from the depths of the Gilden Wood.

Kingdoms and Caverns

Broco, turning his eyes to the high blue mountains far ahead, set out with a skipping heart, his head full of wild dreams of grandeur such as no dwarf before him had ever dared dream. In his fevered mind, he thought how small and puny had been the Delvings of Co'in, and Eo'in, across Calix Stay. The clever work of his sires would be nothing when compared to the kingdom he began to carve in his imagination. And it would all be possible, for he held the power of the very heart of all Windameir, and there would be nothing too much for him to do, nor any goal too large for him to achieve.

He slowed momentarily, thinking of his friends, Bear and Otter, and Froghorn, and Greyfax, and Cybelle, and Lorini, but he soon quickened his pace.

"I'll invite them to visit," he told himself firmly, to quiet the small, uneasy voice that tried to speak deep inside him. "And perhaps I'll have Cybelle for my queen, after all. It would be a good idea, and then all would be well again with the Circle. They shall soon get over worrying about whether or not the Chest will ever be placed in danger of Dorini getting at it. No safer place for it than with me, and once I reach my destination, I shan't be making any more journeys back where she would ever be able to reach me."

A cold wind seemed to spring up in the stillness of the forest, although no leaf, no limb stirred, but Dwarf pulled his cloak up about his neck and hurried on.

"And I shall have a place for my friends to stay anytime they feel like coming for a visit," he went on, to break the clammy feeling that had overcome him. "And I shall even have special honey for Bear, and ripe berries for Otter," he finished, turning as he did so to cast a hurried look over his shoulder.

Were his eyes playing him tricks, he wondered. Or did he imagine the form of a great horse behind him? The vision, whatever it was, sent him scurrying on faster.

Suddenly the thought of meeting Froghorn, or indeed any of the Circle, seemed a very frightening thing to Dwarf, and for reasons he did not fully understand, he left the faint trace of woodland path and kept to the shadows of the bordering trees, moving more quietly now, and with greater care.

"It's important that I keep myself concealed," he told himself, "or else I'll be observed by someone I don't want knowing my whereabouts. It's never too prudent, in these times, to throw caution to the wind."

A slow change of mind came over Broco as he skulked along in the shadows, and with each step he took away from his friends, he seemed to stoop lower and lower, until finally he was moving along in a crablike, sideways gait, glancing nervously about him, his eyes wide and fear-glazed.

"Otter said he and Flewingam had met up with a false wizard that had the identity of Froghorn. And how do I know that the Froghorn I met wasn't the same? Or Otter, or Bear? If it's so easy to take on guises here, how can I be sure who's who, or if anybody is really who they say they are?"

A splintery, barbed fear had begun nibbling at his thoughts, and soon it had grown into a black pit without depths, and with every beat of his pounding heart, he felt himself being drawn closer to the brink.

"My only safety lies in the mountains," he assured himself, half aloud. "I'm sure I can find my old dwelling, and I shall find shelter there. It wasn't such a bad place, and at least I can rest there, and decide what must be done. I can move there more easily, and cross on into the Beginnings, if it seems safe enough."

Dwarf's hand curled into a tight fist around the small object inside his cloak, and without realizing it, his thoughts began turning once again toward his friends, and Greyfax and Froghorn. A fleeting stab of sorrow burned inside him, and he drew up his halting steps and stood staring unseeingly at the wooded path ahead that led on away toward the now invisible mountains.

Dwarf ran a hand across his brow and squinted his eyes shut tightly, and a small sob racked him. He felt as if he had a high fever, and mopped his brow again, with his sleeve.

"What in the name of the great Co'in am I doing?" he blurted, not trying to keep silent any longer. "I've got to get back to Ned and Cranny, and Froghorn, before they miss me."

But this thought lingered on deep inside him, and the other fear came back, and for a reason he could not explain to himself, he felt he wanted more than anything not to be found by Froghorn or any of the others of the Circle. His brow knitted, and his eyes clouded once more, and without realizing why, he set out once again toward the mountains.

His thoughts grew muddled, and all he could think of for a time was Cybelle. Someone, he knew, somewhere in the past hours, or days, or perhaps weeks or years, he could not tell which, had said something about Cybelle being captured by the Dark Queen, and a strong feeling washed over him that he must somehow free Cybelle, and that he, Broco, was the only way her salvation was to be won. And another flicker of memory made him huff proudly, for it had been a lowly spanner of a dwarfish lore master who had outwitted the Dark Queen once and escaped from her dreaded Ice Palace, where none other had ever returned from, except the powerful wizards Greyfax Grimwald and Faragon Fairingay. Yet Broco, simple lore keeper, and of a dwarfish nature, had escaped her grasp also. And at the time, he had held only one of the Sacred Five, and that had been enough.

His hand clutched the Arkenchest.

"Now," he gloated to himself, "I have four of the Secrets, and I shall be unstoppable. Dorini will not be able to keep me from having Cybelle free."

A pale, glazed fire burned in Broco's eyes, and he dreamed of the hour when he might free Cybelle, and the gratitude she would feel toward him. It would not be unthinkable that she would become his queen. It would only be a natural outcome of events.

"Except for that dratted Fairingay!" he suddenly snapped

aloud. "I'd forgotten Cybelle found something to amuse herself with in his company." He scowled. "But then perhaps that was all there was to that. Perhaps she simply found his idle talk amusing, or his wizardry something to keep her from something else of a duller nature."

He tried to think of how it had been in Cypher when the young wizard had been there, and how Cybelle had looked at him, and what she had said to Froghorn, and what he had said to her. Thinking hard, and turning over his memories of Cypher, he convinced himself that he could not remember Cybelle ever saying outright that she cared for Froghorn other than as a dear friend. And with that, he began to think of the knowing looks and secret smiles she had directed at himself, as he sat at table during meals, or during the idle hours listening to the elfin minstrels or singing fountains.

"There was no mistaking it," he concluded. "She simply kept Froghorn led down the garden path, because she is not a cruel sort, and could not bear to see him hurt. She couldn't find it in her heart to tell him before she was stolen away that she no longer loved him, if she ever did, and that her true feeling lay in the safekeeping of Broco, lore keeper, and soon to be king of the new realm where she would be his queen."

And out of his great affection for her, he decided that they would call this new realm Cypher. Even Lorini, if she wished, would be welcome to make her home there, near her daughter.

Dwarf had increased his pace as he thought of these things, as if he might hurry them into reality by hurrying his arrival at his destination. He began to walk faster and faster, and at last he found himself half running, and he began to stumble and fall as he crashed through the thick brambles that grew onto the edge of the path that led through the heart of Gilden Wood, and soon his hands and knees were torn and bleeding from the repeated falls. Broco, his feelings numbed by the fever and flashing dreams that blazed in his head, hurried on, rising to run a few moments, then stumbling and falling, only to rise again.

He had gone on for quite some time in this way when he began to tire, and sitting down heavily upon a fallen log, which was covered by thick green moss and overgrown with wood flowers, Dwarf sat gasping, trying to catch his breath, which was coming in rapid, gasping spurts.

He could not remember how long he had been running, or for what reason, and the time seemed to melt into the sweltering heat of the closeness of the inner forest, and it seemed to Broco that he was near somewhere that he had been before, or that he vaguely remembered from some time or other. His eyes were watery, and tiny sharp droplets of sweat kept rolling over his eyebrows and into his eyes, and he had to squint to clear his vision, although that didn't help either, for his heart was pumping so fast he seemed to have trouble keeping his sight from blurring or making double images. Still, the sensation persisted that he was very near somewhere or something that he knew, or had known, and a strange overwhelming feeling of nostalgia swept over Dwarf and brought him to his feet.

Taking care not to walk too fast on his still wobbly legs, Broco set out to find what he could not remember, groping forward slowly and wiping his eyes every step or two so that he could make out whatever it was he was seeking. On he went, farther still, unable to recognize any landmark or sign, deeper into the depths of the green walls and silence of the wood.

His breathing had quieted at last, and Dwarf, for the first time since the feeling had come over him, was able to make out clearly his surroundings. A vague lump in the pit of his stomach had edged its way toward his throat, and he began to remember. Ahead of him, not more than a dozen paces, was a dark hole that seemed to grow out of the darker shadows behind it, overgrown with berrybush and thorn brake, but still a definite opening into the deeper shadow behind. Dwarf had halted in midstride, and stood gazing at the long-unused cavern mouth, and the forest wall surrounding it. There, in front of the cavern, were the roughhewn logs that had been used as chairs for sitting outside in the fine weather, and the table, although scored by exposure and fallen to rot in a dozen places, was still there too.

Dwarf crept nearer, almost afraid of startling himself into waking from this daydream, and finding these visions only another part of his tortured thoughts. Nearer still, and he stumbled and almost pitched face down over an object that had long ago been mislaid or overlooked. He picked it up and held it to the filtered afternoon sunlight, and studied it closely. All the handiwork was still visible, although time had taken its toll and dark earth and tiny forest growths covered most of the visible surface. He held it in one hand and went forward again, looking about him with wide, remembering eyes, and he sat wearily in one of the hewn log chairs, after first scraping away some of the dark earth and brushing aside a cache of leaves and rainwater that had made a home there. He placed the object he had picked up from the ground on the rotting table, and sat staring in wonder and disbelief.

"It could not be a mistake," he thought. "And I can still see that lummox of a brown lout sprawled out not far from here, with that ridiculous hat and cape he had on, as sound asleep as a lump of dough."

A thin smile cracked Dwarf's features as he recalled when he and Otter had found the sleeping form of Bear here in these woods, so long ago now he had to think very hard to remember it all and to piece all that had happened in between together into a picture he could look at all in order. Flashes ran through his memory, unordered and dim, but as he sat here before the old cave of Bear, the patterns began to slow and fit themselves together, and at long last, he sighed, and somehow the fever that had been raging in his mind subsided somewhat.

He looked about him anxiously, not fully knowing why he was here, or in truth quite how he had come. Bits and pieces of his thoughts earlier came to him, like ghosts emerging from some forgotten night, without substance or order, but it frightened him badly, and he began slowly realizing that something was very wrong with him. It was as if something had taken over his mind and was controlling his actions, and he felt helpless to combat whatever it was or to keep himself from falling back into that same trancelike state that had been the cause of his waking here, in front of his friend's ancient cave.

The thought that something had happened to him in the crossing of Calix Stay occurred to him, although from all his lore study, and from his discussions with Froghorn, it usually was much more pleasant than the tortured thoughts he had been suffering through, or the dark fears that had engulfed him. Vaguely, he recognized that it all had something to do with the Dark Queen, and that somehow, although he could not guess the workings of it, Dorini had managed to pull his thoughts into her reach, and was even yet pulling at the warmth of his heart, beckoning him ever nearer to her cold, icy embrace. In a brief flash of truth and light, he knew that Dorini had been feeding his mind full of the thoughts he had been having, and the crazed dreams he had dreamed were but the crafty work of the Queen of Darkness. Cybelle was not the bride in the dreams, but Dorini. And Dorini was going to rule the three lower worlds of Windameir forever with the capture of the Arkenchest, and there would be no escape and no hope for any of those yet trapped in the darkening worlds that were falling irretrievably under the gathering black clouds of fear and hatred.

With the last remaining strength he possessed, Broco dragged himself to his feet and began struggling his way back the way he had come, calling Froghorn's name feebly aloud, and fighting strong temptation to turn around and go on in the direction he had come in getting to Bear's old shelter. A great compulsion to return and go into the cave itself began to naw at his awareness, and he cried aloud the names of the Circle, feeling his thoughts pulled into the black abyss. He shouted out the name of Froghorn, and fell to his knees, trembling.

Very slowly, he opened his eyes, and another thought occurred to him, and that was that if Froghorn were to answer his call and come to him, he would be punished.

Dwarf quickly got up and scurried as quickly as he could to the entrance of the cave, and without looking back or checking his stride, he entered into the dark mouth of the mustiness of the long-unused tunnel, which led on deeper into a stifling and silent darkness.

Mirrors of Windameir

The Mystery Deepens

The companions sat in a silent circle about Froghorn Fairingay, who stood beside Pe'lon, stroking the tall steed with gentle hands. No one seemed able to speak, and no one dared voice what he feared the most. There had been no cause for Broco to leave unless he had done so of his own accord and for reasons known only to him.

Bear, sitting beside Otter, turned to his small friend.

"It's beyond me, Otter. And I've been with that pesky lump of a dwarf since we started out from here last time. I can't see why he would try to go out alone now, unless he was trying to spare us some new danger that he may have wind of."

Otter looked hopefully at Froghorn. "That must be it," he agreed eagerly, chittering and playing nervously with a stick he had picked up, rolling it back and forth in his forepaws. "I'm sure we don't know what's happened, and the reason Dwarf has gone on without us. But he was always quick to endanger himself if he thought he could spare his friends some peril. That has to be the answer."

"He was always full of them tricks just when we was aneeding 'em worst of all," chimed in Ned Thinvoice, feeling a great deal of remorse over the things he had said and the thoughts he had had earlier, before Broco's disappearance. "And I isn't too sure but what we isn't being spared some grief, seeings as how he has got hiself took off without no fair say why, and since we ain't seed no other folks at all. It looks mighty odd, and I doesn't think our Dwarf would ups and go asneaking off nohow, but what it was to save his friends from acoming to some hurt or other."

"That could," said Froghorn quietly, speaking for the first time. "It might explain certain things that might be a puzzle otherwise. Yet I don't feel any immediate danger here, nor does good Pe'lon, and he is very quick to sense any peril that may be lurking near."

The great horse whickered and pawed the ground, nibbling playfully at Froghorn's gloved hand.

"Whatever the reason, he's gone," concluded Flewingam grimly. "The danger has perhaps been and gone, without our knowing. But what we need is a plan to see us through. Do we follow on and try to find Dwarf, or seek to reach the mountains Froghon has spoken of?"

"It is as well for us to set out in that direction," replied Froghorn. "I think that will be where Broco has set his sights, at least for now. All paths seem to be leading toward the Beginnings, and I suspect that some great new show has just begun, now that all the cast of characters have finally arrived on stage."

"I doesn't knows about no stages, or no character sorts, but what I does know is that I is mighty confused by all this, and whether anybody else is agoing to say it or not, I is. I has been afraid of our Dwarf since we has been ended up here in this place. No sense in any of it, I says, and what with all the gab I has running in and out of my ears, I is awful near athrowing up my hands and washing myself clean of everything to do with all of it." Cranfallow had jumped up angrily as he spoke, and paced furiously about. "I has been as stout a comrade as I is able, but I doesn't hold with no mousy words about what is or isn't, and what is is just as plain as any fool like me can sees. Our Dwarf has plumb taken leave of his senses, and is gone off by hisself, most likely 'cause he figgers he can better hisself in some way, and do it easier than if we was all atagging along."

Cranfallow halted, and faced the silent companions, who were all looking at him.

"Don't just sit there agaping at me, then. Tell me what's the riddle about it all. He was just as ornery as a army mule afore, but I is telling you, it's all somehows turned about since we has been here. I mean he was always griping and anagging Ned or me about too much noise, or not no water, or hasn't we got no plain sense about nothing, but it was different then. Since we has ended up here, it's been just like the old Dwarf we was aknowing was gone somewheres, and we was stuck with somebody who looks like him, fair enough, but all different. He never did snub me and Ned afore, not even when he was fit to be tied."

"Now, Cranny; I doesn't knows if I would go all that far," protested Ned Thinvoice.

"No, let him speak his piece," said Froghorn. "I find this very interesting."

"What I is after saying," continued Cranny, bowing to the young wizard, "is that something has happened to our Dwarf that has changed him up, and he just ain't the same blighter we was after knowing afore all this hocus-pocus about crossing this here river and all."

"I don't think any of us are the same," broke in Flewingam. "Or at least I don't feel the same as I have remembered feeling. And I certainly don't think Broco is doing anything, or acting any differently than he is forced to."

"Well put," said Froghorn, "for that seems to be the case. Our Dwarf isn't the same, as are none of us, as you so quickly noticed, Flew. Broco, we must remember, was a prisoner of the Dark Queen at one time, and has been bearing a burden that is almost beyond enduring. He has been carrying that for quite a long time. All this is taking a toll of him. Men begin to behave in strange ways when they've been under fire a long while, as we all know. And when the mind is strained beyond a breaking point, then strange things can happen."

"You mean you think he has come aloose from his wits?" asked Ned.

Froghorn smiled slightly. "Not exactly, but close to that, Ned. It seems that when the mind is overtaxed, then the heart takes over. It always has worked that way, and it is the way of the nature of things. When Dwarf is taxed hard enough, it will all come to rights, or I have missed my guess."

"Is that what you think, Froghorn?" asked Bear, his brow knitted. "I mean, do you think that all the pressure of carrying the Chest and the Secrets all this time has made him funny? Like maybe he would be thinking a bit odd?"

"Something to that effect, Bear. Whether we know it or not, we all carry the Chest and the Secrets with us at all times. Sometimes we wake up and remember, and then is when we have some trouble. It always looks very interesting, all that power, and we are like the child and the fire. We do not learn without pain that the beautiful flames that look so pretty also burn us badly if we try to hold them."

"I haven't had any Chest carrying," piped in Otter. "And from all I've seen from my small part of it, I don't want to, either."

"You have, my small friend. But that is neither here nor there. Our concern now is what turn our plans shall take, and what road our feet will be set upon."

"Isn't we agoing to be after them mountains everybody is so all-fired worked up about?" asked Ned, looking away over his shoulder at the barely visible range of peaks, their snowcaps glittering in the pale golden light like distant signal fires.

"Eventually, yes," answered Froghorn, sitting down at the side of Pe'lon. "Here we are," he continued, drawing a crude map with his hand, "and here lies Gilden Wood's end, and the start of Gilden Far. Beyond that is Gilden Tarn, then Cheerweir. I think we should set our course in that direction, for I think we shall find news there of a nature that will enlighten us on certain subjects."

"I had a shelter there," burst in Bear. "And that's where I was staying when Dwarf found me. He and Otter."

"That's right," chirped Otter. "And I had just left Cheerweir."

"It don't matter where you was afore," snapped Cranfallow, "or where we is agoing to now. I still has my doubts about what are going on in our Dwarf's head, and I is wondering what it is he has got hisself up to." Cranfallow paused a moment, looking down at his boots. "I is after liking the little bloke a lot more than I lets on, and I guess that are what's gnawing on me. I doesn't want to think it, but if something has happened that is after achanging him around inside, I wants to know. I mean like has he forgot us, or something like that?"

Cranfallow was extremely agitated and very near tears as he finished.

Bear and Otter glanced uneasily at each other, then turned to Froghorn.

"How do you feel about this?" asked the young Master, addressing himself to Bear. "Before we make any further plans or try to see our way clear to do anything, I think we should share our feelings with each other as to how we really feel about this problem that has been handed us."

Bear frowned, and wrinkled his ears into a posture of deep thought.

"I'm not sure. I'm like Cranny, as far as that, and I've known Dwarf a long time. I hate to think or say the worst without knowing what's happened, but I know we must face the truth, whatever it is. And I'm sure that whatever it is that's wrong with Dwarf is something we all have, or have had, sometime or other. Just because he's acting a little more like an ass than usual doesn't mean he won't come to his senses and be blundering his way into camp any moment now."

"I think that's so, Bear," chimed in Otter. "I'm always a quick one to dash off half-cocked about some foolishness or other, but then I usually find out I've been wrong all along. And I feel all funny inside talking this way about Dwarf. He's been a good comrade to all of us, and done loads of good things for us all along, and I don't think talking like this will help us any, or bring Dwarf back."

"It shall at least clear the air a bit," said Froghorn. "And I feel it's good to know where we stand on the matter before we go on."

He turned to Flewingam.

"I stand as Bear said. If Dwarf has taken leave of his good sense, then I feel he'll return, sooner or later. In the meantime, it might be best to try to find him, before he gets himself into some mischief or other."

"That, good Flew, is excellent advice," said Froghorn. "And I think that is the closest explanation we shall likely have regarding our good Dwarf. It is easy to explain to Greyfax or Melodias, for they usually are far ahead and beyond. It is something else, again, to have to put into ordinary words what we feel, one way or another. But be of good heart, gentlemen. We know no defeat, except that which we accept. And this is merely a prelude to the beginning."

Fairingay rose suddenly, and swung into Pe'lon's saddle.

Bear groaned, and put his paw to his muzzle.

"I knew it," he muttered. "Things must be worse than I thought. Dwarf has disappeared again, and now you're leaving. That's always the way it seems to start out, and it always gets worse from there."

Froghorn chuckled. "Good Bruinlen, what would my life be without you to cheer me?" he laughed. "But I promise I shall not be gone overly long this time, and there's nothing I shall be able to do here but give you your direction, which is clearly marked through Gilden Wood. All you need do is stay to this trail, and stay beyond the grasp of Tyron."

"Oh, easy for you," went on Bear, in a hurt tone, "since you're going to be out of harm's way, and safe and snug somewhere with Melodias, or Greymouse, or Greyfax. It's us that has to wear our paws to a nub, and risk the loss of our hides, while you're having tea, or playing tiddlywinks, or whatever it is you do when you're all together."

"We do usually have tea," teased Froghorn. "But I'm surprised you know about our tiddlywinks." His blue-gray eyes crackled with laughter. "However, since you seem so adverse to a nice woodland stroll, with more than an even chance for a little adventure to boot, I shall take you with me upon my errand. Come on, old fellow, use the words I gave you, and come up."

Bear had sat down in a flustered heap, and worked his great muzzle into a perplexed glare.

"You mean you'll let me go with you?"

Froghorn nodded.

The unexpected behavior left Bear speechless for a moment.

"Can Otter go, too?" he asked at last.

"Pe'lon can only carry the two of us easily. However, since Otter is small, he might ride here in front of me, if he'll hang on tightly."

"Well, I'm not so sure I want to go, anyhow," shot Otter, standing on his hind paws and wiggling his whiskers rapidly. "I may want to stay right here and go with Flew, Ned, and Cranny. I'm not against a good walk, as long as it leads out of here and back toward somewhere I want to be."

"But I don't want to go alone, Otter. And I've never heard him make any kind of offer like this before. We always used to get stuck somewhere in the middle of nowhere, with a bag of dry journey cakes that wouldn't feed a bird for a week, let alone us, and a can of water that wouldn't drown a fly, and then were told that we'd have to hoof it just a few hundred leagues or so, just to take in the fine weather, and that there would be someone there on the other end to meet us, which there never was." Bear snorted. "And if there was someone there to meet us, right enough, it was most usually a division or two of Worlughs or Gorgolacs for a greeting party."

Froghorn seemed to find Bear's tirade amusing.

"At least you'll find no Worlughs or Gorgolacs to greet you here," laughed the young Master. "We've got disgruntled elves, and a dwarf that's taken leave of his stiff-necked sense, but all in all, it's fairly easy going, compared to the fare you've been used to at the hands of the Circle."

"Otter, climb on, and let's see where he's off to," pleaded Bear. "It won't be like before, I know, but at least we'll get to see where he's going."

"Well, if that don't tip the pot," complained Ned Thinvoice. "First we has our Dwarf gone aloose from his moorings, and then we sits here arunning our jaws about it and talking all sorts of things about everything that would make me take leave of my poor old brains, and now we is agetting to see just who our real friends is." Ned stuck his nose high in the air and made a wry face. "Goes ahead, we doesn't care none. Flew and Cranny and I is good mates, at least. We'll shoots through, if you'll leaves us enough cakes and water to see us beyond them parts you is jawing about, or gets us to them mountains that has you so interested."

"Ned's right," insisted Otter. "We can't leave them to go alone. I know my way through here, or I know my way once we get a little closer to Cheerweir."

Bear's great muzzle took on a hurt look.

"You mean to say that *I* know my way through *this* part of Gilden Wood," he said. "You don't need to add that I should stick by my friends and do what I ought to be doing, and that's guiding them through the dangerous parts, and on to where a certain lump of a water dog will take over."

Otter started to protest, but Froghorn interrupted the two friends. "Enough, enough, good fellows, we have enough on our hands as it is with our misbehaving Dwarf. Bear, as you say, you know this part of the woods well enough to guide everyone safely through. I think that will be our first order of business. Secondly, Otter, you can take over once you reach Gilden Far and Gilden Tarn. I should be back long before that, or if not myself, then certainly Greymouse or Melodias will meet you somewhere between here and there."

"What if we find Dwarf?" asked Otter.

"I don't think we'll have to worry about that question for now. Our Dwarf is busily embarked upon a scheme to put things into a different light, if I'm not too mistaken. And I don't think his plans at the moment include being found by his friends."

Bear frowned in a puzzled manner.

"You sound as if you know where Dwarf is," he said slowly, trying to work his thoughts into order.

"I may, and then again, I may be all astray," replied Froghorn simply. "But I do know that our tasks draw nearer upon us, and we must make a start if we are to be ready when the curtain for this part of the act goes up."

"Why can't you tell us more?" Otter blurted out, fearing, as so often had happened in the past, that Froghorn was preparing to leave them once more with no word of explanation or instructions.

"I know nothing to tell you, my little friend, except that we shall be where we are supposed to be, and shall do what needs doing. And we all must follow where our paths lead. And mine, at the moment, leads beyond here. But I shall be with you again, and not long from now."

Bear had begun to protest the young wizard's departure bitterly, but even as he opened his mouth to speak, Froghorn had raised a hand in farewell salute and was gone in a blurring white flash of speed and light.

Otter looked around gloomily and saw with a somewhat cheerier mien that they had been left a travel sack, with provisions for them. Bear opened the rucksack and pronounced in an injured tone that they would all starve or perish of thirst within a day.

Cranfallow and Ned buckled their cloaks tighter about them, and with Bear in the lead, set off, with Flewingam and Otter bringing up the rear.

Despite the big animal's grim predictions, they all had a long lunch break after an hour or two on the trail, and the journey cakes filled them, and the wonderful, sparkling water from Froghorn's flask quenched their thirst, and even Bear had grumblingly to agree that he was satisfied. And to add to their enjoyment of the wizard's provisions, they had not heard or seen anything of Tyron's armies.

As Ned Thinvoice sat washing down a last mouthful, he glanced down and let out a startled yelp that brought his friends to his side instantly.

"What in thunder does you make of this?" he asked, pointing with the toe of his boot at the square block letters on the face of a large, flat rock.

It was carved in ancient dwarfish fashion, and carefully done, and it took the companions a moment or two to decipher its rather curling forms.

It read:

In this, the return of Broco, Dwarflord,
Holder of the Secrets
And Bearer of the Sacred Chest,
It is proclaimed that
These woods, and all therein,
Are subject to his reign.

"What is all that blatherguff?" asked Cranfallow, removing his hat and scratching his head in bewilderment.

Flewingam, who had knelt and read the words aloud, turned. "That blatherguff, as you put it, Cranny, is the very thing we all suspected, I think. Our Dwarf is becoming too important for the likes of us."

"I knew he should have taken up gardening or beekeeping," said Bear despondently. "All this business has affected every one of us for the worse. And poor Dwarf seems to be taking it hardest of all."

"I wonder" said Otter half aloud, "what it would be like if any other of us was carrying the Chest. Would we be the same?"

"I don't guess we'll be able to answer that," replied Bear, "unless we try to think what it must be like carrying it."

"Brrrr, no thanks," said Otter. "I'm glad I wasn't the one."

"I is, too," agreed Ned. "Them sorts of things is better left to them wizards. Poor old Dwarf is in deep water, that's for dead sure, and just acause he got to meddling with something he ought to have never had no doings with at all."

"Sometimes we don't have any say in the matter," said Flewingam, and looked again at the carved stone. "What I mostly see here is someone good who has been tested beyond his strength," he went on.

Before he could finish the sentence, a thin wisp of a signal horn echoed through the wood, and the companions turned and left the puzzling message of the stone behind as they raced on through the now rapidly thinning wood toward Gilden Far and Gilden Tarn.

And far ahead of them, Froghorn Fairingay kept watch, his handsome face drawn with the strain of waiting.

Shadows in the Darkness

Broco crept warily into the shadows of the enormous cave that Bear had used for his shelter in the time before he had recrossed Calix Stay and gone once more into the World Before Time.

Upon one side of the tall inner door, which was wide enough that Broco had to grope momentarily to find the wall, there was the large stump of a candle in a holder, and a tinderbox beside that, all neatly arranged. With trembling hands, Dwarf lit the huge candle, and the insides of the old dwelling swam into a golden-gray-colored light, edged at the farther corners in black. There, just as Dwarf remembered, were the rows of books that he had seen when first he and Otter had come to this shelter.

Dwarf walked on tiptoe to the shelves of books, almost afraid he might somehow disturb the memory of his absent friends, and looked at some of the titles. There were strange names and glyphs there, and some all written in the high lore of Bear's kindred, but there were others there too. Some he recognized as the ancient tongues of Mankind, who had flourished, then perished in the earlier centuries of the World Before Time, and even here, in the Meadows of the Sun.

He smiled to himself in a superior fashion, for next to the books on Mankind were the thick and numerous tomes done on the dwarfish realms. They were twice the number of those on Mankind, and each volume was so thick and heavy that Broco had trouble lifting one of them from its niche onto the low stool so that he could thumb through the heavy, leather-bound book. It seemed to have a life of its own as he opened the heavy cover, and the smell of long disuse made him sneeze several times before he could focus and read the titles in the dim, shaking light.

It was an authorized history of Eo'in, first Dwarf elder, and designer of many famous delvings on both sides of Calix Stay, and one of the most ancient of all his forefathers. There were rough sketches there of working models of water canals, such as the one they had found below Havamal that ran from the Coda Pool to the broken and ruined rose fountain. He read about the Coda Pool and the work the people of Eo'in had done for the Elders of the Circle.

He became aware that his heart was pounding, and his hands had begun to leave damp spots on the thick parchment pages of the book.

Angrily, Dwarf slammed the huge volume shut and tried to kick it off its stand, but all he managed to do was stub his toe painfully, which caused him to hop awkwardly around, vowing dwarfish oaths under his breath.

"I shall make even those fools appear as upstarts," he swore aloud, and was somewhat startled at the amount of noise his voice made in the confines of the cavern. Hollow and ringing, the cave made his voice sound as if it were larger, more full, or coming from the very earth itself.

A slow smile spread across Broco's face.

"Maybe I shall use this as the seat to the kingdom I will carve here," he said, smirking. "After all, there are all these books here which would not fare well were they in the hands of the wrong sort. But if I create this as my headquarters for the First Year of the Reign of the Chest Bearer, then there would never be any danger of these books being found by anyone, and no one would ever need know that there was a dwarf named Eo'in, or Co'in, or that there were other realms, or other delvings."

His eyes glittered and sparkled in the faint, flickering candle flame.

"And I shall begin the only story that will have any merit here, and that is the true saga of the adventure of Broco, Dwarflord from beyond the Beginnings, who forged a kingdom that spanned even Calix Stay. This saga will have the entire histories of the Arkenchest Bearer, and of the Dwarf who safely guarded the Secrets, even when threatened by the Dark Queen herself and being imprisoned for a time in the Ice Palace, that most dreaded of all dungeons."

Dwarf paced furiously up and down the length of the smooth cave floor that ran in front of the wall of books. His face had taken on the features of one in either extreme agony or unbearable joy, and his mouth worked itself into a slightly frozen grin.

He knew, of course, that he must make some improvements in the living quarters of his new kingdom, for it was a far cry from what his new queen would want. It was not light enough, and the place smelled of musty disuse and old years that had come to live in the darkness of the caverns. There would be a feast hall to put in, and a larger study, and if there were to be any guests at all, there would have to be a whole separate wing for that purpose, and apart from the everyday living quarters.

Broco had paced to the low, roughhewn table that served as both a desk and an eating place. There, still, after all the events that had occurred in the lives of the three friends, was a half-empty tote keg of honey and the still open volume of magic lore that Bear had been reading on the afternoon Dwarf and Otter had found him.

A strange reaction began taking place inside Dwarf.

His heart, aching and sad, as he thought of Otter and Bear, began to beat wildly, and a vague notion came over him that even they, his closest companions, were out to get all they could from the Chest Bearer, and to make good their quest by pretending to be friends to the one who carried the Secrets.

"I never would have thought treachery was afoot even among my best comrades," he said aloud. "But then, they aren't of my kindred, nor are they of any line that ever could be trusted."

He smashed a fist into his palm.

"By the sacred beard, it's good that I've left them behind. There's no telling how much grief they might do me were they still in my company."

A deep, perplexed look pulled down the edges of Broco's mouth.

"Yet they have guarded me and the Chest when I was unable," he said, his voice taking on the softer quality of gentleness that was in his speech of old. "And why am I here alone?" he cried, looking about him and seeing the fading glimmer of reddish gold and dark brown shadows of the book covers, which seemed to catch the flickering candle flame and spin it into mysterious patterns on the cavern wall.

Some secret part of Broco's soul writhed in anguish as he thought these thoughts to himself, and he bravely renewed his decision to leave this cave at once and set out to find his friends. He screwed up his face into a grim smile, and actually took a step or two in the direction of the opening that led outside.

"I may be falling right into the trap they've set, though," he said haltingly. "This may all be a part of their plot to steal the Chest from me and start their own kingdom. All they need is the Secrets, and they would be able to do anything they wished."

The thought of living in a realm governed by Otter and Bear made Dwarf shake his head indignantly.

"Why, the ninnies don't even have the proper sense to take care of themselves, much less look after all the things that need to be looked after if one is to run a proper sort of kingdom. There are schedules to meet, and speeches to make, and any number of governors and ministers to meet with. And of course, one can't forget that there have to be times to hear from the subjects. Not to mention a certain portion of time that must be dedicated to seeking our new solutions to problems, or turning old solutions to new uses."

Dwarf shook his head emphatically.

"No, the silly lummoxes wouldn't do well at all," he said again, and his eyes narrowed to thin slits.

"And I'm not so sure but that I won't have them answer for this treason. After all, an attempt to depose the proper ruler of any realm is more than just cause for retribution. It may be tempered with a great deal of mercy on my part, of course, but friends or not, they must be made to obey the same laws of the land as every other subject."

After another moment, Dwarf continued on aloud.

"And I think I shall have them give back the power to change form, while I'm at it. I don't think I want to have the place cluttered up with any nasty animals. And they can be vicious sometimes, without any warning at all."

Broco had returned the heavy volume on the stool to its place on the shelf, and he ran his hand lovingly over the other thick books that were chronicles of dwarfish achievements and histories of families and kinsmen that he had studied about at his father's knee for all of his young spanner years. Quickly shuffling through the gilt-edged pages of one of these books, he reread the beginnings and all the middle years of dwarfdom, when the greatest and most glorious of all the kingdoms of Underearth were powerful forces in the affairs of all who dwelt in the lower meadows of Windameir.

Those were the years of Co'in and Eo'in, and those great dwarf lords were the highest rulers in the Golden Years, and all who lived then looked with awe and admiration to those leaders, and counted on them for their strength and wisdom. It had taken the long and weary Wars of the Dragon to corrode those wonderful kingdoms, and after the slaying of the last great worm, the slow and inevitable downfall came, because, Dwarf was sure, the realms of Co'in and Eo'in had been diluted and weakened by their dealings with men and elves. It had been only a matter of time until the last of the glorious kingdoms of Underearth had vanished away into time and dust, just as he himself had witnessed the final disappearance of the First Delving from Atlanton Earth. That, too, reassured him that he was to be the beginning of a new era of power and strength, and the pillar upon which all Dwarfdom would build the new world which now promised to become a reality.

Broco huffed importantly, and enjoyed the thought that his father would be more than proud of him. As a spanner, he had spent his time alone, for the most part, and was not readily liked by the few companions that he came in contact with, who were, like himself, the sons of other lore masters. His life then had been spent at lessons and listening to his father repeat the songs and stories that had been handed down through all the lifetimes of the dwarfish kingdoms that had been created by elders who seemed larger than life and of such charm and genius that the stories did not do them true justice.

And now, after all the childish dreams, he, Broco, was the marked one, the Bearer of the Arkenchest, Lord and Ruler of Underearth, and Holder of the Secrets. It would be Broco that the new songs and stories would be of, and Broco that the spanners of the future lore masters would be reading and studying of.

The dwarfish comrades that Broco had known when he was still in the care of his father were all gone now, he knew. Or if they were still about, it would be on this side of Calix Stay.

After the affair at the Delvings, he knew the last Guardians had gone, returned to their own particular time and place, and he had seen the end of the dragon stone. And remembering that, he felt suddenly very alone.

For the first time he realized that he would have no help in creating the new kingdom, and no subjects to rule over, or to help him carve the new Delving that he envisioned. His heart felt leaden, and all the grand hopes he had brought to life burst and disappeared like so many gray shadows in some darkening gloom.

Another feeling came over him then, one of a new and deeper fear, such as he had known once long before, when he had been in the dungeons of the Dark Queen, far below the hollow emptiness and despair of the Palace of Ice. In his memory, the cold shafts of green and yellow light appeared, and he was once more standing in front of the towering throne of Dorini, and she was demanding of him a thing he did not know he had at the time. A frozen wind stabbed at his heart, and the deathly quiet of Dorini's realms crept into his mind and a terrible silence began, where all he could hear was his own mind and heart. Vivid flashes of greenish light flickered upon the walls of the cavern, and Dwarf blinked away the beads of cold sweat that had dropped into his eyes.

He rubbed his face with his sleeve and started to turn for the cavern door, and the day outside, when he saw the fainter shadow among the deeper gloom off to the side, and farther back against the cave wall. It did not move or speak, and Dwarf uttered a little cry of surprise and made a dash for the safety of the light beyond the entrance. Without seeming to move, the shadow was suddenly directly in front of him, blocking out the golden sun and barring his only hope of escape.

Dwarf clutched desperately at the Chest, and drew the short dagger he carried, crouching into position to defend himself. In his desperateness, he did not fear this intruder, but rather felt relieved that here was something real that could be dealt with. Without realizing it, Dwarf felt a wild surge of joy, for the presence of this invader at least convinced him that he was not totally alone.

Broco's Delving

Clutching his drawn dagger tightly, and wielding the Arkenchest with his other hand, Broco advanced on the menacing shadow that blotted out the sun and stood in the way of his freedom. Dwarf's blood was boiling with fear and rage, and a strange new feeling came to him as he held the Chest out before him, a sensation of being indestructible and totally undefeatable.

He raised his voice to begin an old war cry and to shout out the name of the king of all dwarfish warriors, Brion Brandagore, but before he could utter the words, he called out his name instead, and to his startled ears, it sounded much better than that of the ancient king who was long since gone over the boundaries, and who would be of no help at all to him at this moment, in this combat.

"Broco, Dwarflord, Broco, Chest Bearer," shrieked Dwarf, over and over, and raised his dagger on high with one hand and thrust the Arkenchest out before him like a shield. His eyes had narrowed to gleaming red slits, and tiny drops of white froth flecked his dry lips, and the cold blue steel of the knife's blade reflected back the fragile sunlight that filtered into the gloom of the cave's entrance.

"Broco, Secret Holder," screamed Dwarf, and lunged viciously at the dark thing that fluttered near the door like a large black bat.

At the last moment, the ghostly shadow seemed to vanish, and Dwarf's savage knife strokes sang harmlessly through the empty air. Broco whirled and came face to face with the dark-cloaked figure he had attacked. Shock, and then fear, swept over Dwarf, and he fell back a step, trying to form a word upon his trembling lips.

"Yes, good coz, it's Creddin," croaked the ancient dwarf, unchanged in any way since Dwarf had last seen him, moments before Tubal Hall had crashed upon his lifeless body.

"But you've gone," stuttered Dwarf, his eyes wide.

"Only such a trip as you've found time to take, coz. Seems as if you have a deal of trouble believing your eyes."

Dwarf had lowered the dagger, and replaced the Chest in the folds of his cloak.

"How did you get here?" Broco asked, getting over his fear and beginning to grow suspicious.

"I might ask you the same thing, dear coz. And seeing as how I've been here longest, and am senior of the two of us, I expect that you owe me the courtesy of answering old Creddin first."

Broco frowned, and a seething hatred began to boil within him.

"No one speaks with those tones to the Chest Bearer, Lord of Underearth, Holder of the Secrets."

Broco's eyes danced dangerously, and a pale gleam of red fire played across his brow.

Creddin, his voice old and creaking, cackled gleefully. "So that's the way of it, is it, coz? Old Creddin has had a good look into that pit you're digging. Chest Bearer, indeed."

The bent figure of Creddin doubled over, and he laughed so hard he began to have trouble breathing.

"Chest Bearer, indeed," he gasped again, darting a withered old hand out from beneath his cloak and jabbing it toward Dwarf. "You see this?" he asked, holding it still for a moment. "This gnarled old knobby claw once could count more gold and treasure than even the greatest worm of the dragon horde could imagine. I was given such wealth that not even Co'in or Eo'in could brag of more treasure, nor could their kingdoms begin to touch the vast hoard that I could keep in a single vault of the halls of Tubal."

Creddin cackled, and turned the hand back and forth in the air in front of him,

"And look at this talon now, eh. Nothing to show for having counted all that wealth, or touched all those jewels and necklaces, or fingered the pretty trinkets that I had a fancy for."

"You are a fool, Creddin," shot Broco angrily, for he began to feel very uncomfortable in front of this old dwarf's gaze. "You are and were foolish and unwise. Where you wished gold for yourself, you got only what you paid for. Treachery brought you your end."

Dwarf's reply seemed to touch off Creddin's creaking old laugh again.

"Aye, treachery, and too much appetite for the little pretties that I saw from time to time. Yet I found out what they were worth, in the end. My gold vaults and shiny boxes of ancient silver and mithra were nothing in the way of comfort when it was time to leave that existence. An empty hand is all I took away with me, and an empty heart, to boot."

"You might well add an empty head too," put in Broco. "If you had just been satisfied with enough wealth to see you through, you could have had both your gold and a vast kingdom. But your greed stole everything from you, and the kingdom you inherited was the way we found you then, alone, and miserable in the ruins of a once proud house."

"Miserable, yes," replied Creddin, "but not quite alone. And not miserable for a long, long time. I had had my happy times with my newfound wealth, but much before you found me. All my time was spent in sorting the different baubles and bracelets or necklaces and such. It was afterward that the treasures lost their pleasure. And that is when I began to have my visitor more regularly. He would come, asking if I wanted more, knowing that I couldn't refuse. I needed more, for I already knew every coin and trinket that I possessed. I needed newer things to count and hold, and he knew it."

"Who knew it?" questioned Dwarf, interrupting Creddin in the midst of his speech.

An odd smile crept over the ancient dwarf's face, and he showed his toothless gums as he spoke.

"The one I had made my pact with, of course," he said.

"And who was that?" again asked Dwarf, growing irritable.

"Doraki," breathed Creddin, and his old eyes blazed into a fiery reddish gray, and his face seemed to grow harsher.

Broco fell back a step, his heart drumming in his throat.

The knife he held clattered noisily to the cave floor, and the hand that gripped the Chest trembled so badly, he was afraid he might drop that, too.

"But then you came, coz," said Creddin, his eyes becoming softer and his features falling again into the gaunt, thin lines of extreme old age. "And you had your friends with you, and for some reason you stayed the night with the one who was more or less responsible for the death or capture of countless beings by the Darkness. And for some reason I spared you, and because you made me feel that mercy toward you, I had mercy shown to me, in my own judgment, when I crossed Calix Stay."

"What do you mean?" muttered Dwarf, thoroughly confused, and more suspicious than ever. He had retrieved the small dagger and returned it to its sheath.

"If you remember, I had been expecting someone else when you came to me, and it was none other than the dark underling of Dorini. And I could easily have turned you over, for he did come later, in the night, while I was playing with my little toys in the vaults below the hall. He was there to torment me with the knowledge of everyone I had betrayed to gain that wealth, and to remind me that our bargain was sealed, and that I was going to go on growing older, until I could no longer do anything but feel the terror and remorse in my soul. That was what I had come to know. They had given me all I had asked for, yet the price that I paid was much dearer than I like to admit. I had no choice but to do what they asked, and I could not bear to see what was becoming of me, and what I had become."

Creddin's voice had grown stronger as he talked.

"And then you came, as I said. For some reason, I did not

want to let Doraki have you or your friends. I don't know why. Because you were my kindred, I suppose. But I wanted to save you, and let you escape. Somehow, I knew that if I could do that, things might be different with me. At least I would have one act of decency to remember against all the evil I had been responsible for."

Dwarf's eyes had widened, and he took his hand from the hilt of the dagger.

"You mean Doraki was there that night? In Tubal Hall?"

"And very angry," went on Creddin. "He was more interested in the whereabouts of the two wizards you had seen than he was in you, and I suppose that's why he left you alone that night. He was after the two wizards, for they had displeased his queen, and so there was nothing to be gained at the moment from a dwarf and his two animal companions."

Dwarf shook his head. "If he had taken us that night, I wonder where all this would have ended," he mused aloud.

"The fact is, coz, that he didn't. And I escaped the halls of my ancestors by the route that you witnessed, and since you all were there, and were concerned for me, I ended up making my crossing near here, and have been here since. I have found in the course of my studies that this is the very cave where the bear who was with you lived, and that the otter dwelled not far away. Since their hearts were open to me as I was crossing, I was guided here. And here is where I've stayed."

Broco looked back over his shoulder.

"You mean you've been living here?"

"I stay here sometimes," replied Creddin. "But mostly I spend my time below. There were dwarfish delvings here too, you know. Long before the end of the trouble with the dragons, it seems some of Eo'in's band had crossed and spent some deal of time in these parts. They've fashioned a comfortable dwelling below the cave that your friend used as his shelter."

"You mean to say that Bear, that silly ass, was living in the top part of one of our kinsmen's dwellings?"

"It seems that way. And it explains where he found the books. I have had to come up here often when I need a reference. It appears that when he was exploring some of the tunnels and shafts he found the library, and took some of the books that interested him and brought them here. I was going to return them; then I found it was easier and more enjoyable to come upstairs to do my reading and carry on my studies."

Broco shook his head unbelievingly.

"I can't see how I missed all this before. I knew there was some reason that I took to Bear and felt at home when he invited us to his shelter. And I should have guessed right away, after seeing the books that he had. I can't imagine why I didn't question him about these then."

Broco shook his head again.

"And just now, before you came, I was reading one of our ancient lore books."

"It seems empty heads must run in our kinsmen's blood, coz," remarked Creddin, his old voice creaking into a short snort of mirth.

"But it is all as well," said Broco, his voice taking on a somewhat huffier tone. "Now I know that what I felt was true. There was a reason I was drawn to this place, and a reason that I have come upon you."

"That's all true, coz," replied Creddin. "And there must be more to this than chance, I would say."

"Much more," pronounced Broco in a grand tone, "for it has proved to be where my destiny has chosen to guide me. I had dreams of starting a new delving that would be the beginning of a new life for all of Dwarfdom and a shining new chapter in the lore books of our forefathers. But more, *I* would be the instrument of fate that would open the way for the new birth of our kind."

Creddin, his knobby old form bent with age, scuttled nearer to Dwarf.

"You mean we are going to do this all alone, coz?" he asked. "That's a mighty big chore for two small dwarfs to take on."

"Except, you fool, you forget that I am Arkenchest Bearer and Holder of the Secrets."

Creddin's watery old eyes narrowed again, and he put a gnarled finger to his lips.

"I wouldn't broadcast that about so readily if I were you, coz. Things have taken on a change of color during my stay. And I don't mind saying that some of it reminds me somewhat of all that business on the other side. Of course, it's not so nasty, and I have seen some improvement, but things have gone a little sour."

"What do you mean by a little sour?" asked Dwarf. "Has anyone else been here before me?" Broco's fears had returned, and he eyed Creddin warily.

"No, coz, not to speak of. But I have heard the goings-on in the woods, and I have heard rumors, how true they are I don't know, that that jackanapes of an elf, Tyron, has set himself up as some sort of governor of Gilden Wood. That's going to be a bit tricky, having the two of you busy running the same piece of pie," chuckled Creddin.

"Tyron holds only one of the Secrets," snapped Dwarf. "I'll have no trouble establishing my true power. The Chest shall tell all that I am the Holder of the Secrets, and that I am the governor of these realms."

"This is going to be more than a bit of fun to watch, coz," said Creddin. "I had my lessons to learn beyond Calix Stay, but at least I got the worst of them over before I recrossed. It never has been any good being a slow starter," concluded the old dwarf, clicking his tongue to himself and shaking his bony head.

"That's enough out of you, old bones," said Dwarf bitterly. "Now make yourself useful and lead me to these delvings you spoke of."

"With pleasure, coz," said Creddin. "It'll take your mind off all this nonsense you've been prattling, and at least keep you out of sight, in case any of this new rabble that's been crossing the River lately is about. They all seem to be after the same thing, just like you."

Creddin paused momentarily.

"It must be something that's going around," he mumbled, and began moving away from the sunlit door toward the deeper shadows in the back of the cave. "Come on, then, coz. I'll give you a tour of Bani's delving, where he stayed this side of the River."

"It shall be known from this time forward as Broco's delving," pronounced Dwarf testily, and then he said it again, to try the ring of it. "I like that. Broco's Delving, the Birth of the New Beginning," he said, his eyes misting over and the tiny Chest in his cloak growing warm to his touch.

It was to be a grand undertaking, he thought to himself, and now it seemed he had been sent Creddin to help him carry out the scheme that would establish all Dwarfdom once more in the forefront of Creation, where they rightfully belonged, and from where they had long been absent. Broco intended to change all that, and the time drew nearer when all those who yet remained on this side of Calix Stay would be calling out his name with reverence and awe.

As Creddin led Dwarf deeper into the shafts that ran on toward the delving of Bani, Bear, his great head lifted and testing the air, picked up a confusing and exciting scent of something very familiar, and very near. There was no mistaking the heady smell and feel of an old shelter. It made his heart skip a beat, and without warning, he was racing ahead, away from his friends, his nose high and his ears laid back, bellowing short little calls of greeting to welcome an old friendly cave that he had almost forgotten. Better still, he was sure he had picked up the tart and musky aroma of well-aged clover bloom honey.

"I hope I remembered to cork it properly," he muttered to himself, and at that moment, he raced into the dark oval opening of the shelter he had left with Dwarf and Otter to begin the long and weary journey that had now brought him back full circle, to where he had begun.

An Elusive Greyfax Expounds

"How fares it, good Galen? All as it should be?" asked Greyfax.

"It fares as you said it would, sir," replied Galen Isenault, still somewhat breathless from the long journey that now lay behind him. "Froghorn has met with the companions, and we parted our ways after everyone was safely rounded up and accounted for. The dwarf was out of sorts, somewhat, although we couldn't blame him, after all he'd gone through. And I thought for a moment or two that the otter had gone daft and taken leave of his wits. He was on the point of attacking Fairingay before we got him quieted down. Seems as if he had it through his head Froghorn wasn't who he said he was and had slain some woodchuck or groundhog, or something of that nature. I couldn't make much sense of it, except that there could have been great mischief done if we hadn't gotten the little fellow calmed down. He's as strong as a Worlugh when he's riled up, and as ugly a fighter as any Gorgolac I ever had the misfortune to deal with."

Greyfax laughed, turning to Lorini. "You see? He's not that cuddly, helpless fellow that you are always making him out to be. Otter can be a nasty sort if the need arises."

Lorini smiled. "That can be said of you yourself, dear Grimwald. One would not suspect that the gentle Greyfax would ever be the one moved to raise his strength against anyone."

"I cannot vouch for that, madam. There are some who do not hold your kind opinion of me."

"My sister wouldn't, I don't think," continued Lorini. "Although I daresay she would like to. She has had designs on your alliance in the past, and I think she was greatly disappointed when you refused her."

"Possibly. I can't begin to see what she ever saw in me, though, or of what use I could have been to her."

Lorini laughed loudly, throwing back her golden hair from her face. "That, dear fellow, is exactly what would attract her. That little-boy charm you display so well."

Greyfax reddened, and directed another question at Galen.

"Is Froghorn with the companions now?"

"He was when I left, sir. But Melodias and Greymouse were going to take separate routes once the crossing of Tyron's was sealed. I'm sure they've left Froghorn's party by now."

"I hope so," mused Greyfax. "They have their places to fill elsewhere. And I'm not so sure they probably won't have to make another crossing themselves, to gather their troops beyond Calix Stay."

Lorini's beautiful features took on a more serious look. "You mean again?"

"It may prove to be necessary. The quiet that has fallen there seems to have been broken. I have had word that the beasts are afield again and the Gorgolac hordes are swarming out of the Dragon Wastes into the lands that have been untroubled by their presence before now."

"And you, dear Grimwald? Shall you have to go too? And will I be left alone here, just as I was in Cypher, to see you only briefly, and between your comings and goings elsewhere?"

Greyfax took Lorini's hand and squeezed it gently.

"I don't think that shall happen now. If anything, it will be short trips across the River to rally the Light or advise some army or other."

"That's what you always told me before," pouted Lorini. "And I thought perhaps it was too good to imagine that we would operate here together. It seemed too pretty a picture to paint."

"Here, here, I said I may have to travel across the River again, but I never said a word about when. And if I do have to, it shall certainly not be anytime in the immediate future. We have too many errands here to be thinking about going anywhere."

Greyfax paused, and paced down the long, low room, which was built of comfortable, warm logs, and roofed in the fashion of Broco's old home, with the living green limbs of trees, grown over with grass and clover.

"But go on, Galen," he said, returning to stand before the table where Galen sat.

"As I took my leave, they were heading toward the crossing, to deny it to Tyron. Froghorn hadn't told them yet of what they were to do, except that they were coming, as soon as they were finished, to join you. Froghorn didn't want to risk frightening any of them with another meeting with the River, and he was afraid that after just crossing themselves, they wouldn't be up to facing the closing. But all was well with them, and Froghorn had his instructions, just as you gave them to me."

"Good, good. And did he leave them as planned?"

"I don't know, sir. As I say, I left them before they left to carry out their errand. He did say that the stage was set for the next act, and that he was preparing things as they were given to him to prepare. He told me he was going to place the dwarf in a position that would allow him to fall into temptation, and then allow for a reason for his own departure. I assume that probably Froghorn is on his way to the Lower Gate now. That was his plan as he explained it to me."

"Then everything is as it should be," confirmed Greyfax, nodding. "We shall be ready before long to move into action."

As the older wizard finished speaking, a great clatter of hooves was heard outside the low building, and Froghorn Fairingay entered, his cloak following wildly behind him. He bowed low to Lorini and took Galen's outstretched hand, addressing Greyfax as he did so.

"The snare is laid, although I don't like the bait. Something might go wrong, and then we'd all stand to lose more than I think we care to contemplate."

"It's only natural that we look at it that way," replied Greyfax. "And that is exactly the way Dorini will see it, as well. But little ventured, nothing gained, and so on. And not only is it as it was given to us to play, it is Windameir's Will."

"I'm not arguing, I'm simply saying that I feel uneasy,

knowing that if we fail, not only the Chest, but Cybelle and every other single living thing below Calix Stay is lost, and without hope."

"If we fail, old fellow, then we shall all be without hope," said Greyfax gently. "But as long as we know that it is his Will, then what else could we ask? If Windameir wills that we fail, then I shall have to try to be happy in failure."

"I don't like thinking of that," shot Froghorn, "and I certainly don't think that he would ever will us to go down into the slavery of Dorini."

"No, that's so," smiled Greyfax. "Although we have each one suffered that slavery and known that hopelessness, just as every single living being below Calix Stay is suffering her rule. But it is necessary to stir the heart into action, and to yearn to return Home, where it belongs."

"What is the plan he speaks of?" asked Lorini, looking hard at the older wizard. "Or is it my place to be in on the planning of this campaign?"

Froghorn reddened, and glanced sidelong at Greyfax, who stroked his beard thoughtfully for a moment before he spoke. "There is no intent to keep you in the dark about the strategy of this campaign, my dear. It was thought by us all, Erophin included, that it might be best if the full details of the operation were not known to you. No intention of any sort, except perhaps to spare you needless worry."

"Froghorn said not only the Secrets, but Cybelle and every other living thing below Calix Stay would be lost. What did he mean by that?"

"She has asked a question that is for you to answer, since it was you who brought the subject up," said Greyfax, frowning at his young friend.

"I'm not capable of answering that," muttered Froghorn. "I mean I'm sorry for my hastiness, but I don't know how to reply."

He tried to face Lorini, but his eyes fell away from her steady gaze.

"I think I can put something together of this conversation, although I may find it hard to digest," said Lorini, her hands clenched into tight white fists.

"It is nothing like you imagine, and with none of the overtones you may be thinking," Greyfax hastily assured her. "To put it simply, Erophin was worried about you after your visit, and thought it best if you were able to relax awhile and be spared any further tests of your strength until you were feeling more yourself. He knew, and we all agreed, that you might be somewhat shaky about anything to do with Cybelle or that might concern her fate, and he very wisely suggested that we carry out certain parts of our plan upon these realms without your full knowledge. Not to keep you in the dark, as I said, but simply because he could see no good purpose in telling you, and the rest of us were in accord. If the thing was to be done, it need not be known to any more than the immediate people needed to carry off the plan and those who would be needed later to spring the trap."

Greyfax paused for breath, and met Lorini's steady gaze with his own even gray-blue eyes. He smiled slightly.

"However, I see that perhaps Erophin changed his mind and saw fit to have this impetuous pup spill the whole pot of beans, and thereby give excuse to filling you in on the plan, as the Circle has seen its way clear to formulate, to resolve the turmoil upon these lower planes, once and for all."

"I honestly didn't think, Greyfax," blurted out Froghorn

apologetically, "but I was rather worried, leaving Otter and Bear and the others out there, with no further instructions than just to reach you as best they could. And I'm not at all sure I take to the idea of Broco all alone and without protection."

Greyfax brightened as he spoke. "That's where you are wrong, old fellow. He does have protection. The Chest."

Froghorn glanced at his friend. "But that is exactly the thing that was to tempt him, you said. And it was certainly plain to see that it has, from what dealings I had with him since he crossed Calix Stay this time."

"Exactly. That is the first way that the Secrets can be tried. And if the Arkenchest is not complete, and does not hold all the Five, then it is dangerous to any who carry it, if they are not of our Circle. Dwarf is merely waking up to the idea that with those Secrets that he holds he is capable of great power and is able to sway people and control minds. It is very tempting, that, as we all found out when it was allotted to us to do our turn at carrying the Chest."

"Does he know what's happening?" asked Lorini.

"Broco? No, he knows no more than he knew when he carried the Secret that I had given his father, who in turn gave it to Broco. I little knew then that it was to come to this, for I only had a part of the complete picture myself. I knew it was for me to deliver the Secret I carried from the Chest to Broco's father for safekeeping. And that was true enough. It was for safekeeping."

Greyfax paused, smiling.

"What Erophin, and Cephus, and all the others didn't tell me was that the entire chain of events was mapped and plotted out, and that they knew then that Froghorn and I would meet the son of the dwarf who carried the Secret given him by his father, who had the Secret long before from me. I feel just as you do, my lady, that somehow someone was trying to keep something from me."

Greyfax uttered a small laugh.

"But I see now the wisdom in all the secrecy. Had I known then all I was to find out later, I would not have been prepared to act in the way that was necessary, nor carried out my assigned task as it was intended. And most important of all, I was spared any additional grief that would have surely befallen me had I known the future long before it came to pass. His wisdom in that is, after all, merely proof of his kindness and love of us all."

"No one questions his love," put in Lorini, "and I think you have talked yourself out of telling me whatever it was I questioned you about."

"You've convinced me," said Galen, his brows knitted, a puzzled look spread across his face.

"You're as quick-tongued as ever," shot Froghorn, "and I've never known you to be at a loss for words, except when there was something afoot that you didn't want to share with anyone. Then I'm well aware that nothing could loosen your hold on your thoughts. And it has proved to be maddening on more than one occasion."

"Mere discipline, my boy," replied Greyfax, "and necessary to any operation where the least said gets the most done."

"Then you were the root cause of mountains of action," snapped Froghorn.

"Which brings us back to action, and what we shall be doing here, to see what can be done about our lady's dark sister."

"You've gotten me so confused, I'm not even sure what we're dealing with now," said Lorini, in a cool, even voice.

"We are speaking of webs being spun and laid across the doorway that will have to be used by our actors, and which will surely draw the attention of our good Dorini and her following."

"But the risks are surely too great, Greyfax," protested Froghorn, preparing to take up his argument where he left off.

"Great, yes! Indeed greater than any we have yet undertaken to run. The loss of the Arkenchest is perhaps the one thing that alone could doom the worlds below Calix Stay to the eternal darkness of Dorini's night. And to add to that the loss of Cybelle, herself a Holder of the Light, and daughter of our lady, would surely seal the fate of every living being caught in the darkness of ignorance, with never any hint that there was a way out and a Path that leads Home."

"And what of ourselves, if this plan you speak of fails?" asked Lorini quietly.

"We would have the choice of returning Home and betraying all those left behind, or returning ourselves beyond Calix Stay, to delay the inevitable. Eventually even we would not be able to hold out against her, not if she were successful in her aims."

"That's not much of a choice," broke in Froghorn. "And I'm not sure that that would be an end of it, or that it would turn out in the manner you describe."

"Change a few details, alter a few facts, yet it is still the picture of what would happen if the Circle's influence was broken and the Arkenchest captured," replied Greyfax.

"I see no need to discuss the unlikely events of what would happen were we to fail in our plans," said Lorini, her voice raised to make herself heard from where she had retreated, standing by a low window that opened out over a wide, sweeping view of the high blue peaks, and the distant hazy, golden glow that hung over the beginning of the gently sloping foothills, and the green fingers of the forest that reached up toward the mountains. "What I am still interested in learning is what exactly those plans are that we are discussing, and what they consist of, and what it is we need to do in order to carry them out."

"And that, my dear lady, is what we shall attempt to explain to you now," said Greyfax, bowing to Lorini. "Gentlemen, come, sit down, and help me to explain to our lady the rudiments of the basic scheme of things."

"That won't be easy," murmured Galen, "and I'm not even sure I understand myself."

"Nor I," agreed Froghorn, pulling back a chair and holding it while Lorini sat down.

"Then we shall all benefit from the exercise," laughed Greyfax. Perhaps, even, we shall all understand a bit more as we go on reassuring each other."

"There's nothing amusing in this, Greyfax," said Froghorn, in an injured tone.

"Don't mistake me, old fellow. I'm only laughing at myself. Of course there is nothing amusing, except what we find in our own makeup. I was simply thinking that I would prefer to be face to face with Doraki at Havamal once more rather than seated here, across from this beautiful lady."

"Flattery will do nothing to save you from this, you elusive slow-tongue. Now out with it. Let us hear it all."

Greyfax pulled back his own chair, and prepared to speak.

At the first word, as if on cue, a great commotion broke

out at the door, and an orderly in the uniform of Galen strode hurriedly into the room and saluted smartly.

"Yes? What is it, lad?"

"They've been spotted, sir," replied the messenger.

"Where?" asked Galen.

"Below the Last Gate, sir. Right at the edge of Gilden Far. There's no sign of anyone else, though."

"Who is at the Last Gate?" asked Lorini, turning in frustration to Greyfax.

"Tyron's men and his allies."

"But what are they waiting there for?" she persisted.

"Someone, I fear, has warned them of the escape of a certain dwarf through those sacred woods that are so nobly overseen by the grand and sage Tyron the Green."

"Who has done that?" she asked, her eyes widening.

"Greyfax Grimwald, it seems," said Greyfax, his eyes twinkling and turning a darker gray.

And below the Last Gate, the thinning trees of Gilden Far were filled with the green-and-brown-clad elves of Tyron's band, and pacing angrily below, striding about a small clearing, was the irate figure of Tyron himself, his hands clasped tightly behind his back and his face drawn into a dangerous scowl.

After a time, a noise stirred in the forest at the very borders of the clearing, and Tyron hastened to meet the dark-cloaked figure who lingered in the shadows the tall trees cast.

Broco and Creddin

Deep beneath the floor of Bear's old shelter, Broco and Creddin sat down at an ivory-inlaid table that had been wrought by the master craftsmen of Bani, who had been slain long before, in the last battles of the Dragon Wars. The room in which they sat was perfectly round, with a high dome whose top reached all the way to the surface of the ground, and there, in golden and silver muted light, hung what appeared to be a large star, with mirrored flecks of brilliant red, blue, and green stones that caught the glittering afternoon light and spun it into intricate patterns on the polished walls. The cups the two dwarfs drank from were silver and mithra, and fashioned in the likeness of lions' heads, with raging jaws thrown open and rows of intricately cast teeth sparkling dangerously as the cups were moved about in the light.

Before Broco sat a golden plate of freshly baked dwarf cakes, each in the classic shape of a hammer. Creddin urged another helping of the cakes on Dwarf, who waved them away with a weary hand.

"No more, no more. I've had my fill."

"You must admit my fare here is better than I was able to give you the last time we met, coz. I could hardly offer you a stale biscuit then and a drink of water, much less serve it up on finery like this."

"You had a lot more to serve us then than we suspected, it seems," said Broco churlishly. "I have heard tales and read stories of treachery and ill-gotten treasures, and they were enough to turn my blood cold. And those stories were those of Mankind and those that dealt with Mankind, or the animal kings and kingdoms who dealt with elf or man. It was never heard of, within the span of knowledge that I have, of dwarf against dwarf, or of gains gotten by murdering your own kindred or having them murdered by the Darkness."

Broco snorted disdainfully.

"And I do wish you would address me with a little more respectful term than 'coz.' It doesn't suit me, and I don't think the familiarity is called for. You are, after all, an outcast and a self-professed traitor to Dwarfdom."

Creddin leaned back from the finely wrought table and slapped a brittle old knee with a mighty thwack of his hand. "Well, I never," he cackled, roaring with long gasps of laughter. "Well, bless me," he croaked, catching his breath. "Coz, you do seem to find my funny bone. Here we sit, you and I, all by ourselves in this beautiful old delving, probably the last two of our kind beyond the boundaries, and the pot calling the kettle black."

Creddin doubled over again.

"It pleases me to think that I have a right to call you what I please. After all, I have not been responsible for the death of any of my kinsmen or the capture of any of my own kind by the Darkness. At least I have that dignity. But here you sit, all by yourself, telling me your grand plans to rebuild all the glorious delvings that were before, and that you are going to be the rebirth of Dwarfdom."

Creddin smiled pleasantly.

"But what ever happened to your two friends, the animals who were with you there before, when you came to me at Tubal Hall? The two staunch friends who stood by you in the dangers of crossing Calix Stay, and who were beside you then? Have they gone their own way, or have you perhaps left them in your haste to get on with all these wonderful schemes of yours?"

Dwarf leapt angrily up, overturning the beautiful goblet and spilling the contents of the plate of dwarf cakes onto the polished smooth floor with a loud clatter.

"Blast your meddling old bones, that has nothing to do with you. And it's none of your concern where they are."

"Wouldn't take much of a liking to you in this state of mind, I shouldn't think," went on Creddin. "Our sort often get ourselves worked into this way of thinking sooner or later, it seems. Something, I suppose, to do with all the long hours spent hard at work at the anvils, and the long, hard days spent digging and shafting and finishing out the inner beauty of these underground dreams that our forefathers and their forefathers before them dreamed and passed on to us."

Creddin clicked his tongue.

"A pity, too. Our sort are loyal and trusty, and have more than a passing knack for bending a common thing into a work of grace and motion. And I don't but doubt that almost everything handy and useful in the way of good, sensible tools came from us at one time or other."

Broco had huffed and started to speak, but the old dwarf went on, ignoring him.

"Yet we all do seem to get ourselves into a spot of trouble when it comes to having to deal with dragons, or treasures of any sort, and that usually means Dwarfkind is not far behind, for mostly the treasures there are have been hoarded and guarded by the dwarf lords long before any dragons came about to take a fancy to all the glittering things that took their poor minds off themselves and let them have some happiness in their underground lairs, just as I had to discover the pull of gold and the ultimate agony that it causes."

"You're full of old tales that have no bearing on the here and now, Master Creddin. And you speak of the dragons as if you'd known them personally. Rot! All of it. And how would you know anything of it, anyway? You were never called to serve. You never faced the horror of the dragon, or dealt with the terrible beasts, or lost friends or parents to the greedy, horrible things."

Broco had thrown back his chair in his outburst, and knocked another chair over with a wildly flaying motion of his hand. His voice was raised to a hysterical shriek, and his eyes burned in deep, dim fire that blurred his vision and seemed to make him stagger.

"How dare you compare anyone decent with the horrible things that were spawned by the Darkness and set upon the world in a despicable attempt to terrorize all living things into that black pit of horror that is the abode of Dorini? And you never lost your own mother to the foul things, nor had to watch helpless and unable to aid a friend who had been so unfortunate as to get too close to one of those filthy beasts' claws, or tail, nor watched them eaten alive, or roasted, or crunched by one of the despicable monsters you are so busy feeling sorry for."

Dwarf was pounding the beautiful table with his fists, and his voice had risen to a screaming, frenzied tone.

Creddin, unmoving, studied Dwarf closely, and the ancient dwarf's eyes were deep and troubled, and he reached out a gnarled old hand to touch Broco's arm, to reassure him, but Dwarf flung the bony hand aside and stalked away.

"Yes, you say our kind, or rather *my* kind, has spent long hours delving, or at the thankless tasks of the anvils, or sweating out our hearts at creating these dreams we have from living stone. And it is so that the precious things we made we wished to protect and pass on to the spanners that would be coming behind us. That's true, you traitorous hoardmonger, and it's true the foul things of the Darkness took a liking to our beautiful things too, and their greed overcame them, just as it did you. They had to have more, and more still, until all the treasure in Creation wasn't enough, and they took to the thrill of the kill when they lost interest in their baubles."

Dwarf had flung back his cloak as he spoke, and whirled on Creddin, holding up the Arkenchest in his outstretched hand, his eyes dancing with flashing red fire and a grotesque smile across his haunted features.

"But this, you old fool, don't you see, is the answer! It was the answer all along, only none of us knew it. Eo'in and Co'in delved deeper and tunneled farther than any other of Dwarfdom ever dared go. And they went farther still, and learned the secrets of the Guardians, and called even the spirits of the deepest dwellers up from their slumber, to help in the quest for more beauty and more dreams."

Dwarf's voice broke, and he paused to get his breath.

"But with *this*, old bones, they could have succeeded. They had only a part of what was necessary to do what they dreamed of doing. They had all of the ambition and dreams and grand visions, but they did not have this one thing. *This* is the key to all power, all beauty, all truth, and all existence. And I, Broco, Dwarflord, hold all but one of the sacred trust within this Arkenchest, and before all is done, I shall have the Five, and I shall carve such a dynasty of splendor and beauty that no eye shall be able to look upon it direct, and no soul shall go unmoved by it."

Dwarf, gasping for breath now, and waving the Arkenchest about wildly, turned his feverish glance on Creddin.

"And you, you doddering old traitor, who have been responsible for the loss of the bravest and stoutest hearts of Dwarfdom, and who dare sit there smirking and calling me traitor to my kindred, you are lucky to be allowed in my presence, and fortunate that I have not relieved you of your miserable existence. And this time there would be no soft hearts to guide you to any safe haven. It would be straight to the Darkness for you, where you belonged to begin with, for all the evil you've wrought against all of Dwarfdom."

Broco hovered dangerously above Creddin, one hand clutching the Chest and the other locked upon the hilt of his dagger. The ancient dwarf's eyes met Broco's. "Are you going to do me that great honor, Broco? Will it be you once more that frees me from one scene and leads me on to another? I would welcome your assistance, if that is how it is to be."

Broco's hand dropped harmlessly to his side.

"It is not for me to decide your lot, Creddin. You have your own judgment to meet."

"And you too, coz? Have you your own lot and your own judgment to meet?" asked the withered old figure, pulling his cup back to him and taking another sip of the cool drink, and watching Broco evenly over the rim of the mithra and silver goblet.

"We all have our judgment, you old villain, and well you know it."

"Then how shall you approach yours? Still with a free and high heart, full of innocence and wild dreams? Or will there be things there that you can't quite get shed of, or things that you would rather not discuss in the full light of day?"

Broco whirled on Creddin savagely. "What is it you're accusing me of, you filthy, wretched old assassin? I have paid you back in kind for the doubtful good deed you did me by not turning me over to Doraki that night."

"Temper, temper, dear coz. I accuse you of nothing. I merely asked you where your two companions were. They also were delivered from the Darkness, as well as you."

"They have chosen to be elsewhere. And they have proved to me that they are but self-seekers, along with the rest of that rabble that clung to me. All along I trusted them and held them in comradeship, while the lot of them plotted and schemed how they could best use me, and finally, how they could get the Chest away from me."

Broco's eyes clouded over.

"And even my fine and fancy friends of the Circle had nothing more in mind for me than to carry the Chest when it proved too hot for them, and surrender it back when it came time for all the praise and hoopla. Then I'd be no more than an errand dwarf, who'd served his purpose and was no longer of any use."

Creddin took another drink from his cup. "Then you have broken even with the Circle, have you? That doesn't sit well, coz."

"What does sit well is that I have cast aside all the ones who sought to use me, then drop me, once the hard work was over. It's always good enough to get the dwarf to do the nasty work, and kick him back to his anvil once the going is clear again. But I shall offer my kingdom to Cybelle, and have no fear that she will not accept. It is all she could possibly do, in the light of how things stand."

"And how is that, coz?" asked the ancient dwarf.

"I shall, quite simply, be the one who frees the lady," huffed Broco. "It has been stated as simply as that, and the reason I shall be able to save Cybelle is the fact that I hold the Chest and the Secrets it holds."

"And how are you going to be about all this, if I might ask, coz? Just going to drop by and tell Dorini that she must give up the lady, are you? Or speak at length to Doraki? And just by mentioning it, they'll free Cybelle and all the rest, and surrender up their designs on everything, and vanish away forever, or something like that?"

A deep crimson flush crept over Dwarf's face. "I haven't got the exact plan in mind that I shall use," he blustered angrily, "but I have the means by which to do it, once I've decided what is the best thing to do, and the safest for Cybelle. It's a dangerous task, and one that calls for much tact and caution."

"I daresay it is, coz. It must be, for from all I can make out, and from all I have read of this business from the books here, it even has the Circle stumped. And I wasn't aware, until you said it, that they held Cybelle. That's even more trouble than I had suspected."

"Trouble for some, but not for the Holder of the Chest and the Bearer of the Secrets. I shall work out a scheme by which we shall free her."

"I expect something will come of it all," said Creddin quietly, nodding his old head. The light reflected on his bald head, for he had removed the rumpled hat he wore and laid it on the table beside his cup. He turned to say something further, but Broco was standing frozen in his boots, open-mouthed at something Creddin could not see.

"What is it, coz?" asked Creddin, turning as quickly as he could, trying to see what had caught Dwarf's eye.

"No, turn back this way!" snapped Broco, hurrying to Creddin's side.

Broco took hold of the ancient dwarf's head and turned it back toward the light from the domed window.

"It looks almost like the dragon stone," he muttered, "except that it's been returned."

"That's no dragon stone, that, coz," said Creddin, putting his hat back on. "But it was once an accurate map of the coming and going of Creddin, and a fair chart of how he was feeling."

Dwarf's eyes seemed to clear somewhat. "It's gone, that stone," he said sadly, "along with the Guardians, and the Delvings of Eo'in and Co'in. And that is all past and done, and none of it is any good anymore, except what is here and now."

"Well, coz, for the here and now, what do you suggest we do to get this new kingdom of yours on the road? We can't go on just sitting here at our lunch."

Broco stumped to the other end of the long, low dwarfish table and placed both hands on the back of one of the finely carved dark wooden chairs.

"We shall start by making our plans for saving Cybelle," he pronounced grandly. "And as for starting work here, I think we need not worry. Bani and his craftsmen have done well enough to see us through until we have our work at hand finished."

"That's fine, coz. Then let's be at it. Sooner tended, better mended, or so they say."

Dwarf held up a hand.

"Wait, you old fool. We have to make some sort of plan. Where do you think you're going to go scuttling off to, anyway?"

"Why, to Dorini," said Creddin simply. "She isn't hard to find here. I've seen them both, but they haven't seen me. And if your Chest is as powerful as you say, then there won't be anything at all to getting the lady back, and getting shed of Dorini, too." Creddin shook his old head. "They had their fun with me, those two. And I've learned a thing or so from it."

Broco had paled.

"You mean you've actually seen them going about here?"

"She has set up her throne at the old ruins of Cypher, or so I've heard. And I've talked to a lot of elves and animals that know. And I've had a chance to speak on it to Froghorn Fairingay himself."

"Don't mention his name before me again," snapped Dwarf, an odd fear settling over his heart.

Creddin looked at Broco, his eyebrows raised in unspoken question.

"They're all out to get the Chest, I tell you. And Fairingay is most interested of all. He proved that to me when he pretended he was uninterested in it and made a show of wanting me to keep it. Of course, I see why, now. It is as yet dangerous, and he wanted nothing to do with it until all was safe, and every danger over."

"You've got a strange way of seeing things, coz," said Creddin at last. "Almost as odd an outlook as I held once myself. But I don't think you're being wise in cutting off your allies."

"I have no allies that are trustworthy," said Dwarf. "The only things I can trust are the Chest and the Secrets. Those are our allies."

"As you wish, coz."

"That's as I wish. And I think we should take a look now at the rest of this delving, and go on to this place you've spoken of, where you saw the Dark Queen and Doraki."

"It's rather far. We should start now, if we're to make it there and back by supper, coz."

"Then let's get on with it."

As the two dwarfs left the dining hall of the delving of Bani, a shadow flickered across the domed skylight above the table, momentarily blocking out the sun and casting dark waves washing over the glow of the ivory table and the polished, gleaming floors. Broco's heart quivered violently once, then calmed, and he threw a hurried glance behind him, but saw nothing but the empty room where they had found their meal. Creddin looked oddly at his kinsman, then hurried on ahead, moving with amazing speed.

And far behind, in the tunnels of Bear's old shelter, a familiar voice cried out in delightful surprise at the discovery of a tote keg half full of good clover bloom honey.

There was a second surprised exclamation at the finding of a small but clear footprint of a dwarfish boot in the dusty cave, and more cries and calls as Bear and Otter found another separate set of boot prints, different from the first, and easily identifiable by a marked indentation in the heel of one of the shoes, as if it were very old and extremely worn. The friends could not explain the appearance of another dwarf, any more than they could explain the disappearance of Broco.

Events on every hand seemed to grow more confusing.

Urien Typhon Meets Dorini

A pale and shaken Tyron raised a hand in warning. "What call has brought you here? I don't remember asking for any snooping on your part."

"No, good Tyron, there was no summons from you. I came because I felt you might have need of a friend."

Urien Typhon stood nearer as he spoke.

"I have no use for friendship such as you would offer, Urien. There are no words we have for each other. And I have made it plain what would befall any who opposed my will and entered my domain without my consent." Tyron raised his voice and called out. "Guard!"

"They are not going to raise a hand in anger against me. And I have no blow to deal back. All I have to offer is aid."

"Your price is too high, Urien. You would ask too great a cost for the assistance you would render. You and the rest of your spineless friends. Can't you see all they want is the thing which I hold in trust? They care nothing for me or any of my kindred. They have no provisions for Elfinkind in their Circle. Look what they did to my father. They used him, and wrung everything they could from him and all his followers, and then they expected him to stand by and hand back meekly the payment they had promised him."

"The Secret was no payment to your father, Tyron. You well know that. That belongs to all, and everyone."

"So they would like me to believe," snorted Tyron. "And it appears you've already bought their pack of lies. But they tried the same thing on my father."

"The Circle gave Eiorn the Secret to hold when the Arkenchest was in danger of falling to the enemy. He was to hold it until all was well once more, and then surrender it back to the Chest, where it belongs, along with all the others."

"Then what of the miserable dwarf that has carried the Secret he holds as well as the Chest? How can that be explained away by the Circle? What weak brain thought up those provisions for protecting the Chest?"

"It sounds as if you are well versed in all this, Tyron," said Urien softly.

"I keep my ears turned to those who have something to say," said Tyron stiffly. "And it seems that the only one who has any reason or sense in her speech is Dorini."

"You may well lull yourself into believing that, Lord Tyron. Yet I know well your line of thought, and how you plot to make these woods of yours into a haven. All as your father told you, I'm sure, and I was a friend of Eiorn's court in the better days, before he chose to take the tragic path he took. I still remain a friend of his son's, whether he wills it or not."

Tyron stamped a foot angrily, and spun, showing his back to Urien.

"You call yourself a friend of my father's court? And

me?" He spat out a dull, metallic laugh. "Fine words, but you are too late, Urien. You, with all your highborn wisdom and fair looks, how you've always lorded it over the common wood elf, whether here or below the boundaries. My kind has been forever reminded of Urien Typhon, and all those others of the waterfolk, who were fair to look upon, and whose fair ladies would blind the eye with their beauty. I have lived with the curse of that for all my life, and my father lived with it for all of his. The woodland elf was never as tall, or as handsome, or as well received among the Circle, for we always had our chores to keep us at our work and away from courting favor with the bungling Elders, who had nothing better to do than dodder about Cypher, or beyond the Lower Gate, or wherever they found the fancy moved them to dodder. You and your waterfolk have always been the quick tongues and clever wits when it comes to court manners and fine speech. A thing the Circle liked, and it was easy for your kind to cajole your way into the good graces of Greyfax, and Melodias Starson, and Cephus Starkeeper. They are all old and easily flattered." Tyron smiled strangely. "But there are those younger in court who have found it wiser to look elsewhere for their well-being."

Urien listened silently until Tyron fell quiet.

"And that is supposed to mean that you know some new turn of events that is showing the Circle to be crumbling, and the old order changed, I suppose?"

An ugly scar of humor crept over Tyron's face. "You might say I know what my own eyes have told me and what my own ears have heard."

"The Dark Queen is more clever than you know, good

Tyron. She is more than a match for the best minds of the Elders of the Circle. Do you think you pose any threat to her?"

"She finds my company not so unpleasant," snapped Tyron, reddening. "And she finds it not so disagreeable to go on letting me hold onto what is rightfully mine."

Urien laughed grimly. "I daresay, so long as it suits her purpose for you to hold it. And she is far too wise to take it from you by force, for that would spoil her chances of luring the other Secrets, and the Chest, into her snare."

"That's not so!" snarled Tyron, advancing on Urien with a fist locked tightly around the hilt of a small, finely carved elfin dagger. "Dorini has convinced me that she, like myself, has been taken rude advantage of by the Circle, and that the High Lord of Windameir, if he is still in existence, willed her to rule those lower kingdoms as was put down into the Law. And now, against that Law, the sniveling conspirators that propose to take from her her rightful kingdom also propose to rob me of the payment that was duly paid my father for services he rendered to those scoundrels, in beating off the dragon hordes that were set upon the Creation."

"Well learned, good Tyron. Well learned. And did our good Dorini also inform you who set those dragon hordes free to assault these lower realms?" Urien asked.

Tyron blushed a bright pink.

"Of course, it is convenient as a story to fill up a woodland elf's ear, who stands so ready to believe anything he is told, so long as he doesn't have to give up his precious dream about settling the havens, and has rule of those realms. Or have to admit he has been wrong, and return the Secret he wrongfully holds to its true and proper resting place in the Arkenchest."

Tyron held his breath a moment, and a long, steady hiss of air escaped his tight lips. "You are a most unfortunate fool, Urien. Perhaps none of my subjects will raise a hand to harm you, but there is nothing that prevents me from ridding my presence of such a brazen, treacherous foe of Elfinkind. I do not fear your fairness, or your reported prowess as a warrior, Urien. I know that every lore book of our kingdom is filled with the exploits of you and your sires. It is more than an honest woodland elf can bear, at times. To read the histories, and hear the old songs, you would almost think there *were* no woodland elves at all. As if we never existed."

As Tyron had ranted on, a gathering group of his followers had begun to crowd around their half-hysterical leader.

"Without honor, or remembrance, we woodland elves became outcast, no matter where we settled. No one thought us as clever or as learned as your kind, and so we were shunned almost, or cast aside as mere lackeys to do the dirty work of all who needed it. My father was the first who began to catch on to the treatment we received, and he was a high and respected Elder of the Circle, so they told him, so he began to demand equal rights with those of the waterfolk. No one listened, of course. Except when the bungling idiots of the Council found their precious Arkenchest endangered, they found a good bone to throw to the woodland folk in the entrusting of one of the Five to Eiorn. That was just the thing, they thought, to keep us quiet for a little while."

Tyron threw back his head and laughed aloud.

"Yet now it seems they are all through laughing, and I, Tyron, King of Gilden, yet hold the Secret safe against all enemies. And I count the Circle as enemies, Urien, as well as the waterfolk, who were at one time kinsmen, but no more. I call you not elf, but a puppet of Mankind, and an enemy of Tyron."

An ugly rumor of harsh whispers crackled through the group of woodland elves that had encircled Tyron and Urien. Tyron's eyes were all white, and a tight, drawn smile was painted across the mask of his face. Urien Typhon, without glancing once at the threatening movements of the smaller elves around him, looked at Tyron evenly.

"Do you see what has happened, my friend? Do you hear what you are saying? All lies that the Dark Queen has fed into your mind. You know better than any of the things you say. You well know that the glory of all Elfdom is shared alike by each and every one of us. Your father was highly esteemed by every member of the Council, and every elf who knows the least about his own history knows that the woodland folk and waterfolk have always worked side by side in all their journeys, and on each of their ventures. And there is no truth in what you say of the woodland folk being looked down upon or cast aside. Those are all pure lies that have been planted in your heart by Dorini." Urien gathered his breath and went on. "And you speak strangely, Tyron, when you question whether the Lord of Windameir is still about."

"I shall be my own lord," hissed Tyron. "There is no need to run cowering to some imaginary old goat of a dead idea with my troubles. If I want to see action, and have my problems solved now, and quickly, I shall go to my true sovereign, Dorini. She is the only power in these realms that is worth following. I'm tired of the treachery of the Circle, and the bungling old fools who call themselves Masters. They know nothing, and have never done anything for me or my kindred except when by accident they blundered and let my father have the trust that I now hold. And that trust now is going to assure me this haven forever, and provide a long-unfulfilled promise for my people, who are but simple woodland folk." Tyron's eyes had become glazed and lifeless. "There is no other sovereign but Dorini. She is the ruler of these realms."

A party of Tyron's band leaped forward to seize Urien Typhon, who did not move to resist. Another figure appeared in the midst of the group unnoticed, and now raised a warning hand in a signal for silence.

"You have your gall, my impulsive elf, I shall give you that. It shall not make any difference as to the outcome of your fate, but it has given me pleasure to see," came the smooth, cool voice. "And it shall give me even more pleasure to see what you have hoped to prove by your coming. I know it is the schemes of those Masters of yours that send you into these parts, speaking treason to loyal subjects, but they, too, shall soon beg before me. There is no escape now, and it is only a matter of time until I shall have these worlds sealed forever."

"Your Darkness," barked Tyron, and bowed low to the cloaked figure of Dorini. "I had expected Doraki, or Froghorn."

"They shall be here. Are you prepared?"

"I am, Your Darkness."

"Good. Then our plan shall carry on. But give me the elf. I wish him for my amusement. He should be full of amusing stories, this fellow."

"Give her the puppet," snapped Tyron, bowing to Dorini and hurrying to carry out her command.

Surrounded by the threatening guard of woodland elves, Urien Typhon was escorted to her.

"Are you ready to act on your plan?" asked Dorini, addressing herself to Tyron.

"We are ready," replied Tyron in a surly voice, his eyes falling away from Dorini's glance.

"Have any of the others showed up yet, to entertain our little snare we have spread?"

"No, Your Darkness."

"Then I shall take this poor wretch of an elf and go back to my waiting."

Dorini held out an impatient hand, and Urien fell into a stumbling pace behind her and followed after her as she left the throng of Tyron's band. After a few more moments, and once out of earshot, Dorini turned to Urien and smiled, her dark eyes turning a light gray-blue, as clear and bright now as they had been icy black an instant before.

"You do well at playacting, good Urien. You always were a most amazing fellow."

"Thank you, my lady," replied the handsome elf.

"I only hope we have convinced our stubborn Tyron. Do you think he suspected it was not in truth Dorini, but that weak sister of hers, Lorini?"

Urien laughed softly.

"It was a performance that turned my own blood cold, whatever else it did for poor Tyron. His heart is so closed, all it would take to have him believe is to mention the name of your dark sister."

"He seems quite taken by her, does he not?" asked Lorini,

brushing back the cloak hood that had hidden her long, flowing golden hair.

"He is under her sway, no doubt, my lady. I have never seen him yet this bad. It is as if he were burned with a fever."

"She is a fever, dear Urien. She burns the love from your heart and soul, and fills your mind with the cancer of her hate. Yet even she is incapable of doing otherwise. It is the part she must play out, until it is come to its end. I love her, in spite of it all, although I do find myself at times afraid of her."

"I know it is all of the Purpose, but I do fear her too, my lady."

"I am surprised that Greyfax suggested this, knowing how I feel," went on Lorini. "He had a long talk with me about my feelings toward Cybelle, and I wasn't sure I would be allowed to do anything much beyond wait at the Beginning for all the action to be over."

"Yet he relented when you told him you could fill this part."

"I wanted to so badly," breathed Lorini. "I mean it has all come down to nearing the end, and I desperately wanted to do my part without missing cue, or going off as I did in Cypher. I allowed myself my old selfish emotions then, and I know I must have forgotten all I had learned, wanting Cybelle for my own self-centered reasons, and calling it love."

She smiled sadly, remembering.

"Just as I held on so dearly to Cypher for all the wrong reasons. And I totally forgot that Cypher was not the outside, physical realm at all, but the secret warmth of the heart, which can never fall or change at all, no matter what goes on beyond."

"Greyfax seemed to think you would play a good dark queen," said Urien.

"Yes. And I think I did it rather well. I tried to remember all the feelings, and how she would act. It was good for me to put myself in my poor sister's place."

"And Greyfax? He will be here with us?"

"When he is ready. He said, of course, that if the blow is to be struck, he will be here, along with the others."

"Do you think the dwarf will find his way through?"

"I'm sure it has all been arranged," said Lorini.

"Then I had best be getting back to my men, beyond the glen."

"And I must get on with my play," smiled Lorini.

In a terrifying moment, the beautiful Lorini had darkened, and covered her fair hair with the rough, black cloak hood. Urien Typhon bowed hesitantly, and hurried away into the gloom of the dense wood.

And beyond the stretch of wood where Tyron waited with his band, Froghorn Fairingay smiled to himself, and set out toward the Last Gate.

A Disenchantment

As Urien Typhon and the lady Lorini parted, another sinister shadow form hovered above the glade called Last Gate, and slowly settled down toward the figure of Tyron the Green. A marked change overcame the stocky elf, and his pale features drained. There was no conversation between the two forms, nor was any needed to let Tyron feel the displeasure of the dark Doraki. His empty eyes devoured the elf with a bottomless despair, and Tyron's heart was frozen in the mindless panic of a sheer black void, hollow and beyond ending.

A great, choking cry escaped Tyron, and he fell on his knees before the wispy, elusive form of Doraki.

"What is it you seek?" gasped Tyron, trying to speak above the high, piercing, icy wind that had enveloped him.

"I seek to find an elf with high designs who has abused himself for the last time of the goodness of Dorini's patience. This stupidity will be dealt with harshly."

"I have just spoken to Her Darkness," croaked Tyron, the effort to speak almost overpowering him.

"Blind, miserable scraping of an elf, you have not spoken to Her Eminence. You spoke with that meddling snoop of a sister. Somehow she has managed to poke her nose here, but she will be taken care of. We hold her brat, and that fact shall make the wench cower before us. I shall take the greatest delight of all in explaining to that wretched sister what exquisite plans I have in mind for her spoiled offspring."

Tyron made an inaudible noise deep in his throat.

"Speak out, imbecile! Don't you like our plan? Or do you feel left out? Perhaps we can arrange it so that you will be included in Her Darkness' games, eh. Would you like that? Just like that bungling fool of a Father of yours."

Tyron's eyes went wide, showing nothing but whites and large deep pools of shining black, reflecting the horrible gaze of Doraki.

"That is a lie. My father has gone to the Upper Havens. And I know that is beyond your realms."

Tyron's voice cracked, and he had to clear his throat several times as he spoke. Somewhere, deep in his innermost heart, he feared it was true, just as the horrible Doraki had said, yet he had to hold to that one hope, or all would be lost.

"We have brought you the trinket of your father's that he was so fond of. It was nothing to take it from him. He thought he, too, was to outdo Her Darkness, and would be able to secure his Havens by her aid and blessing. He soon found that one gets only what one bargains for. Her Darkness soon tired of his silly mutterings, and found no further use for him, and he had ceased to amuse her. He is with the rest of the pack of savages that went before him, tending to the less pleasant chores of my good lady's realms."

Doraki's empty gaze pulled Tyron's eyes to meet the terrible darkness.

"Perhaps you may see, if you look hard enough, what your own fate shall be."

Unable to tear his glance away from Doraki's eyes, Tyron felt himself drawn deeper and deeper into the closeness of that bottomless despair.

Distorted visions assailed him on all sides, and huge dragon heads, breathing hot, smoky air, and misshapen forms of Gorgolac warriors enveloped him. Crying aloud, Tyron tried to shut his eyes and cover his face with his hands, but he could not pull away from the disaster and terror of Doraki's mind.

Showering sparks of ugly red-orange flames leapt up all about Tyron, and he knew he was within the prison of Doraki's thoughts, and knew, without a trace of doubt, that he was hopeless, and doomed.

Great battle fires loomed and exploded across Tyron's mind, and scenes of massive chaos and blind fury staggered him and buffeted him about in a reddish-yellow, stinging wind that hurt his lungs as he breathed it. Gaping Worlugh warriors bared their throat-tearing teeth at him, and stretched out their dripping clawed hands to strangle him, and laughed horribly as he frantically backed away, turning this way and that, trying to find some escape from their horrible sounds and smells. Roasting pits of charred flesh appeared all about Tyron, and the spitted grotesque figures were all elves, of his own woodland clan. Tyron screamed and writhed in agony, and cried aloud for mercy from Doraki.

The dark scar of Doraki's mouth broke into an oozing wound of a smile.

"But you have not seen your precious father yet, safe in his Havens," sneered Doraki, and bent his thoughts once more at Tyron.

An aging, withered figure appeared, broken and doubled over from wracking pain and abject terror. Tyron stared at the gnarled figure for a long moment before he recognized something in the pathetic face. His father, Eiorn, seemed to be trying to say something through cracked and parched lips, but nothing came, only the creaking hiss of escaping breath over broken teeth.

Tyron shrieked and fell back a step, his drumming heart lodged in his dry throat. Doraki's brittle laughter clattered like dry bones in the wind, and his dark cape fluttered wildly, as if it were a cloud of skittering bats against the moon.

Tyron could not take his eyes off his father, and the broken old figure kept on trying to mouth a sentence. Nearer Tyron came, reaching out to the stooping thing that was his father, and trying to hear the words the muttering, dry lips tried to utter.

"Give up the trust," at last came the garbled words, barely understandable.

Tyron, shaking his dazed head wildly, tried to get away from the terrible likeness of his father, but the withered elf grappled toward him, holding out his gnarled claws that had once been hands.

"Get away!" screamed Tyron. "You're a trick. Keep away from me!"

Scrambling madly to avoid the deformed elf, Tyron fought his way free, and tried to run.

"It is the only way, son," croaked the thin voice. "You must give up the trust. Then you will be free, and they will let me go, too. I am held here because you will not give them the Secret. It will please them, and I can get away from these horrible places where they keep me, and be rid of these things they torment me with."

"You're not my father, you old thorn. Get away, do you hear? Leave me alone."

A faint glimmer of light brightened the ancient elf's face, and he tried to smile, showing his broken teeth.

"You will give it to them, Tyron. They came for me, where I was, and took me away, and I shall never escape them unless you give them the accursed Secret. It is not worth it, my son. It only led me into trouble, and has gotten you involved as well. Give it to them, and they promise a long and peaceful journey, and rest, without all this torment. Think of it, Tyron. Rest, with no thought of danger, or anything else to upset you. Just peace, dark, deep peace, and nothing to trouble you again."

Tyron's eyes had rolled back in his head, and he was beating the air with his clenched fists.

"Get away, you old fool, stay away. There is no such peace as you speak of, and I know you are a trick to try to pry the trust from me. They know that unless I give it up freely, it will do them no good. Now they try to take it from me this way, trying to trick me with you, you horrible old ogre. I know you are no more than an illusion of Doraki's, and I won't listen."

Tyron clasped his hands over his ears and shut his eyes

tightly, trying to repeat to himself that he knew it was all a plan of Doraki's that lured him into the temptation of giving up the Secret, and that none of what appeared to be happening was reality. But he soon felt the dreadful whirlpool of Doraki suck him into the waking nightmare again, and the old elf motioned to him from behind a high iron-barred gate.

"Wouldn't you like to save yourself all this agony, Tyron?" crooned the buttery voice of Doraki, who was suddenly taking another tack. "It would free your old father from Dorini's games, and enable you both to rest. Then you could give up these futile dreams you have of being responsible for the haven that you are so concerned about."

"This haven is for the good of my kinsmen," shouted Tyron, glad to have to face only Doraki's tongue. The frightening thing to deal with was the cunning, powerful mind of Dorini's underlord.

"Your kindred are not worth all this," assured Doraki. "Look at the lot of them wagging their tongues, and completely worthless for anything but taking up breath. They could not even hold Urien Typhon when he so boldly showed himself, and then to add to the insult of that, you were all taken in by the imbecile sister of Her Darkness, and completely duped. But it is only to be expected of your woodland elves. Urien Typhon and his kind have always represented a more dangerous threat than any number of you or your puny brothers. Woodland elves seem to be of a nature as dense as the trees they take their name from."

Doraki drew back his cruel lips into a snarling laugh.

"It is some clever amusement Dorini has had, listening to the rantings of a half-dwarfish elf, who has the audacity to assume he has anything of interest to offer Her Darkness."

Tyron, turning a deep shade of purple, was beginning to feel his old fierce pride overcome the icy terror he felt of Doraki.

"Perhaps it is just as well that I hold to this trust," he gasped, forcing the words to sound calmer than he was. "I know I am safe from you as long as I hold that Secret in the forepart of my mind, just as I am safe from your dark mistress as long as I can make her doubt that holding the Chest will make her stronger, or enable her to carry out her wicked designs."

Doraki growled, and turned to the cowering band of elves who were standing in a circle about them.

"Look at these miserable gnomes. They are more lumpish than sack potatoes, and as worthless as allies. Just as you are, concerning whatever worth you may think you have to Her Darkness. Fat, and puffed up, just like a dwarf, that's what you are, and the miserable lot of followers who have proclaimed you king of these woods have about as much sense as a stick of firewood. Perhaps less."

"I cannot overpower you, Doraki, or order you to leave," shouted Tyron, "but I can refuse to turn the trust I hold over to you, and I promise that so long as I draw breath, I shall fight you and your queen. You might hold terror and despair over my father, or then you may not. I know you and the mistress you follow will stop at nothing to gain your aim. It may be only a lie you have created to make me believe you do hold my father. I know only to believe nothing I see or hear from you."

"You might well do better to believe more in both," said Doraki softly, in a frozen voice. "Dorini is not going to be pleased when she hears what has passed here. She does not find it in her plans to take mercy on bunglers or the mistakes they make. And she is especially unkind about any matters to do with that weak-willed sister of hers."

"I'll risk her ire," shot Tyron. "And I shall hold my trust intact."

"Even at risk of losing your own father?" asked Doraki coldly, his scar of a smile creeping slowly across his icy features.

"I don't think you do hold him, even though you've given me his ring," replied Tyron. "Anyone could have stumbled across that bier. And it is nothing for you to lie in order to gain your ends."

"We shall see, my fine friend," said Doraki. "I have my orders concerning you. I can't touch you as long as she finds you interesting and your paltry schemes amusing. But she tires quickly, elf, and then I shall find my own way of amusing myself with you."

An ominous note crept into Doraki's voice.

"I've been known to entertain myself with elves for centuries at a time."

Before Tyron could reply, Doraki had fluttered darkly against the wind and was gone, leaving him to double his fists and shake them angrily at the late afternoon stillness.

Beyond the Last Gate

New Directions

Otter stood silent and still on the dust-covered table, and his eyes filled with the long-forgotten memories that came to him in soft, flowing motions, just as the sweep of the water in Cheerweir had once lulled him to sleep as he floated quietly on its glass-green surface. From behind him came low rumbling smacks and growls, and much noise of sticky gulps and slurps. Ned hurriedly poked a thin finger into the honey jar and passed it on to Flewingam, who sat it back on the table where Bear had found it.

"What on earth do you suppose Dwarf has gotten up to now?" mumbled Bear, shaking his huge head. "I had hoped maybe Greymouse was right, and that we would be seeing an end to all this, but I don't see how any of it's going to come out right if we don't get that lump of a dwarf back and get the Chest safely to Greyfax and Lorini, or to somebody, anyhow, who can take it back to the Circle."

"Do you remember this, Bear?" chittered Otter, ignoring what his big friend had been saying.

"Remember what?" snapped Bear shortly.

"When we found you, you had on that silly cape, and that hat that was so small you had to put it between your ears."

"It was a very unusual hat," said Bear indignantly, "and I do most assuredly remember the event you speak of. I was working one of my spells, trying to brush up on my lore learning."

Otter giggled, getting down off the table and walking toward the back of the cavern. He stopped in front of the huge, empty keg that had held the heady bear brew.

"Lore learning, all right," snickered Otter. "You'd had a snootful of lore learning."

"Well, you certainly found out soon enough that you had no business messing about with a bear's brew. If I recall rightly, I had to carry both you and Dwarf to bed and let you sleep it off."

"It was all full of bubbles, and tickled my nose," chirped Otter. "But it wasn't so much fun when I woke up from my nap. It felt like a tree had been standing on my head, then. I'm glad it's all gone, and that we don't have to do that anymore."

"Does I suspects bear brew is sort of likes ale, or that sorts?" asked Ned Thinvoice, coming from the dim cave entrance to stand beside Otter.

"Well, you could say it was something of that nature, Ned," blustered Bear, "although good bear bark brew is more like medicinal tea, or at least it was the way I made it. Nothing fancy, just the good stout recipe that my old sow had given me as a cub."

"Ned had twisted the dry spigot, and stood trying to peer over the edge of the tall keg.

"It don't has nothing to it, drat the luck," he said, turning the spigot so violently the tap came off in his hand.

"That are sure a piece of luck for us," put in Cranfallow. "Seeing as how you never could hold no ale down nohow. And when you did, you was always up to some nonsense or other that would lands you smack in the middle of a drubbing, or worse."

"That's all you knows, Cranny. I has seen you full of the gourd on guard, with your shooter all crammed full of goat cheese and your eyes plumb crossed."

Flewingam had knelt beside the imprint of the dwarf boot as the friends were talking, and was studying the markings intently.

"I think you both may as well give up the idea of any sort of goings-on like that," he said. "At least, it seems that way. And things do get a bit dim, now and then. Like what happened here? And who did Dwarf meet? And where have they gone?"

"It were more fun talking about being full of the gourd," complained Ned. "At least I know'd something about them sorts of things, or I did one time or other. I don't reckon there is anything of them likes on this side of that fool River Dwarf has gotten us acrosst."

"We all feel that way, Ned, but we've got to get to Dwarf before he really does do himself some harm. Or find out where he is, so Froghorn or Greyfax can get to him. And we might as well face the fact that we are going to have to chase him down here, just like we were doing before we crossed Calix Stay. I know that sounds a little much, and I don't understand it all, or why it's happening, but that seems to be what's going on. And Froghorn may have known this was going to happen, and be on his way back now."

Bear snorted.

"When have we ever known of a wizard showing up when he was needed?"

"Sooner or later they always come through," replied Otter defensively.

"Oh yes, fine, after everything's all settled, and the dust has cleared, and there are no more little odd jobs to clear up. That's usually my recollection of the good Greyfax showing up, or the ever clever Froghorn, always popping in right at the moment that everything has been taken care of and all the work is done."

"And it are a mighty strange note for Froghorn to be atootin' off that way," said Ned. "Almost as odd as aleaving us in charge of that damp rag of a dwarf what has spooked hisself into arunning off smack in the middle of an enemy camp, and acoming up with what looks like another what are just like him." Ned moaned and rolled his eyes.

"And look here, Bear," chittered Otter excitedly. "Dwarf, or his friend, or both of them have been reading some part of your old library."

"That would be a most unlikely pastime for someone who is trying to get away from something," said Flewingam, coming and looking at the row of books that had been disturbed.

Flewingam scanned the rows of heavily bound volumes, then turned to Bear.

"Where did you find all these? And how did you get them here?"

"When I made my first camp here, before I ever heard of Dwarf or any of his doings, I found this cave, ready-made, it seemed, for the likes of a bear to move into. It was commodious, and dry, and had unlimited possibilities. So I took up my abode here, and begin straightening, and sorting, and digging, and turning it into a first-class shelter."

Bear paused, and indicated the deeper shadows that filled the rearmost section of the cave.

"Back there, not too far, I discovered that this cavern is but the top part of a very complex system of shafts and tunnels that run all through this part of the woods. I found three or four escape holes, in case I should ever need a spare door or two, and three or four secret ways of getting back and forth to certain places in Gilden Wood, although at that time I never needed anything of that nature, and so promptly forgot most of them. However, I did keep on exploring whenever I got the chance, and I stumbled across this cache of books one day, deep below where we are now. I couldn't for the life of me figure out then how they got there, or who they had belonged to. They seemed to be written in many tongues, so I assumed it must have been Mankind, and that for some reason or other, some purpose had existed for putting all those volumes in so deep a shaft, in such an out-of-the-way place as Gilden Wood."

"Were it some Mankind what done it?" asked Cranny.

"Well, I thought so, and it frightened me for a while, for I thought perhaps it might be the sort of thing that someone would come back for. I sniffed out another safe hiding place or two for myself, but naturally no one ever showed up. It was all my rather vivid imagination that had let me worry about something getting into the Gilden Wood. In those times, it was safe from anything crossing Calix Stay. I don't know what's happened now, but it's different."

"So you found all these books below, then?" persisted

Flewingam, who had paced a few steps toward the wall of darkness that lingered beyond the pale golden fingers of the candles.

Bear nodded.

"And then, after I had waited for a time, and there were no others in the wood, and no attempt made to recover the books, I explored farther, and deeper, down until I felt that the very heart of the earth must be close by."

Bear smiled knowingly.

"Of course, we have gone much deeper, and even met the Roots, but I knew nothing of all that then, and grew afraid to go too far beyond the light of the upper caverns."

"These footprints lead off down that way," said Flewingam. "Wherever Dwarf is bound, he isn't traveling outside."

"What do you mean, Flew?" chittered Otter.

"Look. These tracks head in, and there's no tracks pointing the other way. Clever trackers can always walk backward if they are trying to throw someone off their trail. But look. These footprints are all over here, first the one set, then the other. Now look. All these move off together, in the same direction, going farther on into the cavern."

Otter and Bear both bent and studied the tracks closely, and Ned and Cranfallow joined them.

"Well, if I isn't hornswargled," breathed Ned. "It are another one of them paths what leads down into some snake's kitchen." He snorted disdainfully. "But there ain't agoing to be the likes of old Neddy Thinvoice agoing down there no more. I has learned my lesson, I has. Ain't no rhyme or reason for any living thing to be agetting out of the sunshine, nohow. Leastways, not by agoing down no worm's slide into what should better enough be left alone."

Cranfallow nodded his full agreement with wild nods of his head. "I is still ashaking all over from getting drowned in that washout," he said, "and I ain't about to go back in no more dark holes like this."

"I don't blame you," answered Flewingam quietly. "I don't feel any great urge to have anything to do with this myself, except that we are supposed to be trying to find Dwarf, and to be getting on toward the hills Froghorn showed us."

"And that there are a right proper idea," said Cranfallow. "I think we all is after tagging around in the wrong neck of the woods. What we should ought to be after adoing is agetting ourselfs out of this mess into a stronghold of Froghorn or Greyfax. Then there won't be no sense in none of this here agetting lost, or messing around in areas where old Cranny ought to be aleaving well enough alone."

"Hear, hear," put in Ned strongly.

"But if Dwarf has gone on deeper into somewhere from here, we'll have to follow after him," protested Bear. He hesitated in mid-speech, and his eyes grew wider. "I don't like to think of doing it, but what choice do we have?"

His thoughts had turned to the horrible moments that had followed his fall into the raging torrents of the Under Tide, and the darkness that had filled everything there, until he feared he would never see the cheerfulness of a bright sunshine-baked day again.

"If Dwarf is there, and there's someone with him, we'll have to go on," chirped Otter. "It won't do to leave him or whoever else it is. How would we explain that to Froghorn? Or anybody?"

"Easy. We just tells him the way of it, and hopes he knows

a right lot about dirt holes and such, and then we'll just brings him back here, and he can do all the snooping around he is after doing."

"Ned may have a point," conceded Flewingam. "I have no real desire to go off poking around these tunnels without Froghorn. Maybe we could stay here until he returns, and go on from there."

"How do we know he'll find us?" asked Bear. "And if he does find us, he'll only make us go on in the cavern after him."

Otter had gotten back on the rough, carved table again and whistled loudly and raised a paw.

"Whatever we're supposed to do, I would suggest that we not broadcast it all over these woods. There are enough of those elves out there somewhere, according to Bear, to have the lot of us up for morning pound cake. The question is, where is Dorini? Or Doraki? Things have taken a turn for the worse because we have found out that the Darkness can disguise itself at times and trick all the answers it needs right out of you."

"Well, whatever we're to do, it's not going to keep us safe here forever," said Flewingam. "However, I do see some interesting books to read."

"And that was what we was atalking about when we was astarting out," announced Ned, "Atalking about them books, and what could have happened to our Dwarf."

"This started out to be a real homecoming," said Bear gloomily, hanging his great head, "but now I see it's taken a turn for the worse. And I can see now that the dwarf Broco has met is probably one of the long-lost cousins of the fellows that must have done all the other work that's down below. Some of the tunnels are just like the dwarf-wrought places we've seen, Otter."

"You mean there are dwarf halls below here?" asked Otter, his gray muzzle whiskers wrinkling into a frown.

"I didn't know it at the time," continued Bear, "and I hadn't seen any dwarf delvings, so I naturally thought it was all from Mankind."

"How far down do they go?" asked Flewingam.

"Not nearly so deep as we've been," replied Bear. "Deep is not the same, this side of Calix Stay."

"Then we could do it? Follow him, I mean? And not get anywhere near the troubled parts of the earth?" asked Otter, standing upright on his hind paws.

"Somebody else is agoing to have to does that," said Ned Thinvoice angrily. "I isn't ahaving no more to do with no holes, or no elfs, or no friends what has always been after asnooping around in snake dens." He cocked his head. "And I sure ain't having no truck with no more dwarfs, even if they can wiggle them big ears of theirs and stands on their heads till they is all blue in the face."

"That are a mighty fine speech, Ned," teased Cranfallow. "Only what is we agoing to do if we is hungry, and wants that sack of grub, and our friends here has gone on atrying to find Broco? And that means they is agoing to be a far piece from Neddy and Cranny, unless them two worthless galoots is with 'em."

"I doesn't like it none at all," complained Ned.

"Hush!" cautioned Otter. "There are sounds coming from somewhere below here."

All the companions quietened and tried to listen for the sound Otter had heard, but nothing beyond the dusty silence spoke, and a dark ring of uneasiness began to settle about their hearts.

Prelude

Greyfax Grimwald looked gravely down the long table at Froghorn Fairingay, who sat with his head in his hands. Lorini stood behind him, a slim, fair hand on his shoulder.

"Well played, good Fairingay. It could not have been done better," said Lorini lightly.

"I feel as if I've betrayed the Circle," muttered Froghorn, his voice barely audible.

"I know what you feel, my young whelp," assured Greyfax. "I have had occasion to do what you have done, and I can understand the feelings you are suffering. It is well played, yet it does not sit so well inside."

"And you, my lady?" asked Froghorn. "Do you not feel amiss after you have played the role of your dark sister?"

"I feel something, dear Fairingay. I don't know if it is amiss or not. I have had a new look at my sister, through her own eyes, and I can see the terrible misery and suffering she endures. Perhaps that is what you are feeling about your becoming Doraki for a few moments in your dealing with Tyron."

"I don't quite know what you're driving at," replied Froghorn, knitting his brow and looking sideways at Lorini.

"I mean this. I had an opportunity, and was instructed by the High Lord of Windameir himself, to do this thing that I have done in taking on the identity of my sister. And I began to see as I portrayed her what she must see and feel, and it was frightening and sad."

"I think Lorini has hit upon it, old fellow. Perhaps you, too, are feeling a small bit guilty at your rough treatment of Tyron."

"That, among other things," answered the young wizard. "It was not pleasant to treat the hardheaded elf that way, even though he is capable of driving you mad with his eternal quest to found a safe haven for all those who follow him and his clan. But I certainly didn't want to have to torment the fellow so."

"Your treatment of Tyron was necessary if our plan is to carry through without fail. There is no going back now."

"Greyfax speaks wisely, my young pup, and it has already come to the last dealing now. You heard what Erophin has decreed."

"I heard, yes. But it is hard to believe that it is really so serious as all this."

"It is more than serious, Froghorn. You were not yet of the Council of Elders when we went into these times before. There were dissolutions then, up to the Last Gate, and all was undone that had been done, and we all spent a time above the boundaries, until he saw it best to create these lower worlds once more."

"And that's when it all began with our lady and her sister," said Froghorn. "That much I am familiar with."

"And now it seems it is to come about again, only this time the lower worlds are not to be unmade. The World Before Time shall go on yet longer, and nothing will be undone there. All that will change is that the Arkenchest and the Secrets must remain there, to guide those left to the Path Home."

"And all the others are joining us here," said Lorini. "I hardly dared hope it would come about this way, yet it has surpassed my wildest dreams."

"When are we to meet Greymouse and Melodias?" asked Froghorn, brightening somewhat.

"They are gathering their forces even yet, and proceeding to the Last Gate. And I think we may find Cephus Starkeeper there, too. Perhaps even Erophin." Greyfax smiled, and paused a moment before going on. "So you see, your charade has been necessary, if we are not to disappoint all our friends."

"I still don't feel quite right about it," went on Froghorn, dejectedly.

"It was an experience I'm sure you won't have to repeat again soon, old fellow. Doraki shall be most inclined to portray himself, I fear, from now on out."

"And they shall both be wondering, he and his mistress, what has caused this new and dangerous side of Tyron to emerge. He will probably be a little less than happy when Dorini and her Doraki show up."

"But Tyron has no power over them. What if I've angered him to the point that he does something foolish, and Dorini slays him? Or worse?"

Greyfax stood, and pushed his chair aside before he answered his young friend.

"Dorini already has attacked the mind of Tyron and planted the seeds of her darkness there. He is, to some extent, merely an unthinking tool in her hands, who has no choice but to do her will. And Broco, having been captured and taken to her Ice Palace, is in some cases in danger of the same thing. She has long arms to reach and control those of her followers who fear her and move in the shadows of her hatred."

Lorini broke in as Greyfax finished speaking.

"It is not all hatred. After my experience at becoming my sister, I can see she must be dreadfully afraid for having dared to try to challenge even Windameir. She moves from fear, I can see."

"Fear, yes, if you call blind terror and greed fear. It has crept over her slowly, from the new Beginning. At first she was not too amiss in her dealings below the boundaries, as she governed the lower worlds hand in hand with Lorini, her sister. Then more and more, she came to find the power sweet, and her mind became enamored with controlling all of these lower creations. She attacked and drove her twin, who shared that reign, from her lower worlds. Lorini, after leaving, came to Cypher, to hold the boundaries safe. Now Dorini has made her all-out attack, and knows that she risks all, and is too frightened to leave the Chest, for she knows that as long as it is in existence, her lies will sooner or later betray themselves."

"And then all those she holds sway over will see the truth, and remember where they have come from, and set out upon their journey Home." concluded Lorini.

"Still, Dorini must act, and act once for all. There is one here who carries the thing she dreads the most, yet desires above all things. That is the Arkenchest, and the Five Secrets it holds. She knows if she is to carry on her designs, she must capture the Chest and overpower it, or fall. Those are the choices she has now."

Froghorn wiped a hand across his brow.

"Has she a chance at overpowering the Chest?"

Greyfax frowned, looking away toward the glowing golden sunlight beyond the window.

"The thing is not whether she has the power to overcome the Secrets or the lure of the Chest. We know she can't overcome the attraction of having to know whether or not she can overpower Windameir's Creation. And she has kept the lower worlds long in darkness and ignorance. Look for yourself."

Greyfax turned, speaking slowly.

"Look at all the lifetimes we have spent below Calix Stay, striving to keep alive the knowledge that the Secrets exist and are available to all those whom Windameir has called back onto the Homeward Journey."

The older wizard smiled slightly.

"Yes, I do think she has the power to overcome the Secrets."

Froghorn gasped.

"But I don't know for how long," finished Greyfax.

"That, I think, we shall find out at the Last Gate," said Lorini.

"And that is exactly where it has all been leading, ever since we began again," went on Greyfax. "And it's odd to think of it, though, that it shall come to pass in this way.

Here the very source of all Creation is being carried about by an ambitious elf and a half-crazed Dwarf, who is suffering from the same malady. And the two of them are about to clash, and not merely for rule of Gilden Wood, or Gilden Tarn, but the question is even bigger still, of who, the Darkness or the Light, is going to rule supreme in the lower meadows of Windameir."

"There won't be much Dorini can do without all her armies," suggested Froghorn in a reassuring tone, more to calm his own doubts than any of those held by Greyfax or Lorini.

"Our armies here are not so great either," said Greyfax. "Apart from the boundary guards, and those who have crossed and stay close to the River, there are not many who march to our colors here. At least, not in the sense we are talking of, in terms of armies."

"And we will have Erophin, perhaps. And Melodias, and Greymouse, and Cephus, as well as Galen and Urien Typhon and his host. Not to mention ourselves," offered Lorini.

"Indeed we shall," agreed Greyfax. "We have had all these and the rest of the Circle arrayed against your sister for the length of Creation, and that has not yet stopped her. Dorini is also a child of Windameir, and despite her dark designs, does have all the powers that we possess as his children too. But all our efforts have never seemed to stop Dorini, and I suspect the reason why is that the lady is serving her purpose well. Just, perhaps, as we are ourselves."

"I've never heard this before," said Froghorn, slightly taken aback at the older, graying figure's words.

"I've never said it aloud before," said Greyfax simply. "And I haven't been asked about it either."

Lorini stood studying Greyfax silently.

"You know, my lady," he said, addressing her, "that we have been at this business since before we can remember. It has dragged on for what seems eternities, yet there is neither total Darkness nor total Light in these lower realms. We have come upon the brink of ruin time and time again, yet at the last moment there is always something that turns the tide and wins the day. Or stays the hand of Dorini from taking complete victory for herself."

"What are you driving at, Greyfax?" asked Froghorn.

"I'm driving at nothing. What I'm doing is observing something that just this moment occurred to me."

He returned to his chair and sat once more before going on.

"I don't know why I haven't thought of it before. Too simple, really. And right there under my nose all along."

"What's under your nose?" shot Froghorn, bringing a fist down on the table before him.

"You are always the one, my boy, who knows just how to put a question," laughed Greyfax. "And the answer is that it is all right under our noses, when we finally open our eyes to look at it."

He paused, stroking his beard.

"Or stated in another way, we only see a thing from one point of view at a time. When we get so used to looking at a given object in a certain way, we only see it in that light, even when we are given another side of it to look at. If you show me carrots, and say they are carrots, I will believe you. Now take those carrots away and put other carrots in their place. You still have carrots, yet they are different."

"Don't tease," chided Lorini.

"I'm not, dear lady. I'm merely at my lessons with this

young whelp again, although I don't think I'm bringing my point home."

"That, at least, I can agree with," complained Froghorn bitterly.

"It all comes down to this," said Greyfax simply, "We have all been at exactly what we were supposed to be at. In the interim, those who were ready to go Home were shown the Secrets, and they have long since gone, or are in the process of going. True, Dorini keeps many in the darkness of her worlds, and has for quite some space of lifetimes, yet always, even at the last moment, it seems the Light of Windameir shines through, and total defeat of the Circle is avoided."

"What do you call the, loss of Origin and Maldan then? And half of Atlanton Earth travels now through darkness," said Froghorn.

"Yet it is still not all Darkness, my young friend. Nor is it all Light. But I think we are approaching a time when one way or other it will be settled for all those below the boundaries. Dorini is here for the showdown, and Lorini is here also. It seems as if it is coming to a boil in the Meadows of the Sun."

"And what of Cybelle?" asked Lorini, her voice edged with a slight tremor.

"I suspect that we shall find that out soon enough. The characters in this last act are beginning to find their places, and the curtain is on the point of going up."

"Lorini has asked a good question, Greyfax. What of Cybelle?"

The young wizard faced Greyfax resolutely.

"I would like a clearer answer, for once. If I remember

rightly, we left Cypher then, after she was taken, and have passed more than a few lifetimes on one plane or another, gathering the forces of Light where we could and, I thought, dealing blows to Dorini that would enable Cybelle to escape."

"And that has all come to pass, my dear Faragon. Every single breath we have drawn has had a purpose, whether we realize it or not. And our work there was done just as it was willed. We struck the necessary blows, but now the scene is set for the blows to be felt. Your Cybelle is within a thought of rescue. All we need do now is make ourselves available to help the one who shall lift the latch and free her from the dark shroud of Dorini."

"You know who her deliverer will be?" shot Froghorn.

"Only that he is not to be one of us," replied Greyfax.

Froghorn and Lorini both gasped aloud.

"But for now, we must be off. I feel it is growing time that we place ourselves where our parts demand. Soon our good opponents will be seeking us, to go on with this game we have begun."

Froghorn had started to protest and ask a question, but Greyfax cut him short and delivered new instructions to the impatient young wizard, who stormed out of the room abruptly.

Greyfax and Lorini were left alone momentarily, but soon they, too, were gone, speeding on their way to meet the gathering storm clouds that had begun to build above the Gilden Wood.

And at the crossing known as Last Gate, the scene was set for many final meetings.

Old Wounds Forgiven

In an empty corridor far below the ancient dwelling of Bear, Creddin showed Dwarf the many passageways that led into different parts of the old delving. Some were dusty and unused, and showed no signs of being disturbed.

"Where do those go?" asked Broco, pointing to a tunnel mouth that branched into another opening, then disappeared into the shadows beyond the flickering flames of the torch.

"I'm not sure where all of them go, coz. I've only been at my exploring here for a while. There are some that run on deeper, but I've had no real desire to see them. Too far away from the light. I guess I've had enough of living below the sun."

"There must be hundreds of these that are unexplored," went on Broco, elbowing the old dwarf out of the way and taking the guttering torch from his unsteady hand.

"There are many, for a fact. I've noticed a few that probably lead to the old sleeping chambers, and a few that run on down to the wells. More than one of them reaches right on to the River."

"I have no need of going that far," snapped Dwarf.

"Nor do I, coz," replied Creddin lightly. "Not now, at any rate."

"What about the other entrances that lead on to the outside? Have you found them?"

"More than one. It seems as if someone has plugged some of them up and dug some others open. I've even found some tote kegs of honey stashed in a few of them."

"Bear, the silly ass! He was forever poking any nook and cranny full of food. He probably had intended to use those tunnels as an escape hole, should he ever need one. He was always intent on having more than one entry to any cave he lived in. Otter, too, for that matter. Silly animals, always concerned with having someplace to go. It made heating impossible, and there was always a draft from somewhere."

"Sounds sensible to me, coz," answered Creddin. "I always sleep a bit easier if I know I have more than one door to slip out of if I need it."

"Well, it's all nonsense to me. If you are going around worrying about something coming to get you, then you should have more protection than a few doors. All that means to me is that the more holes there are, the more ways whoever, or whatever, has to get in. Give me a stout dwarf-sealed chamber every time."

"Always by the books, eh, coz? That was what always led us into mischief, that bent for walling everything out. Whatever we didn't want to face, whether it was dragon hordes or greed for treasure, we always held to the idea that we could close it all out if only we dug deeper and delved farther into the earth."

Broco swept the torch before him as Creddin spoke, and burned away a thick layer of spider webs that covered an opening that was taller and somewhat lighter than the rest they had passed.

"Where does this go?" he asked. "And I don't want to know if it's walled or not."

Creddin stopped and looked down the passageway, watching the torchlight dance on the polished golden-colored sides of the tunnel.

"It leads to the outside too," he replied. "I've seen this entrance from the other end. There is a glade there. It's a most unusual place. I was there only once, yet I felt a strangeness. Almost as if I had been there before. It felt very odd, but it was like being someplace and knowing something has happened there that was very important, or that something will happen there that's very important."

"Poppyrot. What it says is that you hadn't the courage to move aside all these nasty things so you could take a look at what's on the other side."

And so saying, Broco held the torch to the sticky webs and burned away the draping strings and gray nets that blocked the passage. After quite some time, he had cleared a space large enough for him to enter into the golden-walled passage beyond.

"Are you going there, coz?" asked Creddin.

"Why shouldn't I? We have to know what we have here before we can see what we shall need to do in the way of renovations. And if this is an exit, I want to see if it can be secured more snugly than by a spider or two stringing a web across it. As you can see, that is not the surest way to keep intruders in, or out, for that matter."

"I'm not sure that I would go out there, coz," said Creddin doubtfully.

Dwarf turned suspiciously.

"Why wouldn't you, you old thorn? I wonder? Have you hidden something here you aren't anxious for me to find?"

Broco's eyes reflected the torchlight, dancing in wild red patterns.

"No, coz, I haven't anything to hide anymore. I left everything of that nature below."

"Then why is it you don't want me to explore this particular hole?"

Creddin's old face took on a younger, softer look.

"Because I fear for you, coz."

Dwarf stared at Creddin a moment, then laughed harshly.

"You? Fear for me? And where, might I ask, was all that fine concern when it came to the fate of all those you led to their death, or gave to the Darkness? That's all well and good, that concern of yours, but if that's the end of it, thank you, I'll rest more at ease."

"I understand your feeling, coz. It has taken me a time or two to accept those things I did in my ignorance, but I have come to the point that I see what those lessons were. But you may accept, or reject, as you like."

"And I do, you old dry bones. I've kept you so long now only because you can be of some use, and perhaps make amends to the memories of all the noble dwarf lords and ladies you saw fit to murder in your greed for the treasures you lusted after. Beyond that, you are Creddin, traitor and butcher, and you stay alive here because I don't want the filth of your life on my hands."

"You make yourself exceedingly clear, coz. And I do understand. I shall try to tread softly, so as not to offend your loneliness."

"You're not much company, either," huffed Dwarf, turning and going on deeper into the new passageway. "Now come on! I don't want to argue with you. There are many things yet undone, and we've no time to be haggling about. This torch is beginning to burn out. Come on, we'd best try to make it to this strange glade you're speaking of."

"If you'd rather, we can go on back to the last storehouses. I know where there are torches there, and good candles that I've found."

"I have no interest in candles at the moment. Now, come on, or stay in the dark, as you wish."

"I'll come, coz, I'll come, but I'm still feeling odd inside. I don't know what it is, but I've got a knot down there, and it won't seem to go away."

Broco turned a questioning look on the old dwarf.

"Have you been up to some mischief? Answer me, you mangy old goat. Is there something down this shaft you know of that you're not telling me about?"

Creddin's old face knotted into a frown.

"I haven't the slightest intention of causing you harm, coz. I don't know of anything down this shaft, except that there is a glade beyond it, and a place that felt strange to me when I was there. And I think the knot is there because I keep wanting you to say you've forgiven me, I guess. Or that's part of it. I keep feeling that once I have your pardon for all the grief I caused in those times before, across the River, I'll be able to rest a lot easier."

Creddin had stepped closer to Dwarf in the bright circle of the torch, his old face creased with worry.

"You have your nerve," hissed Broco, his voice low and cool. "Asking that of one whose kindred were sold into darkness or death by the traitor who stands before me now contrite and sorrowful, and full of pity for himself. There is good reason why your rest is bothered, you snake-tongued old baggage, and even if it were within my power to forgive you, I wouldn't."

Creddin's thin voice creaked, and he had to clear his throat several times. "Is the thing you carry then such a mockery? Is it no more than an empty dream that will wilt away at the first sight of broad daylight?"

Broco's eyes narrowed into slits, and a sharp edge crept into his voice. "How do you think you have any right to mention what I carry? That is only for those who have earned the right to deserve its mercy." Dwarf huffed and went on. "It is a thing for all evil to fear, and it shall strike down all those who would labor to darken its glory."

Broco's voice cracked, and his eyes danced, and Creddin fell back a pace or two.

"There is no room in the heart of the Chest Bearer for forgiveness of those who have forever separated themselves from the Light. There is no returning for the murderer once the innocent blood has stained his hands."

Broco ranted on, swooshing the torch about dangerously, and as he brandished the light back and forth, he did not notice for a moment that the bent old figure of Creddin had disappeared. As the flames flickered and burned more evenly, and as his hand steadied, Broco scanned the tunnel in both directions. There was nothing but the empty, golden walls reflecting back the reddish glow of the torch.

"Where are you?" asked Dwarf, his voice trying to remain even.

A deep inner urge to scream out was welling up inside him.

He asked in a slightly louder tone, "Creddin? I know you're here! There's no need in playing these silly games of yours. Come out now, and I won't be angry. I shall be, if you continue on this way."

There was only silence after the echo of his voice died away, and the faint hissing of the dying torch.

"You miserable old imbecile!" shouted Dwarf. "Come out this instant! I forbid you to leave. No one leaves the Chest Bearer without his permission. I command you to come here."

The echoes from his shouting hurt his ears, and Dwarf whirled around, then back, trying to catch sight of the old form.

"Hiding isn't going to do you any good," shrieked Dwarf. "I know you're here, and I know you're trying to trick me. I won't give it to you, though. No one deceives the Chest Bearer. No one, do you hear me! Now come out! I order you to come out at once!"

The drumming echo beat against his ears, and Broco spun back and forth now, slashing the torch before him into the darkness, trying to make out the shadowy visions that seemed to fill the dark tunnel.

A shimmering movement caught his eye, and without thinking, Broco leapt forward, shoving the flames out before him.

"I've got you now, you rotten old traitor. You can't escape the justice of the Chest."

Shrieking at the top of his lungs, Dwarf swept on, faster still, chasing the vanishing form before him. Still on he went, gathering speed and falling into the new battle cry of calling out his own name. Broco lunged into the darkness of the strange tunnel, slashing and beating the air with the sputtering torch, until with one last fluttering burst of sparks, it coughed and went out, leaving him in a silent blanket of complete, smothering blackness that was almost too heavy to breathe.

Broco's voice came in a whisper now, almost a plea.

"Creddin? Are you there? Light another torch, will you? We have to get out of here."

There was a stillness so deep Broco could hear nothing but his own drumming heart, but as his eyes adjusted to the dark, he saw a pale halo of lighter air just ahead. He flung down the smoking stump of the torch and staggered toward the blue-black hole that loomed ahead of him, flinging his arms before him as he went, thrashing wildly, as if to beat away the thick black night of the golden tunnel.

"Creddin! I forgive you," at last cried Dwarf. "I forgive you! Now come out, do you hear!"

And almost at once Broco stumbled into a solid rock wall, turned away, and fell forward on his knees, facing the sharp outline of the old dwarf, against the bright haze of sunlight at the shaft mouth.

Broco sobbed aloud, and began crawling frantically for the freedom of the open air.

The Upper Boundaries

In the quiet glade of Last Gate, which guarded the upper boundaries of the Meadows of the Sun, Tyron the Green waited, along with his vast army of elves. Tyron himself, pale and haggard, paced about restlessly, while a dozen of his captains watched uneasily. There was no sound except the noise their leader made, and the wind had even held its breath, and no leaf stirred in the deep heart of the wood. At intervals, Tyron would stop his pacing and stare away into some unknowable distance, then resume his walk.

This had gone on for quite some time before a messenger hurried through the rows of elves sprawled about the glade and stepped up to Tyron.

"What is it, Thailwicke? What news have you brought?"

"We met with Greyfax, as you ordered. And we met what we expected. He is not to be dealt with easily."

"I could have told you that. And what did he tell you?"

"That he would, for the moment, accept your terms."

"The blasted bunch of hypocrites," shot Tyron. "They say one thing, and before the words are out of their mouths, they're doing another."

"He did not mention the dwarf again."

"I think we may have been played an ill tune, Thailwicke," said Tyron grimly, a deep frown creasing his even features. "He sent word that the bearer of the Chest was to be found trying to cross the upper boundaries at the Last Gate, yet what I ask myself is why? Did they take my terms well when you met with Greyfax earlier?"

"He acted as you said he would," replied Thailwicke. "He attacked us with his magic, and treated us most rudely, and then he said he would, for the moment, accept your kingdom of Gilden Wood. He did not say for a fact that they would stay beyond our realms, but then he did not say that he would try to enter either."

"It is no easier to deal with a dwarf," muttered Tyron. "I've only had trouble and grief ever since I've had dealings with any folk beyond my own. And the accursed wizards, and the Circle, and Dorini, and the lot of them, understand nothing of what makes a woodland elf what he is, or knows any of the dreams we dream."

"That they don't," agreed Thailwicke. "Greyfax taunted me with the memory of seeing me as a small tad, and tried to play on my emotions, but I wouldn't let him carry off that ploy. He was only trying to throw me off-balance to gain an edge for himself."

"I will say one thing for Grimwald," said Tyron in a softer tone. "He has always been fair in his dealings with me. Of course, I know why, for no one dared anger me, seeing that I have one of their precious Secrets. Only it's no longer theirs, now. They shall all have reason to wonder at Tyron before this scene is played out to its finish."

The small elf laughed bitterly.

"Urien has certainly played an odd game with us. Still, I don't know who or what to believe. As far as I can tell, Dorini is amusing herself with him at this moment, although her underling tried to make me doubt my own eyes and ears and convince me that I did not in truth deal with the Dark Queen. But he will do anything to attain his ends. And I think he overenjoys tormenting his victims. He has tried to make me think he holds my father, and now he tries to make me believe that Dorini is in truth the other sister."

Thailwicke looked hard at Tyron.

"Was it necessary to turn Urien over to her?"

"She demanded the impudent fellow, whoever she was. And I've long thought that Urien Typhon needed his comeuppance. He's lorded it over us all this time now, always egging us on with his bawdy lies about the feats of the waterfolk doing this or that, or bringing up the lore learning of his kindred or their exploits. I think we'll let him stew awhile, wherever he is, then perhaps we will see what we can do about having him freed. I don't care to have him settling in our haven, though."

"No," agreed Thailwicke. "I don't expect that I would like that. He makes me feel too uneasy for that. But I would like to see him freed. No elves, not even waterfolk, deserve to be imprisoned."

Tyron had stopped pacing momentarily.

"You are exactly right, Thailwicke. I shall demand Urien's

release to me. And then I shall take great pleasure in tossing him out of Gilden Wood on his ear. And with that, we shall prove to him once and for all that the woodland folk are mighty, and are as wise and powerful as their snobby cousins."

"That, perhaps, will take some doing," said Thailwicke, lowering his voice.

"We shall have our bargaining tool, if you're worried about that," answered Tyron. "I know that Greyfax doesn't lie. I have dealt with him long enough to know that if he says an event will occur, it will occur. And I think he has finally seen the folly of the Elders of the Circle turning over the Arkenchest to a mere dwarf. I simply cannot see whatever reason at all they might have had for that act of stupidity. Yet I think Grimwald is perhaps coming around to the point of view that the Chest would be better off with us in Gilden Wood, where it would be safe from Dorini, than with this wretched dwarf, who from all indications has come unsettled from his senses."

"I'm in agreement there," replied Thailwicke, "but I wouldn't trust Greyfax any further than that. I'm sure he has something up his cloak sleeve."

"I'm sure he does," said Tyron. "They don't give up easily, and I have dealt with Master Grimwald on more than one occasion."

The elf paused, deep in thought.

"No, the illustrious Greyfax is certainly not going to give away any advantage. Yet what could he possibly hope to gain in this exchange? Except that perhaps I might take the Chest, rather than surrender it to Dorini. That is the only advantage that I can see in this affair, as far as the Circle is concerned. And even with the Chest in my hands, and safe in the confines of Gilden Wood, it will do him no good."

"I think he wants it to be able to win himself the hand of Lorini," snorted Thailwicke.

"Don't underestimate him," said Tyron. "He may be overly clever, and devious, but I don't feel that he is an ambitious man in those realms. Misguided, yes, and a perfect puppet for the dupes that form the Circle. Although that, too, seems coming to an end, for I have had more than one conversation with Faragon Fairingay on the subject of the Circle and the rotten inner core of Elders who are all too old and inefficient to remain in power much longer. And somehow I like the idea better of dealing with Fairingay, rather than with Doraki."

"You mean one of their number is becoming tired of their whitewashed stories?"

"Not merely one, good fellow. I've talked with Cybelle, Lorini's own daughter, and she is with young Fairingay to the fullest extent of her support. They have both made mention that in redividing Cypher, once they come into power, and that will be as soon as I have the Chest safely in my hands, they will be most glad of my good favor, and will willingly concede all on this side of the lower boundaries to me, for use as a haven for all elves that might seek safety."

Thailwicke blew out his cheeks and whistled in surprise.

"That *is* news. Then it must be true, as the rumor runs."

"Which rumor?" asked Tyron.

"The one that runs to the effect that once Cypher has

fallen, all the rest of the Circle will gather for flight. It seems that already we are witnessing the destruction of the Council of Elders, and it is especially interesting that two of the Circle's most trusted and beloved members should be speaking treason to their own cause."

"Reason, good Thailwicke, not treason. It has grown evident that the ancient lies can no longer hold together the web of deceit they have spun. The truth must always out, no matter how long it takes."

As Tyron finished speaking, a party of a dozen or more elves bolted into the clearing, their bows and firearms unslung.

"There is a body of Urien Typhon's host moving toward us from the direction of Gilden Far, sir. And a large company of men and elves from the direction of Eastering Dell. Two of the Circle are at the head of it, and are making all haste to reach us here."

Tyron's dark features drained, and he stood frozen for a moment, his eyes unseeing.

"The dirty swine," he breathed at last. "They are incapable of keeping their word."

An alarm horn, blowing wildly through the glade of the Last Gate, roused the lounging elves there to their feet, and as suddenly as they had appeared, the scores of Tyron's great war band melted into the greenery of the thick wood, leaving no one in sight but Tyron himself and Thailwicke, his second-in-command.

"What do you make of this?" asked Tyron. "Did anything Greyfax say imply that the Circle was going to move against us in force?"

Thailwicke shook his head quickly.

"Nothing. There was no sign at all of any army, or of an immediate move of any sort at all."

Tyron paced back and forth hastily.

"I knew there was more to this than that which meets the eye. There is something else afoot here."

"We shall easily overpower anyone who dares to try attacking us on our own grounds," replied Thailwicke. "I can't believe that they would be willing to risk the heavy losses they would suffer should they fall on us here."

"I don't think I'm so sure they are going to do that, good Thailwicke. I don't know exactly what they are up to, but I don't think an attack is in their plans. It couldn't be, not at this moment. Froghorn said he was going to divert most of the army that is on this side of the boundaries to watching up and down Calix Stay, so there couldn't be too many in this battle host. Yet why are they threatening this way?"

"We can scout them out and see," suggested Thailwicke. "Perhaps we can lessen their number somewhat before they reach us, and thus discourage the thought of attacking us in force in our own woods."

Tyron raised a hand, restraining Thailwicke.

"No, no, that won't be necessary at all. I'm sure Dorini is going to want to see about some of this. And I would rather let her suffer the losses than risk losing any more of our band than we absolutely have to. It is, after all, not our fight here. All we want is a guarantee to a safe haven, and a closed border to all those who try to rob the trust I hold."

"What if she insists on using our forces?"

"We will refuse. There is no need for us to shed any more elvish blood for her, especially if there is no call to. And I think Greyfax Grimwald has more in mind than a brainless attack on us here. He could, after all, have set up a more elaborate plan than that if he had wanted to attack us in force. When he said that the Chest Bearer would be showing up at the Last Gate, trying to cross the upper boundaries, I'm sure he could have arranged a welcoming party here that would not have been to our liking."

Tyron frowned, and paced back and forth absentmindedly. He turned to speak to Thailwicke, and came face to face with the terrible beauty of Dorini, whose eyes danced dangerously across him, touching his heart with a darkness that almost smothered his breath. As he tried to speak, another figure, smaller than the elves, stumbled forward clumsily into a heap at Dorini's feet.

As Tyron glanced up from the new intruder, who had come from a thicket of red dewberry bushes a few steps from his right hand, he saw before him the daughter of Lorini, Cybelle. The Dark Queen, whose angry, piercing stare had rooted him to the spot a moment before, was nowhere to be seen.

"My lady," mumbled Tyron in confusion.

Cybelle was kneeling, putting a cool hand to the red-hot brow of a semi-conscious Dwarf, who was rambling wildly about forgiveness, and who turned suddenly in his wild attempts to pull free from the arms that held him and looked deeply into the beautiful face of Cybelle. Broco's hand clutched hers tightly, and he tried to speak, but his reeling thoughts collided within him, and his heart thumped loudly in his chest, and a thin, soft roof of blue stars and silver moons spread its snowy curtain across his sight, and he slipped away into an unknowing dream of a sleep so long and deep it lulled him into its snoring jaws, and just at the last, as he surrendered to its enticing song, did he see the frozen night spreading all around him, and feel the icy hand of the Dark Queen upon his very soul.

A Final Siege Is Mounted

"Who is this other miserable old baggage?" asked Tyron angrily, pointing a finger at the terrified form of Creddin, who stood frozen at the brush-covered entrance to the tunnel Dwarf had just come out of.

A dozen elves leapt on the old dwarf and dragged him roughly to throw him sprawling at Tyron's feet.

"I think I know that one," came Dorini's voice, speaking from her disguise as Cybelle.

"He gave me a moment or two of sport," added Doraki, who had appeared moments after his mistress. His cruel features were covered by the handsome face of Froghorn Fairingay.

"It's the wretched gnome who used to watch Tubal Hall for us," he went on. "His appetite for treasures never found its end, it seems."

"So it is indeed Creddin, is it?" crooned Dorini. "I think we shall have yet more sport of him before all is said and done."

Creddin, held fast by the stout hands of the woodland elves, looked uneasily at the form of Cybelle, and then at Froghorn.

"I beg your pardon, Your Grace," broke in Tyron, "but we've no time for either sport or pleasure at the moment. I've just received word that a force of Urien Typhon's folk is approaching from one direction, and another, led by some of those dolts of the Circle, is coming from Eastering Dell. I'm not sure what the rascals are up to, but I know it is an ill wind for us, unless we look to our defenses."

Cybelle's fair features darkened, and a harsh, cold laugh spilled from her shapely mouth.

"Indeed, he says, we must look to our defenses! It is almost time, Tyron, that you shall learn what it is to suffer fear, and understand what true power means."

A cruel, icy wind sprang up from nowhere and swirled about Tyron's feet, chilling him to the bone and leaving frosted fingers of snow in his hair and on his eyebrows. His breath came in frozen gasps, and filled the air before him with wispy white clouds.

"We have in our grasp now the most deadly defense of all," she went on. "This cursed filth of Dwarfdom has eluded me for long, and caused me much grief, and cost many lives. Needless blood has been spilled defending it, and it all was the fault of that bungling sister of mine. If the fools would have surrendered what this miserable gnome carries, all would have been settled on Atlanton Earth long ago. We would have had an end to all the chaos she and her meddling friends of the Circle have caused, and seen peace and order established for all."

"And I wouldn't have to worry about those beastly fiends always spoiling my fun," added Doraki. "It is never as much sport knowing that your game can be spoiled by a nosy, meddling wizard who has no sense of gamemanship. I miss my wars and my terror-stricken subjects below. And now it seems as if we'll have things our own way for a change."

"We must wait until he wakes," said Dorini. "I want him to see the hopelessness and despair of his defeat and downfall."

"Take it now, then let's taunt him with it," suggested Doraki. "Or better yet, let him think we haven't found it for a while."

"But what are we to do about Urien's host, and the others? I hear my signal horns now. The enemy is within our perimeters, and coming fast."

Tyron looked desperately at the beautiful form of Cybelle.

"Shall I have my men pull back?"

"No!" ordered Dorini. "Have them commence the attack."

Tyron gasped, and reeled backward a step.

"I cannot, Your Grace. That would be foolishness of the highest order."

"Order them to attack at once," she repeated, her voice iron-hard and echoing in the frozen wind that spun about her.

Thailwicke, who had stood speechless beside Tyron, moved as if in a trance, and put a small, mithra worked horn to his lips, and blew a long, high, strident note that slid up and down several times, then ended on a single short blast. Tyron struck the horn from Thailwicke's hand, but too late, for almost immediately from the woods all about them came the popping report of rifle fire and the elfin war cries as the host sprang to the assault.

All about them, the camp exploded into chaos and disorder. Swarms of elfin soldiers leapt about, firing their weapons into the air and screaming in loud, high-pitched voices their woodland battle calls.

Tyron raced back and forth, shouting orders and stopping elves here and there, but they merely looked at him blankly and struggled free, darting away in the direction of the deeper woods beyond the glade of the Last Gate.

Doraki, in the form of Froghorn Fairingay, turned and spun madly, and laughed long gales of icy, barbed laughter. His hand had gone to his side, and from beneath his cloak he had withdrawn an ugly black whip. Slowly he uncoiled its black tail and shook it out before him. An elf stumbling blindly by, firing his weapon carelessly over his head, his eyes glazed and rolled back in his head, suddenly pitched forward and writhed helplessly about, maddened and crazed, and wracked with the brutal pain of Doraki's lash, which had bitten deeply into him.

Tyron, realizing that all his plans had gone awry, picked up the horn he had knocked from Thailwicke's hand and blew the urgent, plaintive call of retreat and regroup, but the horn's voice was lost amid the fury of the storm that broke all about him. Gunfire and battle cries rang like wind-driven seas gone mad, and the howling, shrieking hosts of Tyron surged through the glade of the Last Gate and on into the deeper wood, crashing like waves on the barriers of the forest, swirling angrily about, then pouring on over all obstacles.

In another moment, a new and different battle horn was sounded, and Tyron knew from the call that his woodland folk were locked in mortal combat with the waterfolk of Urien Typhon. That dam had at last burst free, and the two elfin clans had broken the ties that bound them.

And Tyron felt a sad, lost note from the dreams of his earliest youth falter and drown under the madness and turmoil of the battle. He bowed his head, and a sudden sob wracked his small, wiry frame.

And beside him, Dorini laughed her harsh, cruel laugh that tore into his very heart, and wrung from it all pity and sorrow and put in its place the dull, leaden dagger of hopelessness and despair. The bright fire that had blazed there was slowly extinguished, and the black cloak of Dorini's realm closed swiftly over it, like dark water over a candle. He stood transfixed, staring blindly before him, and the tears that had begun were dried, and his eyes misted over in a dull gray frost of undying death.

And Broco, awakening in the fury of the holocaust that flared all about him, came to his senses, and struggled to sit up.

"What is it?" he cried, his reeling mind trying to take in the mad explosion of sound and noise that burst all about him.

Dorini, in the guise of Cybelle, reached a cool hand to him.

"Come! We must escape this. The forces of Tyron attacked us, and we were taken. We are fleeing now to Froghorn."

"Tyron?" asked the muddled Broco. "Tyron the Green? But he's an elf!"

"There is no time to explain. We must flee. Quickly, I see Froghorn now."

A handsome, cloaked figure appeared beside Dwarf, and his heart leapt with gladness, then quailed. He slowly remembered his flight from his friends, and his fear that all were trying to rob him of the thing he carried. Remembering that, his hand darted into his cloak to clutch the Arkenchest and feel the safety it promised, and all the dreams it held, and the new dwarfish kingdom it would bring to life again, with him at the head of the realm, and greater than even Eo'in or Co'in, who had been the greatest and wisest of all Dwarfdom.

His heart stopped, and an icy hand closed about him.

Frantically, Broco searched through all the pockets of his vest and his cloak, but there was no familiar lump that let him know the Chest was safe, and warm, and next to his skin. His eyes went wide in rage and fear, and he began hammering the air and flailing around in the dirt at his feet.

"It's mine, all mine, I tell you. No one has a right to it but me," he shrieked, crawling blindly about, tearing the cloth from the knees of his trousers and leaving oozing trails of blood on the green lawn of the glade.

After watching this for a moment, Dorini, in the guise of Cybelle, hastily nodded to Doraki, who lunged forward and pinned Broco to the earth.

"It's mine, it's mine, I tell you! You can't have it!" he screamed, and struggled so fiercely even Doraki had to hold hard to Dwarf's arms to keep him from tearing free.

"Search him," ordered Dorini, her voice hard and brittle.

Doraki touched Dwarf with the handle of the wickedly curved whip, and a curtain of black terror descended over his heart and drove all thought from his mind. Broco fell forward onto the cool glade floor, his limbs dancing in wild, unconscious jerks.

Helpless, and completely at the mercy of Doraki, Dwarf was rolled onto his back and searched by talon-like hands. His cloak was shredded, and his cap, and even his boots were torn from his feet and discarded. His vest was ripped open, and his tunic, but there was nothing there that might have hinted at the whereabouts of the object Doraki desired. All the pockets of Broco's trousers were torn away, in a last, futile gesture, but the Arkenchest was not on Broco's person, nor anywhere on the ground about him.

Dorini, once more in her own form, raised a shrieking frozen snowstorm that swirled away upward, high above the Gilden Wood. Her rage exploded into thundering green and yellow lightning, and even Doraki cowered before her. Scores of elves, who had been hurrying to and fro near where she had been watching Doraki search Dwarf, fell senseless to the earth, and in the distance, the firing and din of the joined battle rose to even greater heights. The very air itself crackled and hummed, and a roaring, constant rumble flooded the sky, until the golden sunlight had paled and darkened.

"Give me the Chest!" shrilled Dorini, a green tower whirling high above her, sweeping trees and hapless elves into this violent circle, lifting them away and beyond sight.

Explosions and great, jagged blue-green darts plunged from her eyes, and she raised her terrible voice again."

"Give me the Chest! I command it! I am the ruler of these lower spheres. I demand the Chest! There can be no denial of my order here."

At Dorini's feet, and struggling hard to keep from being blown away by the cyclones of her anger, Creddin, trembling and pale, and whose blurry old eyes were shut tight against the cruel wind, crawled desperately to Broco's unmoving form. Grasping his bare foot, the gnarled old dwarf began painfully dragging Broco back toward the shaft they had emerged from earlier, which was close by, behind the brush and undergrowth that hid the opening from the outside.

Somewhere in his mind, Creddin kept that one thought alive, merely to keep crawling toward the shaft entrance, and to keep tight hold of Broco's foot. Slowly, at a snail's pace, his old bones aching and his knees wracked with shooting pain, he inched forward. His eyes had been tightly closed, and he only forced them open every third tug at the leaden form of Broco. As he looked on his third pull, he thought he saw the bushes that grew before the shaft move and part. Blinking back the tears of pain, and sweat, Creddin tried to focus on what he thought he had seen.

Behind him, and over the howling of the elves and the strident, ugly voice of the gunfire, Creddin heard Dorini's voice again, and tried to hurry toward the only shelter he knew.

"You miserable wretch of a fool. You shall pay dearly for this. I shall have my vengeance on you first of all. I am sending you back to the accursed Light!"

Dorini's hand came up, and a black cloud, formless, except for a curving thing that might have been a claw, leapt out toward Doraki.

"It was not my doing," he cried, his voice thin and reedy, like a great wind that shrieks through dead trees.

A scream, dark and horrible to hear, tore the air asunder with a rasping, grating note that was like an iron shield struck against another, or dying mountains roaring at the sky.

Creddin dared not look back, and closed his eyes once more, making a last, gasping struggle to drag the limp Broco into the shelter of the ancient dwarfish delving of Bani. He was not aware when friendly hands took his burden from him, and he kept crawling stubbornly on, until at last Otter patted his old hand and Bear lifted him to his feet. He opened his eyes and saw Cranfallow offering him a water bag, and Ned Thinvoice's pinched face was worked into what might have been a reassuring smile.

The old dwarf gave out a choked sob.

"She didn't find it," he blurted out. "Broco dropped it when he ran into a turning here. It fell out of his cloak, and I picked it up."

His voice cracked, and he sobbed again.

In the gnarled, bony old hands, which were scratched and bleeding from pulling Broco to the safety of the delving shaft, lay the glowing, pure white Arkenchest, humming and alive in the old dwarf's grasp, and pulsing gently its hope and light into the hearts of those who looked down on it with hushed awe and wonder.

A Bargain Is Struck

A low gray twilight settled over the glade called Last Gate, and the noise and din of the battle that raged back and forth through the wood seemed to die down to sporadic bursts of rifle fire, then silence, followed by shouts and explosions.

Dorini stood stiffly erect in the very center of the clearing, her beautiful, harsh, frozen features clouded and dim. Only her eyes seemed to have life, and they were filled with a smoking darkness that drifted about, as if tossed by storm winds.

Before her stood the unmoving figure of Tyron the Green, and beside him was Thailwicke. Tyron's features were blank, and the useless signal horn hung lifelessly from his fingers. A misplaced lock of dark hair crept down his forehead and covered one eye, but he made no move to brush it away.

A burst of rifle fire erupted from a thicket nearby, and three of the woodland elves raced from the cover of a clump of underbrush and reported breathlessly to their leader.

"Sir, we must fall by and regroup. There were more of Urien's waterfolk than we thought, and those devils of the Circle are with Melodias and Greymouse. We're outnumbered, and undone, if we don't move quickly."

Tyron showed no emotion, and the elf's speech did not seem to register on him.

"Quickly, Tyron, we must have the word! We can regroup and fall back in the direction of the Wells."

"Signal, sir!" pleaded another elf, younger than the first, and wounded in the arm.

"Before we are lost, do something! Don't stand there gawking at us," shouted the first, and he took the signal horn from Tyron's unresisting hand and blew a quick, high trill of notes that were blown away on the wind and noise of the battle. He blew yet another call, and turned to the two who were with him.

"Away, then! This is hopeless. Fen, you take Aoel, and I'll try to get His Grace to the safety of the Wells. It is our only hope now."

As the two other elves made their way past Tyron, his eyes cleared a moment and he made an effort to speak, but no words came. He looked pleadingly at the two staring faces, but they hastily looked down and went on their way.

As Tyron was being led away by the remaining elf, Thailwicke suddenly shook himself violently and sprang at the older elf's back.

"No you don't, you slippery dog. You've begun this, and by the sacred name of Eiorn you'll see it to its finish, whether it be good or ill."

"Hold, Thailwicke," cautioned the elf who held Tyron's weight against him. "He is not himself."

"Nor am I, nor are any of the others," shot Thailwicke. "I have followed him long and faithfully, but I never dreamed it would end in this." Thailwicke waved an arm about wildly. "Look at what it's down to, Cremm. We have attacked our own brothers, and now the Circle rides against us too. Tyron always spoke ill of them, but I never truly thought they would go so far as to attack us, when all we wanted was a safe haven for our kinsmen."

The elf Cremm shook his head.

"Tyron has reached the end of his dream, I fear. Leave him alone, Thailwicke. I am with you in feeling, but it does me no good to lament the knot that is undone. All I can do now is mend what I can, and get us to safety, so that we may see what will come of it all."

"Then I shall come, too."

"You should rally whoever you can," said Cremm. "The others will have need of someone they know and can trust after the battle fever wears thin."

Thailwicke had turned, and was on the verge of trotting back toward the heavy firing that was going on toward Eastering Dell when Dorini, who had been as motionless as stone, suddenly raised her hands and beckoned to Cremm to release Tyron. The elf removed Tyron's arm from around his shoulder, and let the reeling, small figure stagger free.

"Come, my sweet," crooned Dorini, "you have work here yet to do, and I fear it is not time for your miserable band to escape unscathed."

Whirling, icy fingers of wind whipped wildly about the cold form of Dorini, and she took on the likeness of Cybelle once more.

"Back to your battle, Cremm. You will find your haven in the Pits of Doom, beyond Calix Stay."

Cremm shuddered and tried to turn away to fly the terrible figure, but before he could reach out his foot, a blazing yellow-green shaft from Dorini's hand cut savagely through the air and struck the elf. He looked puzzled a moment, and his mouth worked soundlessly, and then, shrieking in a horrible, high voice with his eyes turned blood-red, he raged away toward the firing in the wood, brandishing his firearm dangerously.

Tyron, who had watched helplessly, tried to summon his courage to plunge the short elfin dagger into the cold, ruthless figure of the Dark Queen, who stood before him in the form of Cybelle. His hand froze to the hilt of the knife before he could strike, and he cried out painfully and flung the freezing object away.

"It's been *you* all along," he spat. "I had reckoned on the Circle playing these foul tricks, but I didn't expect it of you."

"Silence, elf. I know what you expected. Foolish dreams for foolish, petty dreamers. All your arrogance shall be repaid in full to you now."

Dorini laughed a short, chilling blast that forced Tyron to close his eyes and cover his face with his hands.

"Your meddling has cost me my goal, and you shall pay for that, too, miserable filth of an elf."

Dorini, still in the beautiful form of Cybelle, took Tyron by a hand and pulled him to her. As she lifted the elf before her, she chanted an ancient rune aloud to the overcast sky, and frozen hail drummed the earth with such fury that the very leaves of the trees in the wood about the Last Gate were broken from the limbs, and a rushing, spiraling whirlwind of ice and freezing fire began growing in the distance, shrieking and tearing at the very heart of the forest, as it neared where Dorini stood.

"I want the Chest, elf. You will give me the Secret, and you will call the Chest to you, from wherever it is now. That filth of a shaft rat no longer had it, curse him, but I know it is here somewhere near. And no one, not even the head of the Circle, can stop your Secret from calling the others to it. That is the Law."

Tyron's head had lolled to one side, and his eyes rolled back in his head, but no sound came from his cracked and broken lips.

Thailwicke, who had been badly dazed by the fury of the frozen hail that Dorini had brought upon the glade of the Last Gate, raised himself to an elbow.

"Don't give it to her, Tyron. Don't give the witch its power."

Dorini raised a finger in the direction of the wounded elf, and a frozen green cloud of wind and ice silenced Thailwicke. Dorini turned once more to Tyron, whose eyes had cleared somewhat.

"Speak, wretch! I have waited too long for my trophy. Call up the Chest. Use the power of the Secret!"

"I can't," croaked Tyron.

"You can, and will, you elfin filth. I have suffered you and your kind for longer than I have need of remembering, and it is nearing time when these lower planes shall be rid of the lot of you meddling, sneaking things."

Dorini snorted.

"You have brought me much agony in your time, you and the miserable waterfolk. My beautiful pets were all slain by your kind, long ago, in the Dragon Wars, when the accursed Circle tried before to deny me my rightful throne. But they didn't succeed, just as you didn't succeed in stopping my war to attain my birthright. These worlds are mine, and I must have the Arkenchest to make certain that they stay within my power, as it is written."

Dorini had raised her voice until she was shouting, and the cold echo rang out above even the battle sounds, which had begun to abate and drift farther away. She paused for a moment and looked quietly at the cowering, broken figure of the elf.

She resumed speaking in a calm, sweet voice that sounded almost like Cybelle's.

"Dear Tyron, we need not torture ourselves this way. I have need of the Secret you hold, to call the Arkenchest. As soon as that's done, I will be satisfied, and all this unpleasantness shall end. You will be free of the terrible burden you've been carrying all this time, and the trust your father gave you will be fulfilled, and the Secret will be well guarded, and it shall not be given back to the Circle, which is what he did not want the Secret to suffer."

Tyron's eyes glazed, and he nodded blankly.

"Father did not want the Secret to be returned to Greyfax. He thought it would be safer with us, here in Gilden Wood, where we were beyond harm's way."

"Good. Now you are beyond harm's way, and it is time for you to rest. Your father is calling you to him to rest. It is time. You are very tired, now. It is almost time to seek your father in his own safe boundaries."

A faint flicker of awareness flooded Tyron's face.

"Home? You mean the Gilden Wood?"

"No, Tyron, your father's Havens, beyond these lower boundaries, where you came from so long ago."

A faint glimmer of remembrance played wistfully through Tyron's memory.

"It is time for you to go there, Tyron, where you will be truly safe, and not have to cross the boundaries anymore. Then you will have no more use for the Secret, for that was what it was for, to keep you from crossing the lower boundaries."

"But my father told me the Gilden Wood was our home."

"It isn't. And your father is there now. You could be, too. All you need do is surrender the Secret and call up the Chest, then you may join your father and all the rest of the elves that have gone on to the Havens before you."

Tyron's face wrinkled into a worried frown.

"I don't think I can do what you ask," he mumbled at last.

"Why not, Tyron? It is so cool and restful there, where your father is."

"He can't give you the Secret he no longer has," came a strong, clear voice from behind Dorini.

She whirled, the fair features of Cybelle melting, and she stood forth once more in her own form. Her eyes fell on the new intruder, and her dark, beautiful head tilted back, and she laughed a long, scathing laugh.

"So it is finally you, is it? I have often wondered how this would play out between us."

"It has been a long time, Dorini. I see you have not changed your tune, nor altered your ways," said Greyfax softly.

"You are a headstrong sort, I will say that," laughed Dorini icily. "But more than that, I can't say. You had a chance, once, to serve me, and share my kingdom equally, yet you refused."

"And I see by doing so I have escaped your poor Doraki's fate."

"An ambitious soul, our Doraki. He would certainly have been dangerous had I left him his freedom in the presence of the Chest. This brainless elf reminded me that the Arkenchest had the power to raise the hopes of even one like Doraki. No matter that his hopes would have been to rule in my place."

"So you have seen fit to return him to the Fields of Light, have you?" asked Greyfax, never taking his eyes off Dorini for a moment.

Her glance sought his briefly, but fell away when she saw the dazzling white glow that burned in his eyes.

"It is the only place it would be safe to send the fool. He was growing dangerous to me. And I had no desire to suffer at his hand"

"And I imagine the place you knew he would hate the most would be the Fields of Light."

"Exactly! Poor Greyfax, you are slow on catching me up."

"Not so slow that I don't know your sense of justice, my good lady."

"Then you do see the reality of my plans?"

Greyfax looked away for a moment, and indicated the raging battle that was going on in the wood about them, and the many still forms that were scattered throughout the glade.

"Your plan is alarmingly effective, dear lady. And it shall remain so, I fear, although it shall not be the darkness of the lower worlds as you had planned."

"You cannot stop me! Nor any of the rest of the wretched bunch you call your Circle. I have Cybelle, and I shall rule supreme in these lower worlds."

"Yes, that's true. You do have Cybelle. But I think there is something that you would give her up for. Something more important to you than a mere hostage."

Dorini's eyes narrowed to frozen slits, and she asked in a calm voice, "Are you making a proposal, or stating a fact?"

"I'm in a position to know where a certain object is that you desire. And I may have access to getting that object to you, in return for the life of Cybelle, and her freedom."

"The Chest?" breathed Dorini loudly, her tone taking on a more confident note.

"Exactly."

She thought for a moment.

"I don't want to exchange anything with you, Greyfax. You are not to be trusted."

"Who, then? Froghorn?"

"None of your pure brothers, or that impossibly simple sister of mine. I want to deal only with someone who is not capable of tricking me or using any of your clever ploys."

"Very well."

"Send me the dwarf," she said, smiling wickedly.

"When do we get Cybelle? And how will we know you've kept your end of the bargain?"

"You shall know."

"Will you release her to the dwarf as soon as you have what you are asking?"

"If that suits you."

"I shall send the dwarf, then, Dorini. But he is protected, and is safe from your wiles."

"Perhaps," crooned Dorini.

Without speaking further, Greyfax returned to the great silver-gray horse, An'yim, and mounted. He whirled once, and the air in the glade brightened momentarily as the horse and rider passed, but the long shadow of Dorini soon spread once more across the clearing of the Last Gate.

And in every direction the battle raged on, elf against elf, and kindred striking kindred.

Dorini watched with delight, and grew strong from the discord and hatred that filled even the Gilden Wood, far beyond the lower borders of Calix Stay, and spilled on below the River and into the darkening horizons of Atlanton Earth. Soon, she thought, with the possession of the hated Arkenchest, she would have her complete victory, and the shadow of her reign would be complete over all the three worlds of the lower meadows of Windameir, and her destiny would at last be fulfilled.

The Circle Unbroken

Broco sat staring at his feet, and his hands played nervously with the torn buttons of his vest. Greyfax had fallen silent, and was studying the small figure carefully. He spoke once more, in a louder voice, to make himself heard over the renewing battle that exploded near the mouth of the ancient tunnel of Bani.

"You are to be the one, Broco. Dorini says she will only accept the Arkenchest from you."

Dwarf looked up at the wizard momentarily, then down again. Without raising his head, his eyes went to the tiny form of the Chest, pulsing faintly in a pearl-colored halo of light. He stared long and hard before he answered.

"Is there no other way to rescue Cybelle?" he asked finally, his voice cracking and hoarse.

"None. It is the word that I have had from the Book, as it was given by Windameir himself. It is to be, and you are to be the one that shall do it."

"I don't want to," huffed Broco weakly. "I don't want to

be the one that is going to be responsible for turning over the last hope of all to the Darkness. You can do it, or let Froghorn. Or Lorini. It's her sister."

"Does the Chest have to be surrendered?" asked Lorini, looking up from gazing at the tiny, shimmering object.

"It is as written," replied Greyfax. "And it is to save Cybelle from the darkness of your sister, among other things."

"But is it the only way? And what of the others left? If the Arkenchest and the Secrets are taken, there will be no hope at all for anyone."

Greyfax smiled slowly, and he took Lorini's hand before replying.

"Things have taken a change, my lady. What would not have answered a short time ago is altered now. We're to be allowed to go Home, you see."

An amazing transformation came over Lorini, and the color rose to her cheeks.

"Oh," she managed, but could not go on.

"Yes. It is from Erophin I hear this news, and Cephus adds that they are preparing the way for us. We shall be spending our time soon biding at their table, before returning to Windameir."

Lorini's gray-blue eyes filled with tears, and she had trouble controlling her voice.

"You mean it's true? We have come to the end of this?"

"It's true, my lady. Froghorn and Cybelle are to remain in Cypher to guide those that yet remain below. And we shall see an answer to the question of whether they have yet some Light to guide them, or some reason to keep hope."

"But sir," blurted out Bear, unable to keep quiet any longer, "if all of you are leaving, then what about us? What's to become of everyone who has been trying to follow you?"

Greyfax laughed.

"You'll keep right on following, old fellow. And I think that once we're out of the way, there will have to be someone else to step up to lead the others onto the Path."

"Well, if this don't cook the grits," mumbled Ned Thinvoice. "I hasn't never seen no sense to none of this, nohow, and now it seems like everybody has come aloose of their sockets. It don't make no sense to go agiving up that dad-blamed Chest to the very person we is supposed to keeps it away from. Why, I has wore down my poor hoofs to nubs, and even been deaded ahanging onto it, or atrying to help this stiff-necked dwarf there to holds it."

"That's true, Ned," replied Greyfax. "And what you've done is exactly what needed to be done at the time. And you and Cranny have served long and well, and bravely. You have earned your right among the Circle."

"Circle!" chorused Ned and Cranny together.

"Yes, my good friends, you have taken the robes of the Circle upon yourselves by the merits of your actions and your undying loyalty to the High Lord of Windameir."

Ned Thinvoice blushed deeply, and he stammered as he spoke. "I hasn't been no such thing," he blurted. "And I has spoke ill of my little friend when he was aloose of his wits, and I isn't nohow worth none of them words you is saying. Cranny has always been the best of us, and if you gives him the cloak, then I'll just tags along after him, if it's all the same."

Cranfallow had raised himself to his fullest height, and pointed a finger at his friend Ned.

"You just look here, Neddy, I isn't having no such talk from that smart tongue of yours. I isn't after no cloak of no sorts, and I says *you* shoulds be the one what gets it, and *I'll* does the tagging along."

Greyfax chuckled softly, and raised a hand to signal silence.

"That shall be resolved for you by Froghorn. Now we need to speed our Dwarf on his errand."

"I don't know about any speed," huffed Broco. "And I still don't feel easy about handing over the Arkenchest to Dorini. If anything goes wrong, it'll all be my fault. No one thinks of anything but himself. And I'm not so sure Dorini would give Cybelle up anyhow. What if she takes the Chest and refuses to give us Cybelle? Then where will we be? Then she'll have both of them, and you know who will carry the blame? Me! Broco, the infamous, Broco, the turncloak."

Lorini came and stood before Dwarf, and knelt.

"You see, don't you, that you are the only one that my sister will trust? She knows that you cannot harm her. Greyfax she knows and fears, as well as myself. So there is none of the Circle who could do this thing. I would, dear Broco, if I but could."

"And I," put in Greyfax.

"Well, fine and dandy," went on Dwarf. "Then you go right on and do it. As for me, I would take the Chest and cross on beyond the upper boundaries, and take it where it will be safe."

Lorini smiled sadly at the small, huffing figure.

"Even that would do nothing to save Cybelle or the others."

"We have to think what's best for the most," replied Dwarf stuffily. "And it would certainly be best if the Chest is carried on beyond Dorini's reach."

"We are thinking exactly of what is best for all," said Greyfax, also coming to stand beside Dwarf.

"And how does the rescue of Cybelle help anyone but you?" asked Broco, looking at Lorini.

"Doesn't your memory serve you better than that, dear Broco? Does Cybelle mean so little to you?"

Dwarf, remembering his grand plans of but a short time before, reddened.

"She means nothing to me," he snorted. "She is a beautiful child, and she has a good ear for music."

"That wasn't the way I had it, coz," interrupted Creddin, raising his head from his hands, where he had been resting it as the conversation went on.

"And what would you know, you traitorous old baggage?"

"Only enough to feel that he should drag you in out of Dorini's way," said Bear defensibly.

Dwarf's face drained, and he looked at the gnarled features of Creddin. His lips worked, but no words came.

"We couldn't get to you for all the rifle fire, and then Doraki tore through all your clothes, trying to find the Chest, and then all of a sudden there was a blaze of green fire and smoke so thick we thought the whole glade had gone. And then when it cleared a little, Doraki was gone, and Creddin here was dragging you along by your foot, trying to get you back to the cave."

"And he found the Chest in the tunnel, even before you

went out. He had it all along. That's why they didn't find it on you," chittered Otter.

"And then Dorini tried to force Tyron into using the Secret he carried into calling the Chest up, but he couldn't, when it came down to it. Tyron's heart wouldn't let him."

"And you expect me to give her all of them?" breathed Dwarf, glad for a reason to look away from his rescuer.

"Exactly, Broco. That's what I'm trying to explain."

"I see Dwarf's point, sir," said Flewingam, who had been silent and still, in the opening of the cave, watching the progress of the battle. "If Tyron wouldn't give up his Secret, then why should Broco? And why is it to be Broco that shall deal that blow to the Light?"

"Good Flewingam, your logic is sound. I see it is somehow thought that our good dwarf spanner is going to be made a kick-goat for the Circle, and that his name will be remembered in all the lore that's left as the traitor who sold out the Light."

"Something to that effect," muttered Dwarf.

"But let me hasten to assure you it won't come to that," went on Greyfax. "And let me assure you that it is necessary to have Cybelle back from the prison of Dorini's darkness."

"You can take on any form you like. Take on mine. Go deliver up the Chest."

"I can do that, yes," agreed Greyfax. "But then everyone is going to see the same dwarf as the one they are going to blame anyhow. So whichever way it is to be done, it shall be done, with your help or without it."

Broco turned his bewildered face to the older wizard, whose features had hardened.

"Would you do that, Greyfax? After all we have been through and seen together? I thought you loved me a little, once. I can see I was wrong."

"And what about all that talk you were going on with, coz, about how they were all using you, and trying to trick you out of what you held, and how none of them wanted anything except to get all they could from you? Is that all forgotten about now?" asked Creddin.

Dwarf scrambled to his feet and paced angrily toward Creddin.

"You keep your tongue to yourself," spat Broco. "I have certain thoughts in that direction, it's true, and I'm still not so sure they're far amiss. But I'll thank you to shut up about things you know nothing of."

"I'll take the Chest, sir," chittered Otter. "If it's possible."

"I will, too," put in Bear. "Otter is always up to his ears in trouble, and if he's going, you'd better send me with him. He'd trip over his own tail, as likely as not, and pitch the Chest across the River, if I'm not along to keep an eye on him."

Otter pinched his friend viciously, but Bear's roar was drowned out by a volley of heavy firing that exploded at the very entrance to the ancient dwarfish delving.

"I'll take the Chest," shot Dwarf testily, after the noise had abated somewhat. "It's been my burden this far, and I feel if anyone is to do this, it's me."

"Make your mind up quickly," said Greyfax. "We haven't long to debate the question."

"At least we'll go with you," chirped Otter. "I don't know why we'd want to, but I guess if I can tolerate your huffing this long, I can get used to it a bit longer."

"Me, too," agreed Bear.

"And I won't be left out," added Flewingam.

Ned Thinvoice slapped a hand to his knee. "Well, you isn't about to leaves old Neddy ahind. And I isn't so hot on astaying in these parts too long, no-how. Them rifles isn't so far off now, and I doesn't even has a rock to throw to takes care of my poor old hide."

"Wherever we is agoing, we had oughts to gets at it," urged Cranny.

"What about you, Creddin?" asked Greyfax.

The ancient dwarf looked at the wizard briefly.

"I'm old, but I have no choice. I shall go with the rest."

Another strange smile crossed Greyfax's face.

"And you shall find it easier to go about soon, my friend. You, too, have earned your cloak, as well as the rest."

Before anyone could question the elusive wizard further, a pale, eerie green shadow fell over the cavern door, and a high-pitched humming noise began to grate the air, like giant boulders moving angrily against the cloak of a mountain.

"It's Dorini," warned Greyfax. "She has become impatient for her prize."

The companions quickly gathered beside Greyfax and Lorini, straining to see what was going on beyond the tunnel door. In the glade of the Last Gate, the frail afternoon sun was darkened to a weak, dull greenish-glowing flame that was almost dimmed by the thick haze that spread about the figure of Dorini. The elf Tyron was motionless before her, and the still forms of many other elves littered the dark floor of the woods in all directions.

"We must ask Windameir to set this right before we go, Greyfax," breathed Lorini softly. "My sister has no power to undo life this side of Calix Stay."

"It shall be as he wills," replied Greyfax. "But I think in this case you speak wisely."

The wizard turned to the others, who crowded around.

"Now, my last instructions, and they shall be brief."

He nodded his head at Dwarf.

"Broco, you shall carry the Chest, just as you have done. It has been a burden, I am aware, and you have served well as Chest Bearer. And the burden shall be lifted from you soon. Do what your heart tells you, and you won't fare far wrong."

He held out a hand and grasped Dwarf.

Tears sprang to Broco's eyes.

"You speak as if you're leaving us again, Greyfax."

The face of the wizard brightened, and he smiled.

"Only for a moment, my friend. No more. You shall see more of what I mean shortly."

He clapped Broco's shoulder gently.

"And you two stout fellows shall have to use your form changing a bit more regularly," he said, addressing Bear and Otter. "And that goes for all of you."

He quickly shook hands with Ned, and Cranny, and Flewingam, and Creddin.

Lorini followed behind him, and placed a tender kiss on each of their cheeks, her gray-blue eyes shining, and deeper than the evening sky.

"I don't understand," stammered Dwarf. "You are both going, and we're here, and Dorini is going to have what she wants, after all."

"Go on, Dwarf. Go on with what you must do. We shall see you all safely through it."

"Free our Cybelle, Broco," went on Lorini gently, her

voice barely audible over the reports and explosions of the battle that filled the wood about the friends.

Broco clutched the Arkenchest to his heart and tried to say something further, but he was unable to get the words to form. His eyes dimmed then, and the terrible darkness that was the voice of Dorini had called him, and the frozen splinter of fear that lived within his innermost being, which the Dark Queen had placed there long ago, began to throb and burn, and his mind was numbed with the awesome call of her unending shadow world. His steps began to falter, then go forward, then falter once more, and Bear went on one side, and Otter on the other, and Ned, Cranny, and Flewingam, with Creddin following, fell in behind, their eyes wide and shining in the greenish fog that swirled and writhed about their feet.

As they neared where the towering figure of Dorini stood, the woods grew suddenly silent, and not a sound was heard except the beating of their own hearts. The comrades had all clutched hands, and pressed forward into the stifling glade.

And as suddenly as the silence had fallen, a terrible frozen wind cut through the wood, shrieking and howling, until their ears and eyes were numb and their hearts breathless within them.

"It's mine!" came the triumphant victory cry of Dorini. "I have won my kingdom here, and shall seal it off from Windameir. I am one with even him! He cannot stop me now!"

Dorini's voice crackled with yellowish-green flames that singed the leaves of the trees and burnt the very air, leaving a dull, scorched smell in the glade.

"Give it to me, foul stench of a tunnel rat. Give me my treasure!"

At her words, the Chest quivered in Broco's hands, and a warmth spread upward through him, and he raised his voice so that the Dark Queen could hear him.

"Where is Cybelle? You shall have your trade as soon as Cybelle is released."

"I make no bargains now, earth filth. I am supreme. I am even as great as Windameir!"

She threw up her bare arms, and a driving, blinding blizzard of greenish-yellow hail and snow tore the Chest from Dwarf's hands.

"It's mine!" shrieked Dorini. "I am greater than Windameir!" she shrilled, and as she reached out to take the tiny object which she had struggled for so long to possess, she threw back her dark, beautiful head in the beginning of a laugh.

Her cold hand touched the Arkenchest, and earth, and sky, and wind, and wave in the Creations of Windameir shuddered and groaned, and the very heart of the Creator quickened from that touch.

One long, blinding tower of a light so terrible and bright blazed forth from the small Chest, and the White Light of the Lord of Windameir burst forth in brilliant, singing rainbow colors across every plane of existence he had created. The Secrets, whirling in that golden-white light, burst forth from the Arkenchest one by one, freeing themselves and exploding into golden halos that seemed to pierce every heart that stood there at Last Gate, and going on beyond, into the hearts of all living things once more.

Dorini, colorless and frozen, writhed in agony and torment as the golden daggers of the Secrets buried themselves once more in her cold soul, and without knowing why, or how, the friends were suddenly aware of the Secrets, and remembered they had had them all along, but forgotten them.

Shrieking in an icy rage, Dorini whirled about herself, whipping the golden-white light into a whirlwind of sleet and freezing snow, and shadow.

"You clever fiends think you've won, but you won't have me. I curse this wretched box, and fling it back in your faces. And I shall keep your darling Cybelle where you'll never find her."

Bear and Otter and the others fell back a pace, but Broco, his eyes glazed over with the frozen gray of the realms of Dorini, slowly shuffled a step forward, toward the beckoning arms of the terrible Dark Queen.

"And you, my pets, shall come with me. Greyfilth will regret this trickery."

Throwing her arms above her head, Dorini prepared to strike a fatal blow upon the small company. A dreadful iron bell rang out, and the sky blackened, and the yellow-green flames of the Darkness leapt up to consume the terrified friends.

Just as they felt the frozen steel claw of Dorini's mind reach out of that vile cloud to devour them, her face brightened, and the freezing darkness began to lift, and as they looked on, the two sisters, such dreadful enemies for so long, stood face to face with one another, and then seemed to merge and become one once more, until after a time they were sure that it was the beautiful and warm Lorini, lady of Cypher, who smiled down upon them. As they watched in wonder and awe, Dorini's face had become transformed.

Broco, shivering and stuttering with fright, called out weakly.

"Is that you, Lorini?"

A kind laugh escaped the lips of the beautiful form.

"It is neither Lorini nor Dorini any longer. I am simply the Truth of the Five Secrets, the five forces of Love. My name is Faith, and Hope, and Forgiveness, and Charity, and Humility, but you may see me or call me as you wish, dear friends, for now all things may heal, and forgiveness cure even the most grievous wounds, for it is so within myself once more. I shall return now to the Light as one, for the Darkness that has been in his plan has served its Master as it had been intended to serve, and the shadows that have fallen across the lower meadows are finally lifted, and the Light, and Life, and Love will flow freely once again, as in the Beginning."

"You mean it's over?" chittered Otter, not believing his ears.

"There is nothing that does not come full into its own time," said the Lady.

"And Cybelle?" breathed Dwarf.

"She will find you very soon."

"What happened?" chorused the others.

But the lady smiled again, and their hearts were full of the Secrets, and that warmth grew and grew, and there was a burning white light that leapt from the ground where the beautiful lady stood, and the soft sound of a reed pipe, high up in the air, filled their ears, and then there was silence.

When the friends came to their senses and looked about them, there was nothing even to remind them that she had been towering above them but a moment before, and the only trace of her existence at all was the tiny white Arken-chest, which was pulsing softly in the grass at their feet, and the new feeling of completion that filled their hearts.

And the shadow of the Darkness was gone.

A Long-awaited Peace

A change came over the glade of the Last Gate, and the sun, which had been almost sinking over the distant blue crowns of the white-capped mountains, now stood brightly above, as if it was midday, and a gentle, snoring breeze stirred the sleeping trees into a forest filled with deep-throated wood music.

The battle fire had been blown away in the whirlwind of Sound and Light that had swept the glade clean, and the woodland elves of Tyron the Green stood silently facing the waterfolk of Urien Typhon. Their weapons were held clumsily in their hands, and after another moment, the elves flung down the useless things, and a great cheer went up.

And as Greyfax had thought, the loving Lord of Windameir had not left Dorini's work as she had unmade it.

All the elves and men who had been taken into the darkness of Dorini's shadow stepped forth once more into the Light of Windameir.

Thailwicke stood looking at Tyron, and Cremm blinked back his tears of joy on the grass beside them.

"We've reached the Havens," said Tyron, watching Urien Typhon ride toward him across the green lawn that but a moment before had been bloody from the raging battle.

"Hail, Tyron, my brother. We are come to it, then."

Tyron clasped Urien warmly.

"We have many camps to build, for I feel we shall have need of more room. The upper boundaries will be seeing many of our kindred, both wood- and water-born, arriving now that the River is open again."

"You are right, Tyron. Calix Stay is unguarded now, and any who wish may cross. There is no need to have sentries where there is no danger."

Urien Typhon smiled broadly.

"The Darkness has been returned to her Home, it seems. Her purpose has been completed, and her errands upon these lower worlds have been done. The beings here are all purged clean of her reign, and those that aren't shall soon be, now that her hand is no longer there to direct them in their ignorance."

As the two elves talked, another figure approached, and alit from the tall silver-gray steed that he rode.

Froghorn reached up and helped Cybelle down from the high saddle of Pe'lon. Her beauty had grown, and the shadow of darkness that had crept over her heart was melted in the brilliant colors of the new day, and her long fair hair fell down across her shoulders like a molten river of gold.

Urien Typhon and Tyron bowed low to her, and each in his turn kissed her hand.

Froghorn smiled easily at the two elves.

"It has indeed fallen out for the best, once the Circle has closed once more. Dorini and Lorini filled their destiny, and the Secrets are once more where they should be, safely in the Arkenchest."

Tyron looked quickly at Froghorn; then a slow realization crept warmly over him.

"It's gone," he muttered. "Or rather not gone, but different."

He looked dazedly at Froghorn, who laughed softly.

"You know all of them now, my friend. They are no longer separate. That's what was always the trouble with the Secrets when they were separated. We didn't realize then where we were on Atlanton Earth—and attacked on all sides—that separating the Secrets would cause the havoc that it did. Of course, it was all intended to be that way by Windameir, for that was the trend of the lessons these lower creations needed, in order to remember which way to go when the lessons were completed.

"So your having merely one of the Secrets was a grave danger to you, for it created a knowledge of all the Power of the Five, but with merely one, or any two of them, an imbalance was created. Dwarf found that out when he bore the Chest and it held yet three, plus the one he had had since he was a spanner, which he had carried all along without knowing of it until much later."

"I'm free, then," said Tyron, his pale blue eyes clear and shining. "I am able to look at you now. It is different."

Urien Typhon clapped the smaller elf on the shoulder.

"Before you get too engrossed in your introspection, I think we should find a camp for this new host of elfen folk that are here," he said, indicating the throngs of elves that were racing about the glade, laughing and shouting in unrestrained joy.

"You may take your clan on beyond the Last Gate, Tyron," said Froghorn. "If they wish it. If not, they may stay on here in the Meadows of the Sun until such time as they do want to cross. Cybelle and I will be staying on in Cypher for a while yet, to help on those from below Calix Stay that shall be beginning their journey Home."

Froghorn turned, and looked directly into the face of Broco.

"And you, my dear old companion, what of you? We have need of eyes and ears on the goings and comings beyond Calix Stay. We have need of guides for the ones who are yet below."

Broco's voice wavered and broke as he spoke.

"I'm not worthy of that task."

Cybelle, who hadn't moved, now went to Dwarf, and kissed him quickly on the cheek.

"Dear old Dwarf, you've been held prisoner by the Darkness just as I was. She had captured you once before, long ago, and beyond the Great River. But that splinter was there that she put in your heart, and it grew as time went on, and it was a part of her, and fed off your own fears and doubts."

Cybelle fell silent, and let Froghorn continue.

"I didn't know it was to be a part of the plan," he said. "And I'm glad I knew nothing of it then. As it was, I was greatly disturbed that you were taken by Dorini, and in a place where none of the Circle was permitted by Law to go. It never occurred to me that you would use the Secret you carried to free yourself. Nor did that occur to Dorini. I don't think she ever truly understood that she was a part of the Secrets herself, just as Lorini was. The light and the dark. The positive and the negative. It takes both to create energy.

Once Dorini put her hand on the Chest and the Secrets, the Law was fulfilled, and both she and Lorini were returned to wholeness, and that, as we know, means a return Home."

"And Greyfax?" asked Otter, coming to stand beside Broco and the others.

"Our close-mouthed friend often told me he was tired of this business, and longed to settle down to his charts and stargazing. And I think he and Erophin have plotted at getting themselves interested in a new project beyond the Golden Tide. He and Greymouse and Melodias are all Home now, and happy with it. They have, after all, been about this since the Beginning, and now that Lorini and Dorini are returned, there is no need for them to remain longer."

"Will we ever see him again?" asked Bear sadly. "Or the others?"

"Oh, I shouldn't be a bit surprised if we don't run across them now and again, after we finish up here."

"Look!" interrupted Creddin, who had stepped out into the circle of friends as they talked. "Look!"

Instead of the ancient, knobby old form, there stood before them a handsome, stocky dwarf, not much older than Broco.

"Is that you?" blurted Dwarf, staring in amazement at Creddin.

"Right enough, coz. Only I don't know what's come over me. I feel as if I wasn't any more than five hundred or so." He leapt into the air and clicked in his heels together to punctuate his words, then fell into a series of back somersaults and kipovers in midair that left the startled friends breathless.

"Enough, enough, hotshoes," laughed Froghorn, raising a

hand for silence. "We must begin the plans for our move, and there will be some of you who will want to return beyond the Last Gate, and others may want to keep us company yet awhile in Cypher. We have much work that shall have to be done there, and we shall have many chores and projects for all and any who might wish to help us. There are the singing fountains that need mending, and the stables, and any number of stone and mortar works that shall have to be done. Any and all are welcome: but we understand, should any of you want to go on beyond the Last Gate."

"I would be honored if I might try my hand at the stone work," volunteered Creddin. "It's been a long year between since I've plied my trade, but I was a fair mason once, and could delve with the best."

"I'll take care of your fountains," offered Urien. "And any others of the waterfolk who care to stay and help me are welcome."

A vast roar went up as the majority of Urien's band indicated their eagerness to go to work.

Those who wished to cross the Last Gate and go on beyond drifted toward a brilliant white shaft of light that blazed in the center of the glade, and entering, were gone quickly and easily, and without creating any pangs of sorrow or loneliness in those that remained behind.

Tyron's host, almost to the elf, had crossed, including their leader, and those who remained indicated that they would take charge of the gardens and forests of Cypher, and all the other growing things that flourished there.

"And you, good Cranny and Ned?" asked Froghorn, "And what of you, Flewingam? Is it to be go or stay? What are your thoughts on this matter?"

"Well, all I knows is that I hasn't never seen nothing at all that would hold a wax candle to none of these goings-on," muttered Ned Thinvoice. "It are enough to plumb pull the ears off a donkey, it are, what with all the hoopla and fal-ta-shoot. What I says is gives me a good simple task, and a honest day's board, and I is up to ahelping you fix up just about any old thing what might need amending."

"Good lad, Ned," said Froghorn. "Cranny?"

"I isn't about to give up the ornery company of old Ned. I wouldn't knows what to do without his alooking at the damp side of things once in a whiles."

Flewingam simply nodded his head in agreement with the others when Froghorn came to him.

"Then you're welcome to stay with us in Cypher. It will take some doing, of course, to return it to its old beauty, but we have nothing but time now, and plenty of able hands to do it."

"I can set your libraries straight, and the lore books," offered Dwarf meekly. "I think a good portion of them have probably been upset after Dorini's stay in Cypher."

Froghorn looked evenly at Broco.

"That is a kind offer, Broco."

Dwarf's heart fell, and the tightness that closed his throat grew stronger.

"I might look after the mending of the dwarfish wares," he muttered in a lower tone.

"That may well be taken care of by Creddin, I'm sure."

"I'm up to that, coz," confirmed Creddin, still carefully exploring his newfound strength.

Broco shuddered, and he broke into long, wracking sobs. No one moved for a moment; then Cybelle went to the forlorn dwarf and reached out a hand to him. He paid no attention to her, and turned to make his departure.

"Will I be allowed to go on?" he managed to ask Froghorn.

"No, Broco. You cannot cross the Last Gate," he said, pausing. "Not yet. Your work is yet below, in the realms of the World Before Time. You have been through all the agonies there are, and you are the one most able to do the job that is given to you to do. You and Bear and Otter shall have the task of returning the Arkenchest to beyond Calix Stay."

"Calix Stay!" chorused the three friends.

"Yes, good comrades. You have guarded the Secrets long and well, and our Dwarf has suffered all one could suffer from the misuse of the Chest. There are no others more capable of this errand than you. And Greyfax told you, I think, that once he and the others were gone, someone would have to step into the cloaks they left vacant. He was speaking to you all. Broco, and Otter, and Bear, and Ned, and Cranny, and Flewingam. They say they want to stay on here for a while, to help us put Cypher to rights, and I think that is as it should be. They will become more accustomed to their work, and I will be able to instruct them in the things that they will be doing as they progress."

"We isn't so sure we wants all this fancy stuff you is atalking about, sir. Can't we just gets on back with our friends, and leaves what is best left alone?"

"No, Ned. You will learn your new trade soon enough. And I shall have more need of you here than they shall have need of you below. Our stout fellows have learned enough between them to handle anything that they will encounter on Atlanton Earth now, since the Darkness is gone. Only the echoes of that shadow remain, and those can be dispelled with the power of the Five. Dorini is gone, and can no longer keep anyone in the prison of her mind, and all those that were are released now. They may take some time to return to the full Light of Windameir, but they have made a beginning just by being free of the Darkness."

"What about those foul beasts, and the Worlughs, and the Gorgolacs?" asked Bear anxiously, not any too eager to return across Calix Stay. "And if all this is to happen, how are we going to get back across? And what provisions do we have if we do?"

"I know the spell of Calix Stay," said Broco, huffing a bit, then going on in a quieter tone. "I do know how to hold the River long enough to cross."

"And I'm sure Froghorn will give us a sack of journey cakes and water to hold us," giggled Otter, watching his big friend's eyes roll up at the thought of arriving across Calix Stay again, hungry and without shelter, just as they had done once long before, in another time, and when all things had been under the dark night of Dorini's own dream of ruling the lower worlds of Windameir alone.

And wondering at their crossing again, Otter's thoughts turned to the plump red dewberries that had grown at the River's edge, and almost at the instant he thought it, he found himself peering over a thick berry bush, staring at the calm, wide surface of Calix Stay, its unguarded expanse a cool blue sea of space and time.

Otter blinked once, and there were Bear and Dwarf beside him, looking somewhat startled.

"Well, here we are again," said Broco at last.

"I knew it. I knew Froghorn wouldn't take the time out to

explain what was going on, or try to do anything about any of it. Leave it to a wizard always to manage to disappear just when you need him most."

"I wonder," mused Otter, and held up the small sack of journey cakes and water that he had found at his feet.

In another moment, marked with brilliant flashes of green, and blue, and red sounding echoes, the three friends stood once more in the fields of Atlanton Earth, and there before them, beside a small, cheery fire, sat the smiling Froghorn Fairingay.

The True Beginning

Pe'lon stood a slight distance from Froghorn, quietly grazing in the knee-high clover that grew like a green lawn down to the very edge of Calix Stay. Away in all directions, the three friends saw the clear blue sky, and the sun high overhead, golden and hot as it warmed them.

Froghorn's cloak was now of a pearl-colored cloth, and his eyes twinkled and laughed as he spoke.

"Well met, friends. I think it has been a turning or two since we talked of our travels on this side of the River."

Bear was gazing away at what appeared to him to be a broad roadway that cut right though the distant wood and ran on until he could no longer see it.

"Where does that lead?" he asked at last, turning to the smiling Froghorn, who appeared somehow older, and who, the friends noticed abruptly, had taken on a definite likeness to Greyfax.

"To the places here that will have need of the Secrets, my friends. To towns, and villages, and the woods and fields, and the mountains and seas of Atlanton Earth. Everywhere there are living things, there will be a time set aside for the Light to arrive."

"But it is too big," Otter began. "We couldn't go to *all* those places, even if we wanted."

"You forget, old fellow, that you now wear the cloaks of the Circle."

"A fancy lot of good that does me," grumbled Bear. "I can't eat it, and it certainly won't do my walking for me, and I doubt very seriously I can live in it."

A soft chuckle escaped Froghorn.

"But it's true, Bear. Remember the things that happened when you first met Greyfax and me, not too far from this very spot? You had a taste for some good comb honey, did you not?"

"Still do," muttered Bear, looking about him hopefully.

"Then there is where the cloak is handy," replied Froghorn, who indicated a tote keg full of sweetcomb that was standing before Bear, next to the fire.

"Did I do that?" asked the rather amazed Bear.

"Indeed you did. And you will find that your walking can be done just as easily, and that shelter isn't any farther from you than a thought."

Bear's brow wrinkled into a great frown.

"But how is all this taking place? I mean why?"

"You have always had the ability to do these things, Bear, and more. So does everyone. It is merely remembering how. And the trick is the use of the Secrets, by completely surrendering to them, and by remembering that all power is Windameir's, and not your own."

Otter had furrowed his whiskers and squinted his eyes, until his companions thought that their little friend was in some agony of pain.

"What is it, Otter? What's wrong?" quizzed Dwarf, reaching out a hand to touch the tiny creature.

"I'm just seeing if I can conjure up a good swim," said Otter, his brow clearing, and he looked about anxiously.

"Does anyone see my weir?" he asked rather shortly.

"Those powers can only be used for others, Otter," said Froghorn. "Bear got his honey, for we're all hungry. And the powers are only to be used to help others find their way to us in Cypher. We'll assist them on from there, as they are ready to leave."

Dwarf cleared his throat, and spoke in a very quiet voice. "Will we know what we are to do this time? I mean, more or less, is there any plan that we are to follow?"

Froghorn's face softened, and he looked at Broco, meeting Dwarf's eyes and holding them.

"Yes, my dear fellow. The plan is simple. Follow your heart. That is the guide that will carry you through your mission here, and bring you safely back to us in Cypher."

He paused a moment, then laughed.

"And the libraries *do* need tending, and I'm sure you'll be able to set them aright on your first visit, and after we have straightened Cypher up a bit."

Tears welled up in Broco's eyes.

"Then I shall be able to, after all?"

"Of course, you silly ass," teased Froghorn. "There's no one else about who knows as much about lore learning and history."

"And I want you to read me all about it, Dwarf, when we

get back. I mean I haven't had a moment to stop and really think about all this. I hope someone has had time to write it all down properly. It must be an interesting story," said Otter.

"More interesting to read than to be involved in," grumbled Bear. "I'd just as soon try roasting acorns, and watching a snow."

"Your part will be the most amusing, Bear," chittered Otter. "I can't wait to hear about it."

"Oh, bother," mumbled Bear.

"It will be an interesting story," mused Broco.

"And it shall be put down, and saved," assured Froghorn. "As soon as you come to Cypher, it shall be ready for the reading."

"Then it will be fun," giggled Otter.

"I don't know about that," said Bear. "And I'm not so sure anyone would get it all down right, except those of us who have been there."

"Exactly," agreed Froghorn. "We shall have the little histories of this journey done up properly. There will be the point of view in Bear's lore, and one in yours, Otter, and yours, Broco. That way you'll all be happy."

The friends fell silent for a while, watching the fire.

"I guess it doesn't really matter, though, except that the main part is that we return as quickly as possible. I'm not so anxious to be here anymore," said Dwarf, looking about.

"I was thinking the same thing," added Bear. "Even with a wizard's cloak, it's not very cheery."

"And I'm already lonesome for Flewingam," chirped Otter, rather sadly.

"And there really should be someone else to be about this business," complained Bear. "I can't fill up a wizard's boots just because the Circle suddenly throws a fancy cloak over my shoulders."

"I'm with you, Bear," whistled Otter. "Besides, I'm an otter, not a magician. All I need is a little water and a mud-slide or two, and the first thing you know, I'm off. That isn't the way I'd want anyone to be acting who is supposed to be an Elder of the Circle. Why, I would have dropped my chinwhiskers if I'd ever caught Greyfax Grimwald, or Melodias, or George Greymouse dancing in a meadow, or taking a nose ride down a stream bed."

"And who on earth ever saw a wizard look like this?" asked Bear, indicating himself with a large paw.

"You have your other forms," reminded Froghorn.

"But they don't fit so well," went on Bear. "They were handy enough when you gave them to us, when we needed them to help us get our Dwarf back. But they don't seem to sit too well now. I get very uncomfortable in that disguise."

"Me too," chittered Otter. "And I know that if we have to be around all those people, and in all those places, then we'll have to use those disguises again."

"I'd much prefer being able to straighten out the library," said Dwarf. "That's more what I'm accustomed to. After all, I'm only a lorekeeper, and a custodian of tales. And I could put together an account of these events that we have seen."

"And we could help," added Otter eagerly.

"Sort of keep everything straight," put in Bear. "I'd want to have a say-so in anything concerning my part, at any rate."

He looked about him, and back at Froghorn.

"And I am rather tired of journey cake, and not enough of that to choke a bird, and all this wandering about."

Froghorn studied the three friends for a long moment, his clear gray-blue eyes shining and deep.

"You have completed the errand that was given to you to complete," he said after a long silence. "It was written that you should return the Arkenchest and its Secrets to the World Before Time, and that you have done. And Greyfax offered you the cloaks of the Circle, which would give you all powers, and enable you to rule any realm, yet you have chosen the desire to return with me to Cypher."

He smiled, and his features seemed to glow.

"And that was the last lesson of all, this business of the cloaks of the Circle. We could not have done anything to alter your decision. Ned, and Cranny, and Flewingam, all displayed no desire in that direction. They have played out their parts below here. We weren't sure, in your cases. We suspected as much, but we had to be sure, and this had to be done."

Froghorn indicated the surrounding countryside, and waved an arm to point on beyond.

"You would have been given those lessons in the cloaks of the Circle that you needed, just as it was. But you say you don't need them, and since that is the case, I see no reason for our remaining here longer. There is a welcoming party in Cypher, I rather imagine, who shall think we are somewhat overdue."

And as quickly as the three friends had awakened beyond Calix Stay, staring about them at the high clover lawn and the distant roads that led on to the horizons of Atlanton Earth, they blinked their eyes and were suddenly seated on the dark blue cushions of Cypher, which eased the weariness of all journeys, and the magic of Cybelle's harp played gently and filled the very air about them with the color and hue of their histories, and the journey that they had begun so long ago came alive with every golden note.

Ned and Cranfallow and Flewingam lined one side of the long feast table in the banquet hall of Cypher, and across from them sat Creddin, flanked by Urien Typhon and various other wood and waterfolk.

Dwarf found himself in the stout hug of Creddin before he realized it, and soon was seated beside him, in deep discussion of how the library wall was to be mended, and how high up the new shelves should run.

Bear had fallen into a slightly cumbersome bear step that told the story of how the mountain had danced with the wind, and Otter, invisible except for the two tiny gray ears that stuck up above the table, was content to roll his fork back and forth across the long white tablecloth and watch the mystery of it all play across the tapestries of Cypher.

And as the golden music of Cypher played on, the Worlds in all the Lower Meadows of Windameir began to listen, and slowly, one by one, each began to hear the Secrets of the Lord of Windameir, which would take them from their lonely waiting and return them to the Life, and Light and Love of their Creator, who waited patiently and with outstretched arms.

And this was as written,

as is always said,

The Beginning

The Journey Home is but the closing of
The Circle.

TOR BOOKS
Reader's Guide

Squaring the Circle

By Niel Hancock

ABOUT STARSCAPE BOOKS

The richly imagined worlds of science fiction and fantasy novels encourage readers to hold a mirror up to their own realities, exploring them in a way that is secure yet challenging and demanding. Whether surviving in a complex alternate universe or navigating life on Earth in the presence of a strange new discovery, the characters in these works help readers realize, through comparison and contrast, what it means to be a true human being. Starscape strives to encourage such critical discoveries by making the very best science fiction and fantasy literature available to young adult readers. From David Lubar to Orson Scott Card and from Niel Hancock to Jane Yolen, Starscape books provide numerous unique universes through which young readers can travel on the critical journey to the center of their own identity.

ABOUT *SQUARING THE CIRCLE*

At the close of *Calix Stay*, Bear, Otter, Dwarf and their comrades were drawn to the river. As the fourth and final Circle of Light book opens, all are across Calix Stay, traipsing through the ruins of Cypher, encountering unfriendly elves, and eventually reuniting with their friends. Bear rejoins Otter, while Ned and Cranfallow are again in the company of the Dwarf known as Broco. Froghorn Fairingay, Greyfax Grimwald, and others from the Circle encourage the friends to carry on, promising all will come to rights. Lorini, finally at peace with the events that must follow her daughter Cybelle's abduction, plays a quiet role as the members of the Circle of Windameir watch events unfold and hold fast to their belief that these happenings will lead to their desired end.

Meanwhile, the evil Dorini forms an alliance with power-hungry elf Tyron. Tyron will hold the Arkenchest within Gilden Wood, safe from members of the Circle, thus ensuring Dorini's continued power over the Lower Worlds. In exchange, Dorini will give Tyron dominion over Gilden Wood to seal off for elves alone. But a promise from Dorini is never sacred. Aided by underlord Doraki, Dorini works terrifying dark magic as she searches for chest-bearer Dwarf, aiming to take the prize that holds the Secrets for her own.

However, Dwarf is considering the value of his burden and plotting to keep the Arkenchest, using its power to found his own new dwarf kingdom. Running from his friends, he comes to Bear's old dwelling where he meets Creddin, a dwarf once in league with Dorini, but now returned to an honorable path. Creddin explains that Bear's dwelling lies atop an ancient dwarf delving and follows the angry Broco as he navigates deep into the dwarfish tunnels and through a long-unused door.

The door leads to the ominous Last Gate where Dorini provokes a hideous battle between water and wood elves. Into the fray a frenzied Dwarf emerges from the delving tunnel. Dorini demands Dwarf turn over the Arkenchest but unbeknownst to Dwarf, Creddin has discovered the prize, mislaid during Broco's crazed journey. With the Arkenchest clutched in one hand, Creddin emerges from the tunnel, pulling the terrorized Dwarf away from Dorini. Back in the delving Dwarf is joined by Bear, Otter, and the others who have been pursuing their wayward friend.

As chaos rages, a bargain is struck between Greyfax and Dorini. Dwarf will bring the Arkenchest to the dark lady in exchange for her prisoner, Cybelle. When the exchange is made, a phenomenal event occurs. In a burst of light, the five secrets of the Arkenchest sparkle through the air and bury themselves in Dorini's soul. Suddenly, the friends remember that the secrets were known to them all along, just forgotten. As she is about to strike her final, terrible blow, Dorini comes face to face with her good sister Lorini and they merge into one being—the essence of the truth of the Five Secrets, the five forces of love—and, as one, the Lady returns to the light.

Having returned Lorini and Dorini, Greyfax, Greymouse and Melodias return Home. Welcomed into the Circle, Bear, Otter, Ned, Cranfallow, Flewingham, Dwarf, and Creddin join Cybelle and Froghorn and begin to rebuild Cypher. In the Lower Meadows around them, all have begun to hear the loving Secrets of the Lord of Windameir. Thus the friends find peace once more, having returned from whence they came, after navigating many perilous corners, to close the circle. Their story ends with a peaceful Beginning.

ABOUT THIS GUIDE

The information, discussion questions and activity ideas which follow are intended to enhance your reading of *Squar-*

ing the Circle. Please feel free to adapt these materials to suit your needs and interests.

ABOUT THE AUTHOR

Niel Hancock was born in Texas and grew up deeply affected by the mystery of Roswell, New Mexico, and the atom bomb experiments at Trinity Site. At an early age, Niel set himself on the trail of what he calls "the Road to the Sacred Mountain." After attending University and some time in Europe, he was drafted into the military. Niel served in Vietnam from July 1967 to July 1968, and was a survivor of the Tet Offensive. After the war, Niel spent time in the Virgin Islands, California, and finally Chihuahua. Winning his own war against drugs and alcohol, he began to write "yams and tales of the things he'd seen and done." His books are complex and detailed fantasy collections which confront the earthly realities of war and injustice while simultaneously gifting readers with a lavishly wrought fantasy world. Today, Niel lives with his wife, potter C.E. Ursin, outside Austin, Texas and enjoys riding Harley Davidson and BMW motorcycles.

WRITING AND RESEARCH ACTIVITIES

I. Explore the Novel

A. Go to your library or online to learn more about the literary form called the *novel* from its origins in the late seventeenth century to its more contemporary forms. Create an informative poster or short report on the novel. Include definitions of the novel's forms, such as comedy, tragedy, romance, satire and epic, variations such as historical fiction and science fiction, and terms such as narrative and point-of-view. Present your poster or report to classmates or friends, explaining how *Squaring the Circle* fits into the scheme of the novel and any special characteristics you might have noted.

B. Create a list of 5–10 novels you would like to read. Choose a theme, such as top fantasy novels, Newbery Medal winners, works by one author, or novels with a specific setting. Write the theme on a sheet of colored paper, and the title of each book at the top of its own separate sheet of lined paper. Staple the pages together. After completing each novel, write a short review below its title. Did the book meet your expectations? Did you learn something? What did you like best or least about the novelist's writing style? Recommend your favorite title to a friend or family member.

II. Dark and Light

A. Images of darkness and light are at play throughout *Squaring the Circle*. On a blackboard, whiteboard, or large sheet of paper, list some words and phrases Niel Hancock uses to describe darkness and light. Add to the blackboard titles of other books, poems, movies, or plays in which dark and light play important roles. Finally, create a brainstorm list of words associated with "dark" and "light." Review your board or paper. What story ideas, questions, or research topics come to mind from your lists?

B. Put darkness and light to work to bring *Squaring the Circle* alive in shadow puppetry. Briefly research this theatrical form's history in Asia and in the Americas. Then, cut the bottom from a large cardboard box and cover the opening with a sheet of thin, white fabric or tissue paper to create a screen. Place the box at the edge of a table. Set a battery-operated lantern, or a lamp with its shade removed, on a chair several feet behind the screen so that when your hand is placed between the lamp and the screen its shadow appears clearly on the other side. Cut shadow puppets from stiff paper, mounting them on sticks or strips of cardboard. While one person reads selected scenes from *Squaring the Circle* aloud, puppeteers seated on the floor between the lamp and the screen can operate their puppets to show the action to the audience seated on the opposite side of the screen. If desired, try creating special effects using shadows and light. Perform your shadow play for friends, family members, or classmates.

III. Deceptive Disguises

A. Doraki pretends to be Froghorn, Dorini disguises herself as Cybelle, Froghorn presents himself as Doraki, and Lorini wears the cloak of her dark sister. Create a chart with columns for "Character," "Disguise," "Motive," and "Result." Complete the chart.

B. Use your imagination to draw a picture of a character from *Squaring the Circle*. Lay a piece of tracing paper over the drawing, securing it at the top or side with a piece of tape. Draw a disguise for your character on the tracing paper. Lift and lower the tracing paper to reveal your true character beneath his or her disguise.

C. Go to the library or online to learn more about disguises in nature. Learn about the stick bug, chameleon or other deceptive creatures. How do animal markings serve to make them blend in with their surroundings? How are the disguises and form-changes utilized in *Squaring the Circle* like or unlike disguises in nature?

D. Imagine that you could take the form of someone you know. How might you use this power? Write a short story in which you disguise yourself as a friend or family member for a party, meeting, class, or other event. What happens? What do you learn?

IV. Learning and Libraries

A. The library in Bear's old dwelling helps bring the story full circle, reminds Dwarf of what he likes about Bear, and hints at the value of learning and lore. Learn about the history of libraries as well as how they are changing in the age of Internet technology. How are libraries in America funded? Do you think libraries receive enough support? Write a letter to an elected official in your state making the case for supporting libraries or volunteer a few hours in your local library to learn more about the work of librarians.

B. Broco and Creddin plan to refurbish the library at Cypher. Design your own perfect library. Does it have comfortable chairs, many computer stations, a fireplace, a snack bar, a special book collection, or other features? How are books arranged? Use a piece of graph paper to sketch a design for your dream library. Label and describe your design.

V. Home

A. Find passages in the novel where "Home" is discussed, noting the various ways Niel Hancock defines this term.

How is "home" defined in your dictionary? At the library or at home, look through a CD collection to find songs which feature the term or theme of "home." Compare the lyrics of several of these songs. Which song best defines home for you? Write your own lyrics to a song entitled "Home" and set it to your own made-up tune or to the tune of a folk song or holiday carol.

B. *Squaring the Circle* ends with beautiful images of light, love and contentment. Choose a favorite word, phrase or paragraph from the final chapters of the novel. Copy your choice onto poster board, using block lettering, script, or calligraphy. Embellish the area around the words with drawings, stamps, images cut from magazines, dried flowers, or other craft materials, and place it in a frame if desired. Mount your embellished saying near your front door or in another welcoming or peaceful place in your home.

QUESTIONS FOR DISCUSSION

1. The opening chapters of *Squaring the Circle* are rife with deception. Who are the elves that Otter and Flewingham meet when they find themselves across the river? What does Froghorn do that makes the friends suspicious of him? What does Bear discover when he follows Tyron? Do the friends feel Greyfax has also betrayed them? To what truth might the friends still cling in the first section of the novel, entitled "Echoes of the Past"?

2. Froghorn tells Bear that there are many entries into Calix Stay—one can be washed in by "a sword stroke, or a bullet, or a bomb, or from a fall . . . or mere old age. All things lead to the river." What, then, is Calix Stay? What or where is one who crosses the river?

3. Why is Dorini called the "Iron Crown at Cypher"? What bargain does Tyron the Green attempt to strike with her? How does this foreshadow a later bargain made in the story between Greyfax and the dark lady?

4. What does Greyfax mean when he says: "It is all as written. We are here awaiting the carrying out of our roles."? Do you think that the ensuing events happen exactly as was prescribed, or predicted, by the Lord of Windameir? Or does Greyfax mean something else? Explain.

5. How does Lorini love Greyfax? How does she love Cybelle? How does she love Dorini? What is she struggling to understand about each of these loves?

6. In the chapter entitled "Relics of the Dragon," Froghorn explains that the Secrets are the Law, and that a holder of the Secrets is able to do unusual things. What types of things is he discussing? How is this empowerment also dangerous? Which characters are holding the secrets even as Froghorn speaks?

7. Both Tyron and Dwarf were given secrets from their fathers. Compare and contrast these histories. Have both come to the same end? What does this reveal about the nature of the Secrets?

8. What do you consider the "rules" of keeping a secret? Do you guard secrets as jealously as Tyron? Do you bear the burden of secrets as painfully as Dwarf? Are there different kinds of Secrets? How do the secrets of the Arkenchest compare with the secrets you have experienced?

9. Lorini seems to be kept from much of the planning and action of the story. Why do you think this is? Is she helpless? Is she dangerous?

11. In the latter half of the book, Bear, Otter, Flewingham, Ned, and Cranfallow have several debates as to whether they should follow Dwarf and continue on their mission. Ultimately, they always elect to support each other and the Circle. What does this say about the friends? If you had been among the friends, would you have agreed with their decisions? Why or why not?

12. Greyfax and Froghorn frequently join and then depart the company of the friends, appearing just in a moment of need and disappearing before providing satisfying explanations. Is this a metaphor for wisdom not quite within the friends' grasp? What else might these brief visits mean?

13. In the chapter entitled "Prelude," Greyfax argues that the Circle has never been able to stop Dorini because she too, is "serving her purpose well." What is Dorini's purpose? Does evil, or darkness, have a purpose in Windameir? Does it have a purpose in today's world? Explain your answer.

14. Near the close of the novel, Dwarf returns the Arkenchest to Dorini. What happens when he does so? Why is this chapter entitled "The Circle Unbroken"?

15. Dorini and Lorini become one Lady, the essence of the Secrets, but how can the cruel Dorini become a part of something loving? How does this moment in the story affect your understanding of the Secrets, their power, and the Light that they can bring?

16. In what ways are Broco, Otter, and Bear tested in the penultimate chapter of the novel? Why do they need to be tested? Do they pass the test?

17. Near the novel's end, Froghorn begins to resemble Greyfax. What does this mean? How does this resonate with name- and form-changes occurring earlier in the story? How does this relate to the characters' crossings between worlds and over the river?

18. On the final page of *Squaring the Circle* are the words "The Beginning." Do you think the Circle of Light sequence simply begins again? What else might Niel Hancock mean by including these words?

19. Is there a difference between a physical home and an emotional, or spiritual, home? Can these places be the same? What do you consider to be your home or homes? Explain your answers?

20. What are the Secrets contained in the Arkenchest? How can Bear, Dwarf, and the other friends in the story have known them but forgotten them? Do you believe there are "secrets" that human beings living today have, perhaps, forgotten?